Worlds Without End
The Mission

Book 1

SHAUN F. MESSICK

EMPYREAN

PUBLICATIONS

This book may be ordered through booksellers or by contacting:

www.EmpyreanPublications.com

ISBN-13: 978-1460910603 (Paperback)
ISBN-10: 1460910605 (Paperback)
ISBN-13: 978-1-257-06045-0 (Hardcover with Dust Jacket)
E-BOOK ISBN: 978-1-61397-358-5 (e-book)

Printed in the United States of America

DEDICATION

To my beautiful wife Tanya and my four wonderful children: Kylee, Bryant, Alexis, and Parker. You have all shown that I can go beyond myself and find strength in areas that I didn't know I had.

Dear Reader,

Thank you for reading the *Worlds Without End* series. As you read this novel, you will discover a strong religious theme. This theme comes directly from my background as a member of the Church of Jesus Christ of Latter-day Saints. In no way does this novel reflect the views of the Church of Jesus Christ of Latter-day Saints. This novel is simply a fictitious tale derived from scripture from the *Holy Bible*, *The Book of Mormon*, *Doctrine and Covenants*, and *The Pearl of Great Price*, as well as from modern revelation.

It is my hope that you will be entertained, uplifted, and your mind opened to the possibilities that lie beyond our mortal understanding upon this Earth. Again, thank you for reading the *Worlds Without End* series. For more information about this series and upcoming books, please visit: www.EmpyreanPublications.com.

Sincerely,

Shaun F. Messick

For we saw him, even on the right hand of God; and we heard the voice bearing record that his is the Only Begotten of the Father—
That by him, the worlds are and were created, and the inhabitants thereof are begotten sons and daughters unto God.

–Doctrine and Covenants, 76: 23-24

And worlds without number have I created; and I also created them for mine own purpose; and by the Son I created them, which is mine Only Begotten.

–Moses 1: 33

And other sheep I have, which are not of this fold: them also I must bring, and they shall hear my voice; and there shall be one fold, [and] one shepherd.

–John 10:16

And verily, verily, I say unto you that I have other sheep, which are not of this land, neither of the land of Jerusalem, neither in any parts of that land round about whither I have been to minister.
For they of whom I speak are they who have not as yet heard my voice; neither have I at any time manifested myself unto them.
But I have received a commandment of the Father that I shall go unto them, and that they shall hear my voice, and shall be numbered among my sheep, that there may be one fold and one shepherd; therefore I go to show myself unto them.

–3 Nephi 16: 1-3

PROLOGUE

Approximately 35 A.D. – Planet of Terrest (22-light years from Earth)

Moriantun stood one hundred feet away from the glorious temple that he and his people of the *Tilicah* tribe built to honor their God. He smiled, admiring the pyramid structure as the bright rays of the noonday sun shimmered off of its gold-plated brick. The view was spectacular. With the sun in its current location, its rays reflected off of the brick to the five silver-plated spires located at each corner and entrance of the pyramid, creating a white-orange glow almost as bright as the light emitted from his Lord.

As Moriantun stared in awe, he closed his eyes and allowed his other senses to take control. A warm summer breeze blew through his long dark hair, causing him to wipe a strand from his tanned face, a result of thousands of hours that he and his people labored to complete the spectacle before him. While he enveloped himself in the warmth of the breeze, Moriantun smelled the sweetness of the air. It was the sweet smell of fresh pine, coming from the forest grove just beyond the temple.

With his eyes still closed, Moriantun walked to the closest spire located just fifty feet in front of the entrance of the temple and slowly opened his eyes. He stared into the silver spire and saw his reflection. He no longer looked tired and aged from the countless hours of prophesying, missionary work, and temple construction that had been bestowed upon him by his

Brother. He now looked like a young man again; almost as young as he was when he had first received his calling. His eyes no longer looked gray. They had transformed back to their normal shade of bright blue, and his black as night hair shimmered once again.

As Moriantun admired the joy he saw in his image, he felt a bead of sweat drip from his forehead onto his hand. Realizing he was now hot from the warmth of the breeze and the heat of the sun, he shrugged off his brown tunic, revealing the white robe that covered his broad frame. As his tunic landed on the freshly manicured grass, Moriantun looked down and tightened the scarlet sash around his waist. After doing so, he slowly raised his head and with his eyes traced the spire up to its highest point upon which his proudest creation rested.

There, on top of the tallest spire, stood the golden statue of a prophet he was commanded to place there. Moriantun still did not know whom the image represented but was told by his Brother that the name would be revealed to him at a later time. Even so, he knew the symbolism to which the statue represented. Pointing to the east, the statue stood barefoot, wearing a flowing robe, and appeared to be blowing into a bugle, which signified the coming of the Lord to the Terrestrian people.

While he looked at the statue with pride, Moriantun felt a warm sensation on his back of mercy, love, and strength so incomprehensible that he immediately knelt down and bowed his head. After a few moments of basking in this warmth that he could not describe, Moriantun slowly opened his eyes and saw his Brother's reflection in the spire. Moriantun was still astonished at how a being could emit so much light. And what was even more astonishing was that he did not have to squint, for the light did not hurt his eyes. On the contrary, the light seemed to radiate comfort to anyone in its presence.

With his head still bowed, Moriantun slowly stood and turned. He lifted his face and immediately met the eyes of his Redeemer.

"Moriantun, blessed art thou," the Brother said as He walked toward Moriantun and placed His left hand on Moriantun's right shoulder.

Looking down on his Savior's hand and noticing the nail print, Moriantun felt the most astonishing energy that he had ever felt flow throughout his body as he recalled the importance of his mission.

For nearly fifty-five years, Moriantun had been prophesying and preaching to the *Tilicah* tribe of *Terrest*, prophesying of a God who would redeem them from their sins and visit them from another world inhabited by their brothers and sisters. At first, Moriantun's teachings were met with criticism and sometimes violence. But with persistence and strength from the Lord, Moriantun was successful in converting nearly the entire *Tilicah* tribe to the Gospel of their Lord and Redeemer.

And now, here he stood in the presence of his God and in front of the most beautiful structure his kinsmen had ever created.

Moriantun slowly bowed his head and said, "Thank you, My Lord."

Jesus gently lifted Moriantun's head and smiled. "Art thou prepared?"

"Yes, My Lord, I have fasted and prayed for three days, preparing my soul for what you would have me do."

Jesus continued to smile at Moriantun, giving Moriantun the reassurance that it was he that was truly worthy of the task he would soon embark on.

"Good, then let us begin," the Savior said.

Jesus walked past Moriantun toward the entrance to His temple. Moriantun followed basking in the warmth and love his Brother emitted. He continued to follow, as they both walked down the stone steps that led to the large oak door separating them from the outside world and the Lord's house. With a wave of His hand, Jesus opened the large door. They both walked into a long, narrow hallway, which was full of light from the candle chandeliers hanging from the ceiling.

As they walked down the hallway, Moriantun glanced at the walls he would soon fill with the writings he was called to record. Reaching the end of the hallway, the Savior turned to His right and walked up another set of stone steps, which ended with another large wooden door. Jesus waited a few seconds for Moriantun to stand at his side.

Moriantun knew that the room they were about to enter was crucial, for the Lord had revealed to him that this room would contain a prophecy that would give comfort and faith to his people at a time when they would surely face utter destruction from an enemy far away. Moriantun still did not understand what it meant, but he was eager with excitement, as the prophecy would soon be revealed to him.

With another wave of His hand, Jesus opened the large wooden door. Jesus and Moriantun both entered the brightly-lit room. Moriantun had to squint as he looked around. Rather than the smooth stone granite used to build the entrance to the temple, this room was constructed of pure white marble, which reflected the candlelight from the gigantic chandelier that hung from the ceiling twenty-five feet above. Once Moriantun's eyes adjusted, he looked around the fifty-foot by fifty-foot room. In the corner and to his right rested the beautiful baptismal font, resting on twelve golden oxen. In the corner and to his left was an altar in which worshippers could kneel in prayer to their beloved God. And directly ahead rested the platform upon which Moriantun would create a statue and background painting, representing the prophecy Moriantun would soon receive.

Even though Moriantun was in charge of the construction of the temple and room, he still stood in awe of its beauty. As he marveled at the beauty of the room, he could feel the eyes of his Savior looking at him. Moriantun turned and met the loving eyes of Jesus and asked, "Do you approve, My Lord?"

Jesus gave Moriantun a smile that exuded a love so breathtaking that Moriantun nearly fainted from its power. "It is well, Moriantun," He said.

"Thank you, My Lord."

"Let us proceed," Jesus said as He nodded and pointed to the spiral staircase that led up to the other rooms in the temple and the top floor, which contained the Holy of Holies – a room only the Savior and those most worthy could enter.

Moriantun and his Savior ascended the gold plated spiral staircase, passing the other rooms of the temple. As they passed each room, Moriantun looked with pride at the fine workmanship each room possessed. Finally after a few moments, Jesus and Moriantun walked into a small room that could barely fit three medium sized adults. In the middle of the room was a ladder that led up seven feet to the ceiling, which contained a trap door. The Savior looked at Moriantun and motioned for him to proceed.

Moriantun's pulse began to quicken, as he knew that soon he would enter the holiest room in the temple. Moriantun climbed up the ladder and unlocked the trap door. He slowly opened it and pulled himself up into the uppermost room. He entered the room and looked around. The view was spectacular.

Although the room was small, each wall within was made entirely of crystal giving its occupant a three hundred sixty degree view of the surrounding landscape. Moriantun looked straight ahead and took in the breathtaking view of the great forest, and then he turned around and saw the sprawling city his people had begun to build.

As Moriantun continued to look in wonder, Jesus slowly ascended Himself into the room. Moriantun turned and looked directly into Jesus' eyes. Jesus returned the look and said, "It is time."

Moriantun closed the trap door and knelt before his Lord at the small altar in the middle of the crystal room. With his Savior standing on the opposite side of the altar, Moriantun closed his eyes and bowed his head. Jesus placed His hands upon Moriantun's head and proceeded to bless him.

After the blessing, Jesus said, "Moriantun, arise."

Moriantun opened his eyes and stood. The room was darker now except for the brilliant light his Savior emitted. Moriantun looked outside the crystal windows and noticed that it was now dark outside with *Terrest's* two moons in full brightness, and the stars so bright Moriantun felt as if he was floating in space with his Savior. How long had the Lord blessed him?

Jesus looked at Moriantun and pointed to the brightest star. "Look."

Moriantun looked. Suddenly, he and Jesus were on another planet. The planet was so beautiful, with lush forests, crystal-blue waters, and green-fertile valleys. He saw the people that inhabited the planet. He turned to his Savior and asked, "Who are these people, My Lord?"

"These are your brothers and sisters, Moriantun."

Moriantun looked again and saw the people. The people worked as one and seemed to have a genuine love for one another and their Lord. They appeared to communicate to one another without speech, and could move matter with just a thought. This civilization also had so many wondrous technologies that Moriantun could not describe.

Moriantun looked at Jesus again. "Are we in Heaven, My Lord?"

Jesus answered, "No, Moriantun. We are on another world not far from your world. Your brothers and sisters on this world are mortal just as you are."

Moriantun looked at the people again with confusion. "But, My Lord how is it that they possess abilities that only You have?"

Jesus looked at His brothers and sisters and with a wave of His hand said, "These people are a blessed people. They have obeyed the words of my Father, and because of their obedience and faith they could not be denied my blessings. They have been transfigured in order to withstand the presence of the Father. These blessings will be passed to their children from generation to generation. But I say unto you, Moriantun, as the generations pass, they will forget the Lord their God and turn to transgression. Due to the covenants I have made with their fathers, their abilities will not be taken away from them. Rather, their blessings will become their curse and undoing."

Moriantun watched again as the generations passed among this people. He saw their once formidable civilization crumble to pieces, and the powers they were given as blessings created jealousy, hatred, and wars among the people. Moriantun continued to observe as the Lord withdrew his protective hand from the planet.

The planet and the people were nearly destroyed. One man, however, achieved greatness among this people. He arose as a strong and powerful leader – a leader that would lead them from their dying world to Moriantun's home world of *Terrest*.

Moriantun and the Savior were immediately taken back to *Terrest*. As Moriantun watched, he witnessed his people on *Terrest* fall away from the Lord as well. It pained him to see his brothers and sisters forget the Lord their God, especially when Moriantun now stood in Christ's presence and could feel the undying love He had for each one of God's children on these two worlds.

With tears streaming down his face, Moriantun witnessed the near destruction of his home world and the enslavement of his brothers and sisters by their more powerful brothers and sisters from the neighboring world.

Moriantun couldn't watch anymore. How could his people fall away? He closed his eyes and bowed his head. After a few moments of silent sadness that seemed to pierce his heart, he took a deep breath and turned to the Lord. "My Lord, is there any hope for my brothers and sisters and these people from this nearby world? Will they lose their salvation?"

Jesus looked upon Moriantun with compassion and said, "Many will fall into wickedness and not repent of their sins. As such, My Gospel will be taken from your world and the world you previously witnessed. An apostasy shall occur."

Moriantun shook his head. He couldn't bear the thought of losing one soul. He had to do something, something to keep the Gospel from being taken away from his brothers and sisters. He looked at Jesus with a determined look. "What can I do, My Lord? How can I prevent your Word from being taken from my people? Surely, I would sacrifice my life so that my brothers and sisters do not fall into iniquity."

Jesus smiled at Moriantun, stepped closer to him, and cupped his face into His hands. "I know the desires of thy heart, Moriantun. That is why I am revealing all to you. For you have a great calling ahead. You are called upon to record My Word upon these temple walls and to reveal how your brothers and sisters can be saved."

Moriantun continued to sob as Christ continued to hold his face in his hands.

"Blessed art thou, Moriantun, for the love you have for your brothers and sisters. For this, your salvation is made sure. Now look," Jesus said as He gently turned Moriantun's head toward another bright star in the heavens. "You see the star before you?"

"Yes, My Lord."

With another wave of His hand, Jesus said, "This is my world, Earth, the world where I bled from every pore to redeem all of Father's children from this world and the worlds without end of which our Father has created. This is the world where I was offered as a sacrifice and nailed to the cross. I arose again in three days so that you and your brothers and sisters might have eternal and everlasting life."

Instantly, Moriantun and the Savior were on Christ's home world. Moriantun witnessed the beginning of the earth all the way to its end. He witnessed the shedding of blood by the Savior, and as he watched, he fell to his knees and wept knowing full well that Christ sacrificed Himself so that one day Moriantun and his brothers and sisters could enjoy eternal life with their Father in Heaven.

While still on his knees and with tears streaming down his face, Moriantun witnessed the destruction of his Lord's Gospel from the face of the earth and the apostasy that soon followed. He then saw a man, much like himself, called of God to restore Christ's Gospel once again.

As the years passed, Moriantun saw the Lord's Gospel spread throughout the earth. As a result, the Lord couldn't deny His children the blessings of incredible technologies and machines. Machines that would take them to other worlds inhabited by God's children and spread His Word.

As Moriantun watched in astonishment, he felt a surge of joy penetrate his body. The joy was so powerful that he could hardly tolerate the emotion, for there was hope for his people. One day, the people of *Terrest* and the people of *Terrest's* neighboring planet would become one and together partake in the joy of the true and living Gospel of Jesus Christ.

Still on his knees, Moriantun looked up at the Lord. "But how, My Lord? How will my people and the people of this nearby planet learn of Thee once again when they will have forsaken everything that is good and pure?"

Christ pointed to the horizon of the earth and said, "Look."

Moriantun looked. He arose with strength and a burning in his bosom, as he witnessed the miracle the Lord would send among the people of *Terrest*, so they would once again enjoy the love of their God and the Gospel of Jesus Christ. And then . . . the vision closed.

CHAPTER 1

May 16, 2017 – Cape Canaveral, Florida

To Adrian Palmer this was the dawn of the future. He sat in the flight-deck of the *Mars I* Space Shuttle and focused his deep-set azure eyes on the sky above. A flow of electric energy surged though his 6'1" agile frame as the thought of what was about to happen in a few short moments excited and terrified him in one surreal emotion. As the sky above began to transform from the night's blackness to the morning's illumination, he contemplated all of the events in his life that had brought him to this point. He thought to himself, *what a privilege and honor this is.*

"Houston to *Mars I*, over."

"Go, Houston," replied Adrian.

"In two minutes, we will be ready for your pre-lift off check."

"Roger that," said Adrian.

Adrian, now 35-years-old, began to feel his pulse quicken. It was just five years earlier when he applied and was accepted to the National Aeronautic and Space Administration's Astronaut Training Program. Little did he know, when he applied, NASA had in the works a top-secret project. That project turned out to be the shuttle he sat in now, and the mission he and his crew were about to embark on. He could hardly believe he sat in one of the most impressive creations ever created by man and was about to lift off on mankind's most historic exploration ever.

When Adrian applied to NASA's astronaut training program, he obviously had dreams of grandeur but this was beyond his wildest dreams. Always a humble and somewhat timid person, Adrian always surprised himself and those around him with his accomplishments. Adrian and his older brother, Kevin by three years, grew up in a small town, in Idaho. At a young age, his parents had instilled a value for education in him and his brother. Kevin had always had an inclination for computers, and Adrian had a fondness for adventure and exploration. No wonder Kevin was the founder and CEO of Compu-Tech Super Computers (CTSC) and Adrian the pilot.

After high school, Adrian received a full-ride scholarship to play football at the United States Air Force Academy. Adrian was torn. He knew that if he accepted the scholarship, he wouldn't be able to serve a mission for his church because the Air Force wouldn't grant him a two-year leave of absence. After much fasting and prayer, he decided to accept the scholarship and sign a commitment to the Air Force. Nonetheless, the thought of not serving a mission for his Lord pained him. Yet, he knew he had received an answer to his prayers and that the Lord had a greater mission ahead for him. What that was, he wasn't sure. Perhaps it was the mission he was about to embark on? Maybe he could be an example of integrity and strength to his brothers and sisters on Earth. Whatever the mission was, he knew that what he was doing was right.

Adrian eventually graduated from the Air Force Academy with high honors and a rank of lieutenant. The thought of this brought a smile to Adrian's face. His first sergeant, when Adrian was a freshman, predicted that Adrian wouldn't make it through the first year because he was so quiet.

Adrian proved his first sergeant wrong. He went on to a stellar career in the Air Force as a fighter pilot and earned the rank of colonel after his accomplishments in the Terrorist War of 2012. That same year, from the encouragement of Kevin and his mother, he applied to NASA's Astronaut Training Program and was accepted.

The thought of his mother suddenly saddened him in this the pinnacle of his career. Just one year after he was accepted, in an ironic twist, his mother and father were tragically killed in an airplane crash. Adrian and his wife, Melissa, were devastated. Adrian contemplated dropping out of the training program now that the foundation of his life had suddenly crumbled. But he stayed because of the faith his wife had in him.

Melissa what a wonderful, compassionate, and loving companion she had been. Melissa became the foundation that he desperately needed. She was the first one he told when he was selected as commander of the new *Mars I* Space Shuttle. The day after the good news, however, Melissa was on her way home from buying Adrian a surprise gift when her car was blind sided by a truck that ran a red light. Melissa died instantly. Jake, then two years old, survived.

With all of the tragedy that Adrian had endured, he could have easily fallen into a deep and dark depression. But he didn't, he had to go on for his son and the memory of his wife who had more faith in him than he had in himself, and not to mention, his faith in God.

After Melissa's death, Jake and Adrian had become almost inseparable. The only time they were apart was when Adrian was working. But that was okay with Jake because he was so proud of his dad. In fact, Jake's kindergarten teacher called Adrian one night to discuss a problem Jake was having in class.

Apparently, Jake would not stop talking about his dad and would not stop saying, "My daddy's so cool. He's going to Mars to find Martians!"

Adrian couldn't help but laugh. But by the urging of his son's teacher, he had a talk with his son. "Jake, you've got to do what your teacher asks you to do, and not talk about me all of the time."

"But Daddy, it's so cool 'cause you get to go find some Martians. Are you going to bring one back?" Jake asked as he jumped up and down.

"Probably not."

"Darn it!" replied Jake, with a frown.

"It's okay, Son. But promise you won't talk about me unless your teacher or someone in your class asks?"

"Okay, Daddy. But I still think it's so cool!" Jake replied.

"Good. And also promise me that you will be a good boy for your Uncle Kevin and Aunt Diane while I'm gone?"

"I will."

"I love you, Son."

"I love you too, Daddy."

Adrian remembered grabbing and squeezing his son in a tight hug, and with his left hand, tickling him under his right knee. They both laughed as they rolled on the floor together.

That was just last week. The thought of Jake nearly brought a tear to Adrian's eye. He would surely miss his son on this yearlong journey. Nevertheless, he knew that Jake would be okay with Kevin and Diane.

Furthermore, the excitement Jake must be feeling at this very moment as he watched with his uncle and aunt from the spectator's area, along with thousands of people awaiting the lift off of man's first mission to Mars.

★ ★ ★ ★ ★

A bead of sweat dripped down from the top of Kevin Palmer's dark brown hair, swiveled its way down his partially tanned forehead, and almost made its way into his hazel left eye before he wiped it away. He blinked twice and pulled at the collar of his designer white shirt as he sat in the V.I.P. section of the Cape Canaveral spectator's area next to his wife, who held Jake in her lap, and Bob Taylor his special guest.

Bob was the Editor and Chief of *Time* magazine and Kevin's friend. Bob thought that it would be a fascinating cover story to interview the man who practically invented artificial intelligence, was a consultant for the development of the *Mars I* Space Shuttle, and whose own brother was piloting this magnificent creation.

"Why are you sweating?" asked the short, pudgy editor, as sweat dripped from his own balding head with a scraggly mix of gray and black hair.

Kevin, dressed in a black pinstripe suit, which anyone could tell, was tailored perfectly to fit his broad toned frame, replied, "First of all, it's blazing hot out here for six o' clock in the morning, I'm wearing this dark suit, and I am excited and nervous. Any more non-journalistic questions?"

"Well excuse me," said Bob with a bit of annoyance in his voice. "Speaking of which, I'm not usually up by this time. I need some coffee. You want some?"

"No thanks."

"Oh yeah, that's right you're Mormon, and you don't drink the stuff," Bob said in a sarcastic tone.

"You knew that, Bob. Besides, it's so hot out here why would you want to drink that hot stuff anyway?"

"Hey, you know me. I live on the stuff. I don't know how you Mormons can stay awake this early without it?"

As Bob strolled over to get his coffee, Diane rolled her chocolate eyes, swiped a strand of blond curly hair from her fair complexion, and turned to her husband, "I don't know why you had to invite that weasel to one of the best days of your life."

"That weasel happens to be one of my friends, and besides, he thought that this would be a good cover story," Kevin answered, as he put his arm around Diane and tickled Jake's leg. Jake looked at Kevin with his bright blue eyes, giggled, and pushed Kevin's hand away.

"Well, as it is, I don't like the man. He's sarcastic, and he always makes fun of you about our religion."

"But when he wrote that cover story on me six years ago after inventing the first smart processor, he showed total and complete objectivity when explaining my religious beliefs. I also like him because we entertain each other."

"I know. I just don't like the way he treats you, that's all."

Bob strolled back with coffee in hand. As he walked past Diane and Jake to sit on the other side of Kevin, Jake blurted out, "Aunt Diane thinks you look like a weasel!"

Diane quickly covered Jake's mouth.

Bob laughed, looked down over his glasses, and said, "She does? Well, I suppose it's better than looking like a j—"

"Watch it, Bob! Little ears around," Kevin said, nodding in Jake's direction.

Bob took his seat next to Kevin, took a sip of his coffee, sat it between his pudgy legs, pulled out his computer notepad, and prepared to interview Kevin.

"Oh, now we're going to be professional are we?" said Kevin sarcastically.

"Hey, you know me. When I'm not working, I'm a jerk, and when I'm working, I am completely professional," Bob said as he looked at Diane with a smile.

Diane rolled her eyes again.

Bob began the interview. "So, K . . . Mr. Palmer, why don't you tell me about this technological wonder in front of us."

"Well, Mr. Taylor, as you know, this creation is an evolutionary advance of the previous shuttles built in the 1970s, 80s, and 90s. As you can see, *Mars I* looks a lot like the former Space Shuttle *Endeavour* built in 1991. The Space Shuttle *Endeavour* was about the same weight and size as an old DC-9 airplane. You do know what an old DC-9 looked like don't you?"

"Yes, yes, I know. It was a small two-engine jet. Now, can I continue the interview, or are you going to keep asking me, the journalist, stupid questions?"

"Oh, sorry, I forgot you were a reporter for a minute," said Kevin, receiving a smile from Diane along with an elbow in the ribs.

"Very funny. Now you're a comedian instead of a computer genius," replied Bob, obviously annoyed. "Now, why is *Mars I* so much bigger than the old Space Shuttle *Endeavour*?"

Kevin answered, trying to impress Bob with his extensive knowledge of the craft. "That's simple, Mr. Taylor. The flight-deck of the *Endeavour* only accommodated seven crewmembers. The flight-deck in *Mars I* needs to accommodate ten crew members: a pilot; copilot; a communications officer; a doctor; a nuclear engineer; a computer specialist; an astronomer/physicist; a payload commander – who is also a civil engineer; a geologist; and a botanist."

"A botanist? Why do you need a botanist on a space mission?"

"Skyler Green, the botanist, is going to develop a green house about the size of a football field on Mars. It will grow the food needed to sustain the crew for the six months on Mars, and he will conduct other various experiments. Anyway, I thought we were talking about the size of this thing?" Kevin asked as he pointed to *Mars I*.

"Oh yeah, go on. I promise I won't interrupt again."

"Yeah, right,' said Kevin in a mocking tone. "In addition, to the expanded flight-deck, we have enlarged the mid-deck as well to accommodate the living quarters for the crew. As you know, Mr. Taylor, scientists have, for a long time, tried to solve the problem of astronauts spending large amounts of time in a no-gravity environment."

"Yes, I know. If an astronaut spends too much time in a weightless environment, he or she will experience muscle atrophy due to the weightlessness."

"Wow, I'm impressed Bob. You know your science."

"Shut-up and go on."

"Well, the scientists at NASA, with the help of the smart processor, have solved that problem," Kevin said with pride, mentioning his smart processor. "We have developed, if you will, a spinning wheel within the mid-deck of the shuttle. Each crewmember has his or her individual quarters, with a sleeping area, bathing area, and toiletries area, located on the outside of the wheel. In the middle of the wheel lies the kitchen area, laundry area, and exercise room. While the shuttle is traveling in space, the wheel will spin, creating artificial gravity – the same gravity we feel on Earth."

"Impressive," replied Bob with sincerity. "What happens if the wheel starts to spin too fast or slow down?"

"I'm glad you asked, Mr. Taylor," answered Kevin with pride in his voice again. "The smart processors in the main computer system of *Mars I* will be able to determine if the wheel is spinning too fast or slowing down within one, one-trillionth of its original setting and then adjust."

"Wow!" said Bob, rolling his eyes.

Kevin noticed, understanding Bob's utter indifference toward science.

"Mr. Palmer, why don't you tell me how these smart processors work and the benefit they will have on the mission?"

"I'll get to that later, Bob. Let me explain the remaining decks first. I thought you were a great journalist?"

"I am. I just thought I'd try to throw you off, so I could get you back to the point. Thus, proving my intellectual superiority," Bob answered sarcastically.

Diane cut in. "I thought you two were doing an interview and not trying to prove who's got the bigger brain?"

Kevin and Bob just glanced at each other speechless, knowing that Diane had the best of them.

"My daddy's going to get some Martians!" yelled Jake.

Bob gave Jake an annoyed look and said, "That's great, Kid. Now . . . go on Mr. Palmer."

"Anyway, along with the flight-deck and the mid-deck, we have added what we affectionately call the nuke-deck."

"Nuke-deck?" Bob asked.

"Yes, the nuke-deck. This obviously is the deck containing the nuclear reactor, which will provide power to the ship. Also, since we weren't sure how a nuclear reactor would work in a no-gravity environment, we built a wheel for it as well."

"So, the reactor is going to spin just like the living area for the crew?"

"Yes," said Kevin, growing more nervous as the external rocket boosters of *Mars I* began to smoke. "The last deck is the payload-deck, which contains the satellite arm, *NightHawk* – *NightHawk* is the landing vehicle for Mars – and the other necessities for the journey. By the way, the flight-deck and the payload-deck are the only decks that won't have artificial gravity. As a result, *Mars I* is ten times larger than the old Space Shuttle *Endeavour* and costs fifteen times as much, roughly 31.5 billion dollars."

Bob let out a slow whistle, obviously impressed. He continued, "Now, you can tell me about your chips."

"Oh, I don't want to bore you with the details Bob, so I'll give you the sixth grade version."

"Funny."

"Basically, the chips my company—"

"You mean you?"

Kevin, a bit embarrassed to be taking all of the credit, went on. "My company developed a new computer processor that learns."

"What do you mean . . . learns?" asked Bob.

"Don't tell me you don't know what the word 'learns' means, Bob? Basically. . . . Why are you asking me about the chips when you got all of this six years ago on your first cover story about the smart processor?" Kevin asked.

"I just like to hear you brag about your invention, that's all. Besides, that was six years ago. Haven't there been any advances?"

Kevin gave Bob an annoyed look and replied, "Of course there have been advances, but I don't want to bore you with the details."

"All right, I'll get all of the chip stuff from my first article. So with that, why don't you tell me how fast this thing can go?"

"The earlier space shuttles were able to travel at a speed of up to five miles per second."

Bob shook his head. "Isn't that faster than a bullet?"

"Yes, traveling to Mars at that constant speed would take a crew six months to get there. But with this thing," Kevin said, pointing to the shuttle, "they will get there in half that time."

"Exciting! But you still haven't answered my question. How fast can it go?"

"Four times as fast as the originals. Roughly twenty miles per second, 1200 miles per minute, 72,000 miles per hour, one mil—"

"Okay, okay, I get it. It's fast!"

Diane jumped in again, "Will you guys quit focusing on yourselves for a minute. They're about to lift off."

Kevin looked up and heard the countdown over the loud speakers.

"T-minus ten . . . nine . . ."

★ ★ ★ ★ ★

"*Mars I* this is Houston. Over? *Mars I* this is Houston. Over? Commander Palmer!

Adrian jumped when he heard the spattering in his earpiece. "This is *Mars I*," he said.

"Is everything okay, Commander?"

"Yeah, sorry, I was just thinking."

"Well, don't think too much. We're ready for your pre-lift off checklist."

"Roger that, Houston."

With a dry mouth and his heart beginning to race, Adrian began his pre-lift off checklist. The checklist was simple. He would simply ask each one of his ten-man crew members if his or her station was ready for lift off. "Gloria, are all communication systems up and running?"

With an obvious edgy voice, Gloria replied, "Roger that, Commander. All systems and satellite links are up and running."

"Are you okay?" asked Adrian with noticeable concern in his voice.

"Yes, Commander. Everything's fine. I'm just a little nervous that's all."

Adrian replied with compassion in his voice, careful not to reveal too much, "Aren't we all."

Adrian had to be careful around the other members of the crew not to reveal his true feelings for Gloria. Not long after his wife's death, Gloria Jackson was the first person he confided in. A strong friendship developed, and just two months ago, that friendship gave way to a full-blown relationship. But he and Gloria knew that they could not reveal their relationship to others in the crew nor to NASA, or one of the two would be scrubbed from the mission and replaced.

It was obvious why Adrian was beginning to fall in love. At thirty-four, Gloria was a brilliant communications analyst, very intelligent, compassionate, athletic, and bull headed. Often during the physical training required for the mission, she would hold her own with the men of the crew and at times beat them in timed drills.

Not only did she have these admirable qualities, she was drop-dead gorgeous. The daughter of a former professional basketball player and brilliant lawyer, she inherited the genes of an athlete, the intelligence of a top-notch lawyer, and the looks of one of Hollywood's A-list actresses. She had silky-smooth, dark skin, bright blue eyes, long brown hair, and an extremely well fit body.

"Gloria, do you have all of your coordinates ready for our communications' protocols with Houston?"

"Roger that, Commander."

During the voyage to Mars, Gloria would monitor the satellite link from *Mars I* to the satellite orbiting Earth designated primarily for communications with the shuttle's crew. Gloria would also be the one to perform the space walk when the crew deployed the satellite that would orbit Mars.

"Good," replied Adrian, as he continued on with the checklist.

"Doc, are all vitals connected and is everything reading okay?"

Doctor Charles Porter answered. "Roger, Commander."

Adrian had always suspected that Doc, as the crew called him, knew something was going on between Adrian and Gloria, but Adrian never told him. If Doc did suspect something, he didn't tell anyone. As a result, Adrian felt an unmistakable, deep respect for Doc and a close friendship.

Doc, who was selected for the astronaut training program as a flight surgeon a year after Adrian, appeared to some to be a menacing, large black man. To a person that didn't know him, that person would be terrified to meet him in a dark alley. But to the people who knew him best, Doc was a large teddy bear, willing to do anything for anyone.

"Copy that . . . Doc!" replied Adrian with a bit of sarcasm.

Adrian continued with the checklist. "Petey, is the reactor ready to go once we exit the atmosphere?"

"Roger that, Commander. The reactor is stable and programmed to turn on once we exit the atmosphere."

"Goo—"

"And might I add, Sir, that this is certainly a privilege to be flying with you and this wonderful crew."

Adrian heard a grunt of annoyance come from his copilot, Donald Garrett, who sat next to him.

To some of the crew, especially Donald Garrett, Peter Sanchez – a 5'7" nuclear engineer of Hispanic descent – was an annoying suck-up. Nevertheless, Adrian liked him for his brilliance as a nuclear engineer and his youthful energy because he was only twenty-four years old. He also admired him because Petey seemed to be the only one who could understand the most advanced nuclear reactor ever developed by man.

This new reactor was the life-source for *Mars I*. A fast-reactor developed at the Idaho National Laboratory just sixty miles outside of Adrian's hometown. This new reactor design convinced nearly eighty percent of the world's countries to convert from conventional energy means to nuclear energy. It was not only the fastest reactor ever developed, it also gave way to almost no nuclear waste.

The reactor worked on a process called pyroprocessing. This process recycled spent fuel, using new technology in which actinides could be recovered from spent fuel and could then be recycled back into the reactor, which delivered one hundred times more energy from available uranium resources. The actinides are bi-products from normal fission reactions – basically the waste of a nuclear reactor. Most importantly, with the recycling capabilities of the fast reactor, the new *Mars I* Space Shuttle had enough power to last one thousand years.

★ ★ ★ ★ ★

Gloria loved listening to Adrian's voice, as he continued with his pre-lift off checklist. *What am I thinking? Gloria you know better than to fall in love with someone you work with.* No matter what Gloria told or thought to herself, she couldn't help the feelings that were growing within her. She admired Adrian from the moment they met, respected him for confiding in her after his wife's death, and cherished how he acted as a father. There wasn't one thing that she could find wrong with the man, and that was what worried her.

"Skyler, are you ready to go?" asked Adrian

Skyler answered with his heavy Texas accent, "I haven't been more ready. I also haven't been this excited since I crossed a rose with a cactus… and, boy howdy, that flower was ugly! Yee ha!"

Gloria giggled. She liked Skyler. He always had on his grease, stained cowboy hat that covered his buzzed, blond crop of hair. She pictured him now, sitting in the flight-deck, holding the old thing for good luck. In fact, that's what she liked about him, he never seemed to be down and he always kept things light in serious situations. It was strange that a cowboy from Texas would be so enamored with plants.

"Sean, are all computer systems a go?"

Gloria pictured Sean Gibson's face in her mind's eye. She smiled as she saw his intense gray eyes hidden behind what looked like eighteenth century spectacles. She also pictured him in front of *Mars I's* main frame, rubbing his hand through his sandy, blond hair while he maintained what he loved the most – the shuttle's computer.

Everyone on the ship got a kick out of Sean's passion for computers, especially with the computer system on *Mars I*, which was embedded with smart processors. Crewmembers could actually interact with this new computer system. At first, the *Mars I* computer system's voice was a male's voice. However, Sean, obviously not having a girlfriend, reprogrammed it to that of a smooth, seductive woman's voice, which he affectionately called *Maggie*. The crew even got the impression that Sean was actually in love with it.

"Roger that, Commander. *Maggie* is ready to go," replied Sean with passion.

Gloria continued to listen in on the pre-lift off checklist. Adrian asked the remaining crew members – Scott Hauler, the payload commander; Isaac Cooper, the mission's astronomer/physicist; and Ted Anderson, the mission's geologist, if they were ready. She heard a continuous flow of "Roger that's."

"Don, are all calculations and trajectories preprogrammed for lift off?"

"Roger that, Commander," replied Don.

Gloria hated the way Don answered Adrian. She pictured the glare he must be giving Adrian at this moment with his piercing brown eyes; along with the smirk he probably had on his bronze face that he constantly tanned to help maintain his ego. She could also hear the disrespect he had for Adrian in his voice. Don was jealous since the first day it was announced that Adrian would be the commander and pilot of *Mars I*.

Don, being a year older and a year longer in the program than Adrian, naturally thought that he would be selected to pilot and command the mission. Nevertheless, NASA chose Adrian. NASA and the entire crew, except for Don, knew that Adrian was the better leader and the natural selection. But, Don insisted that Adrian was selected because his brother helped construct *Mars I*. He even went so far as to express his displeasure to the press. Even so, Adrian still chose Don as his copilot.

Suddenly, Gloria was jerked out of her daydream. She heard Adrian.

"Houston, *Mars I* is ready for countdown."

★ ★ ★ ★ ★

Adrian felt beads of sweat drip to the back of his flight helmet. Even when the crew tested the new shuttle on a flight to the moon, he wasn't this nervous. In fact, that flight had been a record flight. In 1969, it took the

Apollo crew seventy-three hours and twenty-seven minutes to fly to the moon. With *Mars I*, the crew was able to make the journey to the moon in three and a half hours. Everything went smoothly on that mission. Yet, he still did not know why he was so nervous and scared.

"Houston, *Mars I* is ready for countdown," said Adrian, as the shuttle began to tremble.

"Roger that, *Mars I*. T-minus ten . . . nine . . . eight . . . seven . . . six. . . . Ignition. Four . . . three . . . two . . . one . . . zero. . . . Lift-off!"

Adrian began to feel the centrifugal force as the most sophisticated invention of the twenty-first century ascended from the launch pad. He felt as if the front of his chest was now in the seat behind him. He tried with all his might not to black out, and continued communication protocols with Houston while the technological wonder he sat in projected itself into space. His muscles tightened and were starting to ache, especially in his left arm as he held the flight stick of *Mars I*. His fingers wanted to let go and relax along with the rest of his arm. But Adrian had to muster all of the strength he could find. If he were to let go of the stick, his arm would violently fly back and smack his flight helmet, probably breaking his arm. He had to hold on. *Hold on, hold on.* He thought to himself.

Adrian could see the atmosphere thinning and felt his heart in his throat. "Yes, Houston."

"You're right on trajectory, Commander."

A few moments later, Adrian began to see the blackness of space. The take off went smoothly. But why did he still have a feeling that something was amiss? And then a dreadful thought popped into his head. *Was last night the last time he would see and hold his son?*

CHAPTER 2

Three months later, August 20, 2017 – Onboard Mars I…Approaching Mars

Adrian and his crew sat eating dinner in the kitchen area of *Mars I*. The table seated all ten crew members in the middle of the room with a cooking area on one side and the wash area on the other. The room wasn't any bigger than a master bedroom in a modest-size home. When all ten crew members were in the room at once, it felt terribly claustrophobic.

Adrian was trying to choke down his dehydrated roast beef and potatoes. He was sick of NASA's dehydrated food. He couldn't wait until they were on Mars. Skyler could begin his green house, and in a few months, they would all enjoy fresh fruits and vegetables.

Amid the silence, Peter Sanchez finally spoke, "I don't know about you guys, but I can't wait to see Mars tomorrow. Just imagine we're going to—"

Don cut in, "Why don't you just shut-up, Petey! I'm sick of you being positive and constant brown-nosing."

"He wasn't brown-nosing, Don," Adrian said. "And leave him alone. We're all tired because of the long journey. I think it would be good if we all took the night off and retired to our quarters for a quiet and peaceful evening. We've got a big day tomorrow."

Actually, Adrian was glad to give that order. Frankly, he was tired of seeing the same faces day in and day out, except for Gloria's of course.

"I think you're right, Commander. A little R-and-R would do us some—"

Don interrupted again, obviously furious, "There you go again!"

"What?"

"You're brown-nosing again!"

"Leave him alone, Don. You've been riding him for three months. And, to tell you the truth, we're all getting sick of it," said Doc, as he began to rise from the table. "Well excuse me, DOCTOR," said Don in a mocking tone.

Gloria joined in, "Why don't we all just clean up and retire to our quarters for the night. We all need a good night's sleep. It's obvious that we're all agitated."

Adrian could feel the tension starting to build in the room. Ted, Isaac, Skyler, Scott, and Sean all got up without finishing, cleaned their utensils, and began to make their way to each of their quarters.

Adrian was about to do the same when Petey piped up again. "See, those guys have the right idea. I agree with the commander. Let's all—"

"You're doing it again!" said Don, slamming his fist onto the table.

"Doing what?"

"Brown-nosing!"

"You know what, DON!" Petey said. His face flushing red, and fists clenching.

"What?"

"I know what the real problem is here."

"Oh yeah, what's that?"

"You're jealous."

"What? Jealous…That's ridiculous. Why would I be jealous of you?"

Adrian had to admit. He was starting to enjoy this. He could sense that Doc and Gloria were too. After all, they needed a little excitement after three months of testing, analyzing, and preparing. He also noticed that the rest of the crew had come back to watch the argument.

Petey continued. "Oh, you're not jealous of me. I know that."

"Who am I jealous of then?" Don asked.

"Commander Palmer!"

And there it was, out in the open. What everyone had been thinking and feeling the past three years as they trained together as a crew…the truth.

"Wha…you're off your rocker, Sanchez!"

"Admit it. You've been jealous since the day NASA chose Commander Palmer to command this mission over you. Oh, you've never said it to us, but you said it to the press. But we could tell. You're always trying—"

"It's true, at the time I was jealous when I vented to the press, but not now."

It was obvious that Petey had Don catching his tongue. Adrian was impressed that Petey finally had the courage to stand up to Don. They all just sat around the table with smiles on their faces as Don was getting his from the young nuclear engineer.

"Oh, don't lie to me, Don. You're still jealous. That's why you use me as a punching bag for your derogatory comments and constant put-downs. You don't have the guts to say it to the commander!"

With that last comment, Adrian saw Don's face flush red; he gritted his teeth, and clenched his fists.

"Why you—," Don screamed as he jumped over the table and lunged toward Petey.

Plates of food splattered and crashed onto the floor. Gloria's drink splashed in her face. Don hit Petey square in the chest with his right shoulder, and Petey sprawled backwards out of his chair, hitting the back of his head on Doc's knee who was standing behind him.

Don and Petey rolled around on the floor with curse words flying. Don rolled over on top of Petey, straddled him, and raised his right arm ready to deliver the knockout punch.

Just as Don was about to deliver the blow that would certainly knock Petey out, Doc grabbed the back of Don's shirt, lifted him off of Petey, and slammed him into the kitchen wall. "That's enough!"

Adrian decided it was time to step in and take charge as he was supposed to. "All right. . . . You two have had your fun. I am now issuing a direct order. We all go to our quarters and retire for the night, and not another word. As for Petey and Don, you both need to write a letter of apology to one another by the end of tomorrow. If not, I'm putting both of you on report."

"A letter of apology! I wouldn't apologize to that—"

"That's enough!"

Gloria jumped, upon hearing Adrian yell for the first time.

Don ignored Adrian and continued. "Maybe Petey was right. Maybe I didn't have the guts to say it before. But I do believe that I would have been the better commander! I wouldn't have ever let a situation like this happen in the first place! The only reason you're in command of this mission is because your brother helped build this thing!"

Adrian had finally been pushed over the edge. Usually calm in tense situations and the peacekeeper, he clenched his left fist and threw a punch in the direction of Don's right cheek. Don ducked and landed a punch of his own on Adrian's left eye. Adrian fell to the ground, and immediately felt his eye throb with excruciating pain as blood rushed out of broken capillaries.

Doc stepped in front of Don who was about to attack Adrian again. "Knock it off, Don! Go to your quarters now!"

"I don't have to answer to you. You're subordinate to me, remember!"

Doc, now angry, lunged toward Don. Don backed out of the kitchen and ran to his quarters.

★ ★ ★ ★ ★

The next morning, Adrian awoke with a throbbing headache, and he could only see out of his right eye. He threw the blankets off of his body, sat up, and ran his hand through his brown hair. *Why didn't I control myself last night, and why do I keep having this unpleasant feeling that something isn't right*, he thought, as he got out of bed and strolled to the washroom mirror.   Adrian   placed both hands on the washroom sink, slumped over and then raised his head groggily to peer into the mirror. "Ouch," he whispered to himself, as he touched his eye. His left eye was completely swollen shut. It looked as if someone had taped an enormous black and purple bandage over it.

There was a knock at his door.

"Come in."

His door slid open, and Gloria walked in. Adrian turned around, happy to see her beautiful face. "Ouch, you need to get some ice on that thing," Gloria said.

"No, I'll be alright," said Adrian, as he and Gloria embraced each other.

"I came to see if you were okay. I've never seen you get that angry before?" Gloria questioned.

"I usually don't. I guess I should have stopped the argument between Petey and Don before it got out of hand, but I just wanted to see Petey give it to Don."

"Yeah, but Don ended up giving it to you instead."

Adrian let out a small laugh as he turned around and sat on the bed. Gloria sat next to him. "Maybe you were right, Gloria. Maybe I shouldn't have chosen Don as my copilot."

"I know I was right," replied Gloria with a chuckle.

"It seems like he's getting angrier each passing day we're out here. I don't know . . . maybe I should apologize and have a good heart to heart with him. What do you think?"

"I think that's great for you, but I don't think he'll accept your apology."

"Why's that?"

"Because he's a selfish, arrogant, j—"

"Now, let's not go calling anybody names."

"Well, he is."

Adrian laughed again. He always found that Gloria was able to make him feel better no matter the situation. She also seemed to be thinking the same thing as him time after time. He knew that Don was what she said he was, but he couldn't help but think that he and Don could resolve their differences.

Adrian stood up, walked to the sink, and splashed cold water on his face. He flinched as his index finger nicked his eye.

"Careful," said Gloria.

She stood up and walked over to Adrian. She turned him around to face her and lightly blew on his eye. Then, she leaned in and kissed him ever so gently on the lips.

Adrian pulled her in close and kissed her back – a long, passionate kiss. He continued to hold her when their lips separated.

"Adrian, there's something I need to tell you." Gloria looked down and paused, trying to find the right words.

Adrian gently touched her under the chin and raised it, so he could look into her eyes. Gloria tried to turn away. Adrian wouldn't let her. "What is it?" He asked.

Gloria paused again. "I don't know. For some strange reason, I had this overwhelming feeling to tell you this morning. . . ."

"Go on. Tell me. What is it?"

"Adrian, I've never told you this before, and you have told me so many times already, but..."

Gloria struggled to find the words and looked down again.

"Go on. It's okay," whispered Adrian, as he gently lifted her head again.

"Adrian, I love you."

Adrian couldn't help but smile. He had wondered all of these months if Gloria felt the same way he did, and now he knew. He pulled her in closer and said, "I love you too."

They kissed again.

After the kiss, Adrian placed the back of his hand on Gloria's smooth face and asked the question he had been avoiding on their three-month journey, "Have you had a chance to read what I gave you?"

Gloria pulled away and looked into Adrian's eyes. "I have."

"And . . ."

"I don't know, Adrian. . . . I've been reading it on our journey and just finished, but I haven't done what the book asks me to do...What was that scripture again?"

"Moroni chapter ten, verse four."

"Yeah, that one. I . . . I don't know. I mean, how do you know God even speaks to us anymore? I was always taught that God doesn't speak to His children anymore. That His word is revealed through the Bible."

Adrian understood Gloria's concern, as he looked deep into her eyes. After all, the secular belief was that God didn't speak to His children anymore. But Adrian knew better. He had a testimony and truly believed that the Gospel of Jesus Christ was on the earth again, restored through the prophet Joseph Smith and that Joseph Smith translated *The Book of Mormon.*

As Adrian looked at Gloria, he knew without a doubt that she was the one he should be with. Even though she could never replace Melissa, he had a deep and abiding love and respect for her, a love he could only compare to the love he had for his late wife.

He continued to look into Gloria's eyes and knew he had to bear his testimony to her again and tell her of his spiritual experience a few days before their scheduled launch to Mars.

He grabbed Gloria's hand and pulled her to the bed. The two sat side by side as Adrian took a deep breath and then proceeded to speak. "Gloria, I understand your hesitation to ask God if *The Book of Mormon* and these things I have told you are true. But I bear witness to you that God lives and that His Son, Jesus Christ, died for us. And I also bear witness to you that Christ restored His church through Joseph Smith, and through His prophet, *The Book of Mormon* was translated and truly contains the Word of God...."

Adrian paused a few seconds as he felt the manifestation of the Holy Ghost swell within him. A tear ran down his cheek, and Gloria reached up to wipe it away. After she wiped the tear, Adrian grabbed Gloria's hand and noticed her eyes beginning to glisten. He knew that she felt the spirit. He was about to continue when Gloria spoke.

"Adrian," she said in a soft whisper, "I know that you believe what you are saying is true. I get goose bumps every time you tell me, but I am the type that needs to be one hundred percent sure. There needs to be some way to find out. I want to believe."

Adrian smiled and wiped a tear away that ran down from her eye. "There is no way to be one hundred percent sure, Gloria. That's where faith comes in. The Lord wants us to have faith because if all of us knew without a doubt that God existed, we wouldn't be tested."

"I guess you're right," Gloria said as she placed her hand on Adrian's cheek. "I'll try, Adrian. I promise. Tonight, before I go to bed, I will pray about the truthfulness of *The Book of Mormon*. But I still have my doubts."

"I know you do, Gloria. That's why I wanted to tell you what happened to me a few days before we launched for Mars."

Gloria looked at Adrian with confusion. "You never told me anything had happened to you before we left."

"I know," Adrian replied. "I'm sorry. I just didn't want to concern you before we left."

"Concern me with what?"

"I almost resigned my commission as Commander of *Mars I*."

"What!" Gloria said, with a small gasp. "Why?"

"I was really struggling with leaving Jake. I felt guilty, I guess. After all, he lost his mother when he was just two and here I was abandoning him while I chased my selfish dreams."

Gloria grabbed both of Adrian's hands. "You can't feel guilty for that Adrian. Jake is so proud of you. For being so young, he truly understands your mission. And besides, he's in good hands with Kevin and Diane."

"I know that now. But at the time I was really concerned. So I decided to do what any good Mormon does when he or she is struggling with a decision. I fasted, prayed, and went to the temple."

Adrian paused a few seconds to see if Gloria would respond. She didn't. She sat and looked at Adrian with such compassion and love that he wanted to scream from the top of his lungs that he truly loved this woman and wanted to spend the rest of eternity with her. But he could also see her indecision with the truthfulness of Adrian's beliefs. He continued. "Anyway, I went to the temple, and as I proceeded through the sessions and came to the final room, the most amazing thing happened."

"You sacrificed a chicken?"

Adrian let out a small laugh. He knew Gloria was kidding. At one time, however, she truly believed that was what Mormons did in their temples. It wasn't until Adrian explained to her what actually happens in the temples that she changed her way of thinking. He knew that this was how she dealt with serious conversations. She often used humor, and he loved her for that.

"No," he said as he chuckled.

"I'm sorry, Adrian. Go on. I promise I won't joke around anymore."

Adrian gave her a warm smile and continued. "As I was sitting in that temple room, I saw what I think was a vision."

Gloria jerked back and gave Adrian a skeptical stare. She then relaxed and placed her hand on his; giving Adrian the reassurance he needed that she didn't think he was crazy.

"I know it sounds crazy, but I wasn't in the same room anymore."

"Where were you then?" Gloria asked.

"I . . . I don't know. It was as if I was transported someplace else. All I know was that I was in this completely different room. The room was beautiful. It was made completely of white marble, and a beautiful candlelit chandelier hung from the ceiling. There was also a baptismal font in one corner and an alter in the other corner. On the other side of the room was this gold, spiral staircase that must have led up to other floors of wherever I was. But the most amazing thing was that . . ."

Adrian had to stop as he felt his emotions rise to the surface again. When he experienced the vision, the spirit communicated to him so clearly that it left him weak with fatigue. And as he recalled the events again, he once again felt the spirit so strongly that he knew without a doubt that God had communicated with him.

As he looked at Gloria, he saw tears streaming down her face. She watched him with an intensity that told him that she believed what he was saying to be true. And she seemed to wait with sincere impatience for what would happen next. "Well, go on, Adrian. Don't leave me guessing. What was most amazing?"

Adrian gave her a warm smile. "Jake was there holding my hand. . . . At least, I think it was him?"

Gloria cocked her head in confusion. "What do you mean, you think it was him?"

"Well, the boy that was holding my hand looked exactly like Jake but was a few years older, probably seven or eight. But he also had black as midnight hair, and you know Jake doesn't have dark hair. He has brown hair."

Gloria nodded.

Adrian smiled again. He could sense without a doubt that Gloria believed every word he said to her. He knew because he could feel the spirit so strongly in his quarters, she had to feel it as well.

He continued. "Yeah, maybe. But while I was holding his hand, a voice spoke to me. The voice was so clear. It was almost as if the Lord was in the room and spoke directly to me." Adrian waited for Gloria's reaction. This time she didn't flinch in surprise.

"What did the voice say?" she asked in almost a quiet reverence.

Adrian looked down and felt the tears flow from his eyes. Adrian then looked up and looked directly into Gloria's eyes.

She returned his look with a look of love and understanding. Tears began to flow from Gloria's eyes as well as she reached up and wiped Adrian's tears away. "Go on, Adrian. What did Jesus say to you?"

"He said that if I didn't go on the Mars' mission, the vision that I witnessed before me wouldn't come to pass, and then just like that I was back in the original temple room."

Gloria nodded her head and moved in closer to Adrian. She placed her head into his chest and wrapped her arms around him in a tight squeeze. "I'm glad," she said. "If you wouldn't have listened to the Lord, we wouldn't have been together on this mission, and I wouldn't have had the chance to hear your testimony."

The couple sat in silence for a few moments. Adrian smiled and ran his fingers through Gloria's long, brunette hair. It felt as smooth as silk. He was growing to love this woman more and more each day, a love that he knew he could not live without. It was at this moment - whether she decided to join the church or not - that he decided he would ask Gloria to marry him when their yearlong journey was over.

But as the two sat in silence and in each other's loving embrace, Adrian remembered the thought that came to him just as they left Earth's atmosphere.

Gloria, sensing Adrian's thoughts, asked, "What is it?"

Adrian gently placed his hands on Gloria's shoulders and pushed her away. He stood up and took a few steps forward with his back to Gloria.

"What?" questioned Gloria, standing to follow.

Adrian slowly turned and looked at Gloria with a deep sadness in his eyes. "I know that the vision and the voice I heard was from God, but the moment we left Earth's atmosphere, a thought popped into my head, a nagging thought that I can't get out."

"What thought?"

"Was the night before we left Earth the last time I would see and hold my son?"

Gloria moved closer to Adrian and said, "Why would you think that?"

"I don't know maybe something is going to happen to us. I haven't told you, but for the last few days, I have had an uneasy feeling that something isn't right."

"That's ridiculous. Everything has been running so smoothly it's almost gotten boring, except for last night's fight of course."

"That's what I'm afraid of. Everything has been running smoothly. Something's bound to happen."

"Now you're being paranoid."

"I don't think so. I think I'm going to call off your space walk today."

"What? Don't you dare," Gloria said as she grabbed Adrian's hand. "I know what this is. I told you that I love you, and now you're trying to protect me."

"No, that's not it at all. It's just—"

Gloria gave Adrian a stern look and cut him off in mid-sentence. "Commander, you're not calling of the walk! I'll be fine. I've practiced this space walk so many times that I can do it without even thinking. This one will be a piece of cake."

Adrian knew that he wouldn't be able to win an argument with Gloria. When she had her mind set on something, there was no changing it. "Whatever you say."

Gloria smiled at him and gave him another kiss. She pulled away and said, "And besides, you know I'm the only one here who can handle this type of space walk."

"Okay, okay, you've convinced me," said Adrian, as he smiled at Gloria and held his hands up in defeat.

Adrian then walked Gloria to the door. The door slid open, and Gloria stepped out. Adrian walked up to her, grabbed her, and gave her a long kiss.

Gloria pushed Adrian away and said, "What are you doing? Someone's going to see."

"I don't care anymore. I think we should tell the whole crew."

★ ★ ★ ★ ★

Adrian made it to the hatchway that separated the mid-deck from the flight-deck. In a few moments, he would feel the strange sensation of weightlessness. He also dreaded opening the hatch because he knew that Don was on the other side already working. However, he knew that he had to go in and apologize.

"*Maggie*," Adrian said, referring to the shuttle's main computer. "Open the hatchway to the flight-deck . . . authorization code: Charlie, Alpha, zero, one, zero."

"Yes, Commander," the computer said, responding in its seductive voice.

Adrian tried to smile as he floated in through the hatchway. The thought of how Sean had become so captivated with *Mars I's* main computer amused him. He looked up and saw Don doing calculations at his workstation.

"Don," Adrian said in a solemn tone.

Don looked up from his work and responded, "Commander," and immediately went back to his work.

Adrian made his way past the other crew members' stations and buckled himself in his seat at the front of the flight-deck. He turned his seat to face Don. "Don, we need to talk."

"Well, talk then," Don said, not looking up from his station.

"In order for this mission to be a success, we all need to work together and know that we can trust each other." There was an odd feeling of silence as Adrian waited for Don to answer.

Adrian paused and shook his head. "Anyway, I know that a good team starts with a good leader, and so far, I haven't been that leader."

"Ain't that the truth," said Don, still not looking at Adrian.

Adrian shook his head again and disregarded Don's comment. This was going to be difficult. He could see that Don was not in the mood for talking, and obviously wasn't going to accept his apology. "I just wanted to say that I'm sorry about last night. I should have acted more professionally."

No answer.

"Don?"

"What?" Don replied, still involved with his work.

"I'm trying to apologize, and you're acting as if I'm not even here."

Don still didn't answer. He looked up and rolled his eyes.

To this, Adrian clenched his fists as he felt the frustrations from the night before begin to boil to the surface again. "So, for the next year we're not even going to talk. You know we're going to have to communicate sooner or later."

Don finally stopped working, turned to face Adrian, and said, "Fine! You want me to accept your apology?"

"Yes."

"Well, I don't. You know I'm the better leader. I was just trying to prove to the rest of the crew how easily you could let a situation get out of hand."

Adrian was getting angrier. "What, so now you're going to stage a coup and leave me on Mars?"

Don let a wry smile spread across his face and said, "Ah, you know that won't happen. The rest of the crew adores you. It seems that I'm the only one here that's right."

"Don, I don't want to have to put you on report, but I will if—"

"Report! Ha! I should be the one putting you on report!"

"What do you mean?" Adrian asked, wishing the rest of the crew was in the flight-deck to back him up.

Don glared at Adrian and raised three fingers, counting off each one of Adrian's offenses, "First of all, you threw the first punch, remember? Second, you've been preaching that Mormon doctrine of yours to everyone in the crew. I can't count how many times you've offered me one of those stupid Mormon books. This is a government-funded mission. Remember, separation of church and state." Don paused as if another thought had come to him. He hesitated a few seconds.

Adrian, now angry, couldn't wait any longer for the confrontation to occur. He knew what Don was thinking but egged him on, nonetheless. "What, Don. Don't stop! You're on a role."

Don's eyes narrowed into a spiteful stare. "Oh yeah, your brother helped fund part of this mission and helped create this shuttle so maybe you feel that gives you a right to preach to all of us as if we're little kids, not capable of believing in what we choose."

Adrian was about to defend himself, when Don continued.

"I told you," Don said, pointing to his own chest, "that I don't believe in a God. Everything man has created he has done on his own. There's no God, there's no afterlife, so quite trying to push your beliefs on the rest of us." Don stopped, waiting for Adrian to respond.

Adrian was speechless; he didn't know what to say. He knew that Don was an atheist, but Adrian always felt a strong responsibility to preach the Gospel, especially after never having the opportunity to go on a mission. After all, everyone else in the crew accepted Adrian's invitation to read *The Book of Mormon*. His best friend, Doc, even converted and was baptized by

Adrian a month before they left on the mission. Was Don a lost cause?

Adrian was about to speak again, but Don beat him to it.

Don raised his third finger and gave Adrian a malicious smile. "And the third reason I should put you on report . . . you're playing kissy face with a member of your own crew!"

Adrian was taken back. How did Don know? Adrian tried to hide his surprise. "Wha...What are you talking about?"

"Oh, don't play dumb, COMMANDER," Don replied in a mocking tone. "I walked around the wheel this morning and there you two were – lips attached and in full embrace."

Don had Adrian. It was true Don could cite a report saying that Adrian failed to report a relationship with a crew member. Not only did Don have that against Adrian, he had the fact that Adrian threw the first punch, and there were witnesses. Adrian probably wouldn't be able to command another space mission again.

Adrian wanted to unbuckle himself and go after Don, but he knew better. Besides, what kind of fight would they have floating around in zero gravity?

"Do what you feel is necessary. I still thin—"

In mid-sentence, Adrian heard the hatchway door slide open, and the rest of the crew floated in, except for Gloria, Scott, and Petey. Each one buckled himself into his station.

"What are ya'll gabbin' about? Can't ya see we got work to do?" said Skyler, as he pointed toward the flight-deck's plasma shield, which gave the crew a clear view of what was ahead and separated them from the vacuum of space.

Adrian and Don turned and looked. There it was . . . coming up fast, the Red Planet.

"All engines stop! Don, get us into a synchronous orbit around Mars."

"Yes, SIR," replied Don in a sarcastic tone.

Adrian shot Don a look. "You will do what is asked from your commanding officer and without an attitude! Understood!" said Adrian, feeling a small victory for finally taking charge of the situation.

Don simply looked at Adrian and the rest of the crew who were trying not to let their amusement show. "Yes, Commander."

As Don maneuvered the shuttle into place, Adrian spattered out orders to the other crew members. "Petey, are you at your station?"

Petey replied, "Yes, Commander."

"Good, make sure all of your instruments are running smoothly, so we don't get any false readings for when we open the payload doors, and we're exposed to solar radiation."

"All instruments are reading perfectly. I've checked them and double checked them."

"Roger that. Scott . . . you and Gloria get to the payload-deck and get Gloria prepped for her space walk. We're ready to set the satellite."

"We're already in the payload-deck, Commander, and Gloria is ready to go," said Scott.

"Good. Doc, do you have Gloria's vitals online?"

"Yes, everything looks good, except her heart rate . . . it's a little high," said Doc, as he punched data into his computer.

Adrian thought that was strange that Gloria's heart rate was high. In her previous walks, her heart rate was perfectly normal. He wondered if she was nervous from what they had discussed, earlier that morning. "Gloria, is everything okay?"

"I'm fine. I'm just a little nervous that's all."

"Well, you'll be fine," said Adrian, trying to ease her nerves. "You've done these walks hundreds of times without any problems."

"Thank you, Commander."

Sean piped in, "Commander, you know *Maggie* could do all of this automatically, and Gloria wouldn't have to go out today."

Gloria spoke before Adrian could answer, "No, I'm fine . . . really. Besides, we've never tested if *Maggie* could remotely activate the satellite, and I prefer to do it on my own."

Adrian continued. "Coop," that's what the crew called Isaac Cooper, "are your calculations correct for the satellite's orbit around Mars?"

"Yes, Commander, I've been working all morning on them and—"

Isaac stopped talking and looked past Adrian, outside of the flight-deck's plasma shield. Adrian gave Isaac a confused look. Isaac unbuckled himself, floated to the front of the flight-deck just behind Adrian and Don, and pointed. "What is that?"

Adrian turned his seat around and looked. "What? I don't see anything," he said as he looked ahead to Mars at his twelve o'clock. He then turned his head left and right.

"There. Can't you see it?" said Isaac, pointing to Adrian's left.

Soon the other five crew members behind Adrian and Don were out of their seats and floating, looking for what Isaac saw.

"I see it," Ted said, pointing to his left.

Adrian didn't know where they were looking. He couldn't see a thing. "Where? I don't see it."

"Look to your ten o'clock, Commander," said Doc, pointing to Adrian's left.

Adrian looked, and there it was. It looked like a ripple in space, similar to when a person throws a rock in water, and it causes the water to ripple out from the center. "Coop, what is that thing?"

"I . . . I don't know."

Don cut in, "Well, you're the astronomer. You're supposed to know."

Isaac answered back and gave Don a dirty look, "In all of my studies and observations, I have never seen anything that looked like that."

Adrian cut Don off before he could respond, "All of you get to your stations. Coop, analyze that thing and see if it's any danger to us."

"Roger that."

Don spoke up again. "Maybe we should move to the other side of Mars to set the satellite in case that thing is a danger."

It pained Adrian to say it, but Don was right. "Yeah, maybe your right. Sc—"

"Of course, I'm right."

Adrian ignored Don's comment and continued. "Scott, hold on, we're going to move to the other side of Mars to set the satellite."

"Too late. I've already opened the bay doors, and Gloria's already out there."

Adrian grew agitated. Why did he feel as if his crew was falling apart? Was he too polite and not demanding enough? This wasn't how it was supposed to work. He was the commanding officer. His crew needed to follow his orders. "What? I didn't give you the order to open the doors and let Gloria out."

"I'm sorry, Sir. I just thought I would start the next step."

Adrian, obviously frustrated said, "Scott, you need to wait until I give the order. Follow protocol. Understood?"

"Yes, I'm sorry, Sir."

Adrian changed his focus. "All right. Here's what were going to do. Scott and Gloria get that satellite set and get in here quick. Once you're in, we're going to go to the other side of Mars to prepare for our surface landing."

Scott replied with a small quiver in his voice, "Roger that."

★ ★ ★ ★ ★

Scott sat at his station in the payload-deck with a lump in his throat. He didn't mean to upset the commander. He just assumed that the commander would order him to open the payload doors because they had done this so many times before. Yet, he knew that he had made a mistake, and he was determined to make up for it by getting the satellite set as quickly as possible.

He manipulated the shuttle's arm using its joysticks. He would simply lift the satellite from the cargo bay and set it in a stationary position in orbit, so that Gloria could do her work. Gloria was already in position, attached to a lifeline that was attached to a winch. When Gloria finished calibrating and activating the satellite, he would simply pull Gloria in with the winch.

"Gloria . . . once I get this thing out there and make sure it's motionless, I'll let go and you can do your stuff."

"It's okay, Scott. We've done this too many times to count."

"I know. I'm just feeling pressured here because we have to do this quick, so we can move away from whatever it is they are worried about."

"I can see it. It looks like a ripple in water."

"Strange," said Scott, maneuvering the satellite into position. He made sure the satellite didn't have any momentum as he let go of it.

Suddenly, Scott was jolted forward, causing him to hit the joysticks that controlled the arm. The arm swung violently. Scott yelled, "Gloria!"

★ ★ ★ ★ ★

Adrian and the crew in the flight-deck were violently jerked toward the ripple. Adrian heard Scott yell. "Scott! Is Gloria okay?"

Gloria spoke before Scott could answer, "I'm alright, Adrian. I felt the jolt too. The arm barely missed my head, and right now I'm about ten feet from the satellite. But I'm getting pulled. Did you fire the thrusters?"

"Negative. We're checking into it."

Adrian turned to the rest of the crew and asked, "What was that?" "Uh . . . Commander, I'm getting some strange gravimetric anomalies from that space distortion," said Isaac.

Adrian's eyes narrowed into a look of serious concern. "What do you mean . . . anomalies?"

"Well, to put it in laymen's terms. That thing's got gravity and a lot of it!"

"What?" said Doc, as he turned to face Isaac.

Adrian turned to look at the distortion. "Are you telling me, we're being pulled into this thing?"

"We are," Isaac answered.

Adrian quickly shouted orders. "Don, fire the reverse thrusters. Scott. . . . Gloria. . . . I'm going to maneuver the shuttle back to the satellite. Once were in position, Gloria, activate that thing, and Scott, when she's done, get her in fast."

Don fired the reverse thrusters. Adrian and the crew felt another jolt, but for some reason, they weren't moving. Adrian turned and looked at Sean. "Sean, send a distress communication to Houston."

Sean quickly replied, "Roger that."

Adrian was starting to become frightened. The shuttle wasn't moving at all. Between the force of the reverse thrusters and the force from the ripple, the shuttle sat motionless in space.

Sean spoke frantically, "Sir, there's a problem with the communication satellite on the shuttle."

Adrian turned his seat around, and with dread in his eyes, seemed to look straight through Sean. "What do you mean, there's a problem?"

Sean swallowed and shook his head. "I don't know. I'm not getting a signal. It's like it's not even there."

Before Adrian could answer, Gloria spoke. "Adrian, I think the shuttle's arm knocked the satellite off because it's floating past me."

Adrian turned his seat back around to face the ripple in front of the shuttle and slammed his fists down onto his console.

Suddenly there was another jolt, and *Mars I* began to move toward the ripple again. "We're moving again! Don, apply more power to the reverse thrusters!"

Don did as he was ordered, as he punched in the commands. "It's no use. We're being sucked into that thing."

The crew in the flight-deck sat wide eyed with their mouths open as the ripple came to within fifty yards of the shuttle.

"Don, more power!" cried Adrian.

"I can't! I've already got the thrusters to full power!"

Adrian looked at the distortion again. They were moving closer to it. It almost looked as if a giant sea creature was beginning to engulf the entire shuttle. Adrian frantically thought and said, "What if we rerouted all of the power in the shuttle to the reverse thrusters?"

Sean answered quickly, "That might do it!"

Adrian turned and shot a look at Sean. "Do it then!"

Adrian felt the shuttle shake violently as it continued to move closer and closer. Alarms buzzed and beeped everywhere within the flight-deck.

Petey spoke anxiously from his station in the nuke-deck. "Uh . . . Commander, we've got a problem down here."

"What's wrong?"

"With the shuttle shaking so badly, one of the rods has become lodged in the reactor core. I need to shut down all of the power to remove it. If I don't, the core's going to melt down, and then we're going to have bigger problems to worry about."

Adrian had come face to face with a decision he dreaded he would have to make since becoming the commander of man's first mission to Mars; placing the crew in danger of one disaster in order to avoid another.

If he ordered Petey to shut down the power, they wouldn't have enough juice in the thrusters to get away from the nightmare that was about to engulf them. On the other hand, if he ordered that all power be rerouted to the reverse thrusters, he ran the risk of a core meltdown.

Don yelled, "Commander, if we don't switch to auxiliary power now, the core's going to meltdown. . . . Commander. . . . Commander!"

Adrian was not only dealing with his responsibilities as commander, he was fighting with his personal feelings as well.

"Commander!" Don screamed.

"Petey, shut down the reactor and reroute all auxiliary power to the winch, and Scott . . . get Gloria in here fast!"

Don gave Adrian a puzzled look. "But, if we reroute all of the auxiliary power to the winch, we won't have time to reroute the power back and shut the bay doors?"

"You don't think I know that, Don!"

"Don't let your personal feelings get in the way of your duty ...COMMANDER!"

"I won't leave Gloria out there to get sucked into this thing while we shut the bay doors and try to escape!" Adrian paused and shook his head. "I won't let anyone in the crew get hurt. You're all my responsibility!"

"Then you may have just killed us all!" yelled Don.

Adrian did not want to make this decision. And then . . . he heard Gloria.

★ ★ ★ ★ ★

Gloria felt her lifeline to the ship tighten. The lifeline was attached to the back of her spacesuit, so as the shuttle began to drift toward the ripple, she began to move further and further away from the satellite. She could sense the shuttle picking up speed because of her focal point on the satellite. She just prayed that the lifeline wouldn't rip her suit, which would expose her to the vacuum of space.

She continued to drift. The satellite was now fifteen feet away, then twenty, then twenty-five, and so on. Gloria could hear the despair in Adrian's voice as he rang out orders and struggled with the decision to shut the bay doors. She heard Don yell at Adrian, and Adrian pause. She knew what she had to do.

"Adrian . . . have Scott detach the lifeline from the winch and shut the bay doors, so you can attempt to escape."

Adrian replied, "No! I won't let you go!"

"You have to. If you don't, we're all dead."

"No!"

"Adrian, listen to me. There might be a chance I won't even go into that thing if its gravity doesn't catch me. My momentum might carry me over it. If you can maneuver the shuttle out of the way, you can swing around, Scott can extend the arm, and I could try to catch myself on it."

"And if that doesn't work?"

"I don't know if it will work, but it's the only option we have," Gloria said. She waited for Adrian's reply. She could hear him discussing it with the other crew members. "Adrian, you better hurry. You're getting closer to that thing!"

Adrian finally answered with fear in his voice. "Okay. . . . Okay. Scott . . . detach the lifeline from the winch. Once the lifeline clears the bay doors, close them. And, Gloria . . . I love you!"

"I love you too. And Adrian?"

"Yes."

"I believe . . . I believe."

Gloria heard Adrian through her communication link. She couldn't tell if he was beginning to cry or not.

"Gloria," Adrian said. "I won't let you die."

"I know," said Gloria, as tears began to stream down her face.

She heard the click of Adrian's communication link, turned around, and saw her cable detach from the winch within the payload doors.

Gloria could feel the terror of not being attached to the shuttle surge through her body. Who knew how fast she was moving? The thought of not being attached to the shuttle and flying through space at an unknown velocity terrified her.

She also worried about another scenario. What if the shuttle was able to stop its momentum? There was the possibility that she could slam into it.

Gloria watched as she saw the lifeline clear the bay doors. The doors closed. She saw the reverse thrusters firing, but the shuttle wasn't stopping or slowing down. In fact, it was picking up speed. Without the reactor running, there obviously wasn't enough power to stop their momentum. The shuttle was moving farther away.

Gloria heard Adrian yell. "Gloria . . . it's not working! Glor—"

With horror protruding throughout her entire body, Gloria watched as *Mars I* vanished through the ripple.

As soon as the shuttle went through the distortion, it closed, leaving Gloria all alone and traveling at an unknown velocity toward Mars. Gloria screamed with terror. "Adrian! Adrian! Adrian!"

But there was no answer. She was alone.

Gloria contemplated her situation for a few moments. She didn't know what to do. She couldn't kill herself. But she knew that her doom was near as the Red Planet grew larger and larger before her eyes.

Closing her tear-filled eyes and her body trembling with fear, she slowly bowed her head and prayed. "My Father in Heaven, blessed be thy name. I am alone and know that I will soon be with thee again. But I need thy comfort, Father. I need thee to help me know what to do. If I kill myself before I enter Mars' atmosphere, will I be committing murder? I don't know, Father. Help me to know what to do. I also know that thy Son bled and suffered for my sins, and that His Gospel was restored through Joseph Smith. I know that Joseph Smith restored the true church and translated *The Book of Mormon*. But, Father, I am afraid I am too late. Please help me, in the name of thy Son, Jesus Christ, amen."

Just after ending her prayer, Gloria felt the most wonderful and amazing feeling enter into her body. She was no longer shaking. She slowly opened her eyes and saw directly in front of her, her maternal grandmother who had passed away nearly five years before, and behind her grandmother was Mars.

Her grandmother was beautiful and younger. Her spirit gave off such a glow that Gloria almost had to close her sun shield to protect her eyes. Her beautiful long, blond hair seemed to flow along with her white robe in the vacuum of space.

She smiled at Gloria, as she reached out her hand and said, "Fear not, Gloria. I have always been with you. Our Father will not let you suffer like this. Take my hand."

Gloria, feeling a sense of calm and love, reached out and grabbed her grandmother's hand. She could feel the smooth touch of her grandmother's hand. She wondered how she could feel it through the glove of her spacesuit.

She looked and noticed that her hand was bare, reflecting the same light her grandmother emitted. She turned her head and saw her body in its flight suit enter the atmosphere of Mars.

The two, floating in space, watched until Gloria's body was no longer visible. Gloria felt her grandmother's hand touch her face and gently turn it to her.

Her grandmother knew what she was thinking and said, "Fear not, Gloria, for Adrian has been called to his mission."

Gloria gave her grandmother a smile of love and happiness, a smile that told her grandmother that she was ready to join her in the spirit world.

CHAPTER 3

Twenty-three years later, June 6, 2040 – Near Ogden, Utah

The rain pounded the 2040 BMW in gigantic droplets of water. It seemed as if the heavens had opened up. The storm dumped so much water that large puddles began to form on the road, like small lakes scattered to-and-fro throughout the asphalt. The glossy black luxury car, however, managed to maintain a constant speed and its control as it sped north on Interstate 15 from Salt Lake City.

"Computer . . . when the car reaches the guard post, stop."

"Yes, Mr. Palmer."

As Kevin Palmer's car drove toward the guard's post at Hill Air Force Base near Ogden, Utah, he contemplated all of the benefits his smart processor had brought to the world. Every industry from car manufacturers to home appliance companies invested in his little chip. Everything with a computer system from a cell phone to an airplane was now voice interactive. Also, it seemed that nearly every person in the world that could afford it now had an interactive robot in their possession, doing all kinds of work. As a result, the smart processor had made Kevin Palmer one of the richest men in the world, but he still wasn't happy. All of the money in the world couldn't replace what he had lost.

"So Dad, what kind of trouble did Jake get himself into now?" said a voice from the passenger side seat.

Kevin turned and looked at his blonde, twenty-year-old daughter. "Now Ashley, when you see him, don't give him a hard time."

Ashley looked at Kevin with her piercing, baby blues and gave him a smile, flashing her perfectly aligned, white teeth. "Oh, you know me, Dad."

"Yes, I do know you, and I know that you're going to give him a hard time. You two have been at each other's throats since you two were kids. But promise me this time that you won't ride him about getting into trouble again."

"But it's fun," said Ashley, sticking out her bottom lip.

Kevin gave Ashley a stern look and said, "Promise me."

"Alright, I'll try," said Ashley, obviously disappointed.

Another voice came from the backseat. "Hey Dad, is Jake going to get kicked out of the Air Force this time?"

"Computer...Auto-drive."

"Yes, Mr. Palmer," replied the car's computer.

Kevin turned his seat to face his son. Kevin adored his 14-year-old son. Adam reminded Kevin so much of Adrian in looks and personality. "I don't know, Son. That's what this meeting is for."

"I hope he didn't do anything stupid this time," replied Adam who was thoroughly involved with his interactive, holographic video game.

"Me too," said Kevin. He gave Adam a smile and turned his seat around to face the dark road. The rain was coming down harder now. It looked as if sheets of water were being poured over the car, and Kevin turned the wipers to their highest speed.

Adam spoke up again, "Because if he did, I'm going to kick his butt. And, when I'm through with him, Ashley won't need to give him a hard time."

All three laughed.

Kevin was astonished at how much Adam looked up to Jake, even though Jake hadn't always been the best role model.

"Mr. Palmer. The guard post is one hundred feet ahead. The vehicle is preparing to stop," echoed the vehicle's computer.

"Very well," replied Kevin.

The BMW pulled up to the guard post at Hill Air Force Base and stopped. Kevin lowered the window. A guard in his mid-twenties, dressed in green fatigues walked up to the car. "What is the nature of your business, Sir?"

Kevin looked up at the guard. "I'm Kevin Palmer. I have an appointment with Colonel Jepson."

The guard pointed ahead. "Yes, the colonel has been expecting you. Drive ahead about one hundred yards. Take the first left. You will see the base's administration building on your right. The colonel's office is on the first floor. Let his secretary know who you are."

"Thank you," Kevin said as he rolled up the window.

Ashley turned to look at Adam. "Hey, Adam."

Adam, still absorbed in his video game, answered. "What?"

"I'll bet you fifty bucks Jake gets court marshaled this time."

Adam looked up, gave Ashley a dirty look, and said, "Shut-up!"

"Hey you two knock it off," said Kevin, while turning the steering wheel left.

The BMW stopped in front of the base's administration building. All three got out of the car and walked into the building. Once inside, Kevin noticed a short, dark-haired secretary dressed in a navy blue uniform, working at her desk. She looked up. "Mr. Palmer, I presume," she said as she stood up to shake Kevin's hand.

"You presume right."

The secretary gave Kevin a warm smile and pointed to her right. "Your children can wait in the waiting room over there."

Adam looked to where the secretary pointed. "Cool! I can finish my game!" he said as he trotted to the waiting area.

Ashley rolled her eyes and sighed as she followed Adam.

"If you will follow me, Mr. Palmer, Colonel Jepson would like to speak with you alone."

The secretary turned and led Kevin down a narrow hallway with administration offices on the left and the right. As Kevin walked past the different offices, officers looked up and seemed to recognize him. Kevin could tell they knew what was going on because they followed him out of their offices and began to talk to one another.

The secretary stopped at the door at the end of the hallway. Kevin could hear voices inside the door. The secretary knocked and opened the door. "Colonel, Mr. Palmer is here."

"Good. Let him in," said the colonel.

Kevin walked past the secretary and noticed Jake sitting hunched over in one of the chairs in front of the colonel's desk, still in his flight suit. Jake looked as if he had been through the ringer. His chestnut hair, which was longer than standard military cut, was ruffled on top of his head. As Jake glanced at Kevin, Kevin noticed that Jake's eyes had changed from their normal shade of bright blue to a darker shade of gray.

Colonel Jepson, a tall and slim man with white hair and in his late fifties not much younger than Kevin, walked around his desk with his right hand extended. "Ah, Mr. Palmer, it's a pleasure to meet you."

"Please, call me Kevin, Colonel Jepson," Kevin said, shaking the colonel's hand.

"Okay, and you can call me Alex."

Colonel Jepson turned and looked at Jake. "That will be all Lieutenant. You're dismissed."

Jake stood up and saluted. "Yes, Sir."

Jake didn't even look at Kevin as he walked past him. Kevin grabbed Jake's arm and felt the toned muscles within tighten. "You can wait with your brother and sister in the waiting room."

"You mean my cousins," Jake said as he jerked his arm away without looking at Kevin.

Kevin shook his head and looked down as Jake walked out of the room.

"Have a seat, Kevin."

"Thank you."

The colonel walked back around his desk and sat down. "What was that all about?"

"What?" Kevin said with a confused look.

"That thing about Jake calling his brother and sister his cousins."

"Oh, that. Ashley and Adam are his sister and brother by adoption. But ever since his mom . . . uh, his aunt died last year, he has been referring to them as his cousins and me as his uncle. He used to call me . . Dad."

"Oh, I'm sorry. I didn't know your wife had passed away. I haven't had a chance to get to know Jake in the two months he has been here at Hill, other than his discipline issues. He never mentioned anything about his aunt passing away."

"There's no need to apologize, Alex. Diane and I adopted Jake soon after his dad disappeared on the *Mars I* mission."

"Ah yes, Adrian. I knew Adrian. I was in the same graduating class with him at the Air Force Academy. He was a good man and a great pilot."

"Yes, he was." It pained Kevin to talk about Adrian. Oh, how he missed him. "Jake was devastated when he learned that his dad had disappeared. Diane and I didn't have any children at the time, and we loved Jake like a son, so we adopted him. Soon he started calling Diane mom and me dad. But it was Diane that Jake grew the closest to. Diane was his mother."

Kevin watched as Alex sat back in his chair and genuinely listened to Kevin. The colonel spoke again. "If you don't mind me asking, Kevin, how did Diane die?"

"Diane was diagnosed with a brain tumor three years ago. I did everything I could for her." Kevin didn't know why he was telling a stranger such intimate details, but he felt a connection to this colonel. He continued, trying not to show his emotion, "I took her to the best doctors and the best clinics in the world, but it was no use. She finally succumbed to the cancer last year."

"Wait a minute. Didn't that Doctor in Florida discover the cure for cancer about a year ago?" Alex asked.

Kevin tried to hold back the tears. "Dr. Christianson, you mean."

"Yeah, him."

"He discovered the cure two months after Diane passed away."

Alex leaned forward, placed his elbows on his desk with his hands under his chin and said, "I'm sorry, Kevin. Please forgive me. I don't mean to play psychologist here, but I'm just trying to figure Jake out. Jake could probably be a major by now, but with his discipline problems, he has held himself back. He's probably the most talented pilot I have ever seen and has great potential as a leader in the Air Force."

Kevin gave Alex a puzzled look. "Jake? We're talking about Jake aren't we?"

Alex laughed. "Yes, we're talking about Jake." Alex turned to his computer. "Computer . . . retrieve all discipline records for Lieutenant Jake S. Palmer." Alex turned to look at Kevin. "Your invention is amazing. I remember when we had to punch all of this stuff into a keyboard."

Kevin felt a little embarrassed.

"Discipline record for Lieutenant Jake S. Palmer retrieved, Colonel Jepson," the computer replied.

Alex looked at the information on his screen. "Hmm. . . . This is interesting."

"What?" Kevin asked.

Alex turned the computer screen to face Kevin. "Look here, Kevin. Prior to last year, Jake had a spotless record and high recommendations from every superior officer he had. Now, look at his record for the past year. He's been in six fights, arrested three times for disorderly conduct due to drinking, and of course, yesterday's incident . . . hitting a superior officer. Obviously, all of this is a result of Jake grieving from your wife's death. I've given Jake a leave of absence for a while. I'm not going to press charges. I suggest you take Jake home and let him work through this."

It hit Kevin like a lightning bolt. He felt horrible. Why hadn't he realized it before? Had he been that selfish, so involved with his own life and grief that he failed to see the pain Jake was in? Jake was crying for help, and he was ignoring him.

★ ★ ★ ★ ★

Kevin met Jake, Ashley, and Adam in the waiting area. Adam was busy playing his video game. Ashley pretended to be reading a magazine, but Kevin could tell she was biting her tongue, trying not to say anything to Jake. Jake sat in the corner of the room with his elbows on his knees and his head in his hands. Kevin looked at Jake and just wanted to give him a hug, but he knew Jake would not have any of that. "Ashley and Adam, will both of you please wait in the car? Jake and I have to talk."

"But Dad, can't we stay too?" said Ashley, noticeably wanting to be involved.

Kevin shot her a stern look.

"Okay . . . okay, we're going. C'mon Adam."

Kevin turned and watched Ashley and Adam leave the room. He then sat in the chair next to Jake. Jake was still in the same position and didn't even acknowledge Kevin's presence. Kevin shook his head and sighed. "Tough week, huh?"

Jake still did not move or answer. This was going to be harder than Kevin anticipated. "You know, Jake, I wish you would talk to me. It seems like eons since we've had a good heart-to-heart."

Jake lifted his head, sat straight up, and turned to face Kevin. His eyes were red from crying. But he still had a look of defiance on his face. "I've wanted to talk, but you've been so busy, you clearly never wanted to talk to me."

Kevin gave Jake a puzzled look and resisted the temptation to defend himself. "I know I have been busy. But whenever you came home on leave, you seemed as if you didn't want to talk about anything."

"Well, I did."

"Well then why didn't you let me know?"

"Because every time I tried to bring something up, your cell phone would ring, or you would have some important meeting. I couldn't talk to Ashley because she would just belittle me, and I couldn't talk to Adam because he's too young to understand."

"Well, I'm here now, and I think I know what it is you want me to understand."

"Do you?" Jake said as he stood up and took a few steps forward.

"I do. The colonel showed me your discipline record. Before you're mother's d—"

"Aunt!"

"What?"

Jake turned around to face Kevin. "Diane was my aunt not my mother, and you're my uncle, not my father!"

The comment cut Kevin like a knife into his chest. He shook his head and continued. "Yes, I know Diane and I aren't your biological parents, but we adopted you and raised you as one of our own. We love you like a son."

Jake turned around again as he tried to hide the tears and wouldn't look Kevin in the eye. "I know you love me like a son, but . . ."

Kevin stood up, walked over to Jake, and placed his hands on his shoulders. "What is it, Son?"

"I . . . I . . ."

Kevin turned Jake around. Jake resisted and walked away.

Jake turned to face Kevin and finally let go. "For some reason, ever since Aunt Diane's death, I've missed my real mom and dad terribly. I feel alone. I feel lost. I remember bits and pieces of my mom and a little more of my dad. It seems that's all I have been thinking about this past year.

"Aunt Diane was my mother, and I loved her like my real mom. It seems like God is taking everything away from me. First my real mom and dad, Aunt Diane, and . . ."

Jake stopped and looked at Kevin.

"Me?" questioned Kevin, as he moved closer to Jake. "You're afraid of losing me?"

Jake looked down and buried his head into Kevin's shoulder. Kevin wrapped his arms around Jake and squeezed. Jake began to sob. No more words needed to be said. Kevin now realized that Jake was acting out because he was terrified of losing his loved ones. Everyone Jake had loved had left him. No wonder he felt alone.

Kevin and Jake just stood there in the waiting room holding each other for a few moments. Kevin decided he needed to say what had been on his mind for the last year. "You know, Jake, you will see your parents and Aunt Diane again."

Jake looked up and backed away. "Oh don't feed me that crap again, Uncle Kevin. You know I haven't been to church for years. I've even started drinking."

"I know. I . . . I didn't mean to upset you. It's just that I think you would be happier if you went, that's all."

"Not after what God has done to me."

"And what had God done to you?" As soon as Kevin said it, he knew he shouldn't have. He could tell Jake was becoming defensive again.

Jake turned around again. "God has killed everyone I love. I hate Him!"

Kevin shook his head. "I'm sorry, Jake. I didn't mean to upset you. Let's not talk about church or God righ—"

Kevin's cell phone, hidden in his suit pocket, rang. He pulled it out and was about to answer it.

"See, there you go again, business over family."

Kevin stopped before he could answer the phone. "You're right. Whoever it is can leave me a message."

The phone stopped ringing, and Kevin said, "We don't have to talk about this now. What do you say, we go get something to eat, and all of us go to a good movie tonight? Let's forget about our problems for awhile."

Jake thought that was a good idea. He looked up and gave Kevin a modest smile. "That sounds good. I've talked about my problems enough, and I haven't seen a movie in nearly a year."

Jake and Kevin began to walk out of the administration building. Kevin put his right hand on Jake's shoulder as the two strolled out of the doors. Kevin's phone rang again. He ignored it.

"You better get that," Jake said. "Whoever it is must be desperate."

Kevin reached into his suit coat pocket and recognized the face on the other end as he placed the phone to his ear. "Mr. Konrad. . . . What's it been, over twenty years hasn't it? . . . What? . . . Say that again? . . . This isn't some cruel joke is it? . . . You want me to bring Jake? . . . Go to Houston. . . . Okay, we'll be there by tomorrow night. . . . Yeah, good to talk to you too."

Kevin put away his phone and looked up at the sky. The rain had stopped, and the clouds had disappeared, revealing bright stars.

"What was that all about?" asked Jake, with a puzzled look on his face.

Kevin turned slowly and looked at Jake. "That was Michael Konrad. He was the flight director of your father's flight to Mars over twenty years ago. He said you and I need meet him in Houston tomorrow night."

"Houston? Why?"

"He said they've got . . ."

Kevin tried to swallow the lump that had formed in his throat.

Jake put his hand on Kevin's shoulder. "What did they get?"

Kevin looked deep into Jake's eyes and said, "NASA received a message from your dad."

★ ★ ★ ★ ★

June 7, 2040

Jake and Kevin sat at the conference table in Michael Konrad's office at Johnson Space Center in Houston, Texas. The office was large and spacious. Michael's desk was at one end of the office and the conference table was snuggled neatly at the other end, which could seat about twenty people. A large bay window was nestled behind Michael's desk, which provided a view of the entire complex.

"This better not be some sick joke?" Jake asked.

"I don't think they would bring us all the way here to Houston if it was," said Kevin. But Kevin still wondered. *Was it possible that Adrian was still alive? Perhaps, Adrian and his crew landed safely on Mars but were unable to communicate with Earth and somehow survived.*

"If your dad did survive, it certainly would be a miracle. They would have had to have found a water supply somewhere and maintained enough energy to support their greenhouse."

Jake turned in his seat and looked at Kevin. "If he did survive, why didn't we get a message earlier?"

"I don't know. Maybe their communications were down. We do know from the probes they sent to Mars after your dad's disappearance that the satellite the crew deployed was not activated. But there wasn't any evidence of the shuttle anywhere."

Jake hunched over and shook his head. "I don't know what I would do if he's still alive? I've already accepted the fact that my dad is gone, but if he were alive, I . . . I just don't know."

Kevin reached over and placed his hand on Jake's left shoulder. "If he is alive, maybe they're planning some sort of rescue mission."

"But I thought after the disappearance, the government cut funding to NASA, and they were forced to just send satellites and probes into space. There hasn't been an astronaut in space since the *Mars I* crew."

"Maybe congress approved money for a new mission. Who knows?"

Kevin and Jake both looked up as they saw the door of the conference room open and two men walked in. The first man was dressed in a black suit with a white shirt and a red tie. The man looked about the same age as Kevin, in his early sixties. He was bald and slightly overweight. Kevin immediately recognized him as Michael Konrad – Administrator for NASA.

The second man, Kevin did not recognize. This man looked to be about the same age or a couple years older than Jake, possibly thirty or thirty-one. He had black hair and dark, brown eyes. He was dressed in a polo shirt with the NASA emblem on the right breast along with khaki dress slacks. He also looked physically fit.

Michael Konrad walked over to where Kevin sat. Kevin stood up. Michael extended his hand and shook Kevin's. "Ah, Mr. Palmer, I'm sorry to keep you waiting. It's so good to see you. What's it been over twenty years?"

"Call me Kevin. It's good to see you too, and it's been almost exactly twenty-three years."

Michael chuckled and gave Kevin a friendly hit on the shoulder. "Always the analytical one weren't you?" Michael then turned his attention to Jake. "And you must be Jake? Wow, you've grown quite a bit. I remember when you were just a kid running around this place. Remember?"

Jake shook Michael's hand and said, "I can't say I can, Mr. Konrad. I don't remember much about this place. I try not to."

"Please, call me Mike. Yes, I understand. But we may have some good news for you today. Oh, but before we go on, I want you to meet Doctor Steven Hendricks."

Both Kevin and Jake extended their hands to shake Dr. Hendricks' hand. Dr. Hendricks shook both mens' hands and said, "Please call me Skip."

"Skip here is our lead astronomer and physicist and not a bad pilot himself. He's also our resident priest," said Mike, as he and Skip seated themselves at the conference table across from Kevin and Jake.

Jake looked at Skip. "Priest?"

Skip gave Jake a shy smile. "I'm not actually a priest. I went to the University of Notre Dame. At first, I thought that I wanted to become a priest, so I majored in theology. But then I found out that I liked the ladies too much."

Everyone laughed, except for Jake who only gave Skip a small smile.

Skip continued, "I then decided to go into Archeology with an emphasis in Hebrew studies."

Kevin questioned, "Hebrew studies?"

"Yes, I loved the scriptures so much I decided that I wanted to focus on discovering the truth of the Bible. As a result, I can now speak, read and write Hebrew and a little bit of Latin, as well as Egyptian hieroglyphs."

Jake whistled and said, "Wow, you've got quite the resume there. And to top it off, you're a physicist too?"

Skip, obviously a little embarrassed, laughed. "Yep, I decided that I didn't like all of that digging, especially in the volatile Middle East, so I changed to my third passion, physics. As you can see I stuck with it."

Mike turned to Skip. "Are you done bragging now?"

Skip laughed and said, "Yeah, I think that about does it."

"Good," Mike said, giving Skip a small smile. "Well, gentlemen why don't we get down to business? I'm sure my phone call shocked you last night, Kevin?"

"To say the least. Are you serious about receiving a message from my brother?"

"Yes, I am. About a year ago, NASA received a strange signal. The mes—"

Jake held up his hand to cut Michael off. "You mean to tell us you had a message from my dad for over a year and you're just telling us now."

Kevin gave Jake a stern look. "Jake don't interrupt Mike. Let him explain."

Jake turned and glared at his uncle. "I didn't mean too. But if they had a message from my dad and your brother, I just thought that the first people that should know would be his family, not a year after they had received it."

Mike interjected, "We would have told you, but we had to be sure it was your dad and not some hoax. We've analyzed the message for a year, trying to get rid of the choppy video that came with it and to decipher what Adrian is saying."

"What do you mean decipher?" Kevin asked.

"When we got the message, it came without any sound. It . . . well, why don't we just show you the original message? Computer . . ."

"Yes, Mr. Konrad," replied the computer.

"Retrieve video-file one, five, six, nine."

"This file is encrypted and classified. It requires your security authorization code."

Mike pulled his pocket computer from his suit pocket and punched in his authorization code.

"Thank you, Mr. Konrad."

Kevin looked around the room for the computer. Out of the corner of his eye and to his right, two cabinet doors slowly opened and a computer screen about forty-two inches in diameter extended. Kevin let out a small gasp as he saw the frozen image of his brother's face on the screen. Adrian had a gash on his forehead and was bleeding. The plasma screen of the landing craft, *NightHawk*, located behind Adrian's image revealed a green field of grass and beyond that, a forest grove of trees.

Kevin glanced at Jake. Jake stared at his father's image like a robot. He just gazed at the screen with a cold, icy stare. "Where is he?" Kevin asked.

Mike glanced at Kevin and then back at the screen. "That's what we have been trying to determine. There's no way that's Mars. We've also digitally enhanced the video to make sure that person you see there is Adrian. And from what we have gathered, that person is Adrian. We believe this message is authentic and not some sort of hoax."

Kevin turned and looked at Jake. Jake just continued to stare at the screen. Adrian could tell that Jake was trying to keep his composure. "Are you okay, Jake?"

Jake seemed to jump as if awakened from a long sleep. "Wha...oh yeah, sorry. It's just that . . . he looks like I remember him."

"Computer play video-file one, five, six, nine," said Mike.

"Yes, Mr. Konrad," answered the computer.

Kevin watched in amazement as the video played. The video didn't contain any sound. It showed Adrian speaking. Every five seconds or so, the video was interrupted.

When the playback finished, Jake asked, "Is that it? Do you guys know what he was saying?"

Mike turned to look at Jake. "That was the original video, the way we received it from wherever your dad is. It arrived without any sound attached to it."

Kevin could tell that Jake was growing impatient. "What do you mean it didn't arrive with any sound?"

Skip answered before Mike could reply. "That's just it. The message arrived without sound, which leads me to believe, and the other physicists as well; that this message didn't come from Mars. . . . It came from somewhere else."

"What are you talking about?" Jake asked, with impatience growing in his voice.

Skip explained. "Well, Jake. . . . Can I call you Jake?"

Jake nodded.

"Well, we received this message just last year, and as you know, the speed of light travels about 186,000 miles per second."

"Yeah. So."

"So, if your dad had sent this message from Mars, we would have received the video portion of the message between nine and twenty minutes, depending on the orbit of Mars and Earth. But, as you know, NASA didn't get the message then. It came twenty-two years later."

Kevin interjected. "Wait a minute. So, what you are telling us is that my brother may still be alive but on a different planet outside of our solar system?"

"It's possible, Mr. Palmer."

Kevin glanced at Jake. Jake shook his head and said, "I don't believe it."

Skip leaned on the table and looked directly into Jake's eyes. "C'mon Jake. You're intelligent. Think about it. It makes logical sense. You know we measure the distance to other stars and planets outside our solar system in light years."

Jake looked up and met Skip's eyes. "Yeah, yeah, I know. If a planet is one light year away and if I were to travel at the speed of light, I would get to that planet in one year."

"Bingo," Skip said. "And we got this message twenty-two years after your dad's disappearance, so that tells us that he may very well be on a planet that is twenty-two light years away from Earth."

Kevin was stunned. "Not possible. Einstein proved through his Theory of Relativity that nothing can travel faster than the speed of light."

Mike cut in. "True. Skip has a theory on that very issue that he can explain to you later, Kevin. But first, I want you two to watch the enhanced version of the video that we have put together. For nearly a year, our guys have been trying to piece together what Adrian is saying by reading his lips and entering their conclusions into the computer. What you are about to hear is the computer's voice in sync with Adrian. We also edited out the video interference, so overall we got about a thirty-second video. Computer . . ."

"Yes, Mr. Konrad."

"Play video-file one, five, six, nine dash two."

"Your security clearance code is required, Mr. Konrad."

Mike typed in his security clearance code again on his pocket computer.

Kevin watched the screen as Adrian's image from the original message reappeared. He just sat and listened to the computer in astonishment. He wondered, *could this all be true?*

Adrian began to speak but with the computer's voiceover. "Houston, this is *Mars I* . . . I repea . . . oria's dead. We have crash landed on anoth . . . anet . . . has atmosphere conducive to our . . . Cooper thinks that we may have gone through a w . . . we know this isn't Earth . . . tell my brother and son that I lo . . ."

Kevin couldn't help the tears that swelled in his eyes. He knew the last phrase that Adrian was saying was that he loved him and Jake. Kevin turned to see Jake's reaction. Jake had a tear rolling out of his left eye while he tried to sustain his tough-guy, pilot bravado.

Mike spoke, "Well, Kevin and Jake, there you have it. From what we have concluded from this message is that Gloria Jackson is dead, the crew crash landed on another planet with an atmosphere similar to our own, and they may have gone through a wormhole."

Kevin glanced at Jake whose jaw was now taught as he continued to gape at the frozen image of his father on the computer screen. Kevin then turned his attention to Mike. "A wormhole? How is that possible? No one's ever seen a wormhole before. So, how do we know they exist?"

Mike smiled and said, "That's where Skip's theory comes in." Mike turned to Skip. "Skip you have the floor."

Skip stood up and walked to the head of the conference table. "Computer . . . retrieve computer program, Wormhole Theory, authorization code eight, four, three."

"Yes, Mr. Hendricks."

Kevin watched as his brother's image disappeared and a new image of the solar system came into view.

"I know that both of you are familiar with physics and Einstein's Theory of Relativity, so I'll be brief. I don't want to bore you with the details." Skip touched the computer screen and an image of the sun appeared with the earth and other planets in the solar system rotating around it. "As you know,

Einstein established that nothing can travel faster than the speed of light, but he also believed that we live in a four-dimensional, space-time continuum. Three of those dimensions are space, and one is time."

Skip continued as the computer displayed a model of four-dimensional space. "You see this cluster of bright dots in the upper left of the model? This is our galaxy. Now, Einstein theorized that any fold, distortion, or expanse in this four-dimensional space continuum could shorten the distance it takes to travel to other planets and stars. He also claimed that anything that distorts this space continuum has to have a mass."

Jake finally spoke, "Like planets and stars."

"Exactly," Skip said. Skip touched the computer screen again. An image of the sun appeared with the planets rotating around it. The planets looked to be spinning on something similar to a flexible sheet of fabric.

Skip continued, "Even though Einstein believed that we live in a four-dimensional, space-time continuum, our human senses have a difficult time imagining a four-dimensional model. So instead, imagine space as a sheet of fabric. And this sheet is made of a stretchy material like a trampoline. If you take a look at this model of our solar system, the sun is in the middle of the sheet. Since the sun has the largest mass, it creates the deepest depression in the sheet. As a result, the smaller planets spin around this depression. The depression that the sun creates in space causes the planets to stay in their current orbits."

Skip touched the computer screen again. The model changed to a long sheet with several solar systems in various places along the sheet. "Now, imagine every solar system in our galaxy or universe on this same stretchy space material. Einstein theorized that only an object in space with a large mass could create a depression that would in turn create a wormhole."

Skip touched the computer screen and the model of the different solar system was turned vertical. One side of the model hung like a bedspread on a clothesline on the left side of the screen. The other side of the model hung on the right side of the screen.

"If you take a look at this model," said Skip, pointing to the computer screen, "space is like a huge blanket hanging on a clothesline. Our solar system is on the left side of this model."

Skip touched the left side of the computer screen. The model magnified, and an image of Mars appeared. Skip then touched the right side of the model, and another spinning planet magnified.

"Now remember, Einstein said that only objects with a mass can create depressions large enough to create wormholes," Skip reiterated.

Kevin watched with extreme curiosity as the side of the model with Mars began to sink in, and the other side of the model with the other planet sank in as well. Each planet created a deep enough depression in space that the two depressions touched each other.

Skip continued, "As you can see by the model, gentlemen, planets on each side of the space sheet may create deep enough depressions in space that we may be able to travel through them in an instant to other worlds."

Jake interrupted before Skip could go on. "Wait a minute. Are you telling us every planet in the galaxy or the universe, for that matter, may be able to create a depression deep enough to reach a planet on the other side of the galaxy or universe?"

Skip smiled and touched the computer screen again. Every planet on the model created its own depression. The depressions on each side of the sheet touched each other. "What I'm saying, Jake, is that your father may have accidentally discovered the secret to deep-space travel."

Jake slapped his forehead and was about to curse.

Kevin cut Jake off before he could finish his curse word. "So you're telling us that it's possible that every planet in the galaxy or the universe can create a depression deep enough to reach another planet? That's what you're telling us, right?"

Mike laughed. "That's exactly what he's saying, Kevin. And you've got to admit, it makes perfect sense."

Kevin leaned back in his chair and ran his hands through his hair. "Wow!"

Skip continued, "We here at NASA now believe that wormholes are present near every planet in the solar system. Earth may even have its own wormhole. We just haven't found it yet."

"But how can you be sure? I mean . . . where is the actual proof?" Jake questioned.

Skip and Mike looked at each other and gave one another a knowing smile. Mike spoke, "We were hoping you would ask that, Jake. Skip, do you want to show them the video?"

"It will be my pleasure. Computer . . ."

"Yes, Mr. Hendricks."

"Retrieve video-file two, eight, six, seven, three, authorization code eight, four, three."

Kevin watched the screen as Skip's model of the wormhole theory disappeared and an actual image of Mars appeared.

Skip continued, "Three months after we received the message from your brother, we sent a probe to Mars. Using the technology that your company," Skip nodded in Kevin's direction, "has developed, we were able to remotely activate the satellite that the *Mars I* crew placed into orbit twenty-three years ago. As a result, we had feedback from the probe. Now, watch. Computer play video-file two, eight, six, seven, three."

"Yes, Mr. Hendricks."

Kevin watched as the video played.

Skip narrated the playback of the video. "Watch. . . . After the probe activated the satellite, we were able to see through the probe's eyes. Now watch, as the probe starts its orbit around Mars. We edited some of the video for time. After a while, the probe stops. Look." Skip said as he pointed to the screen.

Kevin leaned forward to get a better look. The probe stopped in front of what looked like some sort of ripple in space.

"It reminds me of when you throw a rock into a pond and water ripples out from the center," Jake said.

"Yes," Skip said. "But keep watching. The probe stopped to examine this phenomenon, and then it started to accelerate toward the ripple, and then . . ."

Kevin watched anxiously as the probe accelerated toward the distortion. The ripple grew larger and larger. And then, the video stopped. "What happened?"

Skip looked at Kevin and then Jake. "That's it. We believe the probe got sucked into the wormhole." Skip walked back to his chair and sat.

Mike looked at Kevin and Jake. "I know this is a lot to give you, but we have had our best scientists on this for a year and have come to the conclusion that the *Mars I* crew didn't disappear. They were, in fact, sucked into a wormhole, and may very well be alive on another planet on the other side of our galaxy."

Jake looked down and shook his head, trying to control his emotions. "But . . ." He sighed, trying to hold back the tears. "But . . . how can you be one hundred percent sure?"

Mike leaned on the table and spoke softly to Kevin and Jake. "That's where you two come in."

CHAPTER 4

December 25, 2041 – Cape Canaveral, Florida

Kevin paced back and forth in the hallway outside of the medical unit at Kennedy Space Center in Cape Canaveral, Florida. He was waiting for Jake to finish with his pre-flight physical. He hoped to catch Jake before he was transported to the shuttle that was scheduled to launch in four hours. There was so much that Kevin wanted to tell Jake. He didn't get a chance to talk personally with Jake the night before at his family's Christmas party.

Kevin heard voices inside of the room. The door slid open, and Jake and the doctor both walked out together. "Now, Commander, remember all of the training that you have gone through. It may save your life out there if some unforeseen emergency should happen."

Jake reached out and shook the doctor's hand. "I will, doctor. And, thanks again."

"You be careful out there, and good luck," the doctor said, as he walked back into the unit. The door slid shut behind him.

Jake turned and saw Kevin leaning on the opposite wall with his arms folded. "What are you doing here this early?"

"I'll walk you to the transport," Kevin said, putting his hand on Jake's shoulder. "I came by because we didn't get a chance to talk last night."

"What do you want to talk about?"

"Jake, you know that I love you, right?"

"Of course I do."

"Well, I just don't remember the last time I told you, so I wanted to let you know before you took off."

"Why did you want to tell me now?"

"I don't know. I just thought that I should."

Jake could tell that there was something bothering Kevin. Jake stopped, turned, and looked at the man who had been his father for nearly twenty-five years. "What's bothering you?"

"What? Oh, nothing I just needed to tell you that I love you."

"C'mon, Dad. I can read you like a book and can tell when something is bothering you."

Kevin was stunned and flooded with emotion. That was the first time Jake had called him dad in a long time. "Jake, promise me that you will be careful out there, okay? And if you don't find this so-called wormhole, you will land on Mars do a quick search, and come home. I don't know if I could handle it if I lost you."

Jake felt his emotions rise to the surface again. The last two days were the most he had cried since his aunt's death. Shouldn't he be out of tears by now? "You think something might go wrong up there too, huh?"

Kevin gave Jake a puzzled look. "What do you mean? You don't know if this will work either?"

"Honestly, I don't, but don't let my crew know. This theory that Skip has come up with just seems too outrageous. How do we know the shuttle will even hold together once we enter the wormhole? And, how do we know if the original crew is even alive on this theorized planet on the other side? There are so many things we don't know, and yet, we're still going."

Kevin stopped walking and turned to look at Jake. "If you think that this mission is going to fail, why did you accept to command this mission?"

"I don't know. I think I did it mostly because . . ." Jake paused and lowered his head, "Well, if there's even the slightest chance of bringing my dad back home alive, I would give anything in this world to do it. Even if my dad is dead, and I find his remains on Mars or on some other world, to bring him home for a proper burial would bring closure to all of those years of wondering what had happened to him."

"I know what you mean," said Kevin.

Kevin and Jake began to walk down the long hallway again. There was a long silence between the two until they reached the doors that led to the transport. Jake was about to punch in the code to open the doors when Kevin grabbed his arm. "Before you go Jake, I want to say a prayer with you."

"C'mon. You know I don't believe in God anymore."

"I know, but it will help me feel better."

Kevin prayed with Jake. He felt a little foolish standing in the hallway praying, but he didn't care. He wanted God to watch over Jake and bring him home safely. He also prayed that Jake would find Adrian alive and bring him home. As soon as he had said this, he heard Jake sniffle, as if he was beginning to cry.

Kevin finished the prayer and looked at Jake. Jake had his thumb and index finger on his eyes, rubbing the tears away. "Are you okay, Son?"

Jake looked up and gave Kevin a hug. Kevin hugged him back, not wanting to let go. Jake pulled away. "Yeah, I'm okay. It's just that . . . when you prayed to find my dad and bring him home safely, I had a weird sensation come over me that I haven't ever felt before."

Kevin smiled and said, "You know what that was, don't you?"

Jake frowned. "Oh, don't go telling me that it was the Holy Ghost. I won't believe it anyway."

The door that led to the transport slid open, and Skip stood there with an impatient look on his face. "Jake, there you are. We've been waiting for you. C'mon we've got to get prepped."

Jake turned around and looked at Kevin. He smiled. No more words needed to be said. He turned back and followed Skip to the transport.

Kevin watched as his son walked to the transport. Oh, how he loved that boy. He could remember when he was six-years-old, as if it was yesterday. He remembered how they used to shoot hoops together, toss the football and baseball around, and water ski whenever they had the chance.

As the transport sped away toward *Mars II*, Kevin had a flurry of emotions flood within him. On one hand, he felt good about Jake's ability to return home safely. Yet, on the other, he had an uneasy feeling that this mission was the beginning of something bigger than he or Jake, or for that matter – bigger than anything humanity has ever faced – but he couldn't quite figure it out.

★ ★ ★ ★ ★

Three Months Later, March 25, 2042 – Approaching Mars

Jake was engrossed in reading the scriptures that Ashley had given him for Christmas. He was lying on his bed with his left arm propped up by his elbow and holding the book open with his right hand.

Even though he didn't know for sure if God actually existed, he continued to keep the promise he had made to Ashley of reading the scriptures daily. On the three-month journey to Mars, he had read all of *The Book of Mormon*, *Doctrine and Covenants*, *The Pearl of Great Price*, and was now beginning the *Old Testament*. And, what was even more surprising, he was beginning to feel that maybe, just maybe, there was a God and that God was watching out for he and his father. Every time he thought about it, chills would shoot up and down his spine, leading him to think that he was being guided. But then his logical side would take over, telling him that it wasn't possible. After all, he was a pilot, trained to rely on his own senses, not some unforeseen spirit. Nonetheless, he still questioned, and that was what terrified him the most.

Suddenly, the communicator to Jake's quarters buzzed, snapping him out of his daydream.

"Come in."

The door to Jake's quarters slid open. Skip walked in with a smile on his face.

Jake gave him a curious look. "What are you so happy about?"

Skip grabbed the chair located next to Jake's desk, turned it around and sat, resting his forearms on its back. "It's true, isn't it?"

Jake stared at Skip with confusion. "What's true?"

Skip looked at the scriptures Jake had spread open and nodded. "That *Book of Mormon* of yours. It's true, isn't it?"

Jake sat up, closed his scriptures, and leaned his elbows on his knees. "How do you know about *The Book of Mormon*?"

Skip's smile grew bigger. "Remember, Jake, I majored in Theology at Notre Dame. We were required to read that blasphemous book, as the priests so eloquently called it, and write critiques on how it supposedly contradicted the *Bible*. But I just finished reading it again for like the thirty-third time."

Jake shook his head. "Wait a minute. You brought a *Book of Mormon*."

Skip nodded, glancing down at Jake's scriptures. "Yeah, that sister of yours is very persistent and, not to mention . . . really pretty too."

Jake shook his head and gave a small laugh. "She got to you too, huh?"

A smile, as large as Jake had ever seen, graced along Skip's face. "Yep, she did. By the way, Jake, do you think Ashley will be available when we get back from this mission?"

"Dude, you're what . . . thirteen years older than her?"

"Hey, age doesn't matter in eternity," Skip said with honest sincerity.

Jake sat up straight and looked directly at Skip. "You're serious, aren't you?"

Skip continued to smile, but his tone grew serious. "I am." He paused, looked down and looked back at Jake. His eyes were beginning to glisten with tears. "Jake, I promised Ashley that I would read *The Book of Mormon* with an open mind and then pray about its truthfulness."

Tipping his head to one side, Jake asked, "And how did she convince you to do that?"

"She promised me a date if I did."

Both men, who were becoming very close friends, laughed. After a few seconds of laughter, they sat in silence for a few moments. Skip finally broke the awkward silence.

"Jake, I read it and prayed . . ." Skip paused a few moments, as new tears began to stream down his face.

Jake, waiting for him to speak, began to feel that strange sensation he felt when he and Kevin prayed just before they left on this impossible mission.

Skip continued. "I prayed about it. And Jake, I . . . I can't even describe the feeling. It was like every burden, every weight, everything that I have worried about on this mission disappeared. I felt so light, almost as if I was floating. I had goose bumps and warm chills up and down my body. It . . . It was a feeling I don't think I have ever felt before."

"My uncle would say that was the Holy Ghost testifying of the truthfulness of *The Book of Mormon*."

Skip, with his eyes glistening and still smiling, nodded his head. "Yeah. That was it. God let me know that *The Book of Mormon* is true. Oh, man. Jake, I can't even tell you how happy and joyful I feel right now."

Jake lowered and shook his head. He mumbled, "You won't for long."

Skip's smile quickly disappeared. "Wha . . . what do you mean?"

Jake looked up and with stone cold eyes glared at Skip. "Trust me, Skip. I've been a member of the Mormon Church my whole life. The only thing that church and God have brought me is pain and suffering. He took my mom and dad away when I was young. And, he killed my Aunt Diane, even though I prayed nonstop for her to survive her cancer. Why would God do that? In my opinion, He's either a hateful, vengeful God, or He doesn't exist at all."

Skip quickly stood up and pushed the chair he was sitting in to the side. "Don't you dare speak about our Father in Heaven that way! He loves you more than you know. We weren't placed on Earth to just get by. We are challenged to make us stronger. You, more than anyone and being in the military, should know that. Look at your brother, Jesus; he suffered for you and me. He suffered more than anyone in the history of our planet—"

Skip stopped, and tears poured out of his eyes.

Jake was speechless. He didn't know what to say. Whenever, he offended God or tried to deny His existence to his uncle, Kevin would simply try to console Jake and reassure Jake of God's existence. But not Skip. Here, stood a close friend, almost a brother, rebuking Jake for his lack of faith and ignorance.

Skip quickly regained his composure and pointed at Jake. "Jake, Jesus suffered for you. He suffered so you could return to live with your mom, dad, and Aunt Diane again. If it wasn't for Him and your Father in Heaven, we would be lost forever. So you better get your faith back quick, Jake, because when this mission is over – you're baptizing me."

Suddenly the communicator to Jake's quarters buzzed. Jake didn't respond. Again, it buzzed.

Jake, still looking at Skip like a scolded child, cleared his throat. "Wh . . . What is it, Taylor?"

"Jake, we're approaching Mars."

"All right. We'll be right there."

Jake reached under his bed, pulled out his backpack, unzipped it, and placed his scriptures in it. Both men walked into the corridor in silence.

★ ★ ★ ★ ★

Jake and Skip made their way through the ship to the flight-deck. They entered through the hatchway and saw Taylor sitting at his copilot's station. Taylor Young, a brilliant computer programmer chosen as the third member of the mission, looked at Skip and Jake with excitement in his piercing hazel eyes. Skip floated to his station and buckled himself in his seat behind Jake's. Jake floated to his seat and secured himself in as well. They both looked through the flight-deck's plasma shield and saw the Red Planet growing larger as they approached.

Jake had a feeling of calm come over him. He felt that his dad was near. It was a strange feeling, one that he could not explain.

Taylor turned and looked at Jake. "Well, Jake, you're the commander. What do we do?"

Jake felt a little weird giving orders to Taylor and Skip. Skip was already a dear friend. And on the three-month journey, Taylor had become just as true of a friend. However, Taylor was a little more reserved and quieter than both Jake and Skip. Nonetheless, when Taylor did have something to say it was always positive, and Jake and Skip both respected him for that. Jake didn't consider either Taylor or Skip his subordinates, so when it came time for proper protocol, they all seemed to mock the system.

Taylor spoke again, "*Mars II* to Commander. What do we do, Sir?"

Jake, looking at Mars as he spoke said, "We follow protocol. We do what we have been trained to do. I'll put this thing in orbit around Mars. Taylor, you make sure all computer systems are working properly." Jake then turned to Skip. He gave Skip a small smile, letting him know everything was all right between the two of them. Skip seemed to relax a little and smiled back. "Skip, will you set *Mars II's* computers to scan for any gravimetric anomalies, and see if we can't find this wormhole?"

Skip softly slapped Jake's back. "Yes, Sir. Computer . . ."

"Yes, Doctor Hendricks," the computer replied.

"Retrieve program Operation Wormhole . . . authorization code nine-four-three-dash-alpha, and activate it."

"Yes, Doctor Hendricks."

Jake turned his seat to face Skip. "Are you sure that program that you guys designed at NASA will find this so-called wormhole."

"Don't worry Jake," Skip said. "We used data from the probe that we sent to find your dad when he disappeared. The program is designed to indicate any gravimetric anomalies."

Jake turned back to face Mars. "I hope you're right."

Taylor looked at Jake. "Don't worry, Jake. Everything thing is going to be fine. We'll find this wormhole, go through it, find your dad, and come back."

Jake gave Taylor a skeptical look. "You're a little too optimistic for me, Taylor. I haven't told you guys this before, but I don't have a lot of confidence in this mission."

Skip and Taylor both glanced at one another. Skip spoke first. "We've traveled millions of miles to Mars, and you tell us this now."

"I'm sorry. I just don't know if I believe in your theory, Skip."

Skip put his hand on Jake's shoulder. "You're lucky then."

Jake turned his seat to face Skip. "What do you mean, lucky?"

"You're lucky that I believe in it enough for the both of us, and Taylor believes it too. Don't worry, Jake. You just do your job and pilot us through this thing if we find it. You don't need to worry if it exists or not. That's my job."

Jake shook his head. "That's just it. If this thing exists and we enter it, how do you know we won't be crushed to death or shot clear across the universe?"

Skip smiled and said, "I don't."

"That doesn't help me, Skip."

"I know," Skip said. "Sometimes you just have to have faith."

Jake gave Skip a funny look. "Faith huh. Faith in what?"

Skip laughed. "You know. Faith that God will get us through this."

Jake turned his seat back to face Mars. Deep down, he knew that Skip was right, but he couldn't bring himself to admit it. If they were going to survive this, it would have to be God that helped them.

Jake felt Taylor's hand on his right shoulder. "Yeah. Faith, Jake. That's all we have besides us."

Jake glanced at Taylor and then at Skip. "You know what, guys? I couldn't have asked for better men to go on this mission with. It's an honor."

Taylor and Skip both nodded their heads in acknowledgment. They all had grown extremely close. In fact, each man knew that they would give his life for the other if they had to.

★ ★ ★ ★ ★

March 28, 2042 – In orbit around Mars

After days of orbiting Mars, Jake was becoming frustrated. The computer had not detected any gravimetric anomalies or anything that even resembled this hypothesized wormhole. Jake knew that he had to take action soon. "Okay, guys, I don't know if we're going to find this thing, so I think maybe it's time we switch to plan B. Taylor, keep this thing in orbit. Skip and I are going to take *NightHawk* down to the surface and do a search."

"Roger that, Commander," said Taylor.

Jake pressed the communicator button to contact Houston. "Houst . . . that's weird."

"What?" asked Taylor.

"I can't get a signal for the communication satellite orbiting Mars," Jake said.

Skip spoke, "That's strange. We just spoke with them a few hours ago."

"I know. Maybe the satellite is out. Computer . . ."

"Yes, Commander Palmer," the computer replied.

"Are all communication satellites active and operational?"

"Negative, Commander Palmer. Only the communication satellite orbiting Earth is operational. My scans cannot locate the Mars' satellite."

Taylor interjected, "That's weird. Just two hours ago, we passed it in our orbit, and it was there."

Jake looked confused. "Yeah, I know. Okay, here's what we're going to do. We're going to go back and see if we can't locate it. Even if it's there or not, Skip and I are going to go down and do a quick search. Then we're going to head back home."

Two hours later, *Mars II* was back to where it had passed the satellite. All three crewmen looked around for the missing satellite. "Computer . . ." Jake said.

"Yes, Commander Palmer."

"Are your scans able to detect the satellite now that we are back to its previous orbit?"

"Negative, Commander."

Skip unbuckled himself and floated to the hatchway that led from the flight-deck to mid-deck. "I wonder if it fell out of orbit."

Jake unbuckled himself and followed Skip. "Maybe. Even so, let's get down to the surface and do a search for my dad's re . . . *Mars I's* remains."

Jake had a hard time saying it. Even though he was skeptical about the existence of wormholes, he still hoped that they would find one. He really did not want to go the surface and find whatever was left of his dad's crew.

Skip spoke before he opened the hatchway. "Maybe after our search on the surface we should wait a few more days to see if we can't find the wormhole. I'm still positive it's around here somewhere."

"If the satellite was still here, I would agree with you. But under the circumstances, I want to get back to Earth as quickly as possible. I'm sure they're pretty worried by now."

Skip looked disappointed. He succumbed to the fact that he may not get to prove that his theory was true. "Yeah, you're the commander. Whatever you say."

Jake gave Skip an annoyed look. "Don't patronize me, Skip. I just think that we need to communicate with Earth as soon as possible."

Skip did not respond. He opened the hatchway and went through. Jake followed him as he spoke to Taylor. "Taylor keep this thing in orbit. We'll be in constant communication with you. Once we retrieve our necessities from our quarters, we'll prep *NightHawk* in the payload-deck. Once we're ready to leave, I'll give you the order to open the payload doors."

Taylor turned in his copilot's chair to face Jake and saluted. "Roger that, Sir."

Jake smiled and followed Skip to their quarters to get ready for man's first descent to the surface of Mars.

★ ★ ★ ★ ★

A few moments later, Jake and Skip floated through the payload-deck in their flight suits. They were within fifty feet of *NightHawk*. Jake loved the little ship. Not that it was little. It was only little compared to *Mars II*. Nonetheless, Jake loved to fly it. It flew a lot like the new F-81 Tigers that the Air Force used, which were actually updated versions of the F-22 Raptors. The *NightHawk* could maneuver as well in space as it did in an atmosphere. It also employed hover technology, so there wasn't any need for a runway. In addition, *NightHawk* had a sleek and slim design. It resembled the F-117 Nighthawks of the earlier twenty-first century. The only difference was that *NightHawk* was longer and wider, and could accommodate seven passengers comfortably with a bathroom facility and sleeping quarters for each crew member.

Jake opened the door in the back of the craft, and the two entered. *NightHawk's* computer chirped. "Welcome, Commander Palmer and Doctor Hendricks."

Jake secured his backpack under his seat. He responded as he and Skip buckled themselves into their seats, Jake in the pilot's seat on the left and Skip in the copilot's seat on the right. "Computer, prepare for flight and descent to Mars."

"Yes, Commander," the ship's computer replied as the craft came to life. The computer panels lit up, and the engine began to hum.

"Taylor."

"Yes, Commander."

"Open the payload doors."

"Roger that."

Skip spoke as the doors began to open. "Do you think we'll find anything down there?"

Jake looked at Skip and said, "I hope not."

Skip gave Jake a puzzled look.

Jake continued. "I mean . . . honestly, I wish your wormhole theory was right. I don't want to go down there and find anything because I know that there was no way that my dad and his crew could have survived this long on Mars. If I find my dad is dead down there, I don't know what I would do."

Skip didn't speak. He only nodded in acknowledgement and watched as Jake maneuvered *NightHawk* out of *Mars II*.

★ ★ ★ ★ ★

After a successful descent to Mars, *NightHawk* landed softly on the Red Planet's surface. A surge of energy shot through Jake. He and Skip were about to become the first human beings to take steps on the surface of Mars.

Jake looked at Skip and smiled. "Okay, we both agreed that if we had to come to the surface, one of us would be the first to touch the ground. You got the quarter?"

"Yep," said Skip, unzipping a pocket on his space suit and pulling out a quarter. "You call it."

"Heads."

Skip flipped the coin into the air, caught it, and flipped it over onto the back of his left hand. He looked at it and then looked up at Jake with disappointment. "I guess you win. It's heads."

Jake smiled and said, "Hey, look at it this way, you'll always be remembered as the second person to set foot on Mars, behind the great Jake Palmer."

Skip gave Jake a smirk. "Shut-up."

"Taylor, we're ready to leave *NightHawk* and set up a perimeter to triangulate our position," Jake reported.

"Roger that," Taylor replied.

Jake lowered the ramp, and he and Skip walked to it. The two men stopped before descending down the ramp. They looked at the surface of Mars with awe. These men were the first two men in human history to see the Red Planet with their own eyes. It was a breathtaking sight. A massive mountain range pierced the pale orange skyline directly in front of them. To their right was a canyon and to their left were miles and miles of a flat, red landscape. The wind was blowing ferociously, spitting red dust into the air. It looked like something out of a painting.

Jake took a deep breath and said, "Well, here we go."

The two men slowly walked down the ten-foot ramp, Jake in front and Skip step for step behind him. Just as Jake was about to set foot on the surface, the communicator within his ear crackled with static. He could make out Taylor's voice. Jake stopped before he set foot on the surface, holding his hand up to stop Skip. "Taylor, what's going on?"

Taylor responded but Jake couldn't make out what he was saying through the static. "Com ... ars ... cked ... to ... le ... g ... ack ... ic ..."

Jake tried hard to make out what Taylor was saying, but there was too much interference. "Taylor, repeat! I say ... repeat!"

No answer.

"Taylor ... come in! Come in, Taylor!"

Again, no answer.

Jake turned to face Skip and could see the worry in his eyes. "We've got to get back up there to see if Taylor's okay!"

Skip turned and ran up the ramp, with Jake on his heels.

A few seconds later, the two men buckled themselves into their seats. Jake closed the ramp and prepared for takeoff. He was nervous because NASA was never able to simulate a takeoff from Mars. He just hoped that *NightHawk* would have enough thrust to pull away from the strong gravitational force of the planet. Jake grabbed the flight stick and hovered the ship a few feet off the ground. He looked at Skip and said, "Let's pray this works because if it doesn't, this might just be our burial sight."

Skip nodded and closed his eyes. Jake punched the launch button on the computer panel with his index finger. *NightHawk* shot up like a bullet. Jake could barely keep his eyes open. He wanted to black out. The G-forces were incredible. Never before had he felt such power. Not even in all his training as a pilot and astronaut. For a moment, he thought that the G-forces were going to rip him right through his seat. His breastbone felt as if it was pressing against his spine.

Jake continued to resist the urge to pass out. He couldn't turn his head to see if Skip was okay. He couldn't even talk. How fast were they going?

Soon, *NightHawk* was back in orbit around Mars. Jake and Skip looked at one another. Skip spoke first, "What a rush!"

Jake smiled and shook his head. "I've never felt anything like that before. I thought my body was going to be flattened from the G-forces."

"Yeah, I know what you mean."

Jake turned to scan space for any sign of *Mars II*. There was no sign of the shuttle. "Taylor, come in, over. . . . Taylor, come in."

Again, there was no answer.

Skip pointed to his one o'clock. "Look!"

Jake looked to where Skip pointed. About five hundred yards away was Skip's hypothesized wormhole. "Is that what I think it is?" he said.

"I think so. It looks like the ripple we saw on the video when the probe we sent disappeared. Taylor must have gone through already. . . . Oh no, it's starting to shrink!"

Jake looked, and sure enough, the ripple was beginning to get smaller. "Hold on." Jake grabbed the flight stick and maneuvered the ship in the direction of the ripple. *NightHawk* darted toward the distortion as the heads of the two men within slammed back against their headrests.

"Hurry, it's going to disappear, and there's no telling when it will open again!" Skip yelled.

Jake pushed *NightHawk* to full speed. Its nose entered the ripple just as it closed.

Jake looked around and watched as the stars elongated.

CHAPTER 5

March 28, 2042 – 22-Light Years from Earth

The experience only seemed to have lasted a minute. It was a strange sensation. The stars elongated, and the two men within *NightHawk* looked as if they were moving in slow motion. Jake looked at the rear-view screen and caught a glimpse of the wormhole. As soon as he glanced, the hole closed upon itself and disappeared. Jake wondered. *What would have happened if NightHawk was caught in the middle of the hole when it closed? They probably would have been crushed to death.* The thought shot chills up his spine.

"Look out!" yelled Skip.

Jake looked up. There wasn't any time to move out of the way. The object slammed into the cockpit plasma shield of *NightHawk*. Luckily, since the design of the original *Mars I* space shuttle, every new spacecraft that had been constructed was fitted with plasma shields. The reason plasma was used was to provide the astronauts within larger views, and plasma protected the crews from the vacuum of space.

"What was that we hit?"

"I think it was our missing satellite," Skip replied.

Jake and Skip both looked ahead through the plasma shield. *Mars II* was directly in from them, and below the shuttle was a planet that looked a lot like

Earth. The planet had blue oceans and continents. However, this planet's continents were shaped differently than Earth's.

Jake looked just past the planet and saw two moons. "Uh, I don't think we're in Kansas anymore, Toto."

Skip laughed. "Yeah, I think you're right, Dorothy. This is awesome. We are actually in another solar system! Amazing!"

"And just think, Skip, you are going to go down in history as the man who discovered wormholes."

"I think that honor will go to your dad. He and his crew were the first to travel through one, remember." Skip pointed toward the planet. "Do you think your dad is on that planet?"

"There's only one way to find out." Jake slowly fired the reverse thrusters and shut down the aft thrusters to come to a complete stop. "Taylor. Are you okay? Taylor, come in . . ."

Sadness suddenly overcame Jake. Didn't Taylor survive the transport through the wormhole? Why was he not answering? "Taylor, come in. . . . Tay—"

"Ja . . . Jake is that you?"

"Yes. Taylor, are you okay?"

Taylor sounded groggy. "I don't think so. I was monitoring your . . . uh, descent to Mars when I felt the shuttle shake. . . . Uh, The force was so great . . . it ripped my chair right from its bolts. I think it flew back, and I hit my head on the control panel. . . . Yeah, I think that's what happened. . . . I'm bleeding badly, and there's blood all over the computer panel at the back of the flight-deck. I . . . It must have knocked me out . . . while you were on your way to the surface of Mars . . . um . . ."

"Taylor, are you sure you are okay?" Jake asked again.

"What, oh yeah, what was I saying? Oh yeah, while you were on your way, I deployed a video probe so that NASA could see the shuttle and that we were all right. . . . What happened?"

"Taylor, you were sucked into the wormhole," Jake said.

"I know that. The computer said that it detected it. I . . . I tried to contact you, but your signal was scrambled. Right after that, I felt the shuttle shake. . . . What I meant to say was; where are we?"

"Why don't you look for yourself?"

"Let me get out of this floating chair first . . . Oh, wow! There are two moons. Wait! What are those?"

"What?"

"Look to your two o'clock."

Jake looked. His jaw dropped. "Do you see what I see, Skip?"

"What the . . . They almost look like *NightHawk*," said Skip.

"Yeah they do," said Jake, as he continued to stare at his two o'clock. Speeding their way, were about fifteen smaller versions of *NightHawk*.

The cloned ships stopped and surrounded *Mars II* and *NightHawk*. Jake was able to get a closer look at the ships. The cockpits of the cloned ships seated two pilots, one in the front and one directly behind the first. Jake couldn't get a decent look at the faces of the pilots because their flight helmets, visors, and oxygen masks covered them. Jake wondered if he was actually looking at an alien species.

Jake heard his communicator crackle and then several tones, which almost deafened him and Skip. Suddenly, there was a voice at the other end. The voice spoke English remarkably well. "Identify yourselves."

Jake and Skip looked at each other stunned. How could these aliens know English? Maybe they knew about the crew from *Mars I*?

"I repeat. Identify yourselves."

Jake finally gained his composure to speak. "Uh . . . This is Commander Jake Palmer of the *Mars II* Space Shuttle. We—"

"That does not make sense. What is your unit calling number?"

"My what?"

"You heard me, Soldier! What is your unit calling number, and where did you get this massive ship in front of you? It looks similar to one of our war ships."

Jake was now annoyed. "First of all, I have no idea what a unit calling number is, and that ship in front of me is the *Mars II* Space Shuttle. We are on a rescue mission for the crew of *Mars I* and looking for Commander Adrian Palmer."

Suddenly, Jake and Skip grabbed their space helmets. Jake heard Taylor scream through the comm. Jake felt shearing pain, and ringing sounds shot through his head. He felt as if someone was in his head chopping away at his brain. And then, after what seemed like an eternal pain, it subsided.

The leader of the small ships surrounding them spoke again, "You are human, are you not?"

Jake and skip glanced at one another. Jake said, "Well, yes, we are."

"You are in direct violation of Lord Koroan Chast's law six-three-five: No human shall be in possession of Gnol technology. If said human is in possession, it shall be considered an act of war, and that said human shall suffer imprisonment or death."

Skip looked at Jake who had a look of shock on his face as well. What were these aliens talking about? Jake gritted his teeth together and spoke. "I assure you. These ships we have are our own. Our civilization designed them and built them. We are on a peaceful mission. Please—"

"Enough! No human could ever design or build such technology! Humans are worthless creatures, not worthy to be around Gnols. If I had it my way, you would all be killed. However, since his lordship seems to enjoy using your pitiful kind as slaves, you will follow me now to the nearest slave camp on the surface. If you refuse to follow, you will die."

Jake watched in horror as he saw small gun turrets rise from the wings of the smaller ships. Jake didn't know what to do. He wasn't sure if *NightHawk* could outrun these swifter ships, and he certainly did not want to leave Taylor to the mercy of these aliens.

Out of the corner of his eye, Jake saw *Mars II* move. Taylor's voice crackled through his comm. "Jake! Get out of here!"

Jake saw the massive shuttle bank to its right and take out three smaller ships with its nose. Small explosions penetrated the underside of the shuttle. Jake yelled, "Taylor! What are you doing?"

"Go now! Find your dad and find out what's going on? I've—"

Jake watched as the shuttle took about five more ships out. Jake was frozen. He couldn't speak, and he couldn't move. Finally, Jake felt Skip slap his helmet. "Jake! Go now! Taylor has made a way for us to escape!"

Sure enough, Taylor had created an escape route by taking out eight ships. Jake hit the aft thrusters' button, and *NightHawk* sped away. The remaining five ships moved frantically out of the way of the damaged shuttle. Jake watched in his rear view screen as the smaller ships began to fire what looked like red laser blasts at the wounded shuttle.

"It looks like something out of *Star Wars*," said Skip.

Jake continued to watch in horror as explosions ripped the shuttle apart. Suddenly, there was a massive blast as the shuttle fell victim to its prey. Jake yelled, "No! Taylor!"

Jake felt a sudden urge to turn back and exact revenge on the people or things that killed his dear friend. However, he knew that was impossible. The smaller versions of *NightHawk* obviously had more advanced weapons, and *NightHawk* wasn't equipped with any weapons at all, other than a few handguns in the weapon's locker. But what good were handguns in space?

Skip yelled again, "Jake! Get moving! Two of them! They're on our tail!"

Jake looked and saw two smaller ships closing in. He pushed *NightHawk* to full speed. It wasn't any use. The smaller ships were much faster and closing fast. He decided that they weren't going to outrun them in space. He fired the left side thrusters and banked *NightHawk* to the right. He then fired the right side thrusters, which straightened the ship out. *NightHawk* was now on its way to the planet below.

Jake had to angle *NightHawk* to a forty-degree angle once the ship hit the atmosphere, which caused the ship to slow down. Fortunately, the two ships that followed had to do the same thing. Jake could feel the heat of the atmosphere as atmospheric particles collided with *NightHawk's* heat shield. Outside, he saw the orange glow of the particles combusting. He looked in his rear view screen and saw the orange glows of the ships pursuing him.

Once *NightHawk* was safely inside the atmosphere, Jake leveled it out and hit the control that switched the ship from spacecraft mode to jet mode. The jet engines came to life, and the windshield raised up to replace the plasma shield. Jake said out loud, "Now, I'm in my element. See if you guys can catch me now!"

Jake looked to his left and saw a snow capped mountain range. Jake banked *NightHawk* to its left. "I'm heading toward those mountains. Maybe, I can zigzag my way through the peaks and loose them."

"Whatever you do; do it fast! They're catching up again," Skip said.

Jake looked at the rear-view screen. Sure enough, his two pursuers were closing the distance between *NightHawk* and themselves. It was obvious to Jake that the smaller spacecrafts had jet capabilities as well. Jake glanced at *NightHawk's* speed – forty-five hundred miles per hour – he would have to slow down to about four hundred miles per hour when he hit the mountain range in order to maneuver between the peaks.

NightHawk buckled and slowed down a little. Jake saw red flashes of light dash by the ship.

Skip yelled, "They're firing at us! Did we get hit?"

"I don't know. Computer, damage report," said Jake.

"Minimal damage to the left wing. No critical systems were damaged," the computer replied.

A few seconds later, the two pursuers fired another volley of lasers toward their prey. Jake banked right and then left. The volley missed their target and disappeared into the mountain range ahead.

In an instant, *NightHawk* was in the mountain range. Jake slowed the speeding ship down. His pursuers did too. Jake weaved in and out of the mountain peaks. The ships behind him followed him move for move, all while firing.

Jake was beginning to feel the fatigue as he maneuvered *NightHawk* in and out of mountain peaks. He didn't know how long he could zigzag, and at the same time, dodge laser fire. Suddenly, *NightHawk* shuttered again.

Jake lost control of the ship. Alarms buzzed and beeped throughout the ship as the spinning spacecraft plummeted to the valley floor below. Jake fought, with all his might, to regain control. Finally, the spinning ship leveled out.

Jake pulled back on the stick, and *NightHawk* skied upward.

Skip spoke, "Computer, damage report."

"Damage to the right jet engine. It is still operational."

"Jake, they've swung around, and they're behind us again. We need to do something now, or we're not going to make it!"

Jake leveled *NightHawk* out again. "What can we do? Those things behind us are faster, and we don't have any weapons."

Skip paused for a moment as *NightHawk* was hit by another round of laser fire. The ship luckily held together, and Jake managed to maintain control. "The fuel tank!" yelled Skip.

"What?"

"I've been measuring the time between their volleys of shots. The volley lasts about ten seconds and then there's a ten second delay, probably while their guns recharge."

"So," said Jake, as he dodged another round of laser fire.

"So, after their next round, I will count to seven seconds. On my mark, eject the jet fuel."

"Are you nuts? If I do that, we won't have any fuel left."

"Jake, you're a great pilot, and I know you can glide this thing to a safe but rough landing."

"But—"

"They've fired again," Skip said. He then counted to seven. "Now!"

Jake had enough faith in Skip to know when he was right. He ejected the fuel and both men watched as fuel sprayed out from the tail of *NightHawk*. As soon as the fuel tank emptied, *NightHawk's* pursuers fired. The blasts hit the ejected fuel and ignited. The lead pursuer couldn't get out of the way of the fireball. The fire engulfed the ship causing the pilot to lose control. The ship slammed into the mountain peak ahead creating an enormous explosion. The second pursuer managed to dodge the flame. He pulled up and leveled out, putting himself back in the chase.

Jake slapped Skip on the shoulder. "You're a genius."

"Look out!" Skip yelled.

Jake looked at his rearview screen. The second ship fired another round of laser blasts. Jake banked right and rolled *NightHawk* three hundred sixty degrees, causing the blasts to miss. Jake quickly glanced at the fuel gauge. It read *Empty*.

NightHawk's computer chirped. "The jet fuel is now empty."

Jake rolled his eyes as he struggled to maintain the craft. "Yeah, thank you. I know that. . . . Skip, look around for a flat piece of land. I'm going to have to try to land this thing on its belly. Hover mode is offline."

Jake dodged another round of plasma laser fire.

Skip pointed to his eleven o'clock. "Look! It looks like some sort of city."

Jake looked and saw what looked like a city in the valley below, and just beyond that, a flat field full of freshly fallen snow. "The snow, if it's deep enough, should provide us with some cushioning," Jake said.

Jake banked to his left just when his pursuer fired another round. *NightHawk* was sluggish as Jake yanked the flight stick left. They were lucky they had distanced themselves from their pursuer. Unfortunately, Jake could tell the enemy was closing ground again as *NightHawk* lost speed and altitude.

Jake pointed straight ahead. "You see that building just in front of us?"

"Yeah," Skip said.

"I'm heading straight for it."

Skip's eyes widened. "What? You'll never be able to get out of the way. We don't have enough power, and I don't know if you'll be able to turn, especially with how sluggish this thing felt the last time you turned."

Jake smiled confidently. "Trust me."

Skip looked at Jake and said, "That's what I'm afraid of."

The enemy behind the wounded ship closed in fast. It was now within fifty feet. The enemy pilot focused in on the fuselage of *NightHawk* and readied himself for the kill shot.

Skip closed his eyes as he prepared for impact.

Jake squeezed the flight stick and switched the ship from jet mode to space mode. Before *NightHawk* impaled itself into the tower of the building, he punched the button that activated the ship's right thrusters just as the enemy fired. Jake and Skip felt the force of the ship as it quickly changed its course. The edge of *NightHawk's* right wing was taken off by the building. Jake fought to maintain control.

The blasts from the enemy's ship hit the tower and ripped it from the rest of the building. The enemy didn't have enough time to move as the tower fell backwards and landed on the enemy.

Skip opened his right eye to peek at the rear-view screen. He saw the building's tower land on the enemy ship and then a large explosion. He opened his other eye and yelled, "Yes! You did it!"

"We're not out of the woods yet," said Jake, as he squeezed the flight stick with both hands trying to keep the ship from spinning out of control. He managed to keep the ship level, and the nose of the ship up as it headed for the snow-covered field below. The tail hit first, and then the nose of the ship slammed into the ground. Jake felt as if his head was being ripped from his neck with the impact.

The wounded ship skidded out of control on its belly toward a grove of trees. Jake had no idea how fast they were going. He hit the reverse thrusters' button and hoped that would be enough to slow them down before they hit a gigantic tree in front of them, but it didn't work. Every system in the ship was offline. Jake closed his eyes just before *NightHawk* collided with the massive tree trunk.

★ ★ ★ ★ ★

March 29, 2042 – Salt Lake City, Utah

It was 7 A.M. the day after Kevin received the news about *Mars II* disappearing. Kevin was sitting in his front room watching the news on his sixty-inch, wall mounted television/computer screen. He was still in his pajamas with his robe on and his hair a mess. He wasn't going into the office today. He was too depressed. Adam and Ashley were in the kitchen eating breakfast.

The television went to mute and spoke to Kevin. "Mr. Palmer, you have an incoming call from Michael Konrad, Head Administrator for NASA.

Oh great, now what? He thought. Kevin sat up. "Hello, Mike."

The image of Mike appeared on the monitor. "Ah, Kevin, you don't look so well? Are you sick?"

"No, I just didn't feel like getting ready for work this morning. What do you want Mike? I don't think I can handle any more bad news."

Mike gave Kevin an apologetic look. "I'm sorry to have given you that news the other morning. But, the news that I have for you now just might cheer you up a bit."

By this time, Adam and Ashley had made their way into the living room. Kevin sat up a little straighter and said, "Well, go on Mike. Don't keep me waiting."

"Okay, I'll get right to it. About four o'clock this morning, we received a video transmission from a probe that the crew of *Mars II* must have deployed just before going through the wormhole."

"Wait a minute, Mike. They went through the wormhole?"

"Yes, according to the video they did. Well, let me show you."

Mike's image disappeared from the screen, and the image of *Mars II* appeared in orbit around Mars. In front of *Mars II* was the hypothesized wormhole that Kevin first saw in his first meeting with Mike and Skip.

"What's that, Dad?" asked Adam.

"That, Adam, is a wormhole."

"Cool."

The video played. Kevin, Adam, and Ashley watched as the wormhole grew larger. It seemed to take hold of *Mars II* and take the shuttle through it. A few minutes later, the three saw another ship come up from the surface of Mars.

"Where did that ship come from?" Ashley asked.

"That ship is *NightHawk*. It's the landing vehicle for Mars. Jake and Skip must be in that one, and Taylor must have been the only one on *Mars II*."

They continued to watch as the wormhole began to shrink, and the smaller ship sped up. They held their breath as the nose of the ship entered the wormhole, which caused the ship to elongate. Then, the ship disappeared, and the wormhole closed.

Mike's image appeared back onto the screen. "Well, I hope that's good news for you."

Kevin smiled, stood up, and walked a little closer to the monitor. "You have no idea, Mike."

"Great, I'll let you know when they come back through and contact us," said Mike. Then his image disappeared.

Kevin turned slowly to face his children. "Well, kids, in a few months, you will meet your Uncle Adrian for the first time."

CHAPTER 6

March 28, 2042 – Planet of Terrest

Skip's body flinched, awakening him from his deep sleep. His head pounded as if razor sharp nails scratched across his scalp, and short bursts of pain shot down his left leg. He winced as he lifted both arms slowly to take off his cracked space helmet. When he saw his left hand, it was covered in blood from the elbow down. He took his helmet off and felt his body for any areas that may have been punctured. He felt around his torso, nothing. *Where is the blood coming from?*

Skip looked around to assess the damage. His eyes widened as they regained focus to view the catastrophe he apparently survived. From what he could tell, the center of the fuselage of *NightHawk* was split in two by a massive tree trunk. The tree trunk now rested between the two seats Skip and Jake sat in. In fact, Skip's left shoulder rested snugly against the tree's cold bark. He tried to look around the trunk for Jake. He couldn't see around it.

"J . . . Ja . . . Jake," Skip said as he coughed up blood. "Jake . . . are you okay?"

There was no answer.

Please, don't be dead, he thought.

Another sharp pain shot down Skip's left leg. He wondered if his leg was broken. He looked down. His eyes nearly rolled to the back of his head. He fought to stay conscious. He looked again to make sure what he saw was real. Sure enough, blood trickled out of his leg just above the kneecap. He shook his head to keep from fainting and looked again. His terror was solidified when he noticed why blood was trickling out of his leg.

Just above his kneecap was the jagged edge of his femur bone. Shreds of his quadriceps and hamstring muscles hung loosely off the edge of his seat. He reached down to make sure. It felt like his leg was still there. But, as he felt, his worst fear was realized. The tree trunk must have clipped his knee in the crash and ripped his left leg off just above the kneecap.

Skip looked around for something to tie around his thigh. Then, he remembered there was a first-aid kit in the compartment immediately to his right. He opened the compartment and found the first-aid kit. He ripped a piece of cloth in two, took one strip, and tied it around his left thigh as tight as he possibly could. He hoped it was tight enough to stop the bleeding.

"Jake? Jake?"

Again, there was no answer. He had to get out of his seat and somehow make his way to Jake to make sure he was alive. Skip slowly unbuckled himself. He winced in pain as he tried to get out of his seat. It was no use. He must have lost too much blood. He couldn't muster the strength to pull himself out of his seat. He tried again, and then he heard Jake.

"Shh," Jake whispered.

Skip was relieved. "Jake, are you okay?"

Jake whispered again. "Shh. Somebody's here."

Skip held his breath and heard two voices. One voice was deep and raspy, the other sounded young.

The young voice spoke first in a language Skip could not understand.

The deep voice then spoke in perfect English. "How many times do I need to tell you, Private? You will speak the language of our goddess mother. If his lordship knew you were speaking our primitive tongue, he would have your head."

The young voice responded in broken English. "Sorry . . . Sergeant. Me not have . . . uh . . . learned our goddess mother's language yet?"

"You are lucky it's just your first year in the academy, Private. If you were a commissioned officer, you would be put to death for speaking that primitive tongue. When did you start your language training?"

"Ye . . . Yeste . . . Yesterday."

"Yesterday? You should know at least half of the vocabulary by now. You are behind, Private. If you don't pass the exam by the end of the week, you will be dismissed from the academy and a disgrace to the Gnol way of life."

"Yes . . . S . . . Sir."

Skip wondered who or what learns English in a week. He heard the voices getting closer.

The older voice spoke first. "Now, since this is your first field mission, Private, watch and learn."

"Yes, Sir."

"Good. You're getting better."

"This must be the wreckage from the ship the humans stole. Let's find out if any of these humans survived. Then, we will travel back to *Chast* and file our report."

Skip was anxious. He kept his eyes closed. Maybe they would think he was already dead, especially in his condition. He heard the two aliens walk past him on his right.

The younger alien spoke first. "This human . . . uh . . . look died."

"Yes and the proper phrase is – 'This human looks as if he is dead already?'"

"Yes, Sir. This human looks as if he is dead already?"

"Good," the older alien said. "Let's make sure."

Skip felt his heart thumping harder in his chest. He heard one of the aliens approach. The alien placed what felt like two fingers on his carotid artery.

"This one is still alive," the older alien said.

The alien slapped Skip in face. "Wake up, you human scum!"

Skip did not want to open his eyes. Nevertheless, his curiosity got the best of him. He wanted to see what these aliens looked like. Skip slowly opened his eyes.

"Ah, it is alive," said the older alien.

Skip was shocked with what he saw. Instead of ugly, reptilian like aliens, which he expected, he saw what looked like two human beings in front of him. The older alien was bent over, gazing at him with angry filled eyes. He was a broad man, with a goatee, dressed in red fatigues with black trim. On his feet were what looked like military, issued boots, and on his shaved head was a red beret. On the center of the alien's beret was an insignia Skip did not recognize.

Skip glanced past the older alien in order to get a better look at the younger one. The younger alien was slightly smaller than the older alien. He also has a goatee and looked to be around twenty-years-old. He was dressed the same, but his head was not shaved. He had what looked like a military hair cut.

The older alien grabbed Skip by his throat. "Who are you? Are you a member of the slave resistance?"

Skip managed to speak. "I don't know what you're talking about?"

The older alien laughed and turned to the younger alien. "This one speaks the goddess mother's language, and better than you. Impressive." The older alien turned to face Skip again. He knelt down on one knee on what remained of Skip's computer terminal. He grabbed Skip's left thigh with his black-gloved hand. Skip screamed in pain.

"Don't lie to me, human. You must be a member of the slave resistance because you speak our mother's language so well."

Skip spit blood into the older alien's face. The alien back handed Skip across his face. Blood began to trickle from his left eye. The alien stood up and turned to the younger alien. "Keep an eye on this one. We need him alive for interrogation. I will check to see if this human over here is dead or not. Once I finish, we will find the computer's hard drive and download all of its information. And then, we will take him with us to *Chast*."

"Why . . . not . . . we just probe his mind?" the younger alien asked.

The older alien shot the younger alien an angry look. "Not here, Private! I'm sure the colonel would want the pleasure!"

"Yes, Sir."

Skip watched as the older alien walked around the tree trunk.

Unexpectedly, Skip heard the sounds of two gun shots and saw the older alien fall from behind the trunk. Blood slowly began to seep out from the two bullet holes in his head. The younger alien quickly tried to grab his firearm at his side, but he wasn't fast enough. Skip saw Jake jump from behind the tree trunk with the handgun aimed directly at the younger alien. He fired two more shots directly into the younger alien's chest. The alien landed dead in the snow.

Jake walked up to the younger alien still aiming the gun at him. He placed two fingers on the alien's neck. "They're both dead."

Jake then turned to face Skip and nearly vomited when he saw his dear friend's condition. "Oh man, Skip. If I would have known, I would have helped you sooner."

Jake knelt down to face Skip.

"It's okay. I found the first-aid kit and tied a tourniquet around my thigh. I hope I tied it tight enough to stop the bleeding."

Jake examined Skip's leg. "I think you did. I don't see it bleeding anymore, but you're sitting in a pool of blood. There's no telling how much blood you've lost? We've got to find some shelter fast. It's getting dark, and the temperature is dropping quickly."

"I don't think I can move, Jake?"

Jake stood up and looked around. "That's okay. There are pieces of *NightHawk* everywhere. I'm sure I could make some sort of sled with a left over piece of wing. There's some rope in the weapon's locker."

Skip shook his head and winced in pain. "Are those guys human?"

Jake looked at the two aliens lying in the snow. "They sure seem to be. But the way they spoke . . . I don't know. It's like they have some kind of ability us humans don't have. And, it's obvious they hate humans."

"What were they talking about, some sort of slave resistance? Maybe this resistance can help us?"

"Yeah, maybe. Listen, I better get a sled rigged so that I can pull you to some shelter. I'll grab some food rations and water too. You're going to need some rest.

★ ★ ★ ★ ★

Jake walked to the back of the shattered ship. He grabbed the rope out of the weapon's locker. He then put together a big enough sled out of what remained of one of *NightHawk's* wings.

When he finished the sled and gathered the needed supplies, he then made his way back to Skip. Skip was unconscious. *Oh no!* He thought. He knelt down and placed two fingers on Skip's throat. There was still a pulse. Skip must have been so exhausted he had fallen asleep.

Jake mustered enough strength to lift Skip and gently placed him on the sled. He was grateful the space suits he and Skip wore were environmentally controlled as the sky grew darker and the temperature seemed to plummet. Jake looked at the city they saw just before they crashed. It was dark except for the orange glow from the fire, as a result of the alien's ship that collided with the building's tower.

The building wasn't what Jake would call a skyscraper. It was only about two hundred feet tall. But from the air, it looked taller. He scanned the rest of the buildings. Unfortunately, it was too dark to get a clear visual of them. No lights seemed to be present within the city at all. He hoped there would be someone or something there that could help them.

As Jake walked to the back of what was left of *NightHawk*, he saw what it was that the two aliens arrived in. His jaw dropped, it looked a lot like a black hummer only more aerodynamic, and it didn't have any wheels. Instead, it was held in place by three stands, two in the back and one in the front. Jake looked under the impressive vehicle. The stands seemed to extend like landing gear on a plane from its belly.

Jake checked to make sure Skip was all right and left him at the front of the vehicle. He walked to the door on the right side, opened it, and looked inside. Once inside, Jake saw that it was spacious. The front could seat three people and the back seat could seat four. The seats were made of what seemed like fine black leather. Behind the back seats was a place to hold cargo. Jake thought that would be enough room for Skip to lie down in.

Jake pulled himself up to the driver's seat, which was situated in the center of the front of the vehicle. He looked at the steering device, which wasn't in the shape of a wheel at all. In fact, it seemed like the control stick of an old B-2 bomber, except modernized. He looked around the control panel and was stunned to see that everything was in English. He found the ignition button and pushed it.

The vehicle sprang to life. The three stands on which it was positioned retracted back into its underside. The vehicle hovered in the air about four feet from the ground. He pulled back on the controls, and the vehicle moved in reverse. He then moved to the left and right. *This will do*, he thought.

Jake pushed the ignition button again. The legs of the vehicle lowered, and the soft sound of the engine turned off. He stepped out and walked to Skip who was about fifteen feet away. Skip was awake again, but seemed to be falling in and out of consciousness. He didn't look well at all.

"Skip, are you all right?" Jake asked.

Skip looked up at Jake and nodded. He pointed to the hover vehicle and said, "You—," he coughed and spit up more blood, "you were going for a joy ride and leaving me . . . weren't you?" Skip said, trying to force a smile, but he was too weak.

"Ah man. You're not doing well. We've got to find some help fast," Jake said as he grabbed the rope and pulled Skip to the back of the vehicle. Jake looked for some sort of lever or button that would open the back door. There wasn't one. He went to the front of the vehicle and looked inside. He found the button that said, *Rear Door*. He pushed it and the rear door to the vehicle lowered slowly.

Jake lifted Skip and placed him in the cargo hold. Skip cried in pain.

"Sorry," said Jake.

Jake went back to the wrecked ship and grabbed their backpacks. Jake then loaded up the rations and water. He also grabbed both of the alien's weapons and tossed them into the seat to his right, along with his handgun. He climbed into the driver's seat and started the engine. The vehicle hovered there above the ground for a few moments. Jake pushed the controls forward, and the vehicle moved forward slowly but not at the kind of speed Jake wanted. Jake wanted it to move faster, so he could get to the city in enough time to help Skip. He estimated the city was about five miles away. He looked around and found a lever on his right side. The lever had numbers next to it all the way from zero to two hundred. The lever was set at zero. He moved it forward slowly and the vehicle began to pick up speed. He set it at forty-five.

When Jake reached the outskirts of the city, he had familiarized himself a little with the vehicle. He was also impressed with the technology. When he hit a small river about a third of a mile back, the vehicle hovered over it without any trouble at all.

Jake looked around. Small houses were beginning to appear. It was dark now, but both of this strange planet's moons were full, so it was light enough for Jake to see the details of the houses and buildings. The houses were of a familiar design. "Hey Skip, are you doing all right?"

Skip answered with pain in his voice, "Yeah, I'm just exhausted. But I'm a little concerned. I'm still coughing up blood."

"Hang in there, buddy. We're going to find some help. But everything looks deserted." Jake looked around for any sign of life. "Hey, Skip?"

Skip coughed. "What."

"These houses and buildings look familiar. They look like something out of a history textbook."

Skip pulled himself up to get a better view of the houses and buildings. "Hmm, that's inter—," he coughed again, "That's interesting."

"What?"

"It looks like Baroque architecture."

"What?"

Skip coughed before he answered again. "The Baroque style . . . of architecture was used a lot in Europe . . . during the fifteenth through the eighteenth centuries."

"Makes sense. The lampposts for the streets are set up for what looks like oil-burning lamps. I don't know. Maybe this place is an abandoned city for . . . What did those aliens back there call themselves?"

"I—," Skip coughed again, "I think they called themselves Gnols or something like that."

Jake slowed the vehicle down and meandered up and down the streets, looking for any sign of life that could help them. Some of the buildings were burned from the inside out. Carriages, which looked as if they could be pulled by some kind of animal, were spotted here and there along the streets, some tipped over and burned, and some left unmolested.

Jake looked straight ahead and saw the building that he nearly hit in the aerial chase about two hundred yards away. He steered the vehicle toward it.

Jake was starting to get frustrated and worried. Skip was coughing more frequently, and there wasn't a soul in sight. *Why would a city like this be abandoned?* He thought.

Jake entered what seemed to be an old courtyard, and directly in front was the building he nearly hit. The building was made in the same style as the other buildings but bigger and taller. It seemed to be the biggest building in the city, about three hundred feet in height. It reminded him of the Parthenon in ancient Greece – only bigger. He wondered if this was the city's central government building or some religious center. Jake decided he would get out of the vehicle, go in the building, and take a look.

"Skip . . . how you doin'?"

Skip wheezed and coughed. "I've been better."

"Listen," Jake said. "I'm going to go into that main building in front of us and see if anyone is in there that can help us. Will you be okay for a few minutes?"

"Yeah, I'll be fine."

Jake stopped the vehicle and was about to get out when he saw two headlights approaching from the rear of his vehicle. "Wait," he said. "Someone's coming. Maybe they can help us."

"You better hope that they're not with those guys that found us earlier," Skip said.

Jake stopped himself before he opened the door. "You're right. I'd better wait."

The two headlights stopped about ten feet behind Jake and Skip. The communication system within the vehicle came to life. "Sergeant Rossetlagn!

This is Captain Jamear, why are you and Private Toupast not at the wreck sight of the stolen space craft?"

Jake glanced back toward Skip and looked through the back window for a better look. With the light from the moons, Jake could see the aliens through their front windshield. He could tell that the two aliens were dressed the same as the previous aliens they encountered.

The voice spoke again. "Sergeant Rossetlagn, do you copy?"

Skip turned, looked at Jake, and shrugged. "May . . . Maybe we should make a run for it, Jake?"

Jake shook his head. "I don't know. These guys can probably maneuver their vehicle better than I can. Also, I noticed that these things are equipped with guns or some sort of weapon on the front, just above the headlights."

"I say again! Sergeant Rossetlagn, why are you not at the crash site investigating? You should have reported to me at *Chast* over an hour ago."

Jake quickly made a decision. He lowered his voice and tried to mimic the alien who he thought was Sergeant Rossetlagn, and pushed the communicator button. "Yes, Captain. I'm sorry. We were on our way back, when I decided that I should investigate the other crash just ahead of us."

There was a long pause that caused Jake to become anxious. Jake could see the two aliens discussing something.

"Sergeant, investigating this crash was not part of your orders. Why do you sound different, and who is that in the cargo area of your vehicle?"

Skip quickly lowered his head. "Jake, I don't think they're buying it."

Jake responded. "Sorry, Captain. I thought that it would be a good idea to investigate this cr—"

Before Jake could finish, the captain spoke to him in a language he did not recognize. Then silence. The alien repeated the phrase again.

"Jake, we better make a run for it. I think they've got us figured out," Skip said.

"I think you're right," said Jake, as he noticed one of the aliens get out of the vehicle, beginning to walk toward them, with his weapon drawn. Jake quickly pushed the ignition button. The vehicle's engine roared, and its legs retracted. Jake was about to push the lever that would send them off, when he felt a sudden pain surge through his head. His ears rang and his vision blurred. He screamed in pain; Skip did as well.

The sensation was similar to when they had first encountered these aliens in space. However, this time, he had an overwhelming feeling to shut down the vehicle and surrender to the aliens. It was as if he was outside of his body, and somebody was controlling him with a remote control.

Jake fought the urge to surrender. He heard Skip scream for help, and willed himself to throw the vehicle in reverse. He reached down, his head in agony, and pushed the lever to twenty-five. He then reached for the controls, using all of his strength, as his muscles wanted to resist every command he gave them. Struggling with all of his might, he finally commanded his arms to do what he asked them to do.

Grabbing the controls, Jake pulled back, and the vehicle shot backwards. The alien between the two vehicles tried to get out of the way, but he was too close. The rear bumper of Jake's vehicle hit the alien square in the chest and carried him back into the vehicle behind. Jake glanced at the rear view-screen as he hit the other vehicle and saw blood spatter on the rear window, obviously crushing the alien to death.

Jake pushed the lever all the way to one hundred and pressed the controls forward. The vehicle shot off like a rocket. Jake quickly steered the vehicle to the left, before hitting the main building, and sped off down a narrow street.

Before the other alien realized what had happened, Jake and Skip were already about a mile ahead, but he quickly closed the gap. Jake increased the vehicle's speed and zigzagged its way in and out of buildings, alleyways, and streets, all the while dodging plasma fire from his pursuer.

He heard Skip cough and say, "Jake, toss me your pistol and one of those alien's guns."

Jake liked what Skip had in mind. He quickly reached down, grabbed the guns and tossed Skip the pistol and then the alien's gun. He heard the handgun and glanced behind him as the rear window shattered. He saw Skip pull himself up with his left arm as he screamed in pain. With the alien's gun in his right hand, Skip began to fire plasma lasers at the pursuing vehicle.

Jake turned back and saw a building within ten feet. He quickly jerked the controls to the left, slamming Skip into the right side of the vehicle.

"Aaaaah!"

"Sorry."

"You—," Skip coughed, "—you'd better be. Are you trying to kill me before I slowly bleed to death?"

Jake continued to look for a street that would take him out of the city and into a clearing where, maybe, he could circle around to get behind the alien. Jake looked right and saw a street that would take them out of the city. When he was about to reach the street, he warned Skip that he was turning and to brace himself. Jake turned right and saw that the street did indeed lead out of the city.

The alien fired again. The bolt brushed the side of Jake's vehicle causing him to lose control momentarily. The left side of the vehicle smashed into one of the buildings. Jake regained control but noticed steam spewing out of the hood of the vehicle. Alarms began to sound within, but he continued to maintain speed.

"Skip!" yelled Jake. "You better take him out. I don't think this thing can take much more!"

"I'm trying, but this guy is good. Every time—," Skip coughed yet again. "Uh . . . every time I shoot, he dodges!"

"Use the pistol!"

"Good idea."

Skip pulled himself up a little straighter. With the pistol in his right hand, he pointed it at the center of the windshield of the alien's vehicle. He painted the center of the window with the laser and fired four rounds into it. The windshield shattered, and the vehicle swerved right and then left.

Skip could see the driver now. He was still alive but holding his neck. "I got him!"

Jake glanced at the rear-view screen and saw that the alien lost control of his vehicle and crashed into the building on his right. An enormous explosion ensued. Jake was so relieved that he wasn't being pursued anymore that he failed to notice the alien had fired a round of plasma blasts before he crashed.

One of the blasts clipped the right side of the vehicle. Jake lost control, and the vehicle flipped onto its roof. Jake heard Skip scream in pain.

Jake remembered that Skip was not buckled in. However, he was. He looked ahead and saw a familiar building about fifty yards ahead and approaching fast.

Because of the snow, the upside down vehicle would not slow down. The vehicle skidded to and crashed through some sort of wood fence. Jake closed his eyes and held his arms up to protect himself from flying glass. He opened his eyes again and saw the building getting closer and closer. There was nothing he could do to slow the vehicle down. He just hoped that when the vehicle hit the building it would not explode. He closed his eyes and braced for impact.

★ ★ ★ ★ ★

March 29, 2042 – Just outside the strange city on the planet of Terrest

Jake was awakened by a strong wind and a heavy snowstorm. How long had he been out? He looked around and noticed that it was still dark outside. Upside down and still buckled in the driver's seat of the hovercraft, he saw blood dripping from his head to the roof of the mangled vehicle. He reached up and felt a small sliver of glass sticking out of his forehead and pulled it out. Wincing in pain, he assessed the damage of his injury with his right index finger. The gash was deep, and he knew that he would need stitches, but that wasn't his main concern right now.

He unbuckled himself and caught his body with his hands before gravity pulled him to the roof of the vehicle. He exited through the shattered front windshield. The wind blew ferociously, and the snow fell harder. He stumbled to the back of the crushed craft and looked inside of what was left of the cargo hold. There was no sign of Skip other than the blood from his injuries.

Jake looked back at the path the vehicle had scraped through the snow. The path was now filled with freshly fallen snow. He continued to scan for Skip but couldn't see him anywhere. He noticed the fence the craft crashed through and limped his way to it.

Once he reached the fence, he looked around. He could not see a thing through the blowing snow. It was a virtual whitewash. He was starting to panic. *Oh no! Where could he be? Maybe, those Gnol things came back and carried him off?*

Jake continued to search in the vicinity he thought the vehicle had flipped over, and then, about ten feet to his left, he heard a low moan. He turned and hobbled to the source of the sound. As he approached, he could see the bloodied heap of Skip's body.

Jake knelt down beside his wounded friend. "Skip!"

"J . . . Jake . . ." Skip said, as he coughed, with blood trickling down his lip, ". . . I . . . I don't think I can hold on much longer."

Jake began to feel desperate. He knew first aid, but without the use of modern day medical technology, he knew he could not save his friend. "Hold on, Skip. I'm going to get you into that building. Once inside, I'll get our supplies and get you warm."

Jake got his legs underneath him and lifted Skip onto his right shoulder. He didn't know if he hurt Skip because Skip had become delirious and began to mumble things he could not understand.

Jake stumbled his way to the building. His ankle ached with pain and his head throbbed. The building was only fifty yards away, but with the blizzard and his own pain, Jake felt as if he was going to pass out and fall over.

Finally, Jake made it to the building and stopped. He was able to get a better look. He now knew why the building looked so familiar when he was upside down in the vehicle. The building was actually a pyramid about four stories tall. Surrounding the pyramid were five spires that stood slightly taller than the pyramid. Jake noticed that he was standing next to the spire at the front of the pyramid, the one his vehicle had crashed into. The next two were located next to the front corners of the pyramid, and the last two were next to the back corners of the pyramid.

Jake looked for any sort of entrance. About twenty feet ahead, he noticed an opening in the pyramid. He limped toward it. The opening contained a small staircase that led down ten feet to a large wooden door.

Skip was still mumbling.

Jake reached the door and tried to open it with the large handle. It wouldn't budge. Jake was getting mad now. He knew that if he didn't get inside soon, Skip wouldn't survive at all. Jake gently put Skip down on the ground, and with his adrenaline flowing, he kicked the door twice. On the second kick, the door slowly squeaked open. A rush of stale air gushed out. It was obvious with the smell of the air that no one had been in the building for years. Jake pushed the door open a little more.

The building inside was pitch black. Jake turned, picked Skip up, and walked through the door. Jake felt the stickiness of a cobweb, as he walked a little deeper into the pyramid. He could tell that the hall was narrow, but without any light, he didn't want to go any further. He gently placed Skip on the hard stone floor, and walked back to the wrecked vehicle to get a flashlight from the supplies he had packed.

A few moments later, Jake entered the pyramid with the flashlight illuminated. When he entered the narrow hallway, he shined the light on each wall to get a better look. Along each wall was writing, from the top of the walls all the way down to the floor. It seemed that every square inch of the walls was covered. Jake could not read the language, but the writings had the same alphabetic letters as the English language, mingled with hieroglyphs. He thought that it was strange that an alien civilization billions if not trillions of miles from Earth used the same alphabet.

Jake nearly stumbled over Skip as he continued to be amazed by the writings. He knelt down to see if Skip was all right. "Skip?"

No answer.

"Skip, it's me Jake. Can you hear me?"

Skip turned and tried to open his eyes, but he didn't have enough strength. He responded in a slow slur. "J . . . J . . . ake.

"Stay here, buddy. The hallway splits down this way. I'm going to check and see if there's a place I can make a comfortable bed for you and bandage you up."

Jake walked down the remainder of the hallway. He turned to the right and noticed a staircase that led upward. He didn't have the strength to carry Skip up a flight of stairs, so he turned around and noticed the room to the left of the hallway.

He walked into the room. It was a small room. From what he estimated, the room had a perimeter about fifteen feet by ten feet. In the center of the room was a damaged fountain. In the center of the fountain were the remains of a small statue that had been destroyed. The remains were strewn in the empty basin of the fountain.

Jake then shined the light on the walls. The same writings were on the left wall. On the right wall were five old paintings. He moved in closer to get a better look at the paintings. They were difficult to make out. It looked as if someone had vandalized them. One painting seemed familiar, but because of the damage, he could not make out its image. He shined the flashlight downward and noticed a stone bench encircling the room. It reminded Jake of some kind of waiting room.

This bench will be large enough to hold Skip comfortably, Jake thought. He then retrieved all of their supplies from the doorway where he had left them and proceeded to make at least a semi-comfortable bed for Skip.

Jake then went back to Skip. Skip moaned in pain and mumbled something Jake could not understand. He picked Skip up and almost fell from exhaustion. He carried Skip and placed him on top of the one sleeping bag in their supplies.

Jake quickly searched through the first-aid supplies and found some morphine. He cut away at the left arm of Skip's flight suit and injected the morphine. A few moments later, Skip seemed to fall into a deep sleep as the pain subsided. Jake then commenced to clean and bandage the stub of Skip's left leg. He knew that, in a few hours, the bandage would be blood soaked.

After Jake was finished with Skip, he laid on the cold stone floor of the room with his backpack as a pillow. He felt the tears flood into his eyes as desperation set in.

Is my dad really on this planet? And, if he is, where is he? Can anyone help us? The thoughts flooded Jake's mind. He didn't know what to do. His dear friend was holding onto life by a thread, and it seemed that everyone on this strange planet was an enemy. And for the first time in years, Jake did something that even surprised himself. . . . He prayed.

★ ★ ★ ★ ★

Jake was awakened by a loud bang and then a crash. It surprised Jake that he could hear something outside of the large stone walls of the pyramid. Jake turned the flashlight on and checked on Skip. Skip was still alive and sleeping soundly.

Jake heard the sound again. He grabbed one of the alien's guns and walked slowly to the large wooden door. He opened the door, causing a loud squeak. Jake stopped, hoping that if there were any Gnols outside, they wouldn't hear it.

Jake heard the sound again, but this time it was much louder. Jake quietly stepped up the stairs and noticed that the sun was shining, and there wasn't a cloud in the sky. From what he could tell from the sun's position, it must have been noon on this part of the planet.

Jake heard the sound again along with yelling voices in the background. He crept up to the top stair and knelt down so that no one would notice him. He was able to get a better look at the mangled vehicle he had stolen. He wondered how he had even survived the crash.

The left side of the vehicle was completely sawn off by the spire Jake had hit. He looked at the spire and eyeballed his way up to the top. At the top of the spire were the remains of a gold statue. All that remained of the statue were the carvings of bare feet on top of a gold sphere.

Jake flinched as he heard the crashing sound again. Jake looked through his binoculars about two hundred yards ahead. The vehicles that caused the large crashing sounds were actually demolition vehicles, two of them to be precise. The vehicles hovered about four feet in the air; much like the vehicle Jake had stolen. Only these vehicles had large cranes, and at the end of the cranes were wrecking balls.

Jake flinched again and nearly fell down the stairs, upon hearing a large explosion. He looked just beyond the wrecking balls where the explosion took place. *They are demolishing this city*, he thought to himself. Jake scanned the ground. He saw about a dozen or more Gnols with raised weapons. These Gnols were dressed in all black fatigues with red trim and black berets. The Gnols barked out orders to about fifty or more slaves.

The slaves were dressed differently. They all had on what looked like blue denim shirts and pants with black boots. The clothing reminded Jake of prisoner's clothing back on Earth, and on the left breast of each prisoner's shirt was a number.

Jake was horrified to see that not only were men being ordered to work and clean up the debris of the demolished buildings, but women and children were as well. Some children seemed to be as young as five-years-old.

Jake clenched his jaw in anger upon seeing helpless women and children working in such cruel conditions. The slaves seemed as if they were not even fazed. They almost walked in a trance. Jake wanted to do something, but what could he do?

Suddenly, Jake felt the incredible pain in his head that he had felt twice before since his first encounter with the Gnols. He dropped his weapon and reached up to cover his ringing ears. He screamed in pain.

He had an impulse to stand up and walk to his left. He could not resist. It was similar to the night before when the two aliens found he and Skip in the stolen hover vehicle. Only this time, Jake could not fight the urge. Still holding his ringing ears, he stood up, turned to his left, and began to walk.

Jake had his eyes closed from the pain in his head. He managed, however, to open his right eye, barely. His vision was blurry, but directly ahead, about twenty-five yards away, he saw three Gnols, all with their weapons pointed in his direction. Jake wanted to run, but he couldn't. His body wouldn't do anything his brain told it to do.

Jake was overcome with dread and fear. There was nothing he could do. For some reason these aliens, who looked like human beings, controlled him with their minds. He was now ten yards away, then twenty-five feet, twenty, and fifteen. He struggled to regain control of his body, but it was useless. He was going to be captured or possibly killed.

Suddenly, Jake saw the red flash of a plasma blast. The three aliens all went down. As a result, Jake was free from the mysterious, mind control that enslaved him. He dropped to his knees in the snow with his head still throbbing. Jake looked around. It seemed everywhere he looked there were other human beings – dressed in white fatigues in order to blend in with the snow – running and shooting down Gnols. Jake saw other hover vehicles firing blasts of plasma lasers at the Gnols. He was in the middle of a war zone.

Jake was just about to get up and run back to the pyramid when he saw one of the supposedly dead Gnols struggle to his knees. The Gnol raised his weapon and pointed it at Jake. Jake tried to get up and run, but before he could, the Gnol fired. Jake was thrown backwards, about five feet, and landed on his back in the snow. He clenched his stomach in agony.

Jake felt the warm wetness of his blood on his hands. He looked down at his stomach. There was about a three-inch hole where his belly button should have been. His eyes rolled to the back of his head, and then . . . everything went dark.

CHAPTER 7

March 29, 2042 – Planet of Terrest

Adrian, dressed in a surgical mask and gown, burst through the operating room doors, almost knocking down the two nurses and doctor's assistant who were on their way out. The doctor's assistant all but fell down as Adrian bumped into him. The assistant, however, managed to maintain his balance, sidestepped, stood up straight and saluted.

"General," the assistant said.

Adrian was too focused on Doc and managed a half salute back to the assistant. "Doc!"

Doc, who had just finished up his stitch job on his patient, looked up. He was dressed in a surgical cap, goggles, mask, gown, and gloves, and covered nearly from head to toe in spattered blood.

"Doc, is it true? Could it be?" Adrian asked as he stood next to Doc and looked down at the patient.

Doc didn't answer, but just looked at Adrian.

Adrian could tell that his best friend in life was smiling under his surgical mask. Adrian could always tell because as Doc aged the crow's feet around his eyes grew larger with each smile, and Doc smiled almost all of the time, even after all they had gone through together.

"Doc, are you just going to stand there smiling at me? I need an answer. Is it true what Kylee told me?"

Doc giggled and said, "I ran the DNA test as soon as he came in, and . . ."

Adrian was anxious. He needed an answer now. "And what, Doc? You had better tell me! You may be twice my size, but I'll take you down!"

Doc laughed with his deep voice and paused just a little longer to make Adrian squirm. "Anyway, as I was saying before you threatened me, I ran the DNA test, and it's confirmed. My patient, here, is none other than . . ."

Doc had to stop. As he spoke, his voice cracked as emotion crept in. He cleared his throat and continued in a solemn tone, "Adrian, he's Jake . . . your son."

The tears began to roll from Adrian's eyes. He jumped up and hugged Doc, getting blood all over his surgical gown. "I can't believe it. How did they get here and why?"

"I don't know," said Doc, pushing Adrian away. "I should have known it was your son when the special ops unit brought him in."

"Why do you say that?" asked Adrian, as he moved a little closer in order to get a better look at the son he had missed for twenty-five years.

"Well, look at him. He's just as ugly as you are."

Adrian turned around and laughed, giving Doc a little shove. "Doc, this is a miracle. Is he going to be okay?"

"Yes, he's going to be just fine. He was lucky. The plasma blast for some reason didn't penetrate his stomach, but he came in with a three and a half inch diameter hole in his flesh and muscle. He also lost a lot of blood."

"We managed to find a match in our minuscule supply of blood and give him a transfusion."

Adrian looked at the wound that Jake had suffered. "How did you manage to cover the wound so well?"

Doc walked across the room and pulled a drape away that revealed the exposed body of one of Adrian's soldiers. The soldier had a three and half inch diameter hole cut into his stomach. "This is Lieutenant Comoasa."

"No, not Como. He was such a good leader and had such potential. How did he die?"

Doc, saddened with the death of a young officer, whom they had all gotten to know quite well, walked over to Lieutenant Comoasa's body and turned him on his side. "Kylee told me that as they were loading Jake and his friend into the medical transport, Como was shot in the back of the head by a wounded Gnol."

Adrian shook and bowed his head. "I think I should be the one to tell his father, and he should be honored with a proper military burial."

"I agree," said Doc, as he gently laid the lieutenant's body back down and covered him with a sheet. "Anyway, Como wasn't going to make it, and Jake was in critical condition. As soon as they arrived to the base, I decided to graft a piece of Como's skin and muscle into Jake's missing flesh and muscle."

"Wow, you can do that?"

Doc gave Adrian an annoyed look. "Hey, I can do a lot of things you can't do, SIR."

Adrian ignored Doc's sarcasm and walked back to Jake who was sleeping soundly. He gently brushed the left side of Jake's head with his gloved hand. "I still can't believe it, Doc. I never thought I would see him again. I have thought about him every day for nearly twenty-five years. And, look . . . we are finally reunited again on another planet. There's definitely someone watching out for us, Doc."

"You can say that again," said Doc, as he moved to the right side of Adrian. "Listen, Adrian, the nurses will be in here soon to take Jake to his recovery room. I think we should let him rest. I definitely need some rest. That procedure took nearly thirteen hours, and I'm exhausted. I need to get some sleep before I figure out how to help his friend."

Adrian looked up at Doc. "How is his friend doing? What was on his name badge again? Skip, wasn't it?"

"Yeah, I think so. He's in critical condition right now. He lost way too much blood to even be alive, but he's still fighting. His left leg from just above the knee down was missing when he came in, and he had a broken rib in his left side that slightly punctured his lung. I fixed that already, but I've got to do some more research to figure out how I'm going to fix his leg. I had to remove the rest of his left leg because of infection."

Adrian gave Doc a puzzled look. "What do you mean more research? How are you going to fix his leg?"

Doc smiled and said, "Oh, that's a surprise. Sean and I have been working on something that I think will surprise you."

★ ★ ★ ★ ★

Jake slowly sensed his body and mind coming out of unconsciousness. The last thing he remembered was looking at the gaping, bloody hole in his stomach and then passing out in the snow. Jake opened his eyes slowly and tried to sit up. He couldn't pull himself up and felt sharp pains shoot throughout his stomach. He then felt two hands on his shoulders, forcing him to lie back down, and a familiar voice said, "Careful, Son. It's going to take some time to train the new muscles before you can move very much."

Jake groggily turned his head to the left and looked up to see where the familiar voice came from. Sitting at his bedside, was a familiar-looking man. The man's hair was thinning a little at the top, and his brown hair had gray streaks throughout. Despite the man's hair, he still looked relatively young. The man had piercing, blue eyes that had such a familiarity to them. Behind the man, stood two women, a young man, and a teenage girl.

The older woman was attractive. She had auburn hair and beautiful brown eyes. She was dressed in green military fatigues much like the man sitting at Jake's bedside. To the older woman's immediate left was a beautiful blond, blue-eyed woman. Jake figured that she was in her twenties. Her blond hair was pulled up into a bun and covered with a black military beret. She was also dressed in green military fatigues. In fact, everyone was dressed the same except for the young teenage girl.

"Jake, how are you feeling, Son?"

Jake suddenly snapped out of the trance he was in, trying to figure out who these people were and where he was? "What? Oh . . . I'm feeling okay. My stomach just hurts. Where am I?"

"We'll get to that later, but first, let's get some introductions out of the way."

Before Jake could respond, he suddenly remembered Skip. He tried to sit up from instinct, but he couldn't.

"Careful, Son. What's wrong?"

"There was someone with me. His name is Skip. Where is he?"

Jake felt the man place his hands on his shoulders to comfort him. "It's okay, Jake. Skip is in surgery right now. Doc will take good care of him."

Relieved, Jake relaxed a little and focused more on the people that were in his room. "Who are you? And . . . where am I?" he asked.

The familiar man smiled at Jake and said, "Jake . . . look at me carefully. You know who I am."

Jake took a long good look at the man and looked deep into his blue eyes. The man just continued to smile. Suddenly, it hit Jake like a lightning bolt. "Dad!"

Instinctively, Jake tried to sit up and hug his father, but he couldn't. He didn't need to. Adrian leaned down, hugged Jake and whispered in his ear. "Jake, it's me. It's your dad."

Jake squeezed his father and began to sob. He could feel his father's tears on his ear. He knew that his dad had missed him just as much as he had missed his father.

After what seemed like an hour of hugging and sobbing, the woman with auburn hair walked next to Adrian, placed both of her hands on the back of Adrian's shoulders, and said with a slight accent, "Well . . . aren't you going to introduce Jake to the rest of the family?"

Adrian sat up and wiped the tears from his face.

Jake looked at the three ladies in the room and the young man and said, "The rest of the family?"

Adrian, still wiping the tears away, looked at his family in the room, then back at Jake, and smiled. "Yes . . . the rest of the family." He waved for them to stand around Jake's bed. The woman with auburn hair stood next to Adrian, who was still sitting; the blond woman next to her. The young man walked around to the other side of the bed, as well as the teenage girl. All of them gave Jake warm smiles.

Jake felt a little uncomfortable, being in a vulnerable condition and everyone in the room a stranger on another world. His own father was even a stranger. Nonetheless, here he was being introduced to a brand new family.

Adrian pointed to the woman standing next to him. "This is Anyta, my wife."

Jake looked surprised, even though he knew that if his dad was alive, and if he survived on a planet with another humanoid species, the chances of him finding a mate were pretty good.

Anyta leaned down, gently kissed Jake's cheek, and said, "I am so happy to meet you, Jake."

Jake smiled as he looked into the warm, brown eyes of his stepmother. There was something familiar about her, reminding him of his mother and aunt. "I'm glad to meet you too . . . uh . . . mom."

Adrian pointed at the blond woman standing next to Anyta. "This is Kylee, your sister. She was also in charge of the special ops team that rescued you and the slaves."

Jake smiled warmly at his new sister. Kylee reached down and grabbed his hand. She spoke in perfect English. "Dad has told us so much about you, Jake. I've always dreamed of meeting you . . . big brother."

Adrian also added. "Kylee has proven to be a great leader in our cause. She's been elevated to captain and commands great respect from her troops in her squadron."

Jake looked questioningly at his father. "Cause?"

Adrian smiled. "We'll get to that later, Son. But first, let me introduce you to everyone else." Adrian pointed to the young man standing to the right of Jake's bed. "This young man is your little brother, Bantyr. He's in basic training right now. He's also not a bad pilot himself."

Jake looked at Bantyr and examined his new brother. He had dark brown hair that was cut in the typical military style and chocolate, brown eyes.

Bantyr smiled and shook Jake's hand. "It's good to meet you, Jake."

Jake smiled back, pulled Bantyr in close as he winced in pain, and hugged him. "Don't be so formal, little brother. Give your big brother a hug."

After the hug, Bantyr pulled back and smiled shyly. Jake turned to his father and said, "He almost looks like Adam."

Adrian gave Jake a questioning look. "Adam?"

"We can get to that later, but first, who is this beautiful young lady standing next to Bantyr?"

"This is your baby sister, Jake. Her name is Lexis."

Lexis leaned down and gently kissed Jake on the cheek, her long, blond hair brushing across Jake's face. "I am so glad to meet you," she said as she reached into her dress pocket and pulled out a half torn picture. Jake looked at the picture and instantly recognized it as himself when he was about four years of age. Lexis continued, "Dad always talked about you. So, I asked if I could have the only picture he had of you."

Jake took the picture and looked at it carefully. As he looked at the picture, a flood of emotions swept through him. He remembered the time he spent with his father before he disappeared. Jake began to weep as memories flashed through his mind, and here he was now on a strange planet reunited with his father and his new family.

There wasn't a dry eye in the room as everyone cried with Jake. Jake finally stopped the flood of tears in the room. "I have so many questions for all of you. But first, why is everyone in this room dressed like a green beret, except for Lexis?"

Adrian laughed. "Like I said earlier, we'll get into that later. I want you to rehabilitate that stomach first. Doc said that when he was finished with your friend, Skip, he would stimulate your new stomach muscles with a new medical program that he and Sean had developed. It's designed to help your muscles regain full strength within days as compared to months with normal physical therapy."

Jake was surprised that Doc could do that, but he wanted answers now. "But, dad, I want to know everything that has happened to you."

"I also want to know everything that has happened with you too, Jake. But like I said, I want you and Skip healthy to hear everything. You two have traveled thousands of light years through space and landed right in the middle of a war."

★ ★ ★ ★ ★

An hour after speaking with his son, Adrian pushed open the cold steel door that led to the small room dedicated for sacrament meeting. The small room could only hold a maximum of one hundred people, but it was wired for sound so that thousands of other people inhabiting the underground base could listen to the weekly sacrament meetings.

In the twenty-five years since Adrian crashed landed on this planet, he was successful in converting nearly his entire crew and thousands of natives to the Gospel of Jesus Christ, using his tattered scriptures he had brought with him from Earth.

After entering the room, Adrian walked to the back and knelt before a Terrestrian artist's rendition of Jesus Christ. As soon as his knees hit the floor, Adrian burst into tears. He could hardly control his sobbing as he prayed. He thanked his Father for Jake and for Jake's journey to this new world. He continued to pray and sob, thanking the Lord for everything he was blessed with and to help him with the burden he faced to free the Terrestrian people.

When he finished, Adrian heard someone's feet shuffle. He quickly turned around.

"Sorry, Adrian. I knew you would be in here."

Adrian smiled and walked toward Sean Gibson, the computer specialist from the original Mars mission. Sean, dressed in the same military clothing, leaned against the pew in the first row. Sean was now thoroughly bald but still had the same spectacles he wore twenty plus years ago.

Adrian spoke, "It's okay, Sean. I needed to come in here and thank our Father in Heaven for all of our blessings."

Sean just nodded.

Adrian continued, "Anyway, what did you need?"

Sean stood straight up and walked closer toward Adrian. "I just wanted to know how Jake was doing and whether you had told him or not?"

Adrian bowed and shook his head. "Jake is fine. But I couldn't bring myself to tell him yet."

With frustration in his voice, Sean said, "Adrian, you know he needs to know the truth."

Adrian looked back into Sean's eyes. "The truth, Sean. I don't even know what the truth is. When I spoke to Jake, I felt impressed not to tell him yet. The spirit told me that he wasn't ready."

"I understand, Adrian. But sooner or later, he's going to find out."

Adrian nodded in agreement. "I know, but I just don't think he's ready to know why I am here . . ." Adrian paused, turned, and looked into the eyes of his Savior in the painting on the wall, ". . . and . . . most importantly, why he is here."

★ ★ ★ ★ ★

Five days later, April 4, 2042

Skip was sitting up in his bed. He was in a dimly lit room. The only light provided in the room was by a lamp that looked as if a boy scout, trying to earn a merit badge, made it. The room was small. There was barely enough room for the bed that Skip was in and the other four people in the room. Jake sat in a small wooden rocking chair, in the corner of the room. It was still hard for him to stand for long periods of time as his new stomach muscles were not yet at full strength.

A day earlier, Skip had awakened from the complicated surgery he had undergone. The last thing he remembered was falling asleep in the strange temple with the familiar writings that he wanted desperately to learn more about.

When Skip awoke, standing over him was a large, middle-aged black man with an exceptionally warm and inviting smile. The black man introduced himself as Doctor Charles Porter, or "Doc" as everyone else called him. Skip knew who Doc was the moment he told Skip his name. Doc explained to Skip what injuries he had and how they were mended.

Doc also explained that the reason Skip continued to feel pain in his side was because he had suffered a broken rib that punctured his lung. Doc fixed his rib and told Skip that he would heal quickly from that injury. However, as Skip knew, he had also lost his left leg. Skip was surprised when Doc told him to reach down and feel his left leg. Skip, at first, thought the man was crazy. Didn't he know that he had lost his leg in the crash?

Nonetheless, Skip reached down and felt a leg where just days earlier there wasn't one. He immediately began to cry when he felt a leg, and what astonished him even more, was the fact that the leg had feeling and was covered in what seemed like human skin.

Doc explained that just days earlier, in what Skip thought was a strange coincidence or some divine intervention, Doc and Sean Gibson had developed the technology to produce cybernetic limbs, which would help so many of the rebel soldiers in their war against the Gnols. The cybernetic leg was made out of some kind of metal alloy that was only indigenous to this planet. Doc said that the metal was actually stronger than stainless steel or other metals found on Earth, and it didn't rust. Skip couldn't remember what Doc called it, but continued to be amazed at everything Doc and Sean had done for his new left leg.

Skip learned that smart processors were embedded throughout his new leg. At the top of the cybernetic leg, there was a master smart chip that his nerves were miraculously threaded into. The master chip then sent signals to the other smart chips that acted like a knee, a calf muscle, an ankle, and a foot. As a result, Skip could move his new leg just like his old one without even thinking about it. He also learned that the new leg was hollow so that it wasn't too heavy for his body, and that the outside of the leg was covered with some sort of synthetic rubber that felt like real skin. Skip was even more astonished to learn that he could feel as a result of small sensors placed within the rubber that sent signals to his brain.

After learning about his new leg, Doc had Skip walk on it. Skip broke down in tears of joy because he could walk and run, just like he did before he lost his leg. Skip immediately hugged Doc after testing his leg. The big doctor hugged him back, and the two seemed to hit if off immediately. And now, here he was a day later, almost entirely back to one hundred percent, as well as Jake.

Skip scratched at the ivy in his arm. Doc had told him that he had to continue to receive plasma to help replenish all of the blood he had lost. It was a miracle Skip was even alive.

Adrian broke the silence first. "I'm so glad to see you doing so well, Skip?"

Skip smiled. "It truly is a miracle. That doctor of yours is the best," he said, looking at Doc.

Adrian smiled back. "He is. Except he can have a little ego problem sometimes."

Doc lightly punched Adrian in the shoulder. "Careful, General or you're going to find yourself without a limb, and I won't replace it."

Everyone in the room laughed except for Jake who knew that laughing would be painful.

After the laughing stopped, Adrian said, "There's a reason why we are all here today. I told Jake that when both of you were well we would explain what happened to us, and then you will have the chance to explain what this rescue mission is all about.

"As you both have already figured out, we were sucked through some kind of wormhole while Gloria—"

Adrian suddenly became sad. Jake noticed and expressed his concern. "What is it, Dad?"

Adrian looked at Jake. "Do you remember Gloria, Jake? You were only five-years-old at the time."

Jake thought for a moment. "I remember vaguely. I think I can remember you bringing a woman to the house sometimes while you were training for the Mars mission. I remember she was really pretty and really nice, but that's all I can remember."

"Yes, that was her, Son." Adrian paused and then continued. "While Gloria was working on the satellite that orbited Mars, this circular thing opens up that looks like some sort of water ripple in space."

"That's exactly what it was, General. That was the wormhole," Skip interrupted.

"Please, call me Adrian, Skip. Any friend of Jake doesn't need to be so formal with me."

Skip just nodded and allowed Adrian to continue.

"Well, to make a long story short, *Mars I* was sucked into the wormhole, leaving Gloria behind. When we came through the wormhole, we all assumed that Gloria would either kill herself, knowing that we were gone, and she was left alone in space, or that the gravity of Mars would pull her in."

"What happened after you came through the wormhole?" Skip asked.

"When we came through the wormhole, *Mars I* was in pretty bad shape. *Maggie* was down, and—"

"*Maggie?*" questioned Jake.

Sean broke in before Adrian could answer. "Yes, *Maggie* was the pet name I gave to the computer system of *Mars I.*"

"The computer you were in love with you mean," said Doc.

Everyone in the room laughed again; even Sean laughed, seeing the humor in naming a computer and actually having feelings for it.

Adrian continued. "The computer system was malfunctioning, and we were losing power fast. The reactor was close to meltdown, and Peter Sanchez – our nuclear engineer on the mission – knew he wouldn't be able to repair it. So, I decided that we as a crew would abandon ship. Everyone in the crew agreed, except for Don."

"Donald Garrett, your copilot, right?"

"Yes, Don thought that we should stay on *Mars I* and try to repair her. Once she was fixed, he thought we should wait until the wormhole opened up again and try to return to our solar system. I didn't agree with him. Petey had told me that the core of the reactor was about to meltdown because of a jammed rod, and there was no possible way he could fix it.

"As a result, I had to make a quick decision. I decided that we would all load up into the landing craft and try our hand on the planet below. We didn't even know if the planet would support life, but we had a good reference that it would because it looked a lot like Earth – an atmosphere, continents and islands, and of course oceans.

"However, Don was absolutely opposed to the idea. He was so opposed to the idea that he attacked me in front of the rest of the crew in the flight-deck."

"He attacked you?" Jake asked.

Doc spoke first. "Yeah . . . Don, for the entire mission, had been strongly against every decision Adrian had made. In fact, the night before we went through the wormhole, Don went after Petey and eventually had a fight with your father."

"Wow," said Jake. "That doesn't make for a very successful mission."

Doc continued, "Yeah, it doesn't. But, Don was so jealous of your dad because he had been passed over to command the mission for Adrian, who we all thought was the better leader. And, your dad, with the feeling of inadequacy that he has always had, chose him as his copilot because he didn't believe that NASA made the right decision."

Jake looked questioningly at his father.

"Believe me, Jake. I now realize that NASA made the right decision and I the wrong one. As I was saying, Don attacked me. When I was getting out of the pilot's chair, he pushed himself from his seat and forced us both against the plasma shield of the shuttle. Before I realized what he had been doing, he was strangling me. He would have succeeded too, if it wasn't for Doc."

Skip looked at Doc. "What did you do, Doc?"

Doc gave Skip that glowing smile of his. "Oh, it was nothing. I just ripped my computer monitor off of its station and hit him in the back of the head with it."

Sean laughed. "Yeah, and it knocked him out cold."

Doc laughed as well. "You know I wanted to leave him there while we all went to the surface, but your dad, having that kind heart of his, ordered me to carry that s—"

"Hey watch the language, Doc. My son and his friend are here."

"It isn't anything I haven't heard before, Dad. I'm not five-years-old anymore."

Adrian gave Jake a warm smile. From the smile, Jake could tell that his father wished he was still that five-year-old boy he left on Earth nearly twenty-five years ago.

"Will you guys let me get through the story before the day is over? We've got a lot of other things to worry about," said Adrian. "Yes, I ordered Doc to carry Don onto *NightHawk*. Doc buckled Don into his seat next to me. But just as I was about to exit the payload deck, Don woke up. He must have realized what we did to him because he unbuckled himself so fast that none of us realized he was on top of me again. He hit me as hard as he could in my right eye. That's where this scar came from."

Jake, as painful as it was, stood up and walked over to his father. He looked at his father's right eye. Just under his bottom eyelid, was a scar that extended about half an inch from the bridge of his nose to his cheekbone.

"Wow, that must have been some hit?" said Jake.

"It was. I blacked out for a moment, which caused me to veer left into the payload-deck door. As a result, we lost one of our engines.

"Doc hit Don, knocking him out again. He then grabbed the duct tape in the supply locker and taped him to his seat."

"How did you survive the descent to the surface with only one engine?" Jake asked.

"That was difficult. Somehow, I managed to keep the ship at a forty-degree angle, so we wouldn't burn up. When we were finally safe, I looked for a safe place to land the ship. I spotted a clearing just on the other side of a small forest, within a few miles of a city. In fact, that was the same city where Kylee and her squadron rescued you two. The city's name is *Talead*. It's actually the capital city of this planet."

"What is this planet called?" Skip questioned.

"The planet is called *Terrest*. At least that's what the people called it when we were finally able to understand them."

"You mean there were people in the city when you arrived?" asked Jake.

"Yes. We estimated that the city's population was about one-and-a-half million people. But before I get to that, let me tell you what happened after we landed.

"It was dark when we landed. So, we decided that we would just camp out for the night and make our way to the city in the morning. We even kept Don taped in his chair. When he woke up, he demanded that we let him go. Doc was hesitant, but Don promised he wouldn't attack me again. We cut him loose—"

Adrian stopped as emotion crept into his voice. Jake, sensing that something troubled his father, asked, "What's wrong, Dad?"

"It's just . . . that when we cut Don loose . . . all he did was glare at me and then he said, 'Well, you should be proud of yourself, Commander. You've not only failed one of the most important missions of mankind, you've managed to kill one of your crew members and leave the rest of us to rot on this pitiful planet.' I can still remember what he said word-for-word."

Doc put a hand on Adrian's shoulder. "You've got to forget it, Adrian. The man snapped. He went crazy. And, you know that everything that happened was outside of your control."

Adrian put his hand on Doc's. "Yes, I know, old friend, but I just can't help but feel responsible for what he did next. I mean, as a leader, you're supposed to keep your crew together, no matter what."

"What did he do next?" Skip asked.

"Well, right after he said what he said to me, he just walked off into the night. We haven't heard from or seen him since."

"Wow, he just up and left? The man must have really fallen off his rocker?" said Jake.

"That's what we all thought before he left," uttered Sean.

Adrian forced a small smile, but Jake could tell that his father carried a lot of guilt.

Adrian continued. "The next day, we made our way into the city. The city . . . I mean, *Talead*, reminded us all of a city set in the eighteenth century back on Earth. You should have seen the looks we got from the local population. They were dressed the way people dressed in the sixteenth and seventeenth centuries back on Earth, and here we come into town dressed in our flight suits. People were even scared of us.

"The city was extremely busy. We were astonished to find that the people on this planet were actually human. We were all expecting to find some sort of lizard-like alien species on this planet. You know the kind we saw in science-fiction movies back on Earth?"

Everyone in the room nodded in agreement, but no one spoke a word. They were interested in hearing the rest of the story, including Doc and Sean who lived through it with Adrian.

Adrian continued. "Some of the people that had been afraid of us must have gone and told the authorities because, about thirty minutes after we entered the town, four men, that were dressed like the three musketeers with swords and everything, came riding up to us on horses. Yes, believe it or not, they were actually horses. In fact, this planet seems to be almost identical to Earth. It has different climates like Earth – deserts, jungles, and frozen tundras. The animal life, from what we know so far, is even the same."

Skip, unable to control his excitement, interrupted again. "Incredible, I wonder if this is some kind of mirror world to Earth. Who knows maybe we didn't end up on the other side of the galaxy? Maybe we entered some sort of other dimension?"

"Whoa, hold on there, Skip. Don't go getting anymore theories in your head. Let my dad finish his story before we jump to conclusions," Jake said.

"No. I think your first theory about us being on the other side of the galaxy is correct, Skip. I'll get to that later. But first, the four musketeers actually arrested us. We were taken to the palace in the center of the city—"

Jake interrupted. "That must have been the building that looked like the Parthenon?"

Adrian nodded. "That would be the palace. We were taken to the king. His name was *Adrimd Xuta*. In English, his name was actually Edward Cole."

"Edward Cole?" asked Skip. "How did you decipher an alien name into English?"

"Let me finish first, and I'll get into linguistics later. Anyway, the language barrier prevented us from communicating with each other effectively. The king saw us as a threat and sent us to prison for several weeks.

"After a while, he decided that we weren't a threat at all. He released us from prison on the condition we live with him in the palace and help him. As time passed, we learned each other's languages. We learned from him that this planet was, in fact, unified. We learned the history of *Terrest*. We learned that, at one time, there were warring tribes and countries, very similar to Earth. But about five hundred ten years ago on this planet . . . By the way, a year on this planet is three hundred sixty-five days, the same as Earth's rotation around its sun."

"Amazing," Skip said.

Adrian nodded and continued. "About five hundred ten years ago, *King Xuta's* ancestor – they called him *Juzs Lza Bmail* led a crusade and conquered the planet.

"*Bmail* unified the entire planet under one banner." Adrian pointed to his left shoulder. "This is the banner."

Jake leaned forward to get a closer look. On his father's shoulder was a circular badge. The badge had a black border on the outside and was yellow on the inside. In the middle of the badge was a planet, obviously representing *Terrest*, and in the background were *Terrest's* two moons. Near the top of the badge was a saying that Jake could not read. "What does the banner say?"

"It says, *Esolad Ra Ylisd. Os Uem Jud Ra Lmeyl.* In English, it means *United We Stand. In Our God We Trust.*"

Adrian continued, "*Juzs Lza Bmail* united *Terrest* under one language, which is called *Tilicah*, named after the tribe he came from. He also united *Terrest* under one religious banner."

Skip interjected. "He must have been a tyrant?"

"Actually, he wasn't," Adrian said. "According to *King Xuta*, *Juzs* actually believed in the God of his tribe. His tribe believed in one God. His tribe believed that they were actually visited by their God about two thousand years ago. In fact, the temple where Kylee found you two was a temple built to worship their God."

Jake looked at Skip. He could tell that Skip was dying to ask more questions about the temple, but he seemed to control himself and let Adrian continue.

"*Bmail* continued to worship his tribe's God. To say the least, his ideals created the most peaceful civilization that I have ever seen."

Skip's curiosity got the best of him. He had to ask. "Well, then why are the *Terrest* people at war now?"

Adrian smiled at Skip. "Hold on Skip. I'll get to that part later. Anyway, *King Xuta* was the leader of *Terrest* when we met him. Like I said, after several weeks in prison, *Xuta* released us. Not only did we learn from him, but he learned from us as well.

"After he learned of our knowledge of technology, he placed us in important roles within the government, and we gladly accepted because we knew there wasn't any possible way we could return to Earth."

Adrian placed a hand on Doc's right shoulder. "Doc was named Director of Medicine. He actually started the first medical school on the planet. Sean was named Director of Technology and Computer Development. Using your Uncle's smart chip technology, Sean introduced this planet to the car, established a number of computer centers throughout the planet, and opened a computer school. Peter Sanchez, our mission's nuclear engineer, was named Director of Energy. He developed power plants throughout the planet and is currently working on the nuclear reactor for our second base of operations. Skyler Green, our mission's botanist, was named Director of Science and Biology. Five years later, he was commissioned by the king to travel the planet and identify plants and animals. He kept in contact with us, but when the Gnols attacked, we haven't heard from him since. We assumed that he was either killed or captured and forced into slavery.

"We've been trying to locate him as we free the other slaves, but so far no luck." Adrian said.

"What about Ted Anderson, your Geologist, and Isaac Cooper, your mission's physicist?" Skip asked.

Jake could tell that his father's sadness seemed to deepen when Skip mentioned the men's names.

"Ted soon came down with brain cancer and died a few months after, and Isaac was named Director of Physics. In fact, he and I were working on the planet's first airplane . . ." Adrian paused, and his voice became shaky, ". . . Isaac was killed when the Gnols attacked. He . . ." Adrian tried to hide his emotion, but it was useless.

Jake stood up, walked next to his father, and placed his arm around him. "It's okay, Dad. You don't have to go into details. I know it's painful. Why don't you tell us what *King Xuta* put you and Scott Hauler in charge of?"

Adrian looked at his son, who was now a grown man and a few inches taller, and smiled. "Scott and I were put in charge of *Terrest's* army. He and I were both named generals. As we speak, Scott is at our second base of operations with Petey. His division is getting it ready just in case the Gnols discover this base."

"I'm impressed, Adrian. It sure looks like the seven of you did a lot for this planet." said Skip.

"Yeah, in just ten short years after we arrived, we introduced almost every modern convenience we enjoyed on Earth to *Terrest* like indoor plumbing. You name it, we invented it."

Doc placed his bulging arm on Adrian's shoulder and looked at Jake. "Your father is being modest, Jake."

Jake gave Doc a confused look. "What do you mean?"

Doc gently patted Adrian's shoulder. "Why don't you tell him, Adrian? What you've done for us, and the people of this world, is far more important than any new technology."

Adrian shook his head. "No, we don't need to get into that now, Doc. Jake and Skip want to find out what happened."

Adrian was about to continue, but Doc spoke first. Doc, usually lighthearted, looked solemnly at Jake. His eyes almost welled up with tears as he spoke. "Your dad, Jake . . ."

Jake, growing more anxious to find out what his dad had done to help the Terrestrian people, still had a look of confusion on his face. What could his father have done to help the people of *Terrest* more than what he had done already? "What, Doc? What did my dad do?"

Adrian held up his left hand to stop Doc. "Doc, this isn't the right time. I prefer to speak with Jake and Skip alone on this matter."

Doc shook his head and was about to speak, when he looked at his best friend and realized Adrian was serious. This wasn't the time. Doc nodded his head and said, "Okay, Adrian. Why don't you tell them about Anyta?"

Adrian smiled with the mention of Anyta. "Anyta is *King Xuta's* daughter."

Doc interrupted. "Yeah, your dad married royalty."

"We were married about two years after we arrived," said Adrian, giving Doc an annoyed look. "Doc hasn't wanted to settle down, and believe me, he's had plenty of callers."

Doc chuckled. "I just haven't found the right one yet, that's all."

Skip looked at Sean who was staring at the wall with in a blank stare. "What about you, Sean? Did you ever get married?"

Sean slowly turned to face Skip. "I did. I was married a few days after Adrian." Sean's eyes then reddened with tears.

Skip looked confused. He glanced at Sean and then at Adrian.

Adrian spoke for Sean. "When the Gnols attacked, they captured his wife, *Xmhylit* – Crystal in English – and their son, Luke, who was six at the time." Adrian turned and looked at Jake. "In fact, Jake, Luke would be the same age as Kylee."

Sean finally gained the composure to speak again. "They're still alive. Some of our spies have video footage of her and my son in the jungle mining camp of *Zikf*. We haven't attempted a rescue for that slave camp yet because we don't have the resources."

"We are planning an attack within the next year." Adrian said.

Jake glanced at Sean and could tell that Sean was annoyed with Adrian's answer. Sean was about to speak, but Skip beat him to it.

"Who are the Gnols, and why did they attack?"

"About ten years after we arrived, the entire planet was attacked. It was a simultaneous attack. Every major city on *Terrest* was attacked by ships that looked similar to *Mars I* and *NightHawk*."

"Those were the same kinds of ships we ran into when we came through the wormhole." Jake said.

"Yes, they were. We didn't know for the longest time where the Gnols came from, but about seven years ago, one of their top government agents turned to our side. She has been working on our side ever since, giving us valuable information. The Gnols still haven't discovered that she is working with us. When she turned, she held a private meeting with me and explained the reason behind the attack on *Terrest*.

"She told me that the Gnols came from a planet called *Gnolom*. Their planet is in orbit next to *Terrest*. We estimated that *Gnolom* is the same distance from *Terrest* as Mars is from Earth."

"Amazing," said Skip, obviously captivated.

Adrian chuckled and said, "You'll also find this interesting, Skip. Our source also told me that *Gnolom* is a dying planet. Most of the oceans have dried up. In fact, she showed me pictures and *Gnolom* is beginning to look a lot like Mars. That's why they attacked. The Gnols were looking for a new home."

CHAPTER 8

◆━━━━━━━━━━━━━━━━━━━━━━━━━━━━━━━━━━◆

Two days later, April 6, 2042 – Rebel Base on Terrest

Jake stood in front of the mirror of his small room. The room was small but comfortable. There only seemed to be room for a bed, a sink, and a tiny desk. Every member of the *Terrest* military was given a room such as the one he was in now; some military personnel even had to room with two or three other soldiers because of the overcrowding of the underground base.

Jake adjusted the black beret that rested on top of his head and admired how he looked in his new Terrestrian military fatigues. For a moment, Jake let himself become lost in his thoughts. *Was this all a dream?* He could hardly believe he was on another planet thousands of light years from Earth. And he was even more amazed that his father was the one man who now led the Terrestrian people.

As Jake thought about the respect and loyalty the Terrestrian people had for his father, he couldn't help feeling that his father was hiding something from him; something his father seemed afraid to tell him. Jake shrugged the thought away, thinking that it was nothing. He admired himself one last time in the mirror and began to walk toward the exit. As soon as he walked into the door's sensor, it slid open.

Jake was surprised to see his father standing at the door. His father smiled at him and seemed to shift nervously on his feet. "Uh . . . Hi, Dad. I didn't know you were standing there," he said.

Adrian's smile seemed to turn to a look of concern. "I've actually been standing here for a few minutes trying to figure out how I was going to talk to you."

Jake gave his father a look of confusion. "What do you mean? We've talked plenty, and you never seemed unsure of what to say before."

"Well, this is different," said his father.

"How so?"

"Can we speak in here for a few minutes before we meet with Doc and Skip in the conference room?" Adrian asked as he motioned toward Jake's room.

Jake nodded his head and let his father enter the room.

Adrian walked past Jake with his head down. He stopped, turned around, and said, "Jake, why don't you sit down."

Jake didn't respond. He could sense the concern and worry his father had and obeyed as he sat on the edge of his bed.

Adrian paced back and forth for a few seconds, then turned and looked directly into Jake's eyes.

As Jake looked back into his father's eyes, he noticed such a strength and power behind them, as well as love and sadness.

Adrian continued, "Jake, there's a reason why you are here."

Jake nodded, "Yeah, I know, Dad. I told you already. Skip had a theory about a wormhole, and Uncle Kevin funded a resc—"

Adrian held his hand up to stop Jake. "That's not what I'm talking about, Son."

Jake cocked his head to one side in confusion. "I don't understand, Dad. What are you talking about?"

Adrian paced back and forth a few more times, gaining the confidence to speak. He slowly sighed before he began. "Jake, about fifteen years ago, soon after the Gnols attacked *Terrest*, I had a vision that you would come to this planet. . . ." Adrian paused, as if he wanted Jake to respond.

Jake, sensing his father was waiting for an answer, let out a small giggle. "You mean like a dream, Dad."

Adrian shook his head. "No . . . no, Son. I mean an actual vision. I was wide-awake. It was a few days after the Gnols attacked this planet. I was here in this very base. In fact, I was in the room that is now dedicated for the sacrament. I—"

Jake now held his hand up to stop his father from speaking. "Wait a minute. . . . You have a sacrament meeting room here in the base and on this planet?"

Adrian nodded his head.

Jake then shook his head in confusion. "I . . . I don't understand. You mean . . . you're a Mormon on this planet too?

Adrian smiled. "Why not? The Gospel of Jesus Christ isn't designated only for Earth. His gospel is a universal truth. It pertains to all of our Father's creations."

Jake furrowed his eyebrows and shook his head again. He was confused. It had been so long since he had even been to church let alone had a testimony of the gospel. He questioned a God that would take away the ones he loved so quickly and one that would allow such suffering in the world. This inner turmoil even made him question the mere existence of God.

Adrian, sensing his son's confusion, asked, "Son, you mentioned earlier that Ashley gave you a set of scriptures?"

"Yes, she did."

"Do you have them with you now?"

Jake nodded his head, slipped off his bed to one knee, and reached under the bed. He pulled out his backpack, unzipped it, and grabbed the scriptures that Ashley had given him. Then he handed them to his father. Jake resumed his previous position on his bed as his father opened the scriptures and thumbed through them for what he was looking for.

"Ah, here it is," Adrian said as he handed the scriptures back to Jake. "Jake, I want to read out loud *Moses* Chapter one, verses one through four."

Jake was about to question his father, but seeing the look of determination and passion his father had on his face made him nod and read:

> *"The words of God, which he spake unto Moses at a time when Moses was caught up into an exceedingly high mountain.*
>
> *"And he saw God face to face, and he talked with him, and the glory of God was upon Moses; therefore Moses could endure his presence.*
>
> *"And God spake unto Moses, saying: Behold, I am the Lord God Almighty, and Endless is my name; for I am*

without beginning of days or end of years; and is not this endless?

"And, behold, thou art my son; wherefore look, and I will show thee the workmanship of mine hands; but not all, for my works are without end, and also my words, for they never cease."

After Jake read the verses, he look up at his father with the same confused look on his face. "I still don't understand, Dad. I've read these verses hundreds of times, but I still don't know what they mean or what you want me to see in them."

Adrian sat on the bed to the left of Jake. He pointed to verse four. "Read this verse again silently to yourself. But before you begin, ask the Lord for understanding."

Jake gave his father a questioning look. But, as he continued to notice the fervor in his father's eyes, he obeyed. He bowed his head and said a silent prayer. After he prayed, he opened his eyes and read verse four again to himself.

Jake read it once, then twice. He still could not comprehend what his father wanted him to understand. Adrian sat patiently. Jake decided he would read the verse one more time. As he read, one phrase caught his eye. He then read the phrase over and over again. Each time he read, a flood of emotions swept through him like a wave of truth testifying to his soul that the words he read were true.

Jake felt the gentle touch of his father's hand on his shoulder. Jake looked up. Adrian smiled at him, knowing his son now understood."

"Son, you see," whispered Adrian. "The Lord says, *for my works are without end, and also my words, for they never cease'*. Now, wouldn't it make sense that if the Lord's works don't end and his words never cease, that His gospel would be present on other worlds?"

Before Jake could answer, Adrian continued. "Now, skip down and read verses thirty-three through thirty-nine."

Jake did as he was asked. He began to read:

"And worlds without number have I created; and I also created them for mine own purpose; and by the Son I created them, which is mine Only Begotten.

"And the first man of all men have I called Adam, which is many.

"But only an account of this earth, and the inhabitants thereof, give I unto you. For behold, there are many worlds that have passed away by the word of my power. And there are many that now stand, and innumerable are they unto man; but all things are numbered unto me, for they are mine and I know them.

"And it came to pass that Moses spake unto the Lord, saying: Be merciful unto thy servant, O God, and tell me concerning this earth, and the inhabitants thereof, and also the heavens, and then my servant will be content.

"And the Lord God spake unto Moses, saying: The heavens, they are many, and they cannot be numbered unto man; but they are numbered unto me for they are mine.

"And as one earth shall pass away, and the heavens thereof even so shall another come, and there is no end to my works, neither to my words.

"For behold, this is my work and my glory – to bring to pass the immortality and eternal life of man."

When Jake finished reading, he just stared at the pages of his scriptures. Tears began to stream from his face, as he felt a presence in the room that he never felt before – a presence so powerful that he could not deny the existence of his Father in Heaven and His Son, Jesus Christ.

With tear-filled eyes, Jake looked at his father and now knew. He now knew the actual authority, power, and burden his father carried for the Terrestrian people.

Adrian, with tear-filled eyes as well, smiled. The smile confirmed to Jake that his father knew that he finally understood.

Jake cleared his throat and wiped the tears with his hand. "Dad, y . . . you are the Moses of this world."

To Jake's surprise, Adrian shook his head. "No, Son. I am more like John the Baptist of this world, preparing the way for someone greater."

Jake's eyes widened. "Me? Dad, it can't be me."

Adrian let out a small laugh. "I don't know, Son. But trust me; you are here for a reason. I haven't spoken with the Lord face-to-face like Moses. But I have heard his voice so clearly. I have had conversations with the Lord, Son. Can you believe it?

"Me, your father . . . I have been called by God to prepare a way for the Terrestrian people to be free from bondage and to receive the everlasting gospel of Jesus Christ. And I knew you and Skip would come. I saw the both of you, fifteen years ago, arrive on this planet just as you arrived a few days ago. How else would I have known to send a Special Forces unit to *Talead* that day? I knew you and Skip would be there at the temple that day. You and Skip have very important callings to perform. . . ." Adrian stopped to let the spirit that was so prevalent in the room speak to Jake.

Jake could not help the tears from coming. He now knew without a doubt that Jesus Christ existed. Not only did he exist, but he also knew that the Atonement of his Savior was not only for all the inhabitants of the earth, but for all the inhabitants of every world that had been or will be created, including the world he was on now, *Terrest*.

But Jake still could not understand why he, someone so weak in the gospel and someone so insignificant, would be called of God.

Adrian continued. "Jake, the Lord has revealed to me that you and Skip play a direct role in freeing the Terrestrian people from the bondage of the Gnols."

Jake nodded his head. He knew, by the spirit, that what his father told him was true. But his feelings of guilt and inadequacy left some doubt. Jake wiped the tears away from his face. "Okay, Dad, I understand now, but what I still can't understand is why the Gnols are here and why they seem to be so much more powerful than us?"

"I don't know, Son. The Lord has not revealed that to me. But as I study the first chapter of Moses more and more, I am beginning to understand. I will explain further when I understand fully. But to answer your question, I get the feeling that I was somehow responsible for the Gnol's attack on *Terrest*."

★ ★ ★ ★ ★

Skip was dying of curiosity, mostly about the temple ruins that he and Jake had discovered. However, the last two days, the only people Skip had any contact with were Sean and Doc. They helped Skip control his new cybernetic leg, and now, just after a few days since his operation, he was able to control his new leg without even thinking about it. He was able to run, jump, and walk almost better than he had before. Skip was so grateful to Doc and Sean, but he was also frustrated with them as well. Every time Skip would ask questions about the temple ruins, Doc and Sean would just shrug their shoulders and tell him that they didn't know anything. Skip also got the distinct impression that they were hiding something.

Skip wrapped his fingers on the conference table that actually looked like a large wooden picnic table that sat about ten people. He was growing impatient now. *Where are they?* He thought.

Skip stood up and paced around the conference room. The room was quite large. Not only did the room house the large conference table, it also had two computer terminals at the front of the room with a large viewing screen in the center. A gigantic map of *Terrest* hung on the wall directly in front of Skip. He studied the map in more detail. The map was speckled with purple, red, yellow, orange, and bright green dots. The purple dots represented *Terrest's* major cities. Skip was bored so he counted all of them. He stopped at twenty-three. The only city's name he recognized was the one marked with a purple star, *Talead*. Skip studied the map a little more. He deciphered that the red dots represented the Gnol cities and bases. He commenced to count them. There were sixteen in all.

From the scale of the map, Skip estimated that the red star representing the capital city of the Gnols, *Chast*, was about three hundred miles away from *Talead*. Skip then studied the yellow dots. There were only two of them, and they obviously represented the base he was now in and the second base Adrian spoke of before. Skip looked at the scale and discovered that the base he was now in was only about ten miles away from *Talead* and the temple he was so curious about.

Good. He thought. *The temple isn't that far from here. I wonder if Adrian will let me study the writings in more detail.*

Skip estimated the second yellow dot to be about four hundred miles away from *Talead*. Skip then studied the orange dots. Some of the dots had slashes through them. He counted them. There were fifty-one orange dots, and twenty of them had slashes through them. He looked at the key. The orange dots represented slave camps. The ones with slashes were slave camps that had been liberated and destroyed. In addition, he discovered that the four bright green dots represented farm and manufacturing bases for the rebellion's cause.

Skip looked toward the back of the room. There was a sink, what looked like a refrigerator, and some refreshments. Skip scanned the rest of the room, and for the first time, noticed that the entire room was made of a silver metal. There wasn't a window in sight. In fact, Skip just realized he hadn't seen a window since he had arrived at the base.

The door to the room slid open, and Adrian walked in. He was dressed in the same green fatigues and beret that Skip saw him in two days ago. Jake followed his father. Jake looked just like his father, dressed in the same green fatigues and a similar beret. Skip wondered to himself why he hadn't received a new change of clothing. He was still dressed in a hospital gown and a robe.

That question was quickly answered as Jake tossed Skip a plastic bag containing green fatigues and a beret.

"There you go, Skip," Jake said. "We thought you had better have something on that didn't show your rear-end."

Skip gave Jake a sarcastic grin. "Thanks!"

Skip hurried and changed, and then sat down. Just after he sat down, six other people entered the room. Everyone was dressed the same.

Once everyone entered the room, Doc stayed at the front discussing something with Adrian. Jake sat on Skip's right; on Skip's left was Kylee; and on Kylee's left was Scott Hauler, who had recently returned from the second base. Across the table from Skip was Sean Gibson. Sean sat between two men Skip had never met before.

"All right," said Adrian, as Doc sat down next to one of the men Skip didn't recognize. "Today, I've called this meeting mostly for Jake and Skip. They have some questions that need answered, and I am going to give them positions in the military."

Skip looked questioningly at Jake.

Adrian continued. "We are also expecting our visitor to arrive shortly. Before we begin, does anyone have any questions?"

Skip raised his hand.

"Yes, Skip, go ahead."

"This is a trivial question, but my enquiring mind needs to know."

"And what does your enquiring mind need to know, Skip?"

"Well, I couldn't help but notice that this place doesn't have any windows. Why is that?"

"I'm glad you asked that Skip. Actually that's part of our agenda. We need to discuss how the second base is coming along. But, to answer your question, the reason why this place doesn't have any windows is because it's completely underground. About four years before the Gnols attacked, *King Xuta* wanted a secret military base."

"Why did he want a military base if the entire planet was at peace?" Jake asked.

"Actually, *King Xuta* was worried about a few rebel groups in the south. As a result, he put Scott here," Adrian said, pointing to Scott, "in charge of constructing this secret military base. Like I said before, this base is entirely underground, about two hundred yards underground, to be precise. The entire base is made of *Omutx*, the same metal your leg is made out of, Skip. The base is eighteen thousand square feet; the equivalent of six large five bedroom homes back on Earth.

"The base consists of six wings: a medical wing, an administrative and command wing; the aircraft, vehicle, and weapons wing; the training wing, a supply and storage wing; and the living quarters' wing.

"We were lucky. When the Gnols attacked, the base had just been completed. Most of the military leaders were able to escape to the base, but . . ." Adrian paused and a hint of emotion crept into his voice, ". . . Unfortunately, *King Xuta* was captured and tortured to death for not revealing where his military leaders had escaped."

Skip noticed an eerie silence creep into the room with the mention of *King Xuta's* death. It was obvious that Adrian, Doc, Sean, and Scott had all been very close to the king.

Skip looked at Kylee. Instead of grief on her face, Kylee looked angry, and her eyes looked full of revenge as she stared at the map of *Terrest*.

"I'm sorry. The mention of *King Xuta's* torture and death brings a lot of emotions to the surface." Adrian stopped and looked at Scott. "Scott, give us a report on the progress of our second base."

Scott stood and walked to the front of the room, as Adrian moved to the side out of the way. The lights in the room dimmed, and the view screen just above Scott's head sprang to life. A three-dimensional model of a building's blueprint appeared on the screen.

"If you look at that model of our second base," Scott said as he pointed to the view screen with a laser pointer, "it contains all of the same wings this base does. The only difference is that the new base is thirty thousand square feet."

"Are all the wings ready for transfers?" Adrian asked.

"All of the wings are ready, except for the living area. My construction crew predicts that they will have it finished in about two months."

"Good," Adrian said.

Adrian looked at the man sitting directly across from Skip. Skip didn't recognize the man but felt almost intimidated in his presence. The man seemed to be about 6' 3" tall with broad shoulders and extremely toned arms.

He had midnight, black hair that shimmered from the dim lights of the room, and penetrating brown eyes. Skip quickly turned his gaze from the stranger as the man noticed his stare.

"Colonel Jantear," Adrian said. "Get a team together to organize the move of the civilian population in two months."

"Yes, Sir," the colonel said with a small accent.

Skip turned his attention back to Adrian and spoke before Adrian could continue. "How many people occupy this base, both civilian and military?"

"As we free more slaves, our civilian and military population multiplies dramatically. As we speak, we have approximately seven hundred thirty-four civilians in the base. That includes women, children, and men. The military population at this base is approximately one thousand six hundred two, including us. If you add you and Jake, there are approximately two thousand, three hundred thirty-eight people in this eighteen thousand square foot facility. So, you can see we are busting at the seams here. That's why the completion of the second base is so crucial.

"Not only do we have civilians and military personnel here, we have also established four above ground bases that are well hidden and accommodate about two thousand civilians each. Each above ground base is controlled by military personnel of one hundred soldiers."

Jake raised his hand.

"Yes Jake."

"What's your total military personnel population?"

"We have about one thousand military personnel at the second base, so to date – we have approximately three thousand two people."

Jake shook his head. "That's not much of an army."

"No, it's not. And when you compare that number to half a million soldiers in the Gnol military, you can see we're at a great disadvantage."

"Wow," said Skip.

Adrian walked back to the front of the room as Scott sat back down. "When the Gnols attacked, the population on this planet was five hundred million strong. After the attack, the population was decimated. The Gnols were relentless. Not only did they destroy the major cities, they killed men, women, and children. They enslaved the healthy men, women, and children to do their dirty work. We estimated that the population after the attacks was left to about sixty thousand people planet-wide."

"Incredible," said Jake. "Why were these aliens so ruthless? They look just like us."

"Like I told you before, the Gnols were looking for a new planet. So, what better way to get a new one than kill off the indigenous population of the new planet and enslave the rest? You see, Jake and Skip, the Gnols leader's name is Koroan Chast. Koroan Chast has such a hatred for us, mostly because he feels superior to us and thinks that humans are animals. But, little does he know, he is human too."

Now Skip was utterly confused. "You mean their leader is human and doesn't even know it?"

Adrian gave Skip a knowing smile and said, "Doc, it's your turn."

Doc stood and walked to the front of the room. He switched the image on the view screen from the three-dimensional model of the second base to a split screen. On the left side of the screen was the image of a brain with the majority of the brain glowing in yellow. On the right side of the screen was another image of a brain with less than a third of the brain glowing in yellow.

"These are two brain scans," Doc said. "On the left . . . is the brain scan of our Gnol spy who graciously volunteered for this research. On the right side . . . is Adrian's brain scan. And, as you can see from the evidence, Adrian's not that bright."

Everyone in the room laughed except for Kylee.

"All joking aside," Doc continued. "This brain scan of our Gnol spy shows us that the Gnols use approximately eighty percent of their brain capacity, and we only use about ten percent of our brain." Doc paused and looked at Skip and Jake. "Let me ask you. Did both of you experience any head pain or ringing in your ears when you encountered the Gnols?"

Jake and Skip looked at one another. "As a matter of fact, we did," said Jake.

Doc smiled. "That's because the Gnols have the capability to read our minds."

"What! That's crazy," said Skip.

Doc held out his hand. "Hold on, Skip. Let me finish and you will see that it is possible."

Doc turned and pointed to the brain image on the right. "Our brains have seven primary parts, the frontal lobe, the somatosensory cortex, the central fissure, the motor cortex, the parietal lobe, and the occipital lobe. From the research that I have done on our spy friend and a few dead volunteers, I have discovered that the Gnols have the same brain as us. It's just that they use more of it.

"We humans use almost every part of our brain. It's just that we don't use the full potential of each part. For example, when I was doing research on Adrian, I had him recall childhood memories while I scanned his brain." Doc pushed a button on the computer terminal and an image of Adrian's brain appeared alone. He pointed to the frontal lobe.

"As you can see from the scan, while Adrian was recalling childhood memories, only portions of his frontal lobe were active." Doc then pushed another button and the image of the Gnol's brain appeared. "Now, I conducted the same test on our spy. Well, you can see for yourself the difference."

Skip was astonished. He couldn't believe what he was looking at. The entire frontal lobe of the Gnol's brain was active.

Doc continued. "It was amazing. Our spy could recall almost every detail of her life. I continued to conduct similar experiments, and in every test, Adrian's brain wasn't as active as our spy's."

Jake held up his hand before Doc could continue. "Wait a minute, Doc. Let me get this straight. My dad said that Korean Chast hated us because we were humans, but then he said Chast didn't know he was a human. From what you're telling us, it doesn't look like the Gnols are human at all?"

Doc chuckled with his deep laugh. "Ah, but they are. I examined every dead Gnol that came into this place from their toenails to the last hair on their heads. They have the same organs as us, the same blood types, and the same DNA. However, their DNA contains one gene our DNA does not.

Adrian interrupted Doc before he could continue. "Doc likes to call it the *god-gene*."

"What?" questioned Skip.

Doc continued. "The *god-gene* . . . It's the gene that enables them to use eighty percent of their brain capacity; gives them the ability to live longer; allows them to possess more strength; and enables their telepathic and telekinetic powers."

"In other words, Doc," Skip said. "These Gnols are in effect super-humans."

"I wouldn't say super-humans, Skip. I like to think of them as the more evolved of our species. They are, in fact . . . what we can become."

"Except spiritually," echoed Kylee who still looked angry.

Jake raised his hand again.

Doc pointed to him. "What's your question, Jake?"

"Before Kylee and her unit rescued me, I felt as if I couldn't control myself. I wanted to escape from the three Gnols that were approaching me. But for some reason, I had an uncontrollable urge to yield to their commands they were giving me in my head."

"That's exactly what you felt, Jake. Our spy had told us that some, not all of the Gnols, have the power to, not only read minds, but the power of persuasion as well," said Doc.

"A small percentage even have the ability to move things with their minds," said Adrian.

Skip shook his head. "I don't think I can be surprised anymore. I feel like I've stepped through the looking glass and walked right into a science fiction action movie."

Everyone in the room smiled except for Kylee who still looked like her mind was miles away.

★ ★ ★ ★ ★

A few moments later, Doc walked to the bag he had brought into the room with him, unzipped it, and pulled something out. Jake couldn't tell what he had pulled out because his hand was closed. Doc walked behind Jake and Skip and placed four small, circular computer chips encased in silver metal on the table in front of them. The computer chips were the same size as the tip of the small finger on a human. Two long needles, about an inch long, protruded from the back of the chips.

"What are these? Skip asked as he picked one up and examined it.

"These are *Mind Inhibitors*," Doc said.

"Mind what?" asked Jake, picking one up as well.

"*Mind Inhibitors*," repeated Doc. "These small devices were actually developed by the Gnols. They were developed to keep Gnols from reading one another's minds. The inhibitors are activated when they are inserted into your head."

Jake winced as he looked at the long needles. "Whoa, wait a minute. You're not sticking these things into my head."

Doc put a hand on Jake's right shoulder. "It's okay, Jake." Doc knelt down turned his head and pulled both of his ears to the front. Jake leaned toward the back of Doc's head in order to get a closer look. There behind each one of Doc's ears rested a Mind Inhibitor.

Jake shuttered at the thought of someone sticking the inhibitors into his head. "I hope your putting us to sleep to put those in, Doc?"

Doc stood up and walked to the front of the room. He laughed and said, "Nope."

Jake and Skip just looked at one another with fear on their faces.

"Okay," Adrian said. "Quit fooling around with them, tell them it's painless, and what the inhibitors do."

Doc laughed. "Yes, Sir. Don't worry you guys. When our guest arrives we're going to conduct a little science experiment. The procedure is painless. I'm simply going to numb the area behind your ears with a small shot of Novocain. You'll only feel a small pinch when I give you the shot, and after the Novocain wears off, you will feel a dull ache for a few days along with swelling."

Jake was a little relieved to know that the pain would be minimal.

Doc continued. "When the inhibitors are activated they will create an electrical charge, which creates electrical interference in your brain. But, don't worry. The interference doesn't affect your brain. It just creates interference for when a Gnol is trying to read your mind. It all—"

The door to the room slid open. Everyone in the room looked at the guest who had been expected. Jake sat up straight and was stunned. Suddenly, he felt self-conscious about the stitches he still had in his forehead.

She was the most beautiful woman he had ever seen. She was dressed in a blue ceremonial gown that extended all the way down to her feet, which were covered with black high-heeled boots. Over the gown was a long, shiny black robe. The robe's collar extended to her neck. Hanging from her neck, rested a gold necklace with a blue diamond dangling just a few inches above her chest.

The woman made eye contact with Jake. Jake was suddenly embarrassed as he was caught staring at her, and realized that this could be the science experiment Doc was talking about. But, he didn't think she had read his mind yet because he hadn't felt any head pain at all. In fact, he almost felt like he was in heaven as he looked at her piercing, blue eyes that reminded him of the blue water in a tropical lagoon. He then looked at her hair. Her hair was as black as midnight. It was cut short, extending to about an inch below the collar of her robe. Her hair was tucked behind her ears, revealing the same kind of blue diamond earrings.

Kylee immediately broke into tears, stood up, and embraced the woman. Jake looked at his father with a confused look. Adrian walked behind Jake and whispered in his ear. "Yesterday, Kylee's fiancé was tortured and killed by the

Gnols. He had been working with the woman she's hugging. They killed him because he wouldn't reveal where our base is."

Jake suddenly felt compassion for the sister he never had.

Kylee sat back down. Adrian approached the woman and embraced her as well. "It's so good to see that you weren't discovered, Celeste."

Celeste spoke for the first time. Jake nearly fell out of his seat upon hearing her voice. Her English was perfect, and the sound of her voice was soothing. "Believe me, Adrian and Kylee, I wanted so much to reveal myself to save Malk's life. But, I knew if I did, we would both be killed, and the cause would be lost." Celeste walked next to Kylee, placed both hands on her shoulders, and looked into her eyes. "Kylee, Malk knew that if he revealed where the base was, you would either be captured or killed. He died protecting you."

Kylee broke down into sobs and hugged Celeste again. After a few moments, the two women untangled their arms from one another, and Celeste joined Adrian at the front of the room.

"Celeste," Adrian said. "I would like you to meet my son, Jake, and his friend, Skip."

Celeste smiled at both men as she nodded her acknowledgement. "Yes, I know their names."

"What else can you tell us about them?" Adrian asked as he gave Jake and Skip a deceitful smile.

"Well, let me recall. Skip hardly noticed that I entered the room because his thoughts are on the temple ruins just outside of *Talead*."

Skip looked at Doc. "Well, I'm convinced."

"But, your son, on the other hand, definitely noticed when I entered the room. I will not reveal the thoughts that went through his head because they are too private," said Celeste, giving Jake a knowing smile. "Let me just reassure you, Jake. Those stitches on your forehead do not do anything to diminish your handsomeness."

Everyone in the room shot curious looks at Jake. Some were even giggling. Jake felt his face flush red. He wanted to leave the room. For the first time in his life, someone else intimidated him. He wanted to speak but couldn't. For some reason, he felt tongue tied around this woman and nervous.

Celeste spoke again. "I am sorry, Jake. I did not mean to embarrass you. I am just helping your father with a little science experiment."

Doc stood up, grabbed his bag, and joined Celeste and Adrian at the front of the room. "Okay, Jake and Skip, if you will both come forward," he said, as Sean placed two chairs in front of Doc.

Jake and Skip walked to the front and sat in the chairs. Doc reached into his bag and pulled out two syringes. He numbed the areas behind both ears of Jake and Skip. After a few moments, he placed the inhibitors into the head of each man. "Okay, let's try our second test. Jake and Skip, think of anything you like, and Celeste, see if you can read their minds."

Celeste paced back and forth a few minutes in front of the two men. Both men just followed her with their eyes. Jake tried to control his thoughts, but he couldn't help himself. The woman in front of him was too beautiful.

Celeste stopped in front of Skip. Knelt down and looked directly into his eyes. Skip leaned back as Celeste approached.

"Hmm . . . I cannot read anything from Skip, or it could be that he does not have any brain waves at all."

Skip gave Celeste an annoyed look and said, "Oh funny, a spy with a sense of humor."

Celeste gently placed both of her hands on Skip's cheeks, leaned in and softly kissed him on the left cheek.

"It is good to meet you, Skip," said Celeste, as she pulled away.

Jake felt a sudden emotion of jealousy surge through him as he watched Celeste kiss Skip's cheek. *Why was he having these emotions? What did he need to be jealous about?*

Celeste walked to Jake and knelt down. Jake unexpectedly felt butterflies in his stomach. Celeste placed both of her hands on his cheeks and looked into his eyes. Jake tried to look away, but Celeste gently held his face in place. Jake was impressed with her strength.

"Let me see," Celeste said. "Jake is thinking that I am the most beautiful woman he has ever seen, and would like to have dinner with me three days from now in the mess hall." Celeste leaned in and kissed Jake on the cheek as well.

Jake was stunned. He just sat in the chair with a silly grin on his face.

Celeste winked at Jake and smiled. Then she turned to Adrian and said, "Adrian, the *Mind Inhibitors* are working properly. I cannot read their minds."

"Good," Adrian said. "Now that both of you have met our spy and have been brought up to date about the situation, I am going to give both of you positions in the military and your assignments. We need all of the help we can get. But just to let you know, we do this a little differently on *Terrest*. We treat a calling in the military just like a calling in the church, so Doc, Sean, and I will be using the Priesthood to confer all the rights and responsibilities of your new positions."

Skip held his hand up before Adrian continued. "But Adrian, I haven't been baptized yet."

"I'll let you know what your responsibilities are. Then after we lay our hands upon Jake and confer his responsibilities to him, you can be baptized in the font we have specially dedicated for baptisms here at the base."

Skip smiled and looked at Jake. "I would like Jake to baptize me, Adrian. If you don't mind?"

Adrian seemed to beam with pride. "I don't think that will be a problem." Adrian then turned to look at his son. "Would you like to baptize Skip, Jake?"

Jake looked at Skip with a look of fear on his face and then looked at his father with the same look. "I . . . Uh . . . I don't think I am worthy, Dad."

Adrian moved closer to Jake and placed both of his hands on his son's shoulders. "Son, I know what is in your heart, so does the Lord. Trust me, son, you are worthy."

Jake did not know what to think. He knew the experience he had earlier in the day with his father was the spirit testifying to him that the gospel was true. Yet, he could not help but feel powerless and not worthy to hold the Priesthood. Even though he held the Melchizedek Priesthood, he had never exercised it.

As Jake kept his head bowed, he felt the same feelings come to him again that he experienced earlier with his father. He knew that it was the spirit testifying to him that he needed to baptize his best friend.

Jake slowly raised his head and with a tear in his eye said, "It will be my honor."

Adrian smiled warmly at his son and gave him a tight squeeze. After he let go, Skip came over and hugged Jake as well.

As Skip continued to embrace Jake, he whispered in Jake's ear. "Thank you, Jake. You don't know how much this means to me." Then Skip released his embrace.

Jake didn't respond. He simply smiled and nodded his head.

Adrian then spoke. "Okay, I think we should give these two young men their callings." Adrian turned to face Skip. "Skip, you are hereby commissioned to the office of Colonel in the *Terrest* Army."

Skip turned and looked at Jake and gave him a smile of approval.

Adrian continued. "You will also be in charge of three soldiers, a young civilian female, and a professor of archeology and history."

Skip gave Adrian a confused look. "A female civilian and a professor?"

Adrian smiled. "You are going to need the professor and his daughter because they are the leading experts of ancient religion on this planet."

Skip's grin grew bigger. "You mean, Sir . . . I am going to be able to research the temple ruins outside of *Talead*?"

"That's correct, Colonel. That temple has so many similarities to the Mormon temples on Earth. We had always had the intention of researching the ruins and restoring the temple for use, but the Gnols attacked before we could start. And personally, Skip, I believe that temple has some answers about how we can defeat the Gnols."

Skip nodded his head. "Sir, I gladly accept the position and will find the answers you need." He and Adrian shook hands.

"I know you will, Skip," said Adrian. He then walked and stood in front his son. Jake stood. Adrian placed both of his hands on Jake's shoulders. "Son, we haven't had a lot of time to talk since you have arrived, but I am so very glad you are here. Your talent and leadership as a pilot will add a great deal to the liberation of thousands of Terrestrians. Until you arrived, I was the only trained pilot on the planet, and because of my role as the military commander, I have not had the resources or the time to train new pilots.

"Within the last year, our army has stolen nearly one hundred space fighters from the Gnols; the kind of space ships you encountered when you first came through the wormhole. Until now, we haven't had anyone to fly them, except for me and Bantyr." Adrian paused. "Jake, you are hereby commissioned to the office of General in the *Terrest* Air and Space Force. I am creating a new division of the army, and you are in charge of it. It will be your responsibility to recruit and train new pilots."

Jake smiled at his father and said, "I gladly accept the responsibility, Sir."

Adrian returned the smile and the two hugged.

After father and son embraced, Adrian turned around to face everyone else in the room. "Okay, tomorrow we will have Skip's baptism and that is when both Skip and Jake will receive the laying on of hands."

Celeste spoke, interrupting Adrian before he could finish. "If you will excuse me, Adrian. I have to be going."

Adrian turned and embraced Celeste. "Thank you, Celeste. Will I see you at Sacrament meeting on Sunday?"

Jake looked at Skip with a confused look after hearing his father ask the Gnol spy this question. Skip returned the look and shrugged his shoulders. Jake wondered if the beautiful woman, who happened to be one of the most powerful human beings he had ever met, happened to be a member of the church as well.

"You will," said Celeste, as she turned and made her way to the door.

Before she reached the door, Jake finally had the courage to speak to her. "Wait!"

Celeste turned. "Wow, Jake speaks."

Jake was nervous again. "Umm . . . I was just curious. When you entered the room and read our minds, why didn't I experience any pain?"

"That is a great question, Jake. You and Skip did not experience any pain because I have been trained by the most powerful Gnol of all. In fact, only a handful of Gnols are experienced enough to control their mental powers."

Jake was more and more captivated by this woman. She intrigued him, and he had so many questions for her. "What do you mean the most powerful Gnol of all? Who is that?"

Celeste walked toward Jake. Jake took a step backwards and nearly fell back over his chair. She placed her left hand on his cheek. "The Gnol that I speak of is my father. Now, I cannot answer any more of your questions. I really must be going. We can speak again when we have dinner together three days from now. I must go and join my father. He will become suspicious if I am late for his address to the city."

Jake looked into Celeste's eyes. He had a sudden and overwhelming urge to grab her right there and kiss her, but he controlled himself. Celeste smiled at him as if she could read his mind, turned, and left the room.

★ ★ ★ ★ ★

Two hours later, Professor Jaskead Tomwon sat with Skip in the underground base's mess hall. The Professor sipped his steaming cup of tea. He swallowed and leaned his head back, obviously enjoying the sensation as the hot tea crept down his throat. Clearing his throat, he looked across the table at the young man who would lead the research expedition at the temple near *Talead*. He spoke in an accent. It reminded Skip of a German accent back on Earth. "So Colonel . . . that is what the general told me to call you."

"Please, Professor, call me Skip. And, don't think of me as your superior. We are equals since you have more knowledge about the ancient tribes of this planet," said Skip, looking at the old man more closely.

The professor looked to be in his early sixties. His hair was gray and shoulder length. For his age, the professor still had a full head of hair. The hair looked to be a mangled mess, as was his beard.

The professor was still dressed in his slave uniform, the standard slave uniform of the Gnols. Professor Tomwon was not a big man. In fact, when he and Skip first met, Skip was astonished at how short the man was. Compared to Skip's 5'11" frame, the Professor seemed to be just barely over five feet tall.

"Yes, I will call you Skip," said the Professor. "And, please, call me Jaskead; if you are not going to be so formal, then neither shall I. Now, let us talk business. My daughter shall join us shortly. She is showering and refreshing herself. As you can imagine, being in a slave camp for almost five years does not do well for a person's hygiene."

Skip smiled at the old man. When he met Jaskead, he instantly liked him. He had brown eyes that were warm and inviting. "I can imagine," he said. "But before we discuss the pyramid near *Talead*, why don't we get to know one another a little more."

"Yes, my young friend. That sounds like a great idea. If we are going to work together, then we must get to know each other a little better. Why don't you tell me about yourself first? I am very curious about the planet from which you come."

Jake commenced to tell Jaskead about himself. He told him about his childhood in Springfield, Illinois. He also told him about his various career adventures while he attended the University of Notre Dame. Jaskead was so interested in learning about Skip, his experiences, and Earth that he continued to ask questions. Skip was so involved in answering almost all of Jaskead's questions that nearly a half hour went by.

Jaskead was about to ask another question when a young woman with long, auburn hair walked up to the table in which Jaskead and Skip were sitting. Jaskead stood and embraced the woman. The woman had to bend down to hug the professor. Skip figured the woman to be around 5'6" tall.

Skip stood when he realized he wasn't minding his manners. His mother had always taught him to stand when a woman entered the room.

"Oh, I am sorry, Skip," Jaskead said. "This is my daughter . . . Ariauna. Ariauna, this is Colonel Steven Hendricks, but he prefers to be called Skip."

Ariauna extended her hand, as did Skip. The two shook hands.

Ariauna spoke first. Her accent was barely noticeable. "I am pleased to meet you, Skip."

"I am pleased to meet you too," Skip said. "And . . . I look forward to working together."

The two let go of each other's hands, and Skip sat down. Ariauna walked around the table and joined her father on his side. Skip watched her as she walked around the table. She was an attractive woman. He noticed that she had bright, green eyes to go along with her auburn hair. Her face was thin, and her body looked frail – the result of being in a slave camp for five years. She was not dressed in her slave uniform. She was now dressed in the standard military uniform of the *Terrest* army, the green camouflage fatigues but without the beret. It was obvious that any civilian liberated from a slave camp was issued a military uniform because of the lack of civilian clothing. In fact, as Skip looked around the mess hall, the only way he could distinguish the difference between former slaves and military personal was the way they were dressed. Some former slaves had not yet received their uniforms.

Ariauna sat down and smiled warmly at Skip. "So, what were you two handsome men talking about before I arrived. I hope I didn't miss much."

Skip felt his face flush red. Rarely was he embarrassed around women.

"Skip was just telling me about Earth and his experiences," Jaskead said. "Please, Skip, tell me more."

Skip held up his hand. "No, that's enough about me. Why don't you two tell me about yourselves and more about your knowledge Prof . . . uh . . . I mean, Jaskead."

"Well Skip, Ariauna and I are not from this region of the planet. We are from a city called *Baleal* in the *Yuelzaiylams* region of the planet. The region is in the Northeastern hemisphere of *Terrest*, across the *Unifoy* Ocean. *Baleal* was the capital of the Province of *Sinoy*, one of twenty-two provinces that *Juzs Lza Bmail* established when he unified *Terrest* five hundred years ago."

Ariauna cut in before her father could continue. "Yes, *Baleal* was a beautiful and warm city, not like *Talead*. It's too cold here for me."

Jaskead looked at his daughter. "The general tells me that there are beautiful summers on this region of the planet."

Ariauna looked disappointed. "Well, I like *Baleal* better. It is warm year round."

Jaskead laughed. "I am sure Skip would like to hear about the climatic difference of the planet, but I am sure he is more interested in the temple ruins."

Skip smiled shyly at Ariauna. She smiled back.

The Professor continued. "When General Palmer and his comrades arrived on our planet, almost twenty-five years ago, the news spread around the globe dramatically. As a matter of fact, Ariauna was one the first to enroll in the first English speaking school that was established in our city when she was just thirteen-years-old."

"That would explain her flawless English," said Skip.

"Yes, yes," Jaskead said. "The majority of our civilization has learned English quite well. It's really an easy language to learn."

"That's funny. Back on Earth, people that learn English say that the language is one of the most difficult to learn," said Skip.

The Professor shook his head. "Hmm. When the general and his friends began teaching English to us, it was so easy to learn. The reason for that is that the *Tilicah* language, which *Juzs Lza Bmail* established as the primary language of the Terrestrian civilization, contains the same alphabet, syntax, and sentence structure as English. The only difference is how the alphabet is used."

Skip was intrigued. What were the odds that a tribal language millions and millions of miles away from Earth would have something in common with English? "What do you mean, how the alphabet is used?" he asked.

"Rather than me explain, why don't I write it down for you, so you can see for yourself? Do you have any paper or a pen?"

Skip shook his head. He hadn't seen paper or an ink pen for years, not since his society on Earth went paperless.

"I will get some paper and a pen," said Ariauna, as she stood and walked to the counter at the front of the mess hall. She asked the attendant at the counter for some paper and a pen. A few seconds later she returned to the table with supplies in hand.

Skip looked at the paper and pen. The paper wasn't the normal size of paper that he was used to. The paper looked thicker, a little larger, and not evenly cut. The paper reminded Skip of the kind of paper Earth's civilization used back in the seventeenth and eighteenth centuries, before paper factories began producing paper. The pen was felt tipped and feathered.

"Thank you," said Jaskead. "Oh, I am sorry Ariauna. You forgot the ink."

Skip watched as Ariauna went back to the counter and retrieved the ink that went with the pen. She came back and gave her father the ink.

The Professor said, "Thank you, Ariauna. You will have to forgive me Skip. We have not yet learned how to use those handheld . . . uh . . ." Jaskead turned and looked at his daughter., ". . . What do you call those thinking machines again?"

"Computers," said Ariauna.

"Ah yes, computers. We have not yet learned how to use computers."

Skip held up his hand. "It's okay. It's been awhile since I've seen pen and paper used, but there's no need to apologize."

The Professor didn't respond. He commenced to write on the paper. Skip could see that Jaskead was writing the English alphabet down, and then he went on and wrote the same alphabet, but only out of order.

Skip was a little confused at what Jaskead had written down, but when Jaskead handed him the paper, Skip's eyes widened. *Amazing*, he thought. *How is this possible that an alien civilization would have the same alphabet?* Skip examined the English alphabet and compared it to the *Tilicah* alphabet. There were twenty-six letters in the *Tilicah* alphabet, the same number as English. All of the letters were the same. The only difference was the order:

A = I	N = S
B = N	O = U
C = X	P = V
D = D	Q = B
E = A	R = M
F = G	S = Y
G = J	T = L
H = Z	U = E
I = O	V = W
J = F	W = R
K = C	X = K
L = T	Y = H
M = P	Z = Q

Skip finished examining the sheet of paper. He looked up at Ariauna and Jaskead with a smile on his face. "This is incredible," he said. "What are the odds that an alien civilization would have the same alphabet as a language found on Earth?"

"That's what we thought too," said Ariauna

"Yes," said the Professor. "Not only is the language and alphabet similar, but our months and seasons are as well."

"I know. General Palmer mentioned that this planet rotates around the sun in three hundred sixty-five days, the same as Earth," Skip said.

"Yes, but did the general also tell you that *Terrest* has the same rotation as your planet. In fact, we Terrestrians follow a twenty-four hour day just as your civilization does on Earth," said the Professor.

Skip's scientific mind was now becoming more and more intrigued. *Was it merely coincidence that Terrest had almost the same characteristics as Earth, or was there a higher power at work here?* The thought made Skip more and more curious about the temple ruins and the God that the ancient *Tilicahs* worshipped.

Jaskead continued. "I am also sure you will find this interesting, my young friend."

Skip gave the professor a curious look. "What?"

"Our planet has the same months as yours. For example, January is pronounced *Fiseimh* in *Tilicah*."

"This is very exciting Jaskead," Skip said. "For thousands of years, the majority of Earth's civilization believed that they were the only intelligent civilization in the universe. And now, here I sit, speaking my native language to another human being who grew up on another planet in another solar system."

Jaskead took another sip of his tea, which was cold by now, and swallowed. He smiled and said, "Yes, it is very intriguing. There is so much I would like to learn about Earth. But first, let us discuss the temple for which the general has put us in charge of."

"Yes, let's do," Skip said. "But before we get into details, I wanted to ask you why the general is so interested in the temple when he has so much more to worry about? I hope he just didn't give me this assignment because I am so interested in the temple."

Jaskead chuckled and shook his head. "No, no, my young friend. On the contrary, the general is very interested in the temple. He believes that it may have some answers about not only the Terrestrian civilization but the Gnol civilization as well."

Skip was confused now. *What did the Gnols have to do with the temple?* "I don't understand, Jaskead. What do you mean answers about the Gnol civilization? I thought your people didn't have any contact with the Gnols until they attacked?"

Jaskead was about to speak, but was interrupted by his daughter. "That's true. But when General Palmer learned more about the Gnols from Celeste . . ." Ariauna paused and spoke again, ". . . You have met Celeste haven't you?"

Skip smiled at Ariauna. He liked her. Not only was she beautiful, but she was exceptionally intelligent as well; a trait Skip held in high regard. "Yes, we met. In fact, I think the general's son is quite taken with her."

Ariauna smiled back at Skip but then frowned a little.

"What? Did I say something wrong?" Skip asked.

Ariauna shook her head. "No. It's just that the general's son should be careful."

"Why? Don't you trust her?"

"As a matter of fact, I don't."

"Well, why not? Why would she volunteer sensitive information about the Gnols, if she really hasn't changed sides?"

Ariauna shook her head. Skip could tell that she genuinely didn't want to talk about it.

"Please, Skip, forgive my daughter," Jaskead said. "She is very sensitive when it comes to the Gnols, Especially when she sees Celeste among us."

Skip saw a tear trickle down from Ariauna's eye. She stood up. Instinctively, Skip started to stand up as well, but Jaskead reached across the table and grabbed his arm. "Let her be. She needs time to herself."

Skip felt guilty. What did he do? Did he offend her in some way? He wanted to go after her, as he watched her walk out of the mess hall.

Jaskead, seeing the concern on Skip's face, spoke again. "It is not you, my young friend. Ariauna has a lot of pain on the inside."

Skip turned his attention from Ariauna and looked at Jaskead. "I can understand. Five years in a slave camp would do that to a person."

"That is only part of the pain she feels." Jaskead took a deep breath and leaned on the table with his fingers intertwined in front of him. "You see, Skip, when the Gnols attacked, Ariauna – who was twenty-one at the time – her mother, and I were on an archeological dig about two hundred miles outside of our home city of *Baleal*. We were uncovering the ruins of an ancient tribe called the *Bahirsh*. After our dig, we returned to *Baleal* to find it destroyed."

Jaskead bowed his head. Skip could tell he was becoming emotional by the sound of his voice.

"It was a horrible sight. There were thousands of bodies everywhere, men, women, children, and babies. We had no idea what happened."

"What did you do? Where did you go?" asked Skip.

"We knew that *Talead* had a powerful army because of the general. We assumed that maybe *Talead* was spared. So, we found a group of refugees, and we managed to make our way across the *Unifoy* Ocean into the Western hemisphere of the planet. We were lucky when we arrived. Not far from the beach, in which we landed, there was small base of about twenty-five Terrestrian soldiers who had escaped the attacks."

"The leader of the group made contact with General Palmer. The general, however, advised that we stay put because it was too dangerous to travel. He said that the attackers had eyes everywhere.

"Well, we did as General Palmer ordered. We stayed put. We were stuck in that jungle base for ten years. Every time the leader of the group contacted the general, he received the same orders, to stay put until a rescue party could be organized."

"Wow, you must have felt like you were forgotten about?"

"Yes, it certainly felt like that. However, I communicated with the general myself. He said that he had heard of me from my teaching expertise at the University of *Baleal*. After I spoke with him, he assured me that he was doing everything in his power to organize a rescue party, and he wanted me to research the temple ruins outside of *Talead*."

"Unfortunately, the Gnols discovered the base and attacked. . . ." Jaskead's voice suddenly became shaky. He rubbed both eyes with his left index finger and thumb.

Skip could see that the old man had grown emotional. "Jaskead, you don't have to continue if you don't want to."

Jaskead held up his right hand and shook his head. "No, no, it is all right. Thinking about the attack just brings back horrible memories. You see . . . my wife, Arial, was killed in the attack – right in front of Ariauna. She still has nightmares about the ordeal."

Skip's heart went out to Ariauna. "Oh, I am so sorry, Jaskead. I can certainly understand why Ariauna doesn't trust Celeste."

Jaskead took another sip from his tea and cleared his throat. "Yes, that is the primary reason for her mistrust, but it's not the only reason."

"What's the other reason?" Skip questioned.

Jaskead gave Skip a questioning look. "I thought you knew?"

"Knew what?"

"Didn't the general tell you who Celeste's father is?"

CHAPTER 9

April 6, 2042 - City of Chast

Celeste was relieved. She had managed to make it back in time from the briefing with Adrian for her father's address to the citizens of *Chast* – the Gnol's capital city on *Terrest* – and it seemed, at least for now, that no one had suspected where she had been, nor did they question.

She had questioned herself about going to the briefing with Adrian at the hidden rebel base because of her father's speech to the city. However, she also had received word that Adrian's son from another planet called Earth had just arrived. Despite the risk in going, she went anyway. She knew that she would gain valuable information and more insight into these people who looked like Gnols but obviously didn't have the same intelligence or power.

Celeste had grown to respect the heathen aliens, as her father called them. But, never had any of them made an impression on her as much as Jake did. *Why can I not get him out of my mind?* She thought. After all, Jake was just another human? He wasn't as intelligent or as powerful as her, even though she knew that he had the potential to be. Yet, she was impressed with him and obviously attracted to him when they met.

What am I doing? She thought. She shook her head and regained her focus for the moment at hand.

She was standing beside her mother who sat in one of the royal chairs, placed on the royal balcony of the palace that overlooked the city. Celeste looked down at her mother. She loved her mother very much. She was a selfless woman who had taught her to use sound judgment and to treat everyone with respect, a trait that she obviously did not learn from her father.

Her mother coughed and then wheezed as she tried to take in a breath of fresh air. Celeste knelt down and placed her right hand on her mother's cheek. She was burning up.

"Mother, you should not be out here. You should be resting."

Celeste's mother shook her head and spoke. Her voice was raspy and soft. "No, your father demanded that I be here on this great day of his."

"How could he demand that of you? He knows of your condition. He just wants you here for the look of it. He does not have what is best for you in mind."

Celeste's mother looked up into Celeste's blue eyes and smiled. She reached up and placed her left hand on Celeste's cheek. "You remind me so much of myself when I was young and beautiful."

Celeste smiled back at her mother as a she felt a tear roll down her left cheek. Her mother, Ciminae Chast, was a beautiful dark haired Gnol of royal, tribal lineage back when they were on *Gnolom*. However, that beauty had faded because of a mysterious disease that had overtaken her within the last six months. In fact, there were a number of Gnols that had become stricken with the disease that their doctors could not identify.

Now, Ciminae looked frail. She had lost a tremendous amount of weight. Her once dark, beautiful hair was now a gray tangled mess and thinning. Her silk smooth skin had now become a wrinkled bag of flesh.

Celeste smiled at her mother. She smiled back. Celeste had always enjoyed hearing the stories of her mother's family.

Ciminae would tell her daughter stories about a powerful tribe called the *Girtheal*, from which they descended. Ciminae's father was the tribal chief and a skilled warrior, back before the goddess gave the gift of technology to the Gnols, so they could leave their dying planet and find a new home.

Celeste remembered her former world. She never saw the blue water and green valleys that her mother described. All she saw was dust. Her mother had explained that a generation before Celeste was born; *Gnolom* had been hit with a massive object thrown at them by the evil god of despair – a god her tribe worshipped.

Of course, Celeste knew now that it wasn't a god at all, but an asteroid that had slammed into one of the east oceans and caused dramatic climate changes throughout the planet. *Gnolom*, once a beautiful and lush planet, had begun to die. The water dried up, and the atmosphere began to change.

Celeste's father was the Gnol who was chosen by the great goddess, so the story goes, to lead the escape from *Gnolom* and find a new home. He led nearly two million Gnols on the exodus to *Terrest*. And now, nearly every Gnol worshipped her father as a god – the one who saved the Gnols. Nevertheless, Celeste couldn't help but feel resentment toward her father. *Why would a god, if her father were one, kill and enslave an innocent civilization?*

Celeste stood up and shook her head. She returned to where she stood before and placed her left hand on her mother's shoulder. She looked out over the city that her father began constructing when she was just ten years old – just after the initial attack on *Terrest*.

In fifteen short years since the attack, her father had successfully gained control of *Terrest*, and built his capital, in which he named *Chast* in honor to himself. The city was beautiful. It was astonishing to see, even with all the bloodshed that came with the war. The city housed nearly two hundred thousand Gnols.

It seemed that nearly all of those two hundred thousand citizens were present today in anticipation of hearing their lord's words. Three hundred feet below the balcony, the citizens were crammed in the palace courtyard. Celeste looked everywhere. She couldn't see a patch of ground anywhere. It was a sea of Gnols.

From the balcony, Celeste looked up. She could see the top of the towering palace her father had built in honor to himself. The top of the palace stood nearly one thousand feet from the ground. The base of the palace was almost as spectacular, encompassing nearly forty thousand square feet. The palace was truly a remarkable architectural achievement by Gnol standards. Especially since all of the technology that her father had introduced to them was relatively new.

The palace had thirty-five floors, each floor losing about ten thousand square feet of area, until the top floor, which was only about five thousand square feet, and was off limits to everyone but her father.

The floors of the palace served different functions. The first floor was dedicated to the public for worship of the goddess of light and her chosen one Koroan Chast. The second floor through the thirty-second floor contained different living quarters for hundreds of Terrestrian slaves that served her family, not to mention the thousands of military personnel in charge of protecting the palace. The thirty-third floor contained the living quarters of Celeste, her mother, her father, and her brother-in-law whom she loathed. The floor above that housed her father's military base of operations. And the top floor was the mysterious room her father was only allowed to enter.

Celeste shivered in the cold. *Why did my father have to have this event on such a cold day?* She wondered. It was spring now in this part of *Terrest*, but winter was still trying to hold on.

Celeste looked left as she heard the door open that led from the military conference room to the balcony. Her father's three generals walked out of the doors. The first general was Dorange Gar, her brother-in-law. Celeste cringed at the sight of him. She did not understand what her sister had seen in him, and why her father held him in such high esteem, especially since he was nearly the same age as her father.

Dorange took his place upon the balcony on the left side of the podium from which her father was about to speak. He had an arrogance about himself that made Celeste sick to her stomach. It was obvious to all that Dorange wore his crimson red military uniform with pride, showing off the gold stars on each of his shoulders that symbolized his rank in the military along with various medals of honor adorned on his left breast.

Celeste wished Dorange wasn't wearing the inhibitors behind his ears. Oh, how she wanted to probe his mind to find out what deceitful plots he was planning in his head.

Dorange had proven himself worthy to Celeste's father. His talents with his mental powers and strength were astonishing. Yet, Celeste felt that there was something amiss about the Gnol, even though he claimed to have descended from a royal tribe himself.

Dorange turned around and walked toward Celeste and her mother. His smug smile sickened her. However, she had to admit that Dorange could charm anyone into doing his will especially with his looks and words, which was obviously the case with her sister and father.

Dorange was a stunningly handsome Gnol with long black hair, braided into a ponytail, which came to rest in the middle of his back. Despite being in his early sixties, he looked fairly young. If a Gnol was to meet him for the first time, one would assume he was just in his late thirties.

As Dorange approached, Celeste made eye contact with him. Even though he had sparkling, dark-brown eyes, Celeste could see the deceit behind them.

Dorange stopped within inches of Celeste's face. She backed up a little. Dorange stroked his goatee with his right hand. "Hello Celeste. My, you look amazing. I do believe you get more and more beautiful each day," he said.

Celeste glared at him. She wasn't going to give him the satisfaction of playing to his ego.

Dorange had been trying for four years to court Celeste since her sister was killed in a strange accident. Celeste suspected that Dorange might have even murdered her sister because, at one time, her sister told her that she was afraid of Dorange because of his temper. Unfortunately, Celeste didn't have any proof.

Celeste's own father even encouraged Celeste to pursue a relationship with Dorange. But Celeste made it clear to Dorange and her father that she wanted nothing to do with him.

Dorange then knelt down and spoke to Ciminae. "Mother, how are you feeling today?"

Ciminae looked up at Celeste and rolled her eyes. Celeste knew that her mother despised Dorange just as much as she did.

After neither Celeste nor Ciminae responded to Dorange, he nodded and smiled. He then resumed his position next to the podium.

Not only did Celeste despise Dorange, she hated her father's other two generals just as much. Standing on Dorange's left was General Aralt Thourad. General Thourad was just as arrogant and smug as Dorange. He was in charge of the Gnols' ground army. Thourad stood about six feet tall with short, blond hair and hazy, green eyes. At forty-three-years-old, he was also remarkably well built with rippling muscles.

On Thourad's left was the short and pudgy General Kamferal Ochalt. Kamferal was totally bald, and despite his authority and arrogance, there was something humorous about his stature. In addition, he was in charge of the Gnol Navy.

Celeste heard the door slide open again and out walked Vlamer Kreuk, her father's high priest and second in command only to her father. Vlamer was downed in a ceremonial robe of bright scarlet and black that extended all the way down to his feet. The robe symbolized her father's power and godhood over the Gnol civilization.

As Vlamer walked out, he looked at Celeste and Ciminae with his clear green eyes and bowed his head. The red temple hat, that extended nearly a foot off of his shaven head, nearly toppled. Celeste managed to hide her amusement as Vlamer quickly raised his head and gave Celeste a smile underneath his black goatee. Vlamer then assumed his position on the right of the podium from which her father was about to speak.

A few minutes later, out walked her father, Koroan Chast, Supreme Commander and lord over the Gnols. There was an eerie silence that came over the thousands of Gnols in attendance. Celeste looked out over the sea of Gnols, and it seemed that almost every one of them knelt down on one knee in reverence to their savior and lord.

Koroan turned and looked at Celeste and her mother. He gave them both a warm smile and nod. Celeste and Ciminae nodded respectfully in return. Celeste continued to watch her father as he walked up to the podium. He was an intimidating Gnol. Koroan stood nearly 6'5" tall, with long, black hair that hung straight and loose on his broad shoulders. In addition to his piercing, blue eyes, he had a short black goatee. His appearance was just enough to strike fear into anyone, including Celeste.

Koroan was dressed in his all white robe and red cape that extended past his feet. On the back of his cape was the symbol of the goddess of light. The symbol was of a beautiful blond woman, with long, flowing hair. She was adorned in light and dressed in a light blue dress with her arms outstretched. It was a symbol that symbolized her gift to the Gnols, the gift of technology and of her chosen one – Koroan Chast.

Koroan stepped up to the podium and raised his arms above his head. At that moment, the sea of Gnols in unison all said, "Hail our lord and liberator!"

The sound of the Gnols' voices was deafening.

Koroan lowered his arms and smiled as he looked out over his people. He spoke with a thunderous deep voice into the voice enhancer that he invented, along with all of the other Gnol technology.

"My brothers and sisters, I have called all of you here today at the request of our goddess mother."

The entire crowd bowed their heads in honor of their goddess. Celeste, on the other hand, had a difficult time bowing her head in honor of a goddess that was new to her people. For generations, the people of *Gnolom* worshipped many different gods or goddesses depending upon which tribe they belonged; until the day her father claimed he had been visited by the true goddess of *Gnolom*, who bestowed upon him knowledge of strange and wonderful devices that made life easier and possible for the Gnols to flee their dying world.

After the moment of silence, Koroan continued. "Our mother appeared to me in a vision and commanded that I, the chosen one, should give her people a report on the war with the heathen aliens that have stolen this beautiful world from her. But first, our mother wants me to remind you and reprimand you for rumors that have been circulating. It has been said that I am a tyrant. It has been said that I am a murderer and kill in cold blood. It has been said that I lie and deceive.

"And, who is it that spreads these lies and untruths? It is the rebels. These so called rebels have been spreading these lies to the Gnol citizens. It has even come to my attention that we have had traitors that live among us that have told these rebels these lies."

Celeste's heart felt as if it had suddenly jumped into her throat. She had been careful not to give her position away. *Was it possible that her father knew?*

"But, need I remind you," Koroan continued. "Who was the Gnol chosen by our queen mother?" Koroan waited and a deafening sound resonated from the crowd.

"You are! Our lord, Koroan Chast!"

Koroan smiled. He knew that the crowd was playing into his hands. "Who did the queen mother choose to unite the warring tribes and organize *Gnolom* into a united government?"

There was another resounding response.

"You! Our king, Koroan Chast!"

"And, who was he that our mother chose to give her gift of technology and save us from destruction on a dying world?"

"You! Our savior, Koroan Chast!"

Koroan's smile grew bigger as well as his ego. "Yes, it was I. I was chosen as the one to unite our people. I was the one chosen to develop new technology; technology that was not known to us because of our ability to probe others' thoughts. Thus, there were wars between tribes on our old world that lasted as long as history has been recorded.

"For thousands of years, our civilization was not allowed to progress because Gnols knew others' thoughts and ideas. Evil and deceitful Gnols would steal those thoughts and ideas, and in turn, wars would result. But, I say. What does the ancient scripture say that has been handed down from tribe to tribe, father to father? The ancient scripture says that one day the chosen one would arise. The chosen one would unit two peoples and two worlds and he would be a ruler among them."

Koroan paused again.

"And, who is the chosen one that has fulfilled this prophecy?"

There was yet another deafening response from the crowd.

"You! Koroan Chast, our god!"

"Yes, I am he. I am the god that was prophesied. I have risen up and united our people. I have also united our old world with our new one.

"Our mother appeared to me almost a generation ago. She is the true goddess of our world and universe; not the heathen pagan gods our tribes worshipped. It was she that gave us a new language – her language. It was she that gave me the knowledge to develop devices that would block our brain waves, thus, preventing us from stealing what is most valuable from one another. It was she that gave me the knowledge to develop technology, technology that would take us from our dying world and to her home world.

"Her world was taken away from her by these heathen aliens. Aliens that look like us but do not have the mental power or intelligence we possess. And now, there are those that would dare spread these horrible untruths about me. I have only done what has been commanded of me. I have retaken our mother's world. I have graciously saved these lesser people that did not die in war. I have graciously allowed them to serve us. And they dare spread these lies about me!

"Well, I have a warning for those that dare oppose me and our mother. I also warn those Gnols amongst us that have betrayed me! You will be found. You will not be granted mercy, and you will die as a sacrifice to our goddess and mother!"

There was a resounding cheer from the crowd. It was obvious they were loyal to Koroan and believed he was the chosen one. However, Celeste felt a bone chilling shiver resonate up her spine from her father's words. If it were true that he knew that she and some of her aides were spies for the Terrestrian rebels, he would kill her. The thought of facing her father was terrifying. He was the most powerful Gnol ever. If she wasn't wearing the *Mind Inhibitors* – which luckily he never demanded she take out – he could easily probe her mind and kill her.

Koroan continued but spoke in a softer voice. "But let me give you reassurance my brothers and sisters. To date, we have succeeded in destroying all of the Terrestrian's major cities. We are now in the process of leveling these cities, getting rid of any remnant of the alien heathen. For those heathens that don't resist, they are given the honor of serving you and me. I predict that the war will be over soon, and we will experience the most powerful and peaceful civilization ever."

Celeste resisted the urge to reach up and plug her ears. The cheer from the crowd was so deafening that even Koroan seemed to duck his head from the sound.

After the crowd became quiet, Koroan concluded.

"And now, my brothers and sisters, I bless all of you with my love and bid you farewell. Until we meet again."

In unison, the crowd cheered. "All hail, our lord and savior, Koroan Chast!"

Koroan turned from the podium and walked toward Celeste. Celeste swallowed the lump that was in her throat as he approached.

"Celeste," Koroan said. "Take your mother to her chambers and join me and my generals in the conference room. There is something we need to discuss."

Koroan leaned in and kissed her on the cheek, ignored his wife, and exited the balcony. His three generals and Vlamer followed him like baby ducklings following their mother.

As he approached the door, Dorange made eye contact with Celeste and gave her a knowing smile that sent shivers down her spine.

Celeste quickly turned her head and thought. *Oh no, he knows!*

★ ★ ★ ★ ★

A few moments later, after Celeste had taken her mother to her room, she entered the conference room. There, at the head of the enormous crystal conference table sat her father in his black leather chair. On Koroan's left sat Dorange, and on his right sat General Thourad and General Ochalt. In front of her father was a computer terminal in which he immediately closed flat with the table the moment Celeste entered the room. Koroan and his three stooges stood. "Ah, there she is . . . my beautiful princess. Come. Join us," said Koroan, as he motioned for Celeste to sit at the other end of the table. When she sat, Koroan's three cronies sat as well.

Celeste was relieved a little. At least her father wasn't angry, yet. But, one could never tell with Koroan Chast.

Koroan placed his hands behind his back and walked toward Celeste. He stood behind Celeste and placed both of his hands on her shoulder and began massaging them.

There was a time when Celeste would have enjoyed a little fatherly affection from Koroan, but not today, not anymore.

Koroan leaned down and quietly whispered into her ear. "Celeste, my dear, we know."

Celeste felt her whole body stiffen and shivers ran down her spine. She knew that her father felt it as well. She swallowed the lump in her throat. "Know what?" she asked.

Koroan laughed, and so did his stooges. "Ah, Celeste. Do you not know what I am referring to?" Koroan asked as he resumed his seat at the other end of the table.

Celeste glanced at Dorange who still had a smug smile on his face. "No," she said.

Dorange laughed as well as the other two generals, but Koroan cut them off. "Come now, my dear. You hold a high position in my government, and you have no idea why the generals and I are so happy?"

Celeste was frustrated now. Why wouldn't her father just get to the point and call her out?

"Honestly, Father, I have no idea what you know."

Koroan threw his head back in laughter. Upon doing so, his three ducklings did too. Celeste almost laughed too, but not because her father was laughing, but because whatever her father did, the other three followed.

Koroan's face grew serious again, and he focused his gaze on Celeste. "My, how I wish I could read your mind right now? I do not know if you are being honest with me or not? Or maybe you really do not know what I am speaking of?"

No . . . don't do it, thought Celeste.

Koroan Chast never had *Mind Inhibitors* inserted. For some reason, he had developed the ability to block any other Gnol from probing his mind or using their powers against him. Koroan was the first Gnol, at least that Celeste knew of, with the ability to do it.

"Nevertheless," Koroan continued. "I will not demand you take out your inhibitors because you are my daughter, and I trust you." Koroan paused and then looked directly into Celeste's eyes.

Celeste wanted to look away, but she knew if she did, her father would know she was hiding something.

"If you were one of my subordinates, I would demand that you take out your inhibitors," Koroan said. "But do not worry, my dear. I believe that you really do not know what I am talking about."

Celeste cleared her throat and straightened herself in her seat. "Well then, Father, why don't you enlighten me, so we can quite playing this game?"

Koroan smiled and looked at his three generals. "You see gentlemen; this is why she will succeed me as queen to our people."

Dorange squirmed in his chair at the mention of Celeste as queen.

Koroan continued. "She wants to get to the point. There are no mind games with her."

If you only knew, Celeste thought.

"She knows what she wants, and she gets it," said Koroan, smiling with pride at his daughter. "Well, she will get what she wants." Koroan leaned on his elbows and placed his hands underneath his chin. "Celeste, we know where the rebel base is."

Celeste tried not to show her surprise. In a way, she was relieved that he wasn't suspicious of her. Yet, she felt a deep sadness knowing that her father knew where her friends were located. Celeste gained her composure and responded. "Really . . . Father, I am so happy for you. You have been trying to find those wretched rebels for so long. . . . I am curious though. . . . How did you find it?"

Koroan just smiled at his daughter. He stood again and walked over to the refreshment table that was on Celeste's left about ten feet away. On the refreshment table were various fruits and vegetables that Koroan and his generals enjoyed whenever there were important matters to discuss. There were also various wines and ales that were to Koroan's liking.

Koroan grabbed two goblets that were located next to the wines. He poured one of the wines into the two glasses. Sipping from one glass, he looked at the portrait, which hung on the wall behind the refreshment table. It was given to him by a faithful Gnol. The portrait portrayed Koroan riding down from the clouds in a chariot pulled by fiery horses with revenge in their eyes. Koroan was adorned in the very robe and cape he was wearing now. In fact, the portrait was what spawned the dress Koroan wore. On the ground of the portrait were the Terrestrians, which were portrayed as devilish and deceitful. The Terrestrians were being destroyed by lightning bolts thrown by the so-called savior of the Gnols.

Koroan grabbed the other goblet he had filled, turned and walked toward Celeste. He placed the goblet in front of Celeste. Celeste shook her head.

"You know, Father, that I do not drink anything that will inhibit my mind, which this alcohol does."

Koroan laughed. "Oh yes, that is right. For some reason, someone has taught you this. I do not know whom? Nevertheless, you know that this is the royal drink of our goddess mother." Koroan creased his dark eyebrows and now glared at his daughter. "Let me ask you, Celeste. . . ." Koroan pointed to the portrait. "You see this portrait that a faithful Gnol has painted?"

Celeste was now a little fearful. What was her father getting at? "Yes I do," she said.

"What does it represent?"

Celeste tried to hide her anxiety. "Well, as you explained it, Father, it depicts you conquering this world and shows your power."

"Yes it does."

Koroan took another sip from his goblet as he stood on Celeste's left. "The portrait shows that I am a god." He gave Celeste a questioning look.

Celeste figured she should answer. "Y . . . Yes it does."

"And wouldn't a god know everything?"

"Yes, a god would know everything, Father."

"Good," Koroan said as he levitated Celeste's goblet to Dorange with his telekinetic ability.

Dorange grabbed the goblet in midair with his black leather gloved right hand, and drank sloppily. When he had finished the entire goblet, he wiped his goatee with his left arm and smiled at Celeste.

Koroan seemed amused by Dorange's eagerness to drink the royal drink. He turned and looked at Celeste again. "Yes . . . and I, as a god, strive to know everything." Koroan paused again.

What is he doing? Why is he taking so long to get to the point? Celeste thought.

"Tell me . . . my dear . . . do you know a young Gnol in our military named Malk Vier? I believe he was assigned to your intelligence team, was he not?"

Celeste looked down at her left hand. It was shaking. She grabbed it with her right hand and looked back up at her father. Koroan noticed her movement.

"Y . . . Yes," she said.

"And your intelligence team was the team that was assigned to find the rebel base, was it not?"

"Yes."

"Well then, my dear . . ." Koroan moved behind Celeste again and placed his hands on her shoulders. He leaned in and spoke softly again. Celeste glanced at the three stooges. They were leaning in, all with smiles on their faces, trying to hear Koroan, ". . . Why was Lieutenant Vier seen entering a hidden boulder ten miles west of *Talead*, which is not a boulder at all?"

Celeste felt her muscles tighten again. Two days ago she sent Lieutenant Vier, who was a sympathizer for the Terrestrians as well and Kylee's Fiancé, to the rebel base to get a report on Skip and Jake. Adrian had told Celeste that Lieutenant Vier never came. Celeste soon found out that Malk was captured and eventually tortured and killed by her father. She had feared that Malk might have revealed Celeste's treason when her father read Malk's mind. However, when Celeste asked about Malk's treachery, her father had told her that it was of the highest security, and something she did not need to know about.

"I do not know, Father," she said.

Koroan strolled slowly back to the head of the conference table. "Well, thanks to General Gar, who had followed him, Lieutenant Vier was captured. And it was discovered that this fake boulder is actually a hologram designed to act as a boulder on all scans. There is actually a secret hatchway underneath the hologram boulder with a computer terminal. When Lieutenant Vier was captured, he was entering a secret code."

Koroan stopped and glared at Celeste. Celeste felt her body slump in her chair. There was a long pause, and Celeste began to feel the pressure from everyone staring at her. She managed, however, to regain her composure. She sat up and looked her father dead in the eye. "Father, I do not know what you are insinuating. . . ."

"You do not?" Koroan asked.

"No."

"Well, I find that interesting. Why would one of your subordinates know the location of the secret base without your knowledge?"

"I do not know, Father, but it sounds like you have your spy."

Koroan seemed to look harder into Celeste's eyes. Celeste was fearful that he would demand she take out her inhibitors, but he didn't. However, if he did, she was somewhat confident that she could block some of his mind probe.

"Maybe . . . we do have our spy. But . . . you know what is interesting about this?" asked Koroan.

"No, Father, I do not."

"When I was interrogating him, we took out his inhibitors. I probed his mind and found most of the information I needed . . ." Koroan paused again.

Celeste felt a bead of sweat drip down from her forehead. If her father probed Malk's mind, then he knew that she was the spy. Unless...

"However," Koroan continued, "I was not able to get the most important detail."

Celeste saw a flicker of light in the dark tunnel she was in. If her father wasn't able to get all of the information he wanted, then maybe the training she had secretly provided her three subordinates had paid off.

"For some reason Lieutenant Vier was able to block some of my ability to probe his mind. Now, I do not know about you my dear, but there are only four Gnols that I know of with the ability to block another Gnol's mind probes naturally . . . myself, Vlamer Kreuk, your late sister, and of course . . . you."

The three generals shot Celeste a look. They looked like hungry wolves after they had cornered their prey. Celeste, though, had managed to find strength in the fact that if Malk was able to block a portion of her father's mind probe, then maybe she, being the more experienced Gnol, would be able to block more if her father so chose to probe her mind. She continued to hold her father's cool gaze. "With all due respect, Your Eminence, I do not know what you are insinuating, but I had no knowledge of Lieutenant Vier's treason. If I had, I would have been the first to inform you."

Koroan took a breath and smiled at his daughter. He looked at Dorange. "There you see, Dorange. I told you my daughter would not lie to me. Now, do you feel better knowing that she is on our side?"

Dorange looked disappointed and said, "Yes, Your Highness." Dorange then glared at Celeste. Celeste found pleasure in the fact that he had been humiliated in his accusation of her, even if it was true.

Koroan now moved and stood with authority behind his seat. "Ah yes, I need to inform you, Celeste, that you will be assigned a new recruit to replace Lieutenant Vier."

Celeste hid her emotion well. It was hard for her because Lieutenant Vier was a good Gnol with a lot of potential. He also had a warm heart. "Father, if you do not need me for anything else, I would like to retire to my quarters. It has been a long day," she said, as she shot a deadly look at Dorange.

Dorange glared back.

"Before you go, my dear, there is something else you and the generals should know," Koroan said. "I have planned an attack on the rebel base and the capture of their arrogant leader, Adrian Palmer. The attack will commence at dawn two days from now."

Celeste stopped herself from saying 'no'. *Two days from today. I have to get to the base tonight and warn them*, she thought.

"I have placed General Dorange Gar in charge of the operation," said Koroan.

General Thourad spoke immediately. "But your high—"

Koroan darted a look at Thourad. His face flushed hot red. "You dare interrupt me when I am speaking!"

Thourad immediately ducked his head. "Please forgive me, My Lord."

Koroan abruptly changed his mood again and smiled. "You are forgiven. Now, you may speak."

"Thank you, My Lord," said Thourad like some school age child who had just been scolded by his teacher. "With all due respect, Your Eminence, . . . I am the superior officer of ground forces. May I ask why the superior officer of air and space forces is in charge of this mission?"

Dorange looked fiercely at Thourad. It was obvious to Celeste that General Thoroud and General Gar didn't like each other.

"That is a fair question, General Thourad," Koroan said. "I have placed Dorange in charge of the mission because he surveyed the ground above which the base lies and knows the precise location. I also feel that he is the better leader for the attack."

Thourad looked questioningly at Koroan. "I do not understand, Your Highness? What leadership abilities does General Gar possess that I do not po—"

Koroan switched personalities again and raised his right hand from behind his back where it was resting with his other hand. Using his telekinetic ability, Koroan levitated Thourad out of his chair, startling General Ochalt who pushed his chair back from the table, and fell flat on his back.

There, above the conference table, Thourad levitated with terror in his eyes. Koroan spoke not loudly but with authority. "General Thourad, how many times must you be warned? Do not challenge my authority or decisions." And then with a flick of his wrist, Koroan threw Thourad from his midair position above the table into the refreshment table ten feet away.

Thourad's body crashed into the wooden table holding the refreshments and drinks. He lay there like a limp, unconscious animal drenched in fruits, vegetables, and wines.

Koroan then turned his attention to General Ochalt. "General Ochalt!"

Ochalt jumped up to attention from where he was laying on the floor. "Your em . . . eminence?"

"Take General Thourad to the brig. Maybe a few days in solitary confinement will help him see where his loyalties lie?"

"Yes, Your Highness," said Ochalt, bowing his head. He walked over to Thourad's unconscious body. He reached down, picked up Thourad, and placed him over his shoulders.

Celeste was amazed that the short, pudgy Ochalt could lift and carry Thourad. But she remembered that Gnols were roughly five times stronger than the humans for whom she was spending most of her time with.

Ochalt left the room and Koroan turned to face his daughter. "Celeste, please return to your quarters while I speak with Dorange. I will speak with you later. "

"Yes, Father," Celeste said, as she walked out of the room relieved that her father didn't know.

★ ★ ★ ★ ★

"You see Dorange. I told you that she was trustworthy," said Koroan, as he sat at the head of his conference table with his computer open. "I really should be angry with you because you dare accuse her of being the spy. However, I have to admit, the evidence you presented to me was almost convincing."

Dorange looked disappointed.

"Come now, Dorange, do not look so disappointed. You should be pleased that your future bride is not the spy."

Even though Celeste denied the accusation, Dorange would have loved to see her punished by her father. He knew that if she would have cracked under pressure and admitted to being the spy; her father would not have killed her, but forced her to marry Dorange.

Dorange knew that Koroan desperately wanted a son to inherit the throne, and Koroan had made it known, only to Dorange, that he was disappointed in having two daughters. When Dorange married Celeste's older sister, he had high hopes of obtaining the rule from Koroan when he died. However, when Dorange's wife died, Koroan gave the inheritance to Celeste only upon the condition that she marry a worthy Gnol, thereby voiding all the inheritance rights of Dorange.

Nevertheless, Dorange knew what he wanted, and that was to be heir to Koroan's empire. So, Dorange, being the resourceful and manipulative Gnol he was, convinced Koroan that he was the best suitor for Celeste. Now, if he could somehow trap Celeste into marrying him?

"Why do you not speak, Dorange?"

Dorange was startled out of his thoughts by Koroan's authoritative voice. "Oh, I am sorry, Father," he said.

Koroan smiled. Dorange knew that Koroan liked to be called 'father' because Dorange was the son Koroan never had. Koroan, however, only allowed Dorange to call him father when they were alone, in order to show the other generals that Koroan didn't have favorites.

Dorange continued, "I was just thinking about how I look forward to finally having revenge on those rebels, especially their leader, Adrian Palmer."

Koroan grew serious again. The Gnol seemed to change moods more than a chameleon changed colors. "Yes, that is what I wanted to ask you about? You wanted me to put you in charge of the mission instead of Thourad, and I gladly did because I knew you would succeed, whereas, Thourad would not have. But . . ."

"But what, Father?"

"I am curious as to why you have such a vendetta against this human, Adrian Palmer?"

"Father, I thought you knew?"

Koroan looked questioningly at Dorange. "You know I should know everything, so why do you not inform me of what I do not know?"

Dorange put on his best grief stricken face. "That day our precious Raqel died."

"What about that day?" asked Koroan, as he gave Dorange a look that sent shivers down his spine.

Even though Dorange had learned how to sweet-talk Koroan, the very image of him angry made Dorange nervous.

Koroan continued, "You told me the day Raqel died that she had fallen down the steps of the wall that surrounds my city, and that is where you found her."

"Yes, but I was suspicious of the accident."

"You were? Why did you not inform me of your suspicions?"

Dorange was able to muster a tear and looked apologetically at Koroan. "I am sorry, Father, but I did not want to upset you even more with the grief you suffered from the loss of your oldest daughter."

Koroan gave Dorange a look of appreciation. "Yes, that was wise of you."

Dorange smiled at Koroan, showing he had accepted Koroan's appreciation. "Because I did not want to upset you, I conducted my own investigation."

"And?"

"And . . . one of my agents discovered that she did not die because of her fall down the wall's steps."

Koroan now seemed to grow inpatient. "Well, then how did my beloved Raqel die?"

Dorange managed to look sad again. "She was murdered."

"What!" said Koroan, as he slammed his right fist down on his computer monitor. The monitor shattered into pieces. Koroan looked at his right hand as drops of blood began to drip from it. He ignored it. "Why was I not informed of this?"

Dorange backed away from Koroan. "I am sorry, Father, but I sent Captain Sartel to inform you of our discovery."

"Captain Sartel never informed me of anything!"

Dorange now looked angry. "He did not? Well, for his insubordination, I shall have him killed immediately!"

"Yes, you must. In fact, I would very much like to see you be the one to kill him with your telepathic abilities. I would very much like to see his face as his brain is overloaded and turned to mush."

Dorange had to think fast. "Yes, Father, and I would love to demonstrate my power and ability to do so. But first, you must know why I seek revenge on the rebel leader."

Koroan nodded his head.

"Through my investigation, I uncovered a plot designed by the rebel leader, Adrian Palmer, to have your family murdered one by one. I found documents left behind at the scene that were not discovered when Raqel was found dead. On the documents were direct orders from Adrian Palmer to a secret infiltration group. This group was ordered to infiltrate our society and first murder Raqel, then Celeste, and then your wife. Their ultimate goal was to break your spirit, and in your grief, they had hoped you would let your guard down, so they could murder you."

Koroan sprang to his feet. He grabbed his chair and threw it crashing through the glass doors that led to the balcony. "Why was I not shown these documents?"

Dorange kept calm and tried to hide the smile that began to form at the corners of his mouth. *Yeah right. You are supposed to be some so-called god*, he thought. "Father, Captain Sartel had the documents in hand when I ordered him to report to you."

Koroan had a look of revenge in his eyes. "General Gar! Two days from now when you attack the rebel base, I want Adrian Palmer brought to me alive with his family. I will deal with them personally. Meanwhile, I want you to arrest Captain Sartel and schedule his execution, which you will personally see to for tomorrow. But first, I must go and speak with Celeste."

"Yes, Your Eminence. I will go and arrest Captain Sartel now," Dorange said as he stood and bowed his head.

Koroan nodded his approval. "You are excused."

"Thank you, My Lord," Dorange said, as he turned and walked out of the conference room. As he walked out of the door, Dorange's mind was going a hundred miles an hour. There were a lot of things that he had to accomplish tonight before he supposedly arrested Captain Sartel and planned the attack on the rebel base. He also smiled, as he thought to himself, *all too easy.*

★ ★ ★ ★ ★

Celeste paced back and forth in her room. She was impatient. She had to get to the base to warn Adrian that her father knew the location of the base and planned to attack in two days. She couldn't risk sending an encrypted message through her computer or communicator. She knew with the intelligence teams her father had within the building that such a message would be intercepted. No, she had to go in person.

She stopped and looked at herself in her mirror and adjusted her robe so that the black fatigues she wore underneath would not show. She wanted her father to think that she was going to retire for the evening.

The annoying beeping sound signaled, which indicated that someone was outside her bedroom door. She quickly sat in the chair in front of the mirror, grabbed her hairbrush, and began brushing her hair. "Come in," she said.

Her bedroom door slid open, and Koroan, still adorned in his robe and cape, walked in. "Ah, there she is – my beautiful daughter."

"Hello Father," Celeste said as she turned back to face the mirror and began to stroke her hair again.

Koroan stood behind Celeste and placed his hands on her shoulders. They just looked at each other for a few seconds in the mirror before either one of them spoke.

Celeste was the first to break the silence. "Father, why would you believe Dorange's accusation about me being a spy?"

Koroan smiled at his daughter. Celeste was a little relieved that he seemed to be in one of his unfailing moods, but his moods changed so much that it was hard to tell. "Yes, that is what I wanted to speak with you about."

Celeste turned and looked up at her father. As she looked at her father, she yearned for the days before he was corrupted and maddened with power – the days when she was a little girl on *Gnolom*, and her father was a respectable farmer and warrior in the *Girtheal* tribe. But those days were gone.

Even though Celeste witnessed violence and bloodshed at a young age, her father was different. He was kind and gentle, the total opposite from the Gnol he was now. Did she still love her father? Of course, she did, he was her father. Nonetheless, she had witnessed his tyranny against the Terrestrians and even her own people. She would never be able to forgive him for that.

"What are you thinking about my dear?" Koroan asked.

Celeste stood and walked past Koroan. She took another few steps, turned around, and looked him square in the eyes. "I will be honest with you, Father. I do not like the Gnol you have become," she said, holding his gaze and her composure. It was a bold statement.

Koroan's smile turned downward into a frown, and he furrowed his eyebrows. "Celeste, I have been patient with you. I have noticed your sympathy toward the Terrestrian slaves in our possession and have granted you a lot of freedom. I even trusted you when you told me that you were not the spy of which Dorange accused you of being. But . . ." Koroan paused as he walked closer to Celeste. He grabbed her by the arms and squeezed. Celeste winced in pain, ". . . but do not ever make a statement like that toward me again."

Koroan squeezed a little harder until Celeste apologized. "S . . . Sorry, Father."

Koroan let go and switched personalities again. "Good. Now, let me answer your first question."

Celeste didn't say anything. She just nodded. She had to be careful. If she said any more bold statements like that again, which she often did, she could risk giving herself away.

Koroan continued. "I was suspicious of Dorange's accusations because Lieutenant Vier was able to block some of my mind probe when he was tortured to death."

Celeste hid her emotion. She trusted and learned to love Malk like a brother.

"And as you know Celeste, there are only four Gnols that possess the ability to block mind probes."

"Yes, Father, but have you considered that fact that with nearly two and a half million Gnols on *Terrest* that there just might be another Gnol with the ability to block mind probes?"

Koroan gave Celeste another suspicious look and then changed it immediately to a smile. "Perhaps, but as lord and ruler of our civilization, I would know if that were true."

Celeste managed a yawn and said. "Yes, Father. Now, if you do not mind, I would like to go to the first floor temple, worship our goddess of light and you as well, and then retire to bed. It has been a long day."

Koroan seemed pleased that Celeste would pay homage to the goddess and especially him, which Celeste knew he would delight in. "Yes, my dear. I will leave you alone now to do so. I will see you in the morning. I want to have breakfast with you so that we can discuss this matter further," he said as he walked out of Celeste's room with the door sliding shut behind him.

Now, Celeste felt pressed for time. She looked at her digital clock on the nightstand next to her bed. The clock read 11:16 p.m. The rebel base was three hundred miles away. As a result, she would have to act fast if she was going to be back in the morning for breakfast with her father.

CHAPTER 10

April 7, 2042 - City of Chast

As he made his way through a questionable part of *Chast*, Dorange looked down at the time keeper on his wrist. It read 12:10 a.m. He was in the roughest part of the city. The part where there was the most crime, despite Koroan's heavy hand, and the part where there were the most bars. He knew that Captain Sartel would be in the one bar where Dorange always conducted business.

Dorange walked past two Gnols who had passed out from drinking too much. It was obvious that a lot of the citizens were celebrating after Koroan's moving speech. Dorange rolled his eyes as he strolled into his favorite bar.

Once inside the smoke filled bar, he scanned the room, ignoring the dancers on the stage and the drunk couple to his right. He noticed Captain Sartel at the back of the bar in a booth. There, he sat with two scantily clad female Gnols who were all over him, along with empty liquor bottles on the table. Dorange grunted as he approached. He didn't need his most trusted officer drunk at a time like this.

Sartel, who was laughing hysterically as the women mauled him, saw Dorange approaching. He quickly pushed the female that sat next to him on his left out of the booth. She fell flat on her back, but didn't notice as she rolled over in the fetal position and laughed. Sartel stood to attention and saluted, nearly falling over. He giggled his response. "Gen . . . General Gar! What an honor. Why don't . . ." Sartel stopped as he fell over and caught himself on the table, ". . . Why don't you join us?"

Dorange walked to within inches of Sartel's face and glared at him. It was obvious the Gnol was drunk. He looked Sartel up and down. Sartel, who stood at 5'10" tall, was just a few inches shorter than Dorange. Sartel's bright red hair was soaking wet with drink. His green eyes were glazed over, and his black officer's uniform was filthy.

Dorange yelled, causing the crowd in the bar to turn their attention to the four Gnols in the corner. "Captain Sartel!"

Sartel stood at attention again trying to control his giggling. But, the two ladies only laughed louder. Dorange shot both of them looks that could kill. Seeing his face, the two female Gnols got the hint and scattered.

Dorange grabbed Sartel by his uniform collar and shoved him back into the booth. Then Dorange slid into the seat opposite Sartel.

"What's the deal, General? I thought you would enjoy the little party. As you could see, I had a girl for you." Sartel said.

Dorange grabbed a half-empty bottle of liquor and splashed it into Sartel's face.

"Hey! Wha . . ."

"You had better sober up now, Captain. I have a mission for you."

Sartel laughed as he reached for another sip from his bottle. Dorange grabbed the bottle and threw it against the opposite wall. "I mean it, Sartel!"

"Okay, okay. What's so important that I need to be sober for? I've completed most of my missions drunk anyway."

Dorange looked around to be sure that no one was paying attention. Everyone in the bar had seemed to go back to their drinks. He leaned in closer and spoke softly. "I need you to follow Celeste to the rebel base and record her with this," he said, retrieving a mini digital recorder from his uniform pocket.

Sartel laughed. "Our lordship didn't believe your accusation, huh?"

"Shut-up, you fool! He didn't believe my accusation about Celeste, but he believed my accusation about you."

Sartel stopped giggling and grew serious as he looked into Dorange's eyes. "What are you talking about?"

Dorange leaned back in his seat and placed his right arm over the back rest. "Let's just say that you failed to report and show our lordship the documents that documented the assassination of my lovely wife by Adrian Palmer's special ops unit."

Sartel gave Dorange a questionable look. "What are you talking about? There wasn't any assassination attempt. You—"

Dorange quickly leaned over the table and grabbed Sartel by his ear and pulled. "Listen, you little scum bag. If you want to live to see another day, I suggest you do as you're ordered or our so called god is going to turn your brain to soup."

Sartel grabbed Dorange by the wrist and pulled it from his ear. Sartel gritted his teeth and seemed sober now. "You didn't?" he said.

Dorange smiled and nodded his head. "Oh, I very well did."

"You would sell me out like that? I'm the only one who knows about all of your little secrets. What if I just went to Koroan now and told him everything? Maybe I'll even let him probe my mind just so he knows that I'm telling the truth."

Dorange laughed. "You wouldn't dare. The moment you walk into Koroan's presence, he'd kill you. He partly blames you for my late wife's death."

Sartel now had the look of a caged animal. Dorange thought that Sartel was about to leap over the table and attack, but he didn't. He just glared at Dorange.

Dorange continued, "Besides, if you do this, I promise it will be worth your while."

"How so?"

"If you successfully record our dear princess as the spy, Koroan won't kill her but will force her to marry me."

"You've got high hopes, General. There's no way Celeste will marry you."

"I beg to differ, Captain. The king couldn't bear to lose another of his beloved daughters. So, what better way to keep an eye on her than to force her to marry his most trusted servant? He treats me like a son."

"Yeah, I've noticed."

"So, Captain Sartel, when Celeste is forced to marry me, who will become next in line to the throne? And, where will you be as my most trusted officer?"

A wry smile spread across Sartel's face. He nodded, grabbed the recorder, and scampered out of the bar.

★ ★ ★ ★ ★

"Mr. Palmer."

"Yes," Kevin said as he worked on his computer in his office, which was located in the fifteen story home office of Compu-Tech Super Computers, located in Salt Lake City, Utah.

"You have an urgent message from Michael Konrad of NASA," said Nancy his secretary, located just outside of his office.

Kevin was excited. It had been a week since he had seen the video footage of *Mars II* and *NightHawk* going through the wormhole. *Was this it? Had Jake successfully returned from the wormhole with Adrian?* "Patch me through."

The screen on Kevin's computer screen changed from his work to Michael Konrad's image. "Kevin. How are you doing?"

"I'm okay, Mike. How are you?"

"I'm doing great."

Kevin interpreted Mike's response and body language as good news. "So, Mike, it's been a week since I saw the ships go through the wormhole. Are they back?"

Michael looked a little confused and said, "Yes . . . uh . . . I mean we think so."

"What do you mean . . . you think so?"

"Well, remember the probe that *Mars II* deployed just before it went into the wormhole?"

"Yes."

"Just a few hours ago it picked up some interesting video."

"What kind of video?" Kevin asked.

"Here, let me show you the video footage."

Michael's image disappeared, and the image of Mars appeared. To the right of the screen, Kevin noticed the frozen image of a ship. "What kind of ship is that?"

"Well, we think its *Mars II*."

Kevin leaned in a little closer toward his computer screen in order to get a better look at the ship. It looked a little like *Mars II*. However, the ship was red and black, instead of white and blue. It was also bigger and more streamlined in shape. Kevin noticed that in the wings were what looked like gun turrets, four of them to be precise.

The ship also had different insignias on it. Instead of the traditional NASA symbols and American flags, these symbols were diamond shaped, but the background was white. The symbol, in the center of the diamond, was that of a woman in a light blue dress. She had her arms outstretched and looked to be descending from a light blue sky in the clouds. Kevin thought the symbol was a little strange.

Kevin noticed another symbol on the tail of the ship. The symbol was that of a gray shield. In the center of the shield, there was a red sword and a black sword crossing at the blades. The swords were being held by a man with long black hair and a goatee. The man was dressed in red military fatigues.

After examining the ship, Kevin finally broke the silence. "I don't think that this ship is *Mars II*," he said.

"It may not be. But, Kevin, look at the design and structure. If you take away the size and other modifications, it would be *Mars II*," said Mike.

"Perhaps, but why would they need to modify it and how?"

"Well, you know us. We have a theory for everything. Maybe, this planet is a technologically advanced planet. Maybe the original *Mars II* was disabled after it went through the wormhole, and this alien civilization helped fix and modify it."

"Why the different colors and insignias?" Kevin asked.

"It could be that maybe this civilization wanted to put their stamp on the ship."

"Yeah . . . maybe," Kevin said with doubt.

"We don't know, Kevin, but I'll tell you what. We should know within two days."

Kevin was stunned. "Two days?"

"We weren't able to establish communications with the ship, but based on our calculations it will be in our orbit within the next two days."

Kevin sat straight up in his chair and shook his head. "That's impossible. *Mars II* can't travel that fast."

"No, but . . . here . . . watch the video, and you'll see."

Kevin watched as the ship slowly moved with the probe following. But then, the ship took off like a beam of light. If Kevin blinked, he would have missed it.

Michael spoke after the ship disappeared. "Our mathematicians broke down the video and came up with an equation. . . ." Michael paused as if waiting for a climax.

"What kind of equation?" Kevin asked, getting frustrated.

"Based on the equation, they calculated that this ship is traveling at or around twenty-eight million miles per hour!"

Kevin stood from his seat in shock. "How is that possible?"

"We don't know," Mike said. "But, maybe this civilization has technology that we haven't even dreamed of yet."

"I hope you're right about this civilization, Mike."

"How so?"

"I don't know, Mike. Maybe this is a hostile civilization that has discovered the wormhole?"

"I don't think so. Besides, where's your faith. It has to be them."

"Maybe," Kevin said, again with doubt in his voice.

"I have to go, Kevin. I will notify you when we establish communications with them."

"Okay, Mike. I look forward to hearing from you. See you later."

"Okay. Bye."

The image on Kevin's screen switched back to its original. Kevin sat back in his leather office chair, leaned his elbows on his desk, and cupped his face in his hands. *I hope your right, Mike. For some reason, I don't think that's our ship*, he thought.

★ ★ ★ ★ ★

Celeste was grateful that the temple on the bottom floor of her father's palace was empty, as it was nearing 12:45 in the morning. The bottom floor was dark except for the security lights that gave her just enough light to see.

The temple on the bottom floor was enormous, encompassing forty-thousand square feet of space. A gold statue representing the goddess of light rested at the back wall in direct line with the main entrance. The statue stood about thirty feet tall, and next to the goddess of light statue stood the gold and bronze statue of her father. Her father's statue stood only twenty feet in the air but was magnificent, to say the least. The statue of her father was adorned in a red military uniform and he was holding two swords above his head that crossed at the blades. In his right hand was a red sword, which represented *Gnolom*, and in his left hand was a black sword that represented *Terrest*. The crossing was symbolic of the joining of the two worlds of *Gnolom* and *Terrest* by the mighty Koroan, who it was prophesied would unite two worlds and two peoples.

Celeste rolled her eyes as she looked at her father's statue. She was becoming less and less faithful that her father was actually the one prophesied. Celeste walked slowly down the red carpet that led from the temple entrance to the statues. Each side of the carpet contained gold tables adorned with ancient scriptures from *Gnolom's* spiritual leaders and tributes to Koroan's conquering of *Terrest*. She stopped just in front of the statue of the goddess of light, looked around, and pulled out a heavy black coat with a hood from its hiding place behind the statue. Celeste took off her white robe and placed it neatly in the hiding spot behind the statue. She put on the coat and was grateful she had hidden it for such a purpose just days ago.

As she looked out the window, the cruelty of spring in this part of *Terrest* had just begun to throw down its mighty fist. Large, wet snow flakes began to fall, and she could tell from the slant of the snowfall that the wind was blowing ferociously.

Celeste zipped up her coat, made sure her dagger and plasma gun were secure, put on her hood, and walked toward the exit. As she was about to exit the sliding glass doors, she heard a noise from somewhere inside the temple. She looked around. Nothing.

After exiting the temple, Celeste walked over to the ten, two-man assault hover vehicles. Her father had given her one just after he had invented them. They were a speedy and agile craft, traveling at nearly two hundred miles per hour and could turn on a dime. The outside of the vehicle was designed for the least amount of air resistance possible. The tip of it was almost as sharp as her dagger. The nose of the vehicle was about three feet long. At the end of the nose, the vehicle had five foot slanted wings that extended out five feet. In between the wings was the pilot's and copilot's seats and just behind that the jet engine.

As Celeste approached her metallic silver *Chati*, named after one of the fastest animals on her planet, she noticed that the vehicle reminded her of a mini jet airplane that Adrian had shown her pictures of from his home world called Earth.

Celeste reached into her coat pocket and pulled out a remote that opened the canopy to the cockpit. She climbed inside and fired the *Chati* up. She was grateful that they were quiet machines. She retracted the stands and hovered in the air for a few minutes.

Gently pushing the control stick back, she backed out of the parking area and turned the *Chati* to face the guard post that exited the palace courtyard. She knew that she would have to tell the guard a good story as to why she was leaving so early in the morning.

As she approached the guard post, she noticed the guard appear in her lights with his right hand extended, and his assault weapon tucked neatly under his left arm. She stopped as the guard walked to the left of the *Chati*. Celeste opened the Canopy.

"Oh, Your Highness, I didn't know that was you. Where are you going at a time like this and in this weather?"

Celeste didn't want to make small talk, so she got right to the point. "It is none of your concern, Major."

Major Dent looked disappointed. "Very well, Your Highness."

Celeste managed the best smile she could muster. "Thank you, Major. Oh, and do me a favor?"

"Yes, Your Highness."

"Do not tell my father that I have left. He has retired for the evening and is very tired from his address to the city. I know that if you wake him, he will be very angry. I will not be long. I should return before sun up."

"Yes, Your Highness."

"Good."

Celeste closed the canopy as Major Dent ran into his post and opened the thirty-foot *Omutx* metal gate. Celeste grabbed the stick and sped off into the snow filled night.

★ ★ ★ ★ ★

Captain Sartel was mad at himself. He needed to sober up fast, or he was going to slip up, which he almost did by bumping into one of the displays that honored Koroan Chast. He could see Celeste from his position in the temple but was grateful that he was about one hundred yards away so that she couldn't see him. He supposed that she didn't suspect that he was spying on her.

Just fifteen minutes before, Sartel and Dorange had made their way back into the palace courtyard and managed to sneak back into the temple room without Celeste even noticing. Dorange didn't want Celeste to suspect that he had suspected her being in the temple room at this hour, so he made his way up to his quarters via a secret passageway on the other side of the temple room that Sartel didn't even know was there.

Sartel found a well hidden spot underneath a display and began to record. He was proud of himself because he was able to get a clear recording of Celeste replacing her robe with a heavy coat, and hiding the robe behind the goddess of light statue. Sartel continued to record her until she was out of view.

When he couldn't see her anymore, he crawled out from underneath the display and stood. That's when he felt as if he was going to pass out. He stumbled and bumped into the display, caught himself on the small gold table, and caught the small gold statue of Koroan Chast before it crashed onto the marble floor.

And now, here Sartel stood at the large gold and glass doors waiting for the gate to shut as Celeste sped off. He shook his head. *What a time for a mission like this*, he thought.

As soon as the gate closed, he exited the temple room and ran to his own black *Chati*.

Once inside the craft, Sartel shook his head trying to get rid of the cobwebs from his night of drinking and maneuvered the *Chati* to the gate. He saw Major Dent step out of his guard post and hold his hand up. "Hurry up, you old fool," Sartel said under his breath.

Sartel stopped and opened his canopy.

"Captain Sartel. How was your meeting with General Gar?"

"It went well, Sir."

"Good," Dent said as he stepped closer to the *Chati*. "As a superior officer, I am curious as to why you and General Gar would have an important meeting at this hour?"

Sartel glared at Major Dent. "I am sorry, Sir. That's classified information. I can't tell you."

Dent looked disappointed. Sartel knew that Dent was going to keep pushing for information because he felt out of the loop. The only reason he was a major was because of his age. "Sorry, Sir. But, if you don't mind opening the gate, I have a mission that I've got to do."

Dent now looked more upset, opened his mouth, shut it, shook his head, and walked to the guard post.

Once the gate opened, Sartel took off at nearly full speed. He went in the direction he knew Celeste was going.

After Sartel exited *Chast's* city walls, he spotted the lights of Celeste's *Chati* going over a hill headed northwest toward *Talead.* Sartel quickly shut off his own lights, and pushed on the accelerator to narrow the gap.

★ ★ ★ ★ ★

Sartel kept shaking his head. The trip was starting to get boring, and his eyes were beginning to get heavy. Dorange would probably have him put to death if he failed in his mission. The thought alerted him a little more.

After traveling at a constant two hundred miles an hour for almost an hour and a half, he noticed that Celeste's *Chati* slowed down. He looked down at his satellite read out. *This isn't where the entrance to the base is located,* he thought to himself. *There's still another twenty miles left. Maybe there's another secret entrance?*

Sartel looked up and noticed that Celeste's *Chati* had come to a complete stop. He stopped his own about fifty yards away and turned off the engine.

Because of the snow storm, Sartel could barely see the *Chati* in front of him. However, Celeste had left the lights on as she exited the vehicle and walked to a small wooded area on her left.

"What is she doing?" Sartel said to himself.

Sartel watched until Celeste had disappeared into the woods and then he exited his own vehicle.

As he entered the woods, he pulled out his weapon and set it for stun. Just ten yards in front, he saw the shadowy figure of Celeste pass by. He froze.

Celeste continued to walk deeper into the trees. Sartel allowed her to get some distance before moving so that she wouldn't hear his footsteps in the snow. He was thankful, however, that the wind was howling to mask any noise he did make.

Sartel continued to follow as Celeste walked around a large tree surrounded by smaller ones. He stopped and waited for her to come out, but she didn't. *Maybe that's where the other secret entrance is located,* he thought.

Sartel slowly walked to the large tree with his weapon pointed forward. Once at the tree, he slowly peered around to where Celeste had disappeared. Nothing.

He walked into the small four foot by three foot clearing and kicked at the snow. *Where did she go?*

"Captain Sartel."

Sartel jumped at the sound of Celeste's voice and turned around. He tried to raise his weapon, but Celeste quickly hit his hand with the gun in her hand, causing it to fly out.

Celeste grabbed Sartel by the coat collar and pointed her gun upwards into the bottom of his chin. "I should have known that Gar would send one of his stooges to follow me."

"Wha . . . how did you know?"

Celeste turned her face from the stench of his breath. "Maybe, you were too drunk to notice, but you left your satellite tracking system on, you idiot."

Sartel cursed.

"I could see that someone was following me the moment I left *Chast*. So tell me, Sartel. Why is Dorange so desperate to accuse me of being the rebel spy?"

Sartel glared at Celeste and didn't answer.

Celeste shoved Sartel against the large tree and pushed her gun deeper into his chin. Sartel grimaced in pain.

"Answer me!"

"I don't have to answer to you. I'm just doing as I'm told."

Celeste gritted her teeth and quickly shot her right knee up into Sartel's groin.

Sartel screeched in pain and his knees buckled, but Celeste, as strong as she was, held him in place.

"You had better answer me, Captain, or you are going to be feeling worse than that in a few moments."

Sartel began to laugh.

Celeste back handed him with her gun. Blood began to trickle from Sartel's right eye.

"Take out your inhibitors!" Celeste demanded as she pointed her gun in between Sartel's eyes.

Sartel wiped the grin from his face and looked startled. "Wha . . . Why?"

Celeste smiled. "I know your telepathic abilities aren't any match for mine. So, if you are not going to tell me, I might as well probe your mind to get the information I need, and while I am at it . . . inflict a little pain."

"Okay . . . Okay. I'll tell."

"Good. Now, see what happens when you cooperate with me. But before you tell me, let's take a little walk back to my *Chati*.

★ ★ ★ ★ ★

When they reached Celeste's parked *Chati*, Celeste turned Sartel around and shoved him into the vehicle. His back hit the wing, causing him to grimace in pain. "Now talk," Celeste said.

Sartel rolled his eyes and sighed. "Fine," he said. "Dorange is convinced that you are the spy because you are always leaving at strange times and sometimes you won't come back for days."

Celeste shoved her gun into Sartel's rib cage. "Tell me something I do not know."

Sartel winced as Celeste pushed harder.

"You want to know something you don't know, huh?" questioned Sartel.

"Yes, you fool. What else does Dorange have up his sleeve?"

Sartel smiled and laughed.

"What is so funny?"

"Oh, Dorange has it in his mind that if he can convince your father that you are the spy, your father won't kill you. Rather . . . he will force you to marry Dorange. That way Dorange gets the two things that he lusts after the most, you and heir to the Gnol throne."

Celeste eased on the pressure with her gun. "So, that is what he has planned. Well he should know that I would kill him rather than marry him." Celeste then gave Sartel a questioning look.

"What?"

"Last night I was able to listen in on the conversation Dorange had with my father by placing a small listening device underneath the table. Tell me, Captain . . . Dorange mentioned that you failed to deliver the documents to my father that proved a secret rebel force murdered my sister. Why did you not deliver those documents?"

Sartel laughed again.

"What is so funny?"

"Dorange has both your father and you fooled. You know as well as I do that there was never a secret rebel force that killed your sister. Dorange was an abusive and overbearing husband. Your sister knew something that Dorange did not want your father to know. He killed her and made it look like an accident."

Celeste felt her face flush with anger. She jabbed her gun into Sartel's ribs again. "What did she know that Dorange did not want my father to know?"

"You think Dorange would tell me. That supposedly is only something he and your sister knew. But, I'll tell you what . . . Your Highness?"

"What?"

"Your father won't find out about this conversation either," Sartel said as an evil smile spread across his face.

Celeste looked down just as Sartel began to raise his right hand. She tried to dodge the death blow to her heart, but she didn't move fast enough. Sartel jammed a dagger deep into her left shoulder just below her clavicle. She screamed in pain and fell to her knees.

Celeste looked up at Sartel and raised her gun to shoot. Sartel quickly dove out of the way as the plasma flash from Celeste's gun hit the underside of her *Chati*. Sartel tried to scramble to his feet, but he slipped in the wet snow.

Celeste tried to fire again. However, Sartel noticed her taking aim and threw a side kick right into Celeste's injured shoulder. She dropped the gun, grabbed her bloodied shoulder, and fell onto her back, gritting her teeth in pain.

When Celeste opened her eyes, Sartel was standing over her with her gun pointed right between her eyes. "Nice try, Your Highness, but you can't beat me. It looks like you won't be able to warn your rebel friends about the attack."

Celeste grabbed the dagger in her shoulder and began to pull it out, but as she pulled the blade from her shoulder, Sartel placed his foot on the dagger and pressed down. She screamed in pain.

"Don't even think about it, Your Highness! Let's just use this dagger as motivation," Sartel said as he tossed the gun into the snow, straddled Celeste, and grabbed the handle of the dagger with his right hand. Celeste pierced her lips as the pain shot down her arm. She felt the movement of the razor sharp blade cutting away at her clavicle as Sartel moved the dagger slowly back and forth.

"Wha . . . aah . . . what are you doing?" Celeste asked, struggling to wiggle out from Sartel's straddle.

Sartel, still holding the dagger's handle, leaned in within a centimeter of Celeste's right ear and whispered, "Let's just say that I am going to enjoy this before I kill you." And then, he kissed her ear.

Celeste tried to resist, but she was weak and getting weaker by the minute as blood poured out of her shoulder.

Sartel continued to kiss Celeste on the face and then down her neck. Celeste was repulsed and nearly vomited. The more she struggled, the tighter Sartel's grip became on the dagger. Finally, after a few seconds of struggling, Celeste relaxed. She now knew what she had to do, but the question was – could she?

"That's my girl. Don't fight it."

Celeste ignored his comment and continued to force her body to relax, even though she felt her body shivering from the cold because of the blood loss. She needed all of the energy she could muster now. For years, her father had been teaching her how to do it, but she could only move small objects with her mind. She could never move anything bigger than a small boulder; especially another living Gnol.

Sartel was getting more aggressive. Nevertheless, Celeste forced her body to relax and pictured what she was going to do over and over in her mind. Finally, when she felt like she was ready, she took a deep breath and closed her eyes.

She slowly felt the weight of Sartel's body being lifted from her.

"What are you doing?" Sartel shrieked as he gripped the dagger and pushed it deeper into Celeste's shoulder. Celeste ignored the intolerable pain as she felt the point of the dagger penetrate her shoulder blade and exit her skin on the other side.

There is no pain. There is no pain. Lift him! Lift him! She thought.

Sartel was now an inch above Celeste; then two; then three.

Sartel, however, still had a hold of the dagger and tried to force his body back onto Celeste's, but she held him in place.

Celeste held her right hand up with the palm open and mentally pushed Sartel upwards. Sartel shot up another five feet into the air and pulled the dagger out with his ascent. The pain Celeste felt as the blade exited her shoulder caused her to lose focus. She opened her eyes and saw Sartel beginning to fall back onto the top of her. His eyes were wild with fear.

Quickly, Celeste pulled her knees to her chest with her feet ready to catch Sartel. Celeste caught him in the abdomen and smelled the stink of his breath as air rushed out from the blow. She shot her legs forward and sent Sartel hurling through and air. Celeste heard the crack of his back when he hit the wing of her *Chati*.

Celeste rolled over onto her stomach. She could hardly hold back the tears because of the pain. Staggering to her feet, she realized she had made a mistake by turning her back on Sartel. She quickly turned around and saw

Sartel charging at her with the dagger raised. She quickly raised her right arm and extended her hand and fingers.

Sartel reached out and tried to grab Celeste's arm, but he was too late. Celeste had regained her focus and lifted him to about ten feet in the air. Sartel wasn't scared this time, however. He instinctively flipped the dagger around, catching the point of the blade between his thumb and index finger and threw it toward Celeste's chest.

There wasn't enough time for Celeste to move out of the way. So, paying no heed to the throbbing pain in her left shoulder, she painfully and quickly raised her left arm, while still holding Sartel in place, and mentally caught the dagger. The dagger stopped with the point of the dagger a centimeter into her thick black coat. With a push of her left hand, she mentally withdrew the dagger from her coat, flipped it around, and sent it speeding through the snow filled air toward the center of Sartel's chest.

Sartel's face was no longer angry. It was now filled with terror as he saw his imminent death fast approaching. He tried to move, twisting his body, circling his legs, and moving his arms frantically in a swimming motion. But his efforts were useless. Celeste held him in place until the dagger penetrated his chest and ripped through his back by the sheer velocity she projected it.

With a downward thrust of her arm, Celeste sent Sartel crashing to the ground. She heard the crack of his kneecap as his knee hit a small boulder below.

Celeste dropped to her knees in the snow. Her wound and mental concentration on moving Sartel had exhausted her beyond consciousness. She looked up and noticed that her vision was blurry. Just before her eyes shut and her head hit the cold, wet snow, she thought she saw Sartel's body move.

CHAPTER 11

April 7, 2042 – Just outside of Chast

The warmth of the sun shining on Celeste's head woke her. She painfully forced herself up to her knees and looked at her left shoulder. Her shoulder had stopped bleeding; but from the red snow surrounding her body, she knew that she had lost a lot of blood. She didn't dare move her arm and slowly forced herself to stand. She walked forward about fifteen feet to where she had thrown Sartel's body down.

Sartel wasn't there, but Celeste could tell that he had lost a lot of blood as well because of the blood-soaked snow. Celeste was in too much pain to care where Sartel was. She knew, however, that he wouldn't have survived very long with the wound that she inflicted upon him.

Celeste stumbled to her *Chati*. She opened the canopy and nearly burst into tears from pain as she climbed into the cockpit. She pushed the ignition button. The hover craft rumbled for a few seconds and quit. She pushed the button again – again the same result. The third time she pushed the button, there was nothing.

Frustrated, she remembered what happened just after Sartel had stabbed her. She had fired a shot at him and missed, hitting the underside of her vehicle. She managed to climb out of the cockpit and looked underneath her *Chati*. The snow had melted underneath, and she figured out why. Looking at the underside of the *Chati*, she noticed about a five inch diameter hole. She could see all the way to the cockpit. Surrounding the hole were damaged wires and jagged pieces of metal of what used to be the hover engine module. She moved her eyes to the right and saw that a piece of metal had penetrated the fuel tank. That was why the snow had melted underneath the *Chati*. All of the fuel had leaked out.

She crawled out from underneath her vehicle, slowly stood, and scanned her surroundings. To her right was a snow-covered hill. In front of her was the wooded area where she surprised Sartel. And to her left, she saw Sartel's *Chati* and his lifeless body lying next to it.

Celeste stumbled her way to Sartel's vehicle with the hopes of taking his to warn Adrian. However, her hope turned into despair when she saw what was clenched in Sartel's lifeless hand. He must have known that Celeste was still alive, crawled to his own *Chati*, and ripped out the starter module.

She shook her head and sighed. Without tools, there was no way she could fix the vehicle.

Glancing down at her timekeeper, she noticed that it was just after noon. She was about twenty miles away from the rebel base, injured, and almost eighteen hours away from a surprise attack that would certainly kill or enslave the people she truly cared about.

★ ★ ★ ★ ★

April 8, 2042 – Underground Rebel Base

Jake was exhausted. He had been training new Terrestrian pilots the entire day. Most of them had never flown before let alone operated a mechanized vehicle. Nevertheless, he was amazed at their intuition and ability to fly. Jake was especially impressed with his younger brother, Bantyr. Bantyr had learned how to fly from their father, but he impressed Jake even more because of his instincts and ability to fly without depending on the computer system.

Jake yawned and looked at the clock on the wall in his quarters, 12:30 a.m. He desperately wanted to crawl into bed, but he couldn't because his father would arrive shortly. Jake stretched his body onto his bed and decided that he would get a little shut eye before his dad arrived.

He was about to drift into a deep sleep when the buzzer at his door sounded. "Come in," he said as he quickly sat up and rubbed his eyes.

Adrian walked through the door, and it slid shut behind him. "Oh . . . sorry, Jake. . . . I didn't mean to wake you."

"No, Dad . . . I just thought that I'd get a little sleep before you arrived."

"It's okay. I can come back in the morning, and we can talk."

Jake stood up and pulled the chair that was across the room closer to his bed. "No, Dad. Stay. Please. Since our last discussion, we haven't had a lot of time to talk."

Adrian smiled. He walked to the chair, sat down, and leaned forward smiling at Jake. "So how did the training go today?" he asked.

"It went great. These Terrestrians are amazing, Dad. I haven't seen a group of people work so well together."

"Yeah, they are amazing. How did Bantyr do?"

"I think Bantyr takes after you. His instincts are amazing. When I tested each pilot's skills on manual control without the use of the computer, he was the best, hands down."

Adrian smiled obviously proud of his youngest son. "From the sounds of it . . . it sounds as if he takes after you."

Jake gave his father a questioning look. "How do you know?"

"I talked with Skip about five hours ago just before he left for the temple ruins with his team. He told me about how you outran two Gnol ships when you got here. From what he told me, it sounds pretty impressive. Gnols are skilled pilots and very intelligent. I've only been in an aerial battle once with them about five years ago. They destroyed my ship and wiped out my squadron of twenty ships. Only three of us pilots survived."

"Wow," said Jake, feeling a little proud of his accomplishment. "How many Gnol ships were there?"

"Four," Adrian said in a whisper.

Jake was stunned. He didn't know what to say. If these Gnols were as skilled as his father said they were, then how was he able to out fly two of them?

Adrian sat back in the chair. "So, are they battle ready?"

"Who?"

"Your squadron, of course."

"Oh yeah. I don't think so. Even though they impressed me, I don't think they're ready for a mission, especially with what you just told me about the Gnols' ability to fly."

"Well, you better have them ready in three days."

Jake looked at his father and shook his head. "I don't know, Dad? What's in three days?"

"In three days, I plan to have you lead an attack on the Gnol town of *Ciminae*."

Jake stood, walked to his sink, and splashed cold water on his face. "I don't know, Dad. I just don't think they're ready. Besides, why are you in such a hurry to attack?"

Adrian followed Jake with his eyes as Jake walked slowly back to his bed. He looked exhausted. "Because the city of *Ciminae* is where the Gnols produce their war ships, battle cruisers, short range attack ships, and reconnaissance ships. If we can cripple their manufacturing, we can begin to plan for more offensives."

Jake shook his head trying to fight sleep.

Adrian frowned a little. "I'll let you get some sleep, Son. I'll talk to you in the morning." Adrian stood up and began to walk to the door, but Jake grabbed his arm.

"Don't go."

Adrian turned and looked at Jake. "You're exhausted and need some rest. It's okay. I'll talk with you in the morning."

Jake, still holding his dad's arm, looked his father in the eyes. "You know, Dad, if I would have known that all you wanted to talk about was how my squadron was doing and what mission you have planned, I would have gone to sleep hours ago."

Adrian returned to his chair and asked, "What do you mean?"

Jake sighed. "I mean . . . uh . . . well, we didn't quite finish the discussion we had before. . . . You know . . . about you being a prophet or something like that on this world?"

Adrian smiled at his son. "Ah yes, we didn't . . . did we?"

Jake shook his head.

Adrian continued. "I didn't want to finish because I wanted what I told you before to sink in a little. I know from what you told me about your life that you lost your testimony. Sometimes people that lose their testimony need to be brought back into the fold slowly. If you put too much pressure on them, then you may just lose them forever.

"The Gospel is very simple. Yet, at the same time, it can be very confusing if your heart isn't in the right place."

Jake listened intently to his father. With everything he had experienced since crash landing on *Terrest*, he was beginning to understand. "I think I am beginning to understand, Dad. After you left my room the other night, I began studying the scriptures. I found a lot of references to other worlds and how God has created many worlds. I even prayed about it."

"And?" questioned Adrian.

Jake let a small smile spread across his face. He knew his father wanted so badly for him to gain his testimony again. "Well, Dad . . . I know that the scriptures are true. And . . . I think I am beginning to build a testimony again. But . . ."

"But what, Son?" Adrian said as he scooted his chair a little closer to Jake.

Jake looked down at the floor, searching for the words. When he looked back at his father, tears were streaming down his face. "But . . . Well . . . Why would the Lord take you away from me when I was only five. I mean . . . I have been so angry at him for years."

Adrian placed his hands on Jake's hand. "I know, Son . . . I can't imagine the pain you must have gone through all of those years, not knowing what had happened to me."

Jake looked down and nodded.

Adrian sighed and said, "Jake, we never know what the Lord has in store for us. When I was nineteen years old, I wanted so badly to go on a mission. But the Air Force Academy would not keep a scholarship for me if I left. So I prayed about it, and I felt strongly that I should stay at the Air Force Academy and become a pilot. The Holy Ghost communicated to me so clearly that the Lord had a greater work for me to do.

"Of course, this work He has given me far exceeded anything I could even imagine. I thought maybe he would make me a bishop or mission president or something, not the military and spiritual leader of our brothers and sisters on another world."

Jake allowed himself a small laugh. "Yeah, and who would have thought that I would be here too."

Adrian smiled and placed his left hand on his son's right shoulder. "Jake, I want you to know that not a day went by that I didn't think about you. My heart was broken. I missed you terribly. The guilt I felt every day for leaving you on the Mars mission was at times unbearable. The only way I made it through each day was knowing that we would one day be reunited."

More tears streamed down Jake's face. He needed to hear his father say these words. Yes, it was true he was mad at God for his father's disappearance, but he was also bitter with his dad for leaving.

Adrian continued. "Jake . . . please don't be angry with your Father in Heaven for leading me to *Terrest* and away from you. Be grateful because He has led you safely here to be reunited with me, your new family, and new friends."

Suddenly it hit Jake like a lightning bolt. He had never thought of it in that way before. He had been so concerned about his own feelings that he failed to realize the great blessing the Lord had provided him with. He had a family again and new friends. And what intrigued him the most was Celeste. Why did he feel such a connection when, in his own mind, he couldn't possibly fathom being with a woman from another planet, especially one with so many abilities and powers.

Jake didn't realize he was smiling when he opened his mouth and was about to speak.

Adrian beat him to what he was thinking. "You're thinking about Celeste aren't you?"

"H . . . How did you know?"

"Son, ever since you met Celeste, anyone can tell that she is all you think about."

Jake tried to hide the shy smile that spread across his face, but he couldn't. "Um . . . I . . . don't know what to think. She is so beautiful. I've had girlfriends but never have I had a woman on my mind so much. But . . . "

Jake stopped, stood up, and began to pace around his room.

"But what, Son?" Adrian asked.

Jake stopped pacing and looked at his father. "But how can I be with a Gnol? How do the Gnols fit into the picture of other worlds that God has created? Aren't God's children on Earth and other worlds created in his image?"

Adrian nodded. "Yes, we are. But don't you think God would have the same if not more of the abilities as the Gnols?"

"So, you're telling me the Gnols are gods," Jake said.

"No, I'm not saying that. . . . Son, sit down."

Jake sat on his bed, and Adrian stood. He turned and looked at his son.

"Jake, I had those same questions when the Gnols first attacked *Terrest*. I asked the Lord so many times how the Gnols fit into God's plan. After all, the Gnols have abilities, powers, and strength so much greater than any of

God's other children. So, logically, I wondered if the Gnols were even his children at all.

"I think I asked each day for nearly a year after the initial attacks. Yet, there was no answer. Finally, one day I knelt down to pray. Before I even got the words out of my mouth, a vision was opened up to me."

Jake felt his mouth drop. His mind was finding it hard to believe that his own dad would be a prophet of God on another world. He knew his father's weaknesses and he always imagined a prophet being perfect.

Adrian continued. "The vision took me to another world thousands of years ago. An angel was with me. In fact, the angel revealed to me that these people were so righteous and willing to obey the Lord's commandments that the Lord could not withhold any blessing from them, including God Himself walking and talking amongst them."

Jake's face quickly turned from a look of shock to a look of confusion. "Wa . . . Wait a minute. God lived with the Gnols . . . but . . . how can that be? Most Gnols seem to be evil."

Adrian quickly opened the scriptures he had brought in with him. "Here it is," he said as he gave the scriptures to Jake. "Read *Moses*, chapter 1, verse 11."

Jake looked at the verse and commenced to read:

> *"But now mine own eyes have beheld God; but not my*
> *natural, but my spiritual eyes, for my natural eyes could not*
> *have beheld; for I should have withered and died in his*
> *presence; but his glory was upon me; and I beheld his face,*
> *for I was transfigured before him."*

After reading the verse, Jake looked up with a look that told Adrian his son was more confused than ever.

Adrian smiled and said, "Think about it, Son. Since the Gnols were in God's presence, they had to be changed."

"You mean transfigured," replied Jake.

"Yes, transfigured. The angel showed me that the Gnols were changed. Their bodies were changed with more strength to withstand the presence of the Lord. Their minds were open to one another, and they could move objects just by pure thought."

Jake shook his head. "Well then if the Gnols were blessed by God, how come they are here on *Terrest* and have killed and enslaved most of the Terrestrian people?"

Adrian sat next to his son. "The angel also revealed to me that the Gnols eventually forgot about the Lord. They had become so prideful and arrogant in their abilities that they began to use them against each other. Rather than the Lord taking their abilities away, they became a curse.

"After a few generations, the Gnols lost most of the technology they had created and began to live in warlike tribes. The Gnol people weren't able to advance because they could read each other's thoughts and use those thoughts against each other. Eventually, the lord withdrew his presence and allowed nature to destroy *Gnolom*. But somehow the Gnols were able to escape their dying world."

Jake was captivated. Why would a people so blessed by the Lord turn away from him? But his question was quickly answered as he thought back to *The Book of Mormon* and how the blessed civilizations of the Nephites and Lamanites were destroyed because they turned away from the Lord. "Did the angel reveal how the Gnols were able to develop the technology again to leave *Gnolom*?"

Adrian shook his head. "The angel did not reveal that information to me. I asked, but he said that I needed to discover that on my own. Once I did, that information would help us defeat the Gnols and lead some of them back to the Gospel."

Jake smiled at his dad. He could see the mantle his father carried and the burden that went with it. "So, have you discovered that information yet?"

Adrian shook his head as if in frustration. "No, not yet. But . . ." Adrian paused as he sat next to his son.

"But what, Dad?"

Adrian sighed. "I don't know, Jake. For some reason, I feel responsible for the Gnols being here."

"Dad, how could you possibly be responsible for them being here? You had no idea that the Gnols even existed when you first arrived on *Terrest*."

"I know, Son. It's just—"

Adrian's communicator beeped before he could finish his sentence. He reached down, pulled the communicator from his belt and flipped it open. "This is General Palmer."

"Adrian, this is Sean. We have an emergency."

"What is it, Sean?"

"Do you remember those emergency distress beacons I gave to Celeste and her people to use if they were ever in danger?"

"Yes."

"Well, Celeste's beacon has been activated about five miles Southeast of the base."

"Five miles southeast? I thought she was in *Chasf*?"

"Me too, but that's where her signal is originating from."

"Okay, Sean. Contact Doc and have him meet me and Jake in the hangar."

"You got it."

Adrian flipped his communicator shut, looked at Jake, and the two ran out of the room together.

★ ★ ★ ★ ★

Five minutes later, Doc came running into the vehicle wing of the underground base. He was pulling on his black jacket, with his medical supply bag in his left hand. "What's going on, Adrian? I was having a great dream about two gorgeous Polynesian women from Hawaii, and then I get a call from Sean. He just told me to meet you here. Well, here I am. What's going on?"

Adrian ignored Doc's obvious aggravation about being awakened from his dream. "Jake, you drive. Doc, I'll prep you with details on our way. We've got to go now!"

"Hold on," said Doc still trying to pull his jacket over his massive frame.

Once the three men were inside the hover vehicle, Jake in the center driver's seat and the other two men in the seats behind Jake, he slowly maneuvered the craft out of the vehicle wing's bay doors that opened two hundred yards above into the star filled night of *Terrest*.

The vehicle was similar to the one that Jake had taken from the two Gnols he and Skip had encountered when they first crashed on *Terrest*. This one had some differences, however. This hover vehicle had the capability to camouflage itself according to the time of day. Jake reached down to his control panel and pressed the night camouflage button. The vehicle morphed from a pure white snow color, for which it had been used previously, to a color black as midnight.

"So, what's going on?" Doc asked, just as Jake sped off toward Celeste's supposed position.

"Celeste is in trouble," Adrian said.

"What kind of trouble?"

"Do you remember those distress beacons that Sean gave to Celeste and her people to use if they were ever in trouble?"

"Yeah."

"Celeste activated hers about twenty minutes ago. She hasn't moved from her location, so I'm assuming that she is either injured or . . ." Adrian paused and looked at Jake just as Jake glanced back at him, ". . . or she's dead."

Doc grabbed his medical bag and quickly began making preparations for what they would find.

Adrian grabbed Jake's shoulder. "Is the satellite readout clear?"

"Yeah, we're about two miles away from Celeste's beacon . . . wait a minute."

"What?" asked Adrian, as he glanced at the monitor.

Jake pointed to just above Celeste's location. "It looks like we're going to have some company."

Adrian looked a little closer at the monitor. "It looks like a squadron of about twenty ground assault vehicles, fifty *Chaties*, and one-hundred aircraft."

"How long before they reach Celeste's position?" Doc asked.

"I'm guessing another ten minutes. We've got to act fast," Adrian replied.

"Dad, how many people do those ground assault vehicles carry?" Jake asked, slowing down as they neared Celeste's position.

"They carry about fifty soldiers each . . ." Adrian stopped and shot a look directly at Doc, ". . . You don't think they . . ."

Doc nodded his head. "Why else would they bring a battalion of that many soldiers to our position?"

Adrian quickly grabbed his communicator and flipped it open. "Sean, this is Adrian!"

"You're clear, General," Sean replied.

"Code red! I repeat! Code red! Get three pilots to the civilian shuttles! Load them up with as many civilians as they will hold! Women and children first! Warn Scott and Petey at base two to be prepared for the shuttles. Get each team to their battle stations now!"

Sean hesitated. "Why? What's going on, Adrian?"

"Don't ask questions! Just do as you're ordered, General! You're in charge until I get back. Also, warn Skip's team at the temple ruins that the base is going to be under attack and not to return."

Adrian heard Sean curse. "Yes, General."

"I'll notify you as soon as we have Celeste and are prepared to return to base." Adrian flipped his communicator shut and looked at Doc who was frantically putting together a plasma I.V.

"Dad . . . look," Jake said, pointing directly ahead.

Adrian looked and saw what the vehicle's lights had rested upon. About twenty feet ahead, Celeste's body lay motionless. She was sitting upright, resting against a large boulder. She looked dead.

Jake stopped the vehicle and was the first one to Celeste while Adrian and Doc grabbed the stretcher from the rear of the craft. Jake skidded to a halt and knelt down next to Celeste. She was unconscious and covered in blood. Jake could see the wound that caused her blood loss.

Celeste opened her eyes and looked at Jake just as Doc and Adrian arrived with the medical supplies and stretcher. She forced a smile, reached up, and slid the back of her hand along Jake's cheek. "Well . . ." She coughed, ". . . How are you, handsome?"

Jake returned her smile and moved out of the way, so Doc could get to work.

"She's lost too much blood," Doc said. "She's going to need a blood transfusion when we get back to base."

While the three men placed Celeste onto the stretcher, she flickered in and out of consciousness. They loaded Celeste into the back of the vehicle. Doc crawled in and began to monitor her vital signs. Jake and Adrian ran to the other side of the vehicle and were about to climb in. "Shh . . . Dad. Listen," Jake said.

Adrian stopped just as he was about to open his door. Sure enough he heard the rumble of engines in the distance. Both of the men looked straight ahead and saw the lights of a massive number of attack vehicles making their way over a hill. Jake heard what sounded like a small explosion emit from the massive army that was about to overtake them, and then . . . an explosion.

The blast didn't damage the hover craft, but it threw Jake and Adrian back about seventeen feet from where they stood. After Adrian regained his wind, he rolled over and saw that Jake was alright. Both men jumped to their feet and sprinted toward the hover craft. Jake jumped into the passenger seat behind his father who had secured himself into the driver's seat.

"Now, you get to see your old man in action," Adrian said as he fired up the craft and sped off. "Doc, do you have Celeste and yourself buckled in!"

"Yes!"

"Good, because it's going to be a bumpy ride!" Adrian yelled as he sped off back to the base.

Jake glanced behind and saw that four small lights had broken off from the large group of attack vehicles. "Dad, I think we've got company."

Adrian looked at his rear view screen and saw what he was dealing with. "Attack *Chaties*. They're faster than this huge thing, but they don't have as much shielding."

"How long before they catch up to us!" Doc yelled.

"I'd say about another minute or two."

"That's not enough time to get back to base, Adrian."

"I know that, Doc," Adrian said as he put his headset on. "General Gibson. Come in, Sean."

"Go, General."

"We have Celeste and are on our way back. E.T.A. three minutes."

"Got it. I'll open the bay doors precisely at your arrival."

"Also, get four pilots to four attack *Chaties* and send them our way. We've got some unwelcome guests coming to stop us."

"Yes, General. Gibson out."

Jake continued to watch the *Chaties* that were narrowing the gap. He heard Celeste say something and looked down at her. Celeste was looking at Jake and said something he couldn't understand. He leaned down over the seat to where his face was within a few inches of hers. "My father . . . my father . . ." Celeste groaned in pain, ". . . he knows where the base is."

★ ★ ★ ★ ★

Skip was too excited to sleep. He and his team had arrived at the temple ruins almost four hours ago and had already made surprising discoveries; discoveries that he never would have imagined even in his wildest dreams.

From the moment they had begun to decipher the writings on the walls of the temple, they had found out that the writings followed the chronology of *Terrest*. The writings that had shocked Skip the most, however, were the first ones he deciphered on the left wall of the narrow hallway just inside the entrance. In *Tilicah*, it read:

"*Os lza najossosj Jud xmailad lza zaiwas isd Terresta.*"

In English, the writing read:

"*In the beginning, God created the heavens and Terresta.*"

Skip was astonished. The only word that didn't translate was *Terresta*, which Skip presumed to mean the planet of *Terrest*. Was it possible that the writings that he was deciphering within this temple on another planet were, in fact, the *Bible* of *Terrest*?

And that wasn't the only discovery. Skip had made his way half way down the narrow hallway and discovered that many of the writings were similar to the Holy Bible. The only differences were the names and places. He had just made another discovery that the *Tilicah* tribe were the chosen people of the God of *Terrest*, much like the tribes of Israel being the chosen people of God on Earth, when his communicator beeped.

Skip put down the scriptures he had borrowed from Jake. He grabbed his communicator and flipped it open. "This is Colonel Hendricks."

"Skip, this is General Gibson. Is everything alright there?"

Skip looked around. "Yeah, everything's fine. Why?"

There was a pause. Then, Skip heard Sean sigh. "Good. Adrian, Jake, and Doc had to go and rescue Celeste. She's been injured."

"Is she okay?"

"She's still alive. But I have more bad news. Within minutes, the base is going to be under attack by Gnol forces."

Skip jumped to his feet. "Do you need us to return to base?"

"Negative, Colonel. Your orders are to stay put until further notice. We are evacuating as many civilians as we can to the second base. If you need to reach us, you can send a message through the encrypted codes I gave you for the communicators."

"Yes, General. Contact me as soon as you can."

"I will, Skip. General Gibson out."

Skip slowly closed his communicator. How could he stand by and let his friends fight a more powerful enemy, while he fulfilled his curiosities? He had to do something.

Skip slowly bent down and opened his communicator again. "Captain Morasea."

"Yes, Colonel."

"You and your men come back into the temple and meet me in the temple room with the fountain in five minutes. We have an emergency."

"Yes, Sir."

Skip flipped his communicator shut and sprinted to the temple room with the fountain; the same room he and Jake slept in their first night on *Terrest*. Once inside the room, he awoke both Ariauna and Jaskead.

Jaskead, who had been sleeping on the floor with just a thin blanket for cover, rolled over groggily. "Wha . . . What is it my young friend."

Skip with fear in his voice said, "Our friends are in trouble."

★ ★ ★ ★ ★

Adrian quickly banked the hover craft to the right as he saw one of the Gnol *Chaties* fire a plasma bolt in his direction. He had managed to dodge the blast, but Jake was thrown to the left of the vehicle and cracked the back of his head against the window. "You better get buckled in, Son. Like I said before, this is going to be a bumpy ride."

Jake rubbed the bump that was beginning to form on the back of his head and hurriedly buckled himself in. He glanced back and noticed that two black *Chaties* were within ten feet of the vehicle. The other two weren't far behind. One of the *Chaties* fired. "Look out!" yelled Jake.

But it was too late. The blast hit the right end of the vehicle. Adrian lost control for a moment and almost struck a large pine tree. He managed to veer to his left. The right side of the vehicle scraped along the bark of the tree.

"Hey, can't you hold it together up there!" Doc yelled.

"Doin' the best I can, big guy," Adrian replied. "Sean, where are those *Chaties* that I ordered you to send out?"

"They should be at your position now, General. We only had two pilots that were ready to send out immediately."

"Well, I don't see them. Where are they?"

"We're here, Dad."

Adrian looked ahead into the darkness and saw two lights approaching. "Bantyr. Is that you?"

"Yes, and Captain Shaonal . . . Dad . . . I have a lock on one of the Gnols. On my mark, bank to your right."

"You got it."

"Now!"

Adrian banked to his right just as Bantyr fired two hot red flashes of plasma. The bolts nailed the Gnol *Chati* that was closest to Adrian's tail, and it exploded into a brilliant orange fireball.

Adrian looked left and then right. He saw the two red *Chaties* dart by. He noticed that two of the three remaining Gnol *Chaties* veered off and chased the two rebels. The other Gnol *Chati* was closing the gap and maneuvering for a position to fire. "Sean, we're almost to the doors. When I tell y—"

"No!"

Adrian stopped and looked at his rearview monitor and caught a glimpse of one of the red *Chati's* wings clip a tree, which sent it hurling out of control and crashing into a small clearing. "Bantyr! What happened?"

"General, this is Captain Shaonal. Bantyr is down. . . . I repeat. . . . Bantyr is down."

"Adrian, you're almost on top of the base. I'm opening the bay doors," said Sean.

Adrian was in a trance. He had heard Sean but couldn't register what he had said. He couldn't bear the thought of losing Bantyr.

"General! I repeat! I am opening the bay doors now!"

Adrian felt a slap on his shoulder.

"Dad!" Jake yelled.

Adrian shook his head and snapped out of his despair. He looked up and saw the bay doors beginning to open. The artificial trees, rock, and soil that had been placed on top of the doors as a camouflage split in two. Adrian glanced at the rear view monitor to check where the remaining Gnol *Chati* was.

The *Chati* fired and veered off avoiding a crash with the bay doors. Adrian frantically looked up and noticed that he would not be able to bank left or right, or he would slam into the bay doors. He took a direct hit in the backside of the hover vehicle. Because of the superior shielding of the larger hover craft, the plasma blast didn't penetrate, but the force of it threw the vehicle into the left bay door.

Adrian tried to regain control, but the force of the collision with the bay door flipped the hover craft upside down. It began its two hundred yard descent down to the floor of the vehicle/aircraft wing of the base.

Adrian could barely move his arm to grab the controls and flip the vehicle back over. He heard Celeste scream in pain and Doc curse. Finally, after what seemed like an hour of fighting with the controls, he was able to regain control again. But, it was too late. He managed to flip the large hover craft over just enough to have it impact the floor of the base on its right side.

Adrian felt the impact and his shoulder harness snap. His body hurled into the right side of the vehicle, with is shoulder hitting first, then his head, and then darkness.

CHAPTER 12

April 8, 2042 – Temple Ruins outside of Talead

Skip, Jaskead, and Ariauna sat in the fountain room of the temple, waiting for Captain Morasea and Lieutenants Ishae and Tapal to come in from the guard post outside of the temple. The room was well lit from the lights they had brought with them from the base. As Skip scanned the room, he noticed the details of all of the writings he couldn't wait to decipher. But, he felt guilty for being somewhat safe in the temple while his friends were about to be under attack.

Skip heard voices and saw the three soldiers that were in charge of guarding his research enter the room. Captain Morasea was the first to enter. He was a tall Terrestrian, just over six feet with black, short hair that was covered with the black, battle helmet he had on his head. Captain Morasea looked to be barely over the age of twenty. He saluted Skip and sat down on the bench on the other side of the fountain.

Lieutenants Ishae and Tapal soon followed. Both men looked to be in their late teens and dressed in the same black fatigues and battle helmet that the captain was wearing.

Skip liked all three men. They were loyal and subordinate to every order Skip gave them, even though Skip felt more like a civilian than a colonel in the Terrestrian army.

Captain Morasea was the first to speak. "So, Colonel . . . what's the emergency?"

"I just received word that the base will be under attack soon by the Gnols."

The three guards looked at one another. Lieutenant Tapal was about to speak, but Ariauna beat him to it.

"You mean the Gnols know where the base is?"

Skip looked at Ariauna. She still looked beautiful even after sleeping. "Yes," he said. "Apparently, they found it and are going to be on top of it within minutes."

"What were you ordered to do, Colonel?" the captain asked.

"General Gibson told us that our orders were to stay put and to continue our research. They will notify us when they reach *Base 2*."

"That's if they reach the second base," said Lieutenant Tapal.

Captain Morasea shot Tapal a look. "Where's your faith, Lieutenant? General Palmer is a great strategist. If anyone can defend the base, he can."

Tapal looked shocked that Morasea would reply like he did and said, "I know it's just tha—"

"Don't argue with me, Lieutenant!"

Skip raised his hand to stop the two from getting into an argument. As he lowered his hand, he noticed Tapal give Morasea a dirty look. "Hold on guys. There's no need to get into an argument about it. Frankly, Captain, I agree a little with the Lieutenant." Skip noticed that Morasea looked disappointed.

"I know General Palmer is a strong leader, but I have also seen these Gnols in action. . . ." Skip paused, stood, and paced back and forth.

Jaskead saw the indecision on Skip's face. "Forgive me for interrupting, my young friend, but what are you proposing to do?"

Skip turned around and looked at Jaskead, a man who now seemed more like a father. "I don't know. I know that we were ordered to stay here, but . . ."

"But what?" Ariauna asked.

"But . . . I feel guilty for working on this project while our friends are in trouble. I think we should go and help."

Captain Morasea looked surprised. "But, Sir . . . your orders were to stay here until notified."

"I know, but I feel like the general gave this project to me because he knew how curious I was about the temple."

Ariauna, seeing the indecision on Skip's face, stood and walked toward him. She placed both of her hands on his shoulders. "Skip, this isn't just some selfish research project. For centuries, the truth about the *Tilicah* tribe's religion has been lost. And you heard it directly from the general's mouth. He believes that within these walls is the key that will defeat the Gnols."

Skip smiled shyly at Ariauna. The more he got to know her the more he liked her. "I know, but I can't help but feel like we're abandoning them."

"Nonsense," Jaskead said. "You have been put in charge of a very special mission. A mission the general knew you were capable of accomplishing because of your experience and skills. So, my young friend, think of it like this. You may not be on the front lines of the actual physical battle to defeat the Gnols, but on the front lines of the spiritual battle to find the key that will finally free our planet from their tyranny."

Skip smiled at Jaskead. "You're right, Jaskead." He turned and looked at the three guards. "Captain, you and your men resume your posts outside of the temple. Notify us immediately if you suspect any Gnol activity."

Captain Morasea and his men stood and saluted. "Yes, Sir," Morasea said, and the three men left the room.

Skip looked at Jaskead. "You're right, Jaskead. I have a feeling there is something in here that will help us defeat the Gnols. I don't know what it is, but it's in here. And from what I've found already, there are so many similarities to the Christian religions on Earth."

Jaskead patted his hand on the stone bench he sat on and motioned for Skip to sit beside him. "So, my young friend, tell us what you have discovered so far."

★ ★ ★ ★ ★

Bantyr slowly opened his eyes. He noticed that outside of his cockpit dawn was fast approaching. He grabbed his head, which felt as if a hundred horses had trampled over it. Slowly pulling his hand away, he noticed blood and felt a large gash across his forehead. He winced in pain and kicked his canopy open.

As he crawled out, he felt two hands grab him from under his armpits and yank him out of the mangled *Chati*. Whoever grabbed him threw him about twelve feet to the left and into a tree. His head slammed against the bark, and he felt the skin of his scalp give way. He looked up and saw two

Gnols, dressed in black battle suits and black battle helmets with tinted visors covering their eyes, approaching.

Bantyr quickly tried to grab his sidearm, but it was kicked away by the first Gnol to reach him. The Gnol raised his rifle, swung down hard, and caught Bantyr on the right jaw with its butt. Bantyr fell to his left and spit blood and a tooth into the wet, melting snow.

"Knock it off," said the second Gnol. "General Gar will want to question this one."

Bantyr tried to scramble away, but the Gnols' strength was too much. They grabbed Bantyr under each arm and dragged Bantyr along the snowy, muddy ground.

A few moments later, the two Gnols dropped Bantyr at the feet of another Gnol. Bantyr looked up and saw that the Gnol was dressed in the same black fatigues and battle helmet. However, this Gnol had two gold stars on each shoulder and a long black braid extending out of the back of his helmet. Behind the Gnol was a massive army of Gnols, assault vehicles, *Chaties*, and aircraft.

The Gnol pulled his helmet off, reached down, and grabbed Bantyr by the collar of his red flight suit. Bantyr was within an inch of the Gnol's goateed face and stinking breath when the Gnol spoke. "So, we have another one do we?"

Another one. Who else do they have? Bantyr thought.

Bantyr let his eyes scan to his left and his right. On his right, he saw Captain Shaonal on his knees in front of another Gnol who had his plasma rifle pointed directly between his eyes. Bantyr noticed that Shaonal had his hands tied behind his back and looked to have been beaten severely.

The Gnol holding Bantyr pushed Bantyr away. Bantyr could barely stand, feeling the effects of his head wounds and the blow to his face.

"Do you know who I am?" said the Gnol with the goatee.

Bantyr didn't answer. He just put his chin to his chest and looked down. His father had taught him not to speak if he was ever captured.

The Gnol laughed and began to walk around Bantyr. Bantyr still held his head in the same position.

"Well if you won't tell me, I'll tell you who I am. I am Dorange Gar. Commander and General of the Gnol armed forces. I answer only to our lord and savior Koroan Chast."

Bantyr still did not speak. He glanced at Shaonal who slowly glanced back and nodded groggily. Suddenly, Bantyr felt a blow to his right kidney. He fell to his knees and tried to regain his breath.

Dorange walked back to face Bantyr, grabbed him by his left ear, and pulled him up. "Is it my mistake, or isn't it a common courtesy that when someone has introduced himself, the other should introduce himself as well."

Bantyr continued to stay silent and kept his face down.

Dorange continued. "Oh well, there's no need to introduce yourself. I can see your name on your flight suit."

Bantyr stole a quick glance at Dorange and noticed that he looked surprised as he read Bantyr's name.

"Captain Bantyr Palmer. So, . . . you must be related to the famous rebel leader, Adrian Palmer?"

Bantyr still did not answer.

"Answer me!" Dorange yelled as he threw a right hook into Bantyr's already swollen face.

Bantyr managed to maintain his balance. There was no way he was going to give any information to this Gnol scum.

"Well, if I can't beat any information out of you, perhaps you will be persuaded to talk some other way?" Dorange looked at the Gnol who held the rifle to Captain Shaonal's head. "Commander, when I count to five . . . kill Captain Palmer's friend."

The Gnol holding the plasma rifle gave Dorange an evil smile and replied, "Yes, General."

Bantyr looked up, opened his mouth, and then closed it again. He noticed that Shaonal looked petrified.

Dorange turned his attention back to Bantyr. Bantyr met and held his gaze.

"One . . . two . . . three . . ."

Bantyr looked back toward Shaonal and the Gnol. The Gnol with the rifle began to squeeze his trigger.

"Four . . . fi—"

"Alright! Alright."

Dorange smiled. "Now, see Captain Palmer that wasn't so hard was it."

Bantyr looked back at Shaonal who looked disappointed.

Dorange continued. "I will repeat my question, Captain Palmer. Are you related to General Adrian Palmer?"

"Yes."

"How so?"

"He's my father."

Dorange's face seemed to gleam with Bantyr's response. He looked back at his men who were surrounding him. "I will speak to Captain Palmer alone." Dorange looked back at the Gnol with Shaonal in his deadly sights. "Commander, when Captain Palmer and I reach that tree . . ." he pointed to his right, ". . . over there about fifty feet away, kill Captain Shaonal."

"No!" Bantyr screamed.

"Yes, General," replied the commander who now seemed happy to finally be given permission to kill someone.

Dorange grabbed Bantyr by the arm and forced him to the tree. Bantyr struggled, but he was too weak from the blows he had already suffered.

When they made it to the tree, Dorange slammed Bantyr against it. Bantyr felt a small, jagged branch penetrate the flesh on the back of his left arm. He heard a blast and looked past Dorange just in time to see the lifeless body of Captain Shaonal fall to the wet, muddy ground.

Dorange grabbed Bantyr's face. "Let me ask you. What do you know about your father?"

Bantyr gave Dorange a look that could kill. "I know that he is a great man; the man that's going to lead the defeat of all the Gnols."

Dorange laughed. "A great man...you don't know him at all."

"What are you talking about?"

"Tell me, Bantyr . . . do you know where your father comes from?"

Bantyr gave Dorange a puzzled look. "Of course I do."

"Where?"

"He comes from *Talead*."

Dorange laughed again. "Maybe you didn't hear me right. I am asking, where does he come from? Because . . . I know for a fact, it's not from this planet."

Bantyr's eyes widened. "How would you know that?"

"Oh, there's a lot I know about your dear father. Tell me Bantyr, did your father ever tell you how he arrived on this planet?"

Bantyr didn't answer. How would a Gnol know that his father didn't come from *Terrest*?

"Answer me!"

Bantyr now felt a surge of energy. He didn't care anymore. He knew that Dorange would kill him anyway. He rapidly lunged for Dorange's throat with his hands. Dorange side stepped, which caused Bantyr to fall on his chest.

Bantyr quickly turned around in just enough time to catch the boot of Dorange's right foot in the chin. Bantyr felt two of his bottom teeth crack as he fell back into the wet snow.

Dorange lifted Bantyr back to his feet and slammed him into the tree again. He held Bantyr in place as he put his face within a few inches of Bantyr's. Dorange gritted his teeth and spit as he spoke. "Now listen, you little punk. There won't be any heroics today.

"If you won't answer me, then I'll tell you where you father came from. He came from a planet called Earth. He arrived here almost twenty-five years ago. It was his fault. He was the reason we were stranded here on this planet."

Bantyr's eyes widened as he began to realize what Dorange was saying. He reached up and wiped the blood that dripped from his mouth. "You're . . . Donald Garrett!"

"You catch on quick. And . . . I can see that your father told you about me. But no worries . . . in about 30 minutes . . . I will get my revenge."

★ ★ ★ ★ ★

Adrian took a deep breath, opened his eyes, and quickly sat up. His wife grabbed his shoulders and gently tried to lay him back down onto the bed. "Where . . . wha . . . what happened?"

"Shh . . . you're alright," Anyta said.

Adrian tried to get up again, but this time he felt the effects of the collision with the base floor. His head throbbed, and his shoulder felt like someone was stabbing it. He lied back down and spoke. "What happened? Is everyone okay?"

Anyta smiled at him as she spoke. Adrian loved Anyta's smile it seemed to make everything better even when certain disaster loomed. "Everyone's fine. You're the only one that suffered any injuries besides what Celeste already had. You've been out of it for almost two hours. Doc said you sustained a concussion and a separated shoulder. He popped your shoulder back into place, but said you will have to keep your right arm in a sling for a few days to keep it from popping out again. . . . All of you were lucky. If those air bags in the hover craft wouldn't have deployed, all of you would have been killed." Anyta stopped, leaned down, and gently kissed Adrian on the cheek. Adrian felt her tears.

"What about Celeste? How is she doing?"

"She's fine. Doc just finished operating on her. She's resting now, and Doc is helping Jake with battle preparations."

Suddenly, the entire sequence flashed through Adrian's mind. "Oh no! Bantyr! I don't know what happened. I saw his *Chati* go down. Is he okay?"

"We don't know," Anyta said as more tears began to roll down her cheeks at the mention of her son. "Sean has been trying to reach him, but there's no reply."

Adrian managed to sit himself up. He embraced Anyta. "I'm sure he's okay. He's been trained well."

Anyta began to cry. "I pray that you are right."

★ ★ ★ ★ ★

"Major, I want my squadron ready and in their fighters within the next ten minutes," Jake said as he pulled on his red flight suit.

"Yes, Sir," replied the major.

Jake watched as Major Ducal left the dressing area to prep the fighters. Major Ducal was the officer in charge of the entire fleet that Jake's father had amassed throughout the rebellion. The fleet was confiscated from various victories against the Gnols. Most of them were damaged, but repaired and painted red (to distinguish the rebel ships from the black Gnol ships) due to Major Ducal's genius mechanical expertise. All in all, the fleet consisted of three shuttle transports that reminded Jake of smaller versions of the *Mars II* space shuttle, thirteen hover crafts that Jake had become so familiar with, fifty *Chaties*, and thirty-five space and air fighters that the Major affectionately called *Wildcats*.

The *Wildcats* sat only one pilot and were smaller, modified versions of the *NightHawk*, which surprised Jake. So much of the Gnol technology was similar to the designs of the *Mars* Space Shuttles, and other military vehicles on Earth; the difference being, of course, the hover technology that the Gnols possessed, weapons, and other modifications.

Unfortunately, the fleet was only a fraction compared to the hundred thousand ships and vehicles that were estimated to be in the Gnol fleet. Also, the Terrestrian rebels did not have the *Wildcat II*, as Ducal named it. The *Wildcat II* was the same design as the *Wildcat* but sat two pilots instead of one. In addition, the rebels did not possess the various ground vehicles that the

Gnols did: the ground assault vehicles, which carried ground forces, and the hover tanks.

Jake finished dressing, grabbed his red flight helmet, and jogged to the hangar. The hangar seemed to be in chaos. Military personal and civilians were scrambling everywhere, trying to make their way to where they were supposed to be. Jake spotted Sean, Doc, Kylee, and his father – who must have just awakened after being knocked unconscious from the crash – near the computer terminal area of the hangar.

"Dad, how are you feeling?" asked Jake, as he embraced his father.

Adrian hugged Jake with his free right arm. "I'm feeling a little dizzy, but I'm doing fine."

"You let me know if you feel any head pain," Doc said.

Adrian looked at Doc and just and gave him a frustrated look, just as a little boy would his overprotective mother.

Jake turned his attention to Doc. "How's Celeste."

"She's recovering in the medical wing. I immobilized her shoulder, and she has had a successful blood transfusion. In a few minutes, I'm going to go back and get her so that we can put her in one of the transport shuttles."

"Good," Adrian said. "Now, how many forces are we dealing with?"

Sean pointed to the satellite image on the computer monitor. According to the readout we're dealing with twenty ground assault vehicles, which carry fifty soldiers each, forty nine *Chaties*, and thirty-five *Wildcats*."

Adrian took a deep breath and looked out across the hangar. "Well, the good news is I don't think they realize the number of troops we have here, or they would have brought more. The bad news, however, is we don't have enough aircraft for the number of people here, three of our pilots are already designated to the transport shuttles, Bantyr and Captain Shaonal are missing . . ."

Jake noticed the sadness in his father's eyes.

". . . That leaves you with only twenty-five pilots including yourself, Jake."

Jake nodded and said, "Each transport is crammed with women and children . . . Dad, did Anyta and Lexis get on one of the shuttles?"

"Yeah, Anyta protested and wanted to stay and help fight, but I finally forced her on the last one."

"Good," Sean said. "Each shuttle is able to hold two hundred people. We were able to cram two hundred fifty into two of them, and two hundred thirty-one into the third shuttle." Sean smiled. "We were able to get all of the civilians into the shuttles."

Adrian looked surprised. "Great! Okay, the only problem is how do we safely get those shuttles to *Base 2*?"

"We've been looking at that," Jake said. "According to the radar, they only have thirty-five *Wildcats* that will be able to attack the shuttles from the air."

"What about ground plasma cannons," Kylee interjected.

"We've accounted for them too," responded Jake. "Our plan is to launch the forty-eight *Chaties* we have left—"

Adrian raised his hand to stop Jake. "Wait. We don't have enough experienced pilots for the *Chaties*."

Jake nodded. "I know. After we got back and Doc declared me okay, I grabbed forty eight volunteers and began training them immediately on the *Chaties*. There wasn't much room for them to maneuver in the training wing, but they got the basics down."

Adrian looked impressed. "Very good. Go on."

"Anyway, the plan is to launch the forty-eight *Chaties* first. Their primary targets will be the sixteen ground plasma cannons located at the various positions as indicated by the satellite readout," said Jake, pointing to another computer monitor. "It seems, Dad . . . that whoever the Gnol leader is, leading this attack, that he has seriously underestimated what technology we have available."

Adrian didn't respond. He just nodded.

Jake continued. "After the *Chaties* launch, my squadron will launch to provide cover for the shuttles. Once the shuttles are out, the remaining vehicles we have in the fleet will launch."

"Go—," Adrian began to say, but Kylee cut him off.

"What if the Gnols blast the doors open. We're going to have debris in the way of the ships taking off."

Sean spoke before Jake could answer. "That won't happen. The only thing that will blast those doors open is a thermo-nuclear blast, and the Gnols wouldn't risk losing any of their forces. Their computers must have analyzed that option already."

"What happens if they drop explosives in after the doors open?" Kylee asked again.

Jake looked at his half-sister. He hadn't gotten to know her at all in the weeks he had been on *Terrest*. Ever since she lost her fiancé, she had been quiet and withdrawn. "We've accounted for that too," he said. "Each special ops team is going to surround the walls of the hangar. If anything enters the doors, your orders are to open fire."

Kylee scowled at Jake. Adrian noticed. "You will do as you're ordered, Captain!"

Kylee quickly shot her father a look and said, "Yes, General." Then she walked away.

Jake looked at his father. "What was that all about?"

Adrian shook his and followed Kylee with his eyes. "I don't know."

"Celeste!" yelled Doc.

Everyone turned toward the direction Doc looked. Celeste was walking to the group, freshly dressed in green fatigues.

"Why are you up? And, where's your sling?" Doc asked with frustration.

Celeste, who still looked to be in pain, simply looked at Doc and smiled. "I am fine. Besides, I need to be here to help in the battle."

Adrian shook his head. "I don't think so, Your Highness. You're going to be placed on a shuttle and transported to bas—"

Celeste raised her hand to keep Adrian from speaking. "Forgive me for interrupting, Adrian, but I can be more use to you here in the battle."

"What do you mean? You're recovering from a serious wound. You'll only be sure to suffer more," Doc said Doc, obviously getting frustrated with Celeste.

Celeste turned and looked at Doc. She smiled and didn't say a word.

"What?" Doc asked.

Celeste just continued to smile at Doc. Doc looked around at everyone to see if he had missed the joke. Celeste closed her eyes and slowly raised her right arm with her palm upwards and fingers extended.

Doc felt his body slowly start to rise. He looked at everyone in surprise. Sean, Jake, and Adrian just looked dumbfounded. The military personnel surrounding the group stopped working and looked just as surprised.

"Woa . . . okay . . . okay, you have me convinced!" Doc shrieked as he flapped his arms and legs five feet in the air.

Celeste slowly lowered Doc back to the floor and opened her eyes.

Jake looked at Celeste with admiration. He was so drawn to this woman. He noticed that Celeste stole a quick glance at him and smiled. Jake then turned to his father. "Dad, I don't think you're going to convince her to get on the shuttle."

204 Shaun F. Messick

Adrian, whose mouth was still open, shook his head. "You're right." He then focused his attention on Sean. "All right, is everyone ready?"

Sean nodded. "On your mark, I will open the bay doors."

"Good, Celeste, you stay here with me. I will stay until every last vehicle and troop has left."

Jake quickly looked at his father. "No!"

"It's okay. The troops that are left will be led by Major Halem out of the back entrance. Fifty other troops, me, and Celeste will take the last remaining assault vehicle."

Jake was beginning to protest again, but Celeste grabbed his hand. He turned and looked into Celeste's eyes.

"He will be fine. I will not let anything happen to him," she said.

Jake wasn't so sure and tried to protest. "Bu—"

Celeste put a finger up to Jake's lips. "Shh." She looked deep into his eyes. Jake shyly turned away. "Look at me, Jake."

Jake slowly turned his gaze to look into Celeste's bright, blue eyes. *She is so beautiful*, he thought.

Celeste continued. "Trust me. I will not let anything happen to him, and that is a promise."

Jake felt a little better, especially after seeing what Celeste did to Doc. He managed a smile and nodded. He then turned toward his father. "I will stay in constant radio contact with you."

Adrian walked to his son, grabbed him, and squeezed tightly. "Promise me, you will be careful out there, okay. I don't want to lose another son today."

Jake pulled away, smiled, saluted, and said, "Yes, Sir!" He then turned and sprinted off to his fighter.

Adrian watched his son – who he didn't want to let out of his sight – get settled into his fighter. He then turned his attention to Doc, Sean, and Celeste. "Okay, everyone . . . battle stations! Sean, you and Celeste stay here with me to command the defense. Doc, get yourself and your people onto the last shuttle. I want you to be ready at *Base 2* when we have casualties." Adrian stopped and looked two hundred yards above at the bay doors. "And . . . we're going to have a lot."

★ ★ ★ ★ ★

Bantyr sat with his back against a small tree, his hands and legs bound. Bantyr knew the tree was only about five yards away from the artificial ground that covered the bay doors. He saw Dorange, or Don as he knew now, walk to the center of the doors with one of his colonels and kick at an artificial rock. Bantyr wondered if any of the other Gnols knew that Dorange was actually one of the despised humans that Koroan Chast hated so much. He also wondered how he was able to get away with deceiving Koroan all these years. He was tempted to yell out, revealing who Dorange truly was, but he knew that was useless. What Gnol would believe him? It was obvious that Dorange had the respect and loyalty of his subordinates.

Bantyr strained to listen as he saw that Dorange was about to speak. "So, Colonel . . . you're telling me that we can't blow through these doors?"

"Yes, that is correct, Sir," the colonel said.

"I'm sure the rebels know that as well. That's why I planned for a little surprise."

"Sir?"

Dorange looked past the colonel and waved at another Gnol. The Gnol nodded and ran to the back of the rows of vehicles and aircraft. Within seconds, a gigantic hover craft, larger than any Bantyr had seen before, made its way through the fleet. Bantyr's eyes widened as it approached Dorange's position.

The vehicle was gigantic. The bottom portion was rectangular. Bantyr noticed a window along the front and what looked like about three Gnols within. Bantyr scanned upwards and saw two monstrous metal arms that extended to what seemed like five hundred feet into the air with claws at each end of the arms.

When the vehicle reached Dorange's position, it stopped. The entire bottom portion covered almost the entire surface area of the bay doors, which, Bantyr recalled, were about four thousand square feet each!

Bantyr tried to examine the craft further, but the hover engines from the vehicle were sending debris his way, pelting his body. He heard Dorange yell. "Colonel, move the prisoner to the prisoner frigate!"

A few moments later, Bantyr felt two Gnols grab his arms and drag him away from the gigantic monster that was about to rip the bay doors wide open. As the Gnol dragged Bantyr further away, he stole another quick glance at the arms and noticed small protruding segments about every five feet from each other. *Oh no!* He thought. *Plasma cannons!*

★ ★ ★ ★ ★

Despite the number of soldiers and rumbling aircraft within the hangar, there was an eerie silence as the entire rebel force sat listening to what was happening two hundred yards above. Adrian turned and gave Sean a confused look. Sean looked back and shrugged his shoulders. Adrian turned his eyes up toward the bay doors. He could hear what sounded like a massive engine rumbling, and metal clashing against metal.

Out of the corner of his left eye, Adrian saw Celeste slowly make her way to the center of the hangar. "Celeste! Get back here!" he yelled.

Celeste ignored him.

Adrian heard what sounded like thunder and jerked his eyes back to the bay doors. He saw two enormous, metallic claws penetrate the center of the doors. Suddenly, he realized what going on. "They're pulling them apart," he whispered.

"What?" shrieked Sean.

Adrian looked at Sean with fire in his eyes. "They are ripping them apart!"

Sean cursed.

"*Chati 1* . . . do you copy?"

"Yes, General," replied the *Chati* squadron leader.

"As soon as those doors are ripped open, your squadron is to launch and engage your primary targets!"

"Yes, Sir!"

Adrian continued to watch in horror as the morning sun began to sneak its rays through the penetrated doors. The claws continued to pull the doors further and further apart. Then, without any warning, the clawed arms dropped down to within one hundred feet of the hangar floor.

"What the . . ." Sean said.

"*Chaties* . . . engage, now!" Adrian ordered.

Adrian saw the red *Chaties* speed their way up to the surface. All of a sudden, the arms began to fling thousands of red plasma bolts in every direction.

"Adrian yelled as he hit the deck. "All units . . . open fire! I repeat . . . open fire!"

Within the hangar, there were thousands of plasma blasts and explosions as the rebel fleet was depleted within seconds. "Jake . . . engage now!"

"Already done, General!"

Unexpectedly, the plasma blasts and explosions stopped. Adrian and Sean slowly made their way to their feet and looked over the computer monitors. There, in the center of the hangar with her eyes shut and her arms extended, was Celeste. Adrian scanned up and saw what she was doing. "Unbelievable," he said.

"This is not right." Sean said in an eerie tone. "If her father is supposed to be more powerful than this, we're in trouble."

Adrian didn't respond as he watched Celeste bend the massive arms with her mental powers. Everyone froze and watched in astonishment. The arms continued to bend upwards until they cracked. A loud explosion permeated throughout the hangar. Adrian shot his eyes back to Celeste. She had fallen to the cold, metallic floor, unconscious. "Kylee . . . get two of your men to Celeste and get her back here with me and Sean," he said.

"Yes, General!" Kylee said as Adrian saw her order two of her men to Celeste with a wave of her arm.

The two soldiers rushed to Celeste, grabbed her by each arm, and dragged her back to the computer terminals. As soon as the soldiers arrived, Sean rushed to her and checked for a pulse. "She's still alive," he said.

Adrian took a deep breath. "Good," he replied. He then turned his attention to the three transport shuttles. "Shuttle leader . . . go now!"

"Roger that!" the shuttle leader replied as two of the shuttles slowly ascended to the exit and sped off.

"General, this is *Shuttle 3*. One of our engines was hit in the initial attack."

Adrian looked at the last shuttle his wife, daughter, and Doc were on. A crew of about five soldiers were there trying to put out a fire at the back of the spacecraft. "Major Ducal . . . can you fix that?"

Ducal's response came back through the communication device in Adrian's right ear. "That's a negative, Sir. I don't have any spare spaceship engines lying around."

Adrian slammed his fist down onto one of the computer monitors. "Kylee . . . order three of your men to escort the people on that third shuttle to the medical wing. That should keep them safe . . . at least for a while."

"We have incoming!" Sean shouted as he ran next to Adrian and pointed upwards.

Adrian looked up as black *Chaties* swooped down from the hangar entrance. Adrian and Sean hit the deck again. Adrian glanced at Celeste who was still unconscious. "Open fire!" he screamed.

The entire hangar was again ablaze with plasma fire and orange fireballs from explosions.

"This isn't going so well, Adrian," Sean said.

Adrian shook his head. Sean was right. *How were they going to get out of this?*

★ ★ ★ ★ ★

Shuttle 1 to *Wildcat* leader. . . . I repeat . . . *Shuttle 1* to *Wildcat 1*. Get them off my tail!"

Jake heard the pleading of the shuttle pilot within his flight helmet. He turned his head to locate the shuttle. There it was, speeding its way south. Behind it, were three Gnol fighters within firing range. "*Wildcat 2*," he said. "I repeat . . . *Wildcat 2* . . . come in."

"Sir, this is *Wildcat 7*. We've lost nearly twenty *Wildcats* so far."

Jake cursed. "*Wildcat 7* help those *Chaties* take out the two remaining plasma cannons. I'm going to help *Shuttle 1*."

"Roger that."

Jake jerked on his flight stick and felt the G-forces as he banked right. He straightened it out and shot off toward the three Gnols that were chasing the shuttle.

Suddenly, he saw a gigantic fireball burst on his left side.

"*Shuttle 2* has been hit. I repeat . . . *Shuttle 2*, h—"

Jake strained his neck and saw another large explosion and three Gnol fighters escape from the flames. Jake turned his attention back to *Shuttle 1* and felt a deep sadness. *No, they wouldn't. They had to know that the shuttle was full of women and children*, he thought to himself, as he gritted his teeth. He then hit his accelerator for more speed.

"Get them off!" demanded the *Shuttle 1* pilot, as one of the Gnol fighters fired. The hot red plasma bolt just missed the right wing as the shuttle's pilot banked left.

Jake was within firing range on the middle Gnol when his alarm went off within his fighter. Jake looked at his rear monitor and saw that another Gnol was behind him and had just fired a missile.

Jake grabbed his flight stick with both hands and banked left. He held the stick and rolled the fighter three hundred sixty degrees with the missile just missing the underside of his *Wildcat*. Jake saw the missile clip the tail of the Gnol fighter he was about to fire on. There was a bright explosion as the middle fighter ahead of Jake careened out of control into the fighter on its right. Both ships fell to the ground in bright, red fireballs.

"I'm hit!"

Jake looked ahead and saw that the one remaining Gnol fighter trailing the shuttle had landed a shot on the left wing. "Is it bad?" he asked the shuttle pilot.

"Negative . . . I still have control."

Then Jake saw brilliant, red flashes buzz by on each side of his canopy. The Gnol trailing him was still on his tail. Jake maneuvered his *Wildcat* back and forth while trying to get a missile lock on the Gnol ahead of him.

Suddenly he heard a loud explosion. He glanced at his monitor and saw that the Gnol chasing him had burst into flames. "What the—"

"You're good to go, General."

Jake continued to look and saw one red *Wildcat* fly through the flames.

"*Wildcat 7* is that you?" he asked.

"Negative, Sir, this is Captain Mechlis, *Wildcat 10*. You'll never guess what happened?"

Jake, who was still trying to get a lock on the Gnol ahead of him, felt annoyed. *Why was this captain trying to play guessing games at a time like this?* "Just tell me, Captain!" he ordered.

"General Hauler from *Base 2* just arrived with an entire squadron of assault vehicles and hover tanks. They're taking out everything."

Jake was stunned. "What? . . . Where did they get hover tanks?"

"I don't know, but he has them."

A smile grew on Jake's face.

Jake then noticed that the Gnol ahead of him was beginning to get in line for another shot. Jake tightened his grip on his stick and banked right to follow the Gnol fighter. Then, he heard the tone he was waiting for – missile lock. He squeezed the trigger, and a missile fired out from under his left wing.

The Gnol must have heard his missile warning. He tried to bank left and then right, but the missile kept him in its sight. The missile hit the Gnol fighter directly in the tail engine causing it to explode into a bright, red and orange fireball. Jake and Captain Mechlis both banked left to avoid the flying shrapnel.

"*Shuttle 1* . . . this is General Palmer."

"General."

"You're free. Captain Mechlis and I will escort you to the second base. E.T.A. twenty minutes. Your orders are to unload all civilians, and we will escort you back to *Base 1*. We need another shuttle for the civilians that were on *Shuttle 3*."

"Roger that."

★ ★ ★ ★ ★

Adrian and Sean continued to lie on the metal floor of the hangar. Everywhere, Adrian heard explosions and screams of agony. He knew that his entire force was being depleted one by one. "Kylee," he said. "Come in, Captain Palmer."

Adrian heard the static in his ear piece and the slurred speech of his daughter. "Da . . . Dad . . . I've been . . . I'm hurt."

Adrian's first instinct was to jump to his feet and find his daughter, but Sean grabbed him to keep him safe from the plasma fire. "Kylee, where are you?" he asked.

"I . . ." She coughed, ". . . I'm not . . . not far from you."

"Where!" demanded Adrian.

"Dad, it hurts."

"Where are you?"

"I'm . . . I'm about fifty feet from your position . . ." Kylee coughed again, ". . . I'm behind the two burning assault vehicles."

Adrian slowly raised his head above the computer terminals and looked to his right. There they were, the two burning vehicles in the corner of the hangar. He looked at Sean. "I'm going after her. Order the retreat for all remaining soldiers to exit the base at the primary entrance."

Sean grabbed Adrian's left arm before Adrian could leave. "You'll get yourself killed!"

Adrian jerked his arm away and pointed to Kylee's position. "That's my daughter over there! Do as you're ordered, General!"

Adrian jumped over Celeste's unconscious body and sprinted toward Kylee. A plasma blast hit the floor just in front of him. The impact threw Adrian to his right, slamming him into the wall. He jumped to his feet again, determined to make it to his daughter.

When he made it to the burning heap of metal, he saw a boot sticking out from behind the mangled mess. He ran around the two burning vehicles and slid to a stop on his knees right next to Kylee. His daughter's body was shaking.

Kylee opened her eyes and looked into her father's eyes. "Da . . . Dad, it hurts so bad."

Adrian, holding back the tears, looked at his daughter's body. The left side of her body had been burned. Her left arm and hand were black as charcoal, and the left side of her face was red and blistered. Adrian continued to scan her body for anymore injuries.

In his earpiece, he heard Sean issue the retreat.

He gently turned Kylee and found a piece of hot shrapnel from the damaged vehicles lodged about two inches into her lower back. "Shh . . . it's going to be okay," he said.

He grabbed the shrapnel but quickly pulled his hand back because of the heat. Grabbing his left breast pocket on his shirt, he ripped the cloth off and wrapped it around his hand. He grabbed the shrapnel and quickly pulled it out. Kylee screamed in pain.

Adrian jumped to his feet in a squatting position, and ignoring the pain in his left shoulder, he took his sling off and threw it to the side. "Okay...I'm going to lift you."

Kylee nodded her response.

Adrian gently placed his arms under Kylee's right side, so as to avoid her wounds, and lifted his daughter into his chest. Kylee cried in pain.

Once Kylee was secure in his arms, he darted off back toward Sean and Celeste's position behind the computer terminals. When he arrived, he gently placed Kylee next to Celeste and looked at Sean. "Report."

Sean looked up at Adrian. "Captain Listin has your wife, Lexis, Doc, and all of the Civilians crammed in the medical wing. But . . ."

"But what, Sean?"

"But we have lost an estimated eight hundred troops."

Adrian dropped his body down next to Sean and placed his face into his hands. He was beginning to feel the fatigue of his sixty-year-old body. Holding back the tears, he looked at Sean. "Are the remaining troops retreating through the primary entrance?"

"Yes. And, we—"

Both men looked up and saw the roaring engines of two black assault vehicles descending to the hangar floor. Adrian looked at Sean. "I think it's time we left." He pointed at Celeste. "You carry Celeste, and I'll carry Kylee."

Sean and Adrian gently lifted the two women. They made their way to the spacious hallway that led past the medical wing and to the primary exit of the base. But, as soon as they entered the hallway, they were met by Captain

Listin. "Captain, why aren't you with the civilians in the medical wing?" Adrian asked.

Captain Listin didn't respond and turned his head toward the medical wing. Out of the wing, came Anyta, Lexis, Doc, and all two hundred plus civilians. They were followed by several Gnol troops with weapons raised. Behind them, came the remaining retreating troops with arms raised to their head. They were also followed by several Gnol troops.

Captain Listin turned his head back to Adrian and shook his head. "They penetrated the primary entrance just as we were about to exit."

CHAPTER 13

Adrian gently lied Kylee down on the floor of the hangar. Adrian, family, friends, and troops were all gathered to the center of the hangar by the Gnols. Celeste and Kylee were left near the computer terminals. All around, there were burning ships, as well as dead and wounded soldiers.

The two black assault vehicles had finished their descent and landed next to the mass of prisoners. About fifty Gnol troops emerged from each vehicle. The last soldier off of the second hover craft seemed to Adrian to be the leader. He was dressed in all black fatigues with large gold stars on each arm. His eyes were hidden because of the black helmet and visor on his head. He had a long black braid of hair extending out from the back of his battle helmet and a thick black goatee. He briskly walked toward Adrian and stopped within a foot of Adrian's face.

"General Palmer, I presume."

Adrian didn't respond. He just nodded.

"No response, very well. . . . I'll do the talking. General Palmer, do you know who I am?"

Adrian shrugged his shoulders and looked at his wife who was crying, but trying to hold back the tears. He then turned his attention back to the Gnol leader. "I presume you are Dorange Gar, Koroan Chast's right hand man."

Dorange threw his head back as he laughed. "That is a good guess. But, do you know who I really am?"

Adrian gave Dorange a puzzled look. *What kind of game is this Gnol trying to play?* He thought. "How would I know who you really are?"

Dorange laughed again. He then stepped closer to Adrian, reached up, and grabbed the bottom of the visor on his helmet. He was just about to take off the helmet when the communicator on his belt chirped. He stopped and grabbed the communicator. "This had better be important, Colonel."

"It is, Sir," the colonel replied. "We have a problem up here."

"What is it?"

"Another squadron of rebels has just arrived."

Dorange seemed annoyed. "Well then, Colonel, you know what to do! Take care of it!"

"That will be a problem, Sir."

"How so?" Dorange questioned.

"The squadron contains approximately thirty assault vehicles—"

"So! We can take those out!"

". . . and fifty hover tanks!"

Adrian quickly looked at Sean and Doc. Both men returned his look with the same astonishment and shrugged. He wondered where Scott and Petey got tanks from.

"What?" Dorange bellowed as he snapped his finger and motioned for one of his officers to stand next to him.

The colonel at the other end of the communicator continued. "The tanks have taken out almost all of our fighters and *Chaties*!"

Dorange cursed, slammed his communicator shut, and looked at the officer who was now standing next to him. "Major . . . take fifty troops and return to the surface for support."

"Yes, Sir," the major said as he whirled around and motioned for troops to follow him to the first assault vehicle.

Dorange then turned his attention to another nearby officer. "Captain."

"Yes, General."

"I will personally accompany General Palmer back to the palace," Dorange said as he turned his attention back to Adrian and smiled. "Our lord, Koroan Chast, will take care of him personally."

"And what about the rest of the prisoners, Sir?" The captain questioned.

Dorange paused for a moment and looked around the hangar at the two hundred plus prisoners. "We don't have time to bring the prisoner shuttle down . . . so . . . kill them all!"

★ ★ ★ ★ ★

Skip, Ariauna, and Jaskead had already deciphered nearly all of the writings on the bottom floor of the pyramid. The three were now at the top of the narrow stair case that split right of the narrow hallway on the first floor. Jaskead was writing with an ancient feather pen on parchment, he preferred this to one of the laptops Sean offered to give him. Ariauna was cleaning the right wall, so they could get better readings of the writings. Skip, with Jake's scriptures beside him, was going back through the deciphering he had written on his laptop.

He scrolled down and found what he was looking for. "Look at this," he said.

Ariauna and Jaskead stopped what they were doing and moved to each side of Skip to get a better view of the screen.

"What is it?" Jaskead asked.

Skip smiled and looked at the old man. "There isn't a doubt in my mind that the same God the *Tilicah* tribe worshipped is the same God that my religion worships back on Earth."

"You mean . . . this Jesus Christ you speak of," Jaskead said.

"The One and the Same."

Ariauna interjected before her father could continue. "But we haven't found his name mentioned in any of the writings . . . you know, the name . . . What was the name he used in your Old Testament?"

"Jehovah."

"Yes, Jehovah. That name hasn't been mentioned either."

"I know, but remember all of your religions on this planet have the same creation story. You know, a supreme being created a man and a woman. The man and woman partake of a forbidden fruit and are cast out of paradise."

"Yes, that is true," Jaskead said. "But I do not understand how that proves this Jesus is the same God you and the *Tilicah* worship."

"No," said Skip, as he turned his attention to Jaskead. ". . . it doesn't. But, remember every religion on this planet puts its creation story about six thousand years ago. That coincides with the creation story of my religion."

"So, what you're saying," Ariauna said. ". . . is that both *Terrest* and Earth were created about the same time according to their religions."

"Yes," Skip said. "And according to the scripture I found on the wall earlier . . . Well, here I'll just read it to you:

Verily, Verily I say unto you. The Son of Man shall be born of the Holy Spirit to a Virgin. He shall come at the end of the four thousandth year from the fall of man. But behold, the Son of Man will not be born upon this body, but upon another.

Verily, Verily I say unto you. The Son of Man will be a sacrifice to wash away the sins of man and return him to the spiritual glory the Father has bestowed upon him. Yea, the Son of Man's sacrifice will not only be for those upon his body, but for man on all Celestial bodies, Amen.'"

When Jake finished reading the scripture, he looked at Ariauna who looked just as confused as her father. He sat his laptop down and stood up. "Here, let me explain," he said with excitement in his voice. "Jesus' name is mentioned here. An—"

Ariauna interrupted and pointed at the monitor. "No it isn't. I don't see the name of 'Jesus' anywhere."

"No, it's not mentioned literally. But in the scriptures my religion reads, 'Son of Man' is another name for 'Jesus' or 'Jehovah.' And remember the story I told you about Jesus?"

Jaskead's eyes began to beam as he began to understand what Skip was saying. "Yes, yes . . . you said that Jesus was born to a virgin, suffered in a garden, and was crucified to save men from their sins."

"Yes, Jaskead," Skip said, becoming more excited. "But according to this scripture that we deciphered, Jesus not only died for the sins of men on Earth but for the sins of men on all worlds."

Ariauna continued to look at Skip with bewilderment. "I don't understand," she said. "This scripture doesn't mention the word 'worlds' at all. It only mentions 'body' and 'bodies'."

"My point exactly," Skip said as Ariauna shook her head. "You see . . . Well, what's another word for 'world'?"

Ariauna shook her head again. "I don't know. Um . . . globe, orb . . . I don't know."

"Body . . . body is another word for 'world'," Skip said as he knelt down and pointed at the computer screen. "Here, 'body' is used as a reference to 'world' or 'worlds.' In other words, God not only created Earth, he created other worlds and populated them with human beings. And Jesus, his Son, was the sacrifice that will enable all of us to return to our Father in Heaven. He saved all of us from physical death, and if we accept him as our savior and follow his commandments, he will save us spiritually, and we will return to live with him again."

Jaskead stood next to Skip and put his arm around him. "Yes, now I see, Skip. This Jesus you speak of is the God of both of our worlds. That would make you my brother."

Skip looked at Jaskead and smiled. "Yes, Brother," he said as he put his hand on Jaskead's. Skip then paused and looked down at his computer monitor in thought.

"What is it?" Jaskead asked.

Skip looked back at the professor. "Jaskead, approximately how long ago did you say that the God of the *Tilicah* tribe visited them?"

Jaskead pulled his arm back from Skip and stroked his beard as he thought. "That would be about two thousand seven years ago. Why?"

Skip's eyes sparkled. "Listen, my world's calendar follows the Gregorian Calendar. Earth's yearly dates go from the time of Jesus' birth, which begins around 1 A.D. The date on Earth, as of today, is April 8, 2042. Two thousand forty-two years from the birth of Christ."

Ariauna stood and looked even more confused. "I don't understand," she said.

Skip had to concentrate to slow down his speech. He was so excited about the discoveries in the temple. "Your father said that the God of the *Tilicah* tribe visited them about two thousand seven years ago. That would put Earth time at 35 A.D.. It is estimated that Christ was crucified around 32 A.D.." Skip stopped and looked at Jaskead. "And what did I tell you happened to Jesus three days after he died?"

Jaskead's smile grew bigger. "He was raised from the dead. What did you call it? Uh . . . resurrected."

Ariauna raised her hands before Skip could speak. "Okay, hold on. What you're saying is that this Jesus visited the ancient *Tilicah* tribe after he was resurrected."

"That's exactly what I'm saying."

Ariauna shook her head in disbelief. "I don't believe it. Why would a God visit a world he wasn't even a part of?"

Skip gave Ariauna a frustrated look. In the short time he had gotten to know her, he had grown fond of her intuitiveness and beauty. But at times, she was often skeptical about every theory Skip and her father suggested. It was, at these times, that she seemed also angry and aloof toward Skip.

Before Skip could speak, Jaskead spoke. "Come now, Ariauna. Look at what Skip has deciphered so far. The writings on these walls have so many similarities to the scriptures that Skip has brought with him from Earth. And the time frame that Skip mentions makes perfect sense."

"I don't know, Father. I just find it hard to believe. With these writings, there's no mention of Earth, and with the exception of this one scripture . . ." She said as she pointed to the laptop, ". . . there's no mention of any other worlds."

"Okay, wait a minute," Skip said as he bent down and picked up Jake's scriptures. He then showed the scriptures to Ariauna while he placed his other hand on top of them. "These scriptures are Jake's. Remember we belong to a Church called the Church of Jesus Christ of Latter-day Saints. Other people on Earth call them Mormons.

"Yes . . . so."

"Well, the Mormons believe in the *Holy Bible*, *The Book of Mormon*, the *Doctrine and Covenants*, and *The Pearl of Great Price*. We believe that these books were given to us by God as a witness of Christ."

Ariauna seemed determined not to follow what Skip was saying, even though he knew she was just trying to frustrate him. "So," she said. "I don't see what those books have to do with *Terrest*?"

Skip had hoped she would ask the right question, and she did. "Great question," he said as he flipped open the scriptures and found what he was looking for. He read a few lines and looked at Ariauna. "Here," he said, pointing to the book. "It says here in *Doctrine and Covenants* section 76, verses twenty-three through twenty-four:

> *'For we saw him, even on the right hand of God; and we heard the*
> *voice bearing record that he is the Only Begotten of the Father—*
> > *That by him, the worlds are and were created, and the inhabitants*
> > *thereof are begotten sons and daughters unto God.'"*

Skip stopped reading and looked at Ariauna. She was about to speak, but Skip held up his hand to stop her. "And . . ." He said as he flipped to the back of the book, ". . . it says in *Moses* chapter 1, verse 33:

> *'And worlds without number have I created; and I also created*
> *them for mine own purpose; and by the Son I created them, which is*
> *mine Only Begotten.'*

"So you see, Christ, under the direction of God the Father, created worlds without number. So, it makes perfect sense; why wouldn't he visit a world he has created?"

"Maybe so," said Ariauna. "But—"

"Okay," Jaskead cut in. "That's enough, Ariauna. I know you believe what Skip is telling you, so quit trying to frustrate him."

Ariauna backed away from Skip and smiled at her father.

Skip looked at Jaskead first and then Ariauna. Why did she always do this? She had a knack of getting Skip excited about one of his theories, and then totally frustrating him while he tried to prove them. Maybe it was her way of getting to know him better?

"All right," she said. "You convinced me. But these scriptures still don't tell us how the Gnols are involved or how they can be defeated."

"You're right," said Skip, as he looked at the writings on the wall behind Ariauna. He moved closer to the wall and blew away the dust. After examining the writings for awhile, he turned and stared at the other wall in thought. "Okay, so far all of the writings we have deciphered have followed a chronological order, from the creation up until this point."

Skip stood, stroked the stubble on his face that was beginning to form under his chin, and paced back and forth. He looked at Jaskead. "Jaskead, every prophet on this planet has foretold of events that have occurred on *Terrest*, such as *Juzs Lza Bmail's* conquering of *Terrest*. Ancient prophets on your planet have even prophesied about the coming of a God that visited the *Tilicah* tribe. But up until this point, there hasn't been anything mentioned about a race of super humans enslaving the Terrestrians. . . ."

Skip stopped pacing and whirled around to face the wall behind Ariauna. He shook his finger at the wall in thought. After a few seconds, he spoke. "Wait a minute . . ."

"What is it?" Jaskead asked.

"I . . . wait . . ." Skip moved in closer to the wall, knelt down, and began deciphering some of the writings as he mumbled. "I think this wall contains the prophecies of Jesus Himself when he visited the *Tilicah* tribe two thousand years ago."

Skip whirled around again. "Come here, Jaskead. You're faster at deciphering these writings than I am."

Jaskead grabbed his feathered pen and parchment paper. He knelt beside Skip and began translating the writings from *Tilicah* to English. After several minutes of writing and translating the entire wall up to the solid oak door, he put down his pen and looked at Skip with a huge grin spread across his face.

Skip grabbed the parchment and began reading aloud:

"For behold, I am he who has been prophesied to come. I am Alpha and Omega. I am the Beginning and the End. I am the Son of God."

Skip looked up with the same grin that Jaskead had. "I knew it."

Skip read aloud with such an excitement that every once in awhile Ariauna had to calm him so that he would slow his reading down. There wasn't a doubt in Skip's mind that the writings he was reading were Christ's actual words. He continued to read until he came to a shocking prophecy. He stopped reading and looked up at Ariauna and Jaskead.

"What is it?" Ariauna asked as she looked at her father who already knew what Skip was about to read.

"Listen to this:

Behold, I say unto you. The people of this body will one day fall into iniquity. Yea, verily, I say unto you. They will forget the Lord their God and forget it was He who has saved them.

But behold, the people of this body will fall into captivity due to their wickedness. Ye shall be overcome by another body, another body that has the appearance of God. But behold, this body will seem to be as God, but it is not. Yea, verily, verily, I say unto you. This body are your brothers and sisters in me. They also have I created, but they have also forgotten me.

This body that is spoken of will overcome thee. Nevertheless, this body will not destroy thee. For behold, you shall one day again be given the knowledge that I am he who has died for your sins.

You shall be liberated. A Sav . . .'"

Skip looked at Jaskead. "Wha . . . where's the rest?"

Jaskead shrugged his shoulders. "I do not know. The writings ended at this door," he said as he pounded on the gigantic wooden door.

Skip knelt down beside the writings on the wall and examined them with his right hand. He followed them until his hand stopped at the door. He stood, grabbed the circular, rusted out metal handle pulled. It didn't budge. "It's no use," he said as he backed up and looked at the door. "The door's locked and too big to break into with one person. We're going to have to blow it down."

He stopped and looked at his two partners. "The answer we're looking for is behind this door."

★ ★ ★ ★ ★

"No," yelled Adrian, as he lunged for Dorange. But he was immediately hit in the back of the head with a butt of a plasma rifle. He fell down, grabbing the back of his head. Doc then reached for the Gnol that hit his best friend, but another Gnol hit him square in the face with the butt of his rifle.

"That enough!" Dorange yelled as he walked back to Adrian. He forced Adrian to stand by grabbing his hair.

Adrian looked at Dorange with vengeance in his eyes. He couldn't get a decent look at Dorange's eyes because of the tinted visor on his helmet.

"General Palmer. I think you should witness this, so you will always remember how your family died," Dorange said.

Adrian shook loose of Dorange's grip and looked back at the mass of prisoners that this deranged Gnol was about to execute. He looked first at his beautiful wife. Anyta looked back with tears streaming down her face. She mouthed the words, *I love you,* back toward Adrian.

Adrian gritted his teeth. He looked at his youngest daughter who was sobbing in her mother's arms. He then looked at his best friend. Doc nodded his acknowledgement back with fiery eyes as he put his arm around Anyta. Adrian glanced at Sean. Sean had his head down and arms around a sobbing mother with her newborn child, trying to console her.

"Captain, get your men into position," Dorange ordered.

The captain he was speaking to hand signaled the other Gnol soldiers. About fifty Gnol troops encircled the two hundred plus prisoners with plasma rifles raised. Dorange grabbed Adrian by the arm and jerked him along to the outside of the circle.

Adrian tried to pull away, but it was no use. He was physically and emotionally drained. *How could he live knowing that his family, friends, and those he was sworn to protect were about to be brutally murdered by a mad man?*

Adrian suddenly felt a burst of energy. He didn't care anymore. If everyone he loved was going to die, then he was going to die along with them. He quickly pulled his arm away and threw a roundhouse kick directly into Dorange's chest. Dorange flew back about three feet and slammed into the black assault vehicle that he emerged from.

Adrian frantically looked around and saw a plasma rifle lying next to one of his dead soldiers. He lunged for the rifle. But before he could get to it, he heard a shot and instant pain in his right arm. He rolled over in agony.

Adrian rolled back onto his back and saw another Gnol step over him and point his weapon directly between his eyes.

"No!" Dorange shouted. "Don't kill him! Lord Chast would be most displeased."

The Gnol soldier straddling Adrian nodded in acknowledgment and stepped away from him. Dorange then walked next to Adrian and landed a direct kick into his left side. Adrian felt one of his ribs crack as the air rushed out of his lungs.

Dorange bent over and grabbed Adrian by the throat. Adrian tried to wiggle free, but it was useless. He was out of strength now, especially with the added wounds to his arm and ribs.

"Noble . . . but stupid," Dorange said as he slammed Adrian into the black assault vehicle. "Next time you try to be a hero, I will kill you, myself!"

Dorange turned to the captain whom he ordered to encircle the prisoners. "Captain, on my mark . . . open fire."

The captain let a wry grin spread across his face. "Yes, Sir."

"Ready!"

Adrian felt so helpless. There was no way he could handle watching the mass murder of everyone he loved. But what could he do? They were all going to die, and he was going to be alive to see it.

"Aim!"

Adrian tried to hold back the tears. He tried to be strong, but he couldn't help it. He put his head down and began to close his eyes when he saw movement out of the corner of his left eye. He glanced up and saw Kylee and Celeste moving about thirty yards away near the computer terminals. Kylee was sitting up wide eyed against the wall with tears streaming down her face, and Celeste slowly making it to her feet.

Adrian looked back at Dorange to make sure he didn't notice them. He didn't.

Adrian closed his eyes again. He was about to witness the deaths of his loved ones, especially his wife. He knew that if he lost her to a tragic end there was no way he could stay sane. He had already lost two women that he loved very much to tragedies. *Why was he being punished like this? What did he do to deserve this?*

"Fi . . . Wha . . . Who?

Adrian opened his eyes and looked in astonishment. The Gnol soldiers that had the mass of prisoners within their sights were elevated about fifteen feet off of the floor. Their weapons were still in their hands, but their arms were raised, unable to get clear shots at the prisoners.

Adrian looked at Dorange. He seemed frozen but could still speak and move his eyes. Adrian saw Dorange's eyes move toward him and look beyond. "Celeste!" he yelled.

Adrian turned to look. There she was with her arms raised and a fierce look of determination on her face.

"Adrian!" She hollered. "Go now! I can't hold them much longer!"

Adrian turned back to the mass of petrified prisoners. They were all frozen in amazement. "Sean!"

Sean shot a look of fear at Adrian.

"Get as many people as you can into that Gnol assault vehicle . . ." Adrian shrieked, pointing at the black hover ship, ". . . and then go and help Doc get Kylee and Celeste!"

Sean paused. He seemed unsure of what to do.

"Go now!"

Sean scrambled and began barking orders to the civilians to load into the vehicle. The mass of prisoners sprinted toward the craft.

"Doc!" said Adrian, as he turned and looked at his best friend. "Grab a weapon and go and protect Kylee and Celeste! She won't be able to hold them for long!"

Doc nodded, grabbed a weapon, and sprinted toward Celeste and Kylee.

Adrian ran to Anyta and Lexis. He hugged and kissed them both, so grateful they were still alive, at least for now. He led them to the hover vehicle and made sure they were secure. As soon as he stepped off of the craft to help other civilians, he saw Celeste's legs tremble, and then she collapsed to the floor.

The Gnol troops fell to the ground and scrambled to their feet with weapons raised. They began firing volleys of blasts into the civilians who had not made it to the hover craft yet, hitting a few. Adrian grabbed a gun from the floor and fired at the troops.

Suddenly, there was a large explosion in front of the Gnol troops. A handful of the fifty plus troops were thrown into the far wall of the hangar. Adrian looked up and saw two *Wildcats* and a shuttle swoop down into the hangar. The shuttle landed on top of the other Gnol troops that were struggling to get away as the two *Wildcats* hovered above and provided cover fire. The remaining civilians and rebel troops scattered to the shuttle.

Adrian turned his attention back to Doc. "Do . . ."

Adrian stopped as he saw that one Gnol soldier had seized Doc's weapon. The soldier was escorting Doc back to Adrian's position. Adrian noticed that Celeste was unconscious again, and his daughter unconscious as well. He prayed that they weren't dead.

Adrian raised his gun as the soldier approached with his weapon pointed at Doc's head. "Let him go!"

"I don't think so," said a voice from Adrian's left.

Adrian turned around. Dorange stood about two feet away with his weapon pointed at Adrian's head.

Adrian raised his arms and dropped the gun.

"Well done, Corporal," Dorange said as he nodded at the soldier who had captured Doc.

The corporal escorted Doc next to Adrian and stood next to Dorange. Both Gnols continued to keep their weapons on Adrian and Doc.

"You thought you could get away," Dorange said. "You need to understand something, General Palmer. This is a war you can never win. . . . Corporal!"

"Sir?" said the young Gnol.

"On my mark, we will execute these two resistance leaders together. But first . . ." Dorange reached up and grabbed the visor of his battle helmet.

"No!" yelled Doc. He reached out, grabbed the corporal's arm and twisted. The gun fell to the floor as the Gnol's arm cracked. The young corporal screamed in pain. Dorange turned his weapon and took aim at Doc. But before he could get a shot off, the gigantic doctor picked the corporal up and threw him into Dorange.

The corporal and Dorange fell to the floor.

Doc grabbed Adrian, and they both ran to one of the assault vehicles. "Go now! I will get Celeste and Kylee onto the shuttle."

Adrian jumped into the vehicle and turned around. Doc was about to run toward Celeste and Kylee when Dorange grabbed him and threw him against the craft. Dorange then grabbed Adrian and pulled him out of the vehicle and raised his gun to Adrian's face. "I have been waiting so long for this," he said.

Adrian tried to break free of Dorange's grip, but his injuries had finally caught up with him. He didn't have any more strength. Adrian saw Dorange slowly squeeze the trigger on his gun. He closed his eyes.

"No!"

Adrian opened his eyes and saw Doc barrel his two hundred fifty pounds of muscle into Dorange. Dorange flew to his left. Doc then grabbed Adrian and threw him into the assault vehicle. "Get ou—"

Adrian looked and saw his friend, with his eyes wide open, slowly fall to the hangar floor. Blood began to flow from his mouth. "No!" he shrieked as he looked up and saw Dorange with the smoking gun in his hand.

Dorange was about to get another shot off when Adrian hit the button that shut the door. The door slid shut just as Dorange fired. The plasma bolt sparked against the armored door.

As the remaining rebel force ascended out of the hangar, Adrian looked down with tear filled eyes. He first saw the lifeless body of his best friend, the friend who had sacrificed his life to save his. He scanned the rest of the hangar and saw several Gnol soldiers and Dorange encircle Celeste, Kylee, and Sean.

Adrian felt his wife slide into the seat next to him. She hugged him, and the two sobbed together. "I am so sorry, Anyta. I pray that we will see them again."

"When will this ever end?" Anyta said as she kissed his forehead.

Adrian shook his head. "I wish it was over now. I don't think I can take this anymore, Anyta. Bantyr's missing. Kylee, Celeste, and Sean have been captured. "And . . ." Adrian wiped the tears away that were flowing from his eyes, ". . . Doc's been killed. I can't take losing the people I love anymore. Why am I being punished? Where is God?"

Anyta didn't respond. She embraced her husband, and they both sobbed in each other's arms.

CHAPTER 14

April 9, 2042 – Earth-Salt Lake City, Utah

Kevin stood along with Adam and the rest of the restless crowd within the arena that bore his company's name, Compu-Tech Arena. The arena was built five years ago and was the new home of the NBA's Utah Jazz. On this night, the Jazz were playing the Los Angeles Lakers. The game was tight in the fourth quarter, and Sam Johnson, the Jazz's all-star shooting guard just made a spectacular lay-up and was fouled.

The entire crowd was frenzied. The shot was incredible and brought the Jazz to within one point of the Lakers. Kevin looked at his sixteen-year-old son. Adam screamed and shot a fist into the air. Kevin clapped and smiled. This was a pleasant break from work and his worries about Jake and the strange shuttle he saw just two days earlier.

The crowd continued to stand, but became deathly silent as Sam Johnson made his way to the free-throw line. Kevin's cell phone vibrated. He flipped it open to see who was calling. It was Michael Konrad from NASA. He lifted the phone to his ear. "This is Kevin Palmer."

"Kevin. Good. Your daughter said you were at the game. I hate to interrupt your fun. I have the game on here at the office. It's good. But anyway, this is important. I—"

The crowd went nuts as Sam Johnson hit the free throw that tied the game.

"Mike . . . I can't hear you! Let me go out into the concourse!" Kevin turned and began to make his way out when Adam grabbed his arm.

"Where're you going, Dad! You can't miss this!"

Kevin showed Adam his phone. "Got an important call from Michael Konrad!"

Adam nodded and turned his attention back to the game.

A few moments later, Kevin was out in the concourse, away from the noise of the crowd. He looked at the visual image instead of holding the phone to his ear. "Go ahead, Mike. I can hear you now."

"Sorry, but this is important. The FBI, the CIA, the military, and not to mention the President have been on my butt all day."

"What? Why would they be questioning you?"

"The shuttle we saw go through the wormhole just beyond Mars a couple of days ago . . . well . . . it arrived today."

"And . . ."

"Well, you were right, Kevin. This shuttle isn't a modified version of *Mars II*."

"Well then . . . who or what is it?"

"I don't know. But this shuttle wasn't shy about avoiding our satellites. In fact, that's why the government is questioning me. The government saw what we at NASA saw as well."

"What did you see?"

"The shuttle orbited Earth for a few hours. During its orbit, it dropped off about two hundred small probes."

"What kind of probes?"

"We don't know. We tried to contact the shuttle in every language known to man, but no response. That's why the government is questioning me. They think we launched some sort of secret shuttle without their permission."

"Where is the shuttle now?"

"Well, as soon as it dropped off the probes, it took off back toward Mars. We're tracking its course."

Kevin was frustrated. This was clearly not the news he was hoping to hear. "What about Jake? Have you heard anything from Jake?"

"Sorry, Kevin, we're monitoring the wormhole twenty-four-seven. It's even opening and closing more frequently. The only shuttle that has gone through was the shuttle we saw a few days ago."

Kevin shook his head. His worst fears were beginning to come to fruition. Maybe Jake and Adrian were stranded on some strange planet, or worse – dead. "It's not your fault, Mike. Just keep me posted, okay."

"I will. And, by the way, when are you going to be in Washington D.C. next?"

"I have to meet with the Senate Technology Committee in June. Why?

Mike seemed uncomfortable on the other end of the phone. He sighed and said, "Well, President Galbraith and his advisors want to meet with you personally about the shuttles you helped design."

Kevin gave Mike an annoyed look. "I kind of figured."

Mike nodded. "Kevin, they're not blaming us. They're just suspicious that's all. . . . Yeah . . . listen Kevin, I've got to go. I'll talk to you later."

"Yeah. By Mike."

Kevin flipped his phone shut. He turned to go back into the arena, but he didn't feel like it, even though the crowd was frenzied and the game was coming down to the wire. He sighed and turned toward the exit.

Once outside, he sat on the steps leading up to one of the entrances and buried his head in his hands.

Kevin lifted his head and looked up at the stars. He didn't know the answers to his questions, but he knew where he could go for guidance. Kevin sighed, stood up, and began to walk the five blocks east to Temple Square.

Kevin glanced at his watch when he reached the southern entrance of Temple Square. 9:30 pm. Kevin was grateful that the square was still open to visitors. As he entered the square, he looked up at the magnificent structure that had stood for nearly two hundred years. No matter how many times Kevin looked at the temple or walked through its halls as he attended sessions, he was still amazed at the beauty of the building and how it continually brought thousands of visitors from the world every day.

Kevin continued to stare in awe at the brightly-lit temple as he walked into the garden on his left. Once in the perfectly manicured garden, he found a small area secluded by fresh flowers and two trees. On this night, Kevin noticed that there weren't that many visitors in the square.

Knowing he wouldn't be seen or heard, and appreciating the solitude, Kevin knelt on his knees and began to offer a fervent prayer to his Father in Heaven. In his prayer, he gave thanks to everything that he had been blessed with in his life. He then asked for answers to the questions that had been plaguing him since the discovery of the strange wormhole.

For years, many members of the church began to question whether Christ was actually going to return like He had promised. After all, scholars and members alike had been predicting that the Lord's return was imminent. But with the passing years, the entire world relatively at peace, and all of the nations open to missionary work, many members were beginning to apostatize, questioning the Church's doctrine on the Second Coming. He wondered . . . *could this wormhole, be a strange sign in heaven as predicted in Helaman chapter fourteen, verse six?*

When Kevin finished his prayer, he continued to kneel and sat in silent reflection as he looked at the temple.

"The day or the hour no man knoweth; but it surely shall come."

Kevin jumped up from his kneeling position and whirled around toward the direction of the voice. "Oh, President Scott, I . . . I didn't know you were there."

President Christopher A. Scott – a distant relative of Richard G. Scott and current prophet, seer, and revelator – gave Kevin a warm smile and walked toward him. "I'm sorry, Brother Palmer. I like to take walks around the temple at nights. It's a great time to feel the spirit and ponder."

Kevin nodded his head as the current President of the Church stood on his left and looked at the temple. Kevin turned around but did not look at the temple. Instead, he turned his head back and forth looking for the prophet's security.

"Oh, they're around, Brother Palmer, watching us. You don't think I would be foolish enough to walk around here alone do you?"

Kevin let out a small giggle and relaxed a little. He had met President Scott on several occasions but never actually had the chance to speak with him one-on-one. As he looked at President Scott, he was amazed at how young the seventy-four year old prophet looked. The light from the temple reflected off of the small white streaks of gray that were beginning to form in his thick brown hair. The prophet turned and met Kevin's gaze with his sincere hazel eyes.

"Wha . . . what did you say before?" Kevin asked.

President Scott continued to give Kevin a warm smile as he spoke. "I quoted *Doctrine and Covenants* section thirty-nine, verse twenty-one. No man knows when the Lord will come again, Brother Palmer. Not even me."

Kevin looked a little disappointed. "You heard my prayer?"

"Sorry, Brother Palmer, I was walking by when I heard someone speaking in the garden. I stopped and listened. I didn't mean to eavesdrop on your prayer. But I could feel the spirit so strongly while you prayed."

"I felt it too, but I am still confused more than ever." Kevin said.

With a small sigh and a nudge on Kevin's arm, President Scott said, "Come. Walk with me."

As the two men began to walk, Kevin noticed the prophet's security guards surround them.

"You know, Brother Palmer, I have been following your story in the news. I know the questions you have about what happened to Adrian and where he is now."

Kevin stopped suddenly and looked at his spiritual leader with sadness in his eyes. President Scott noticed and continued. "What if I were to tell you that Adrian and Jake are being watched over by the Lord?"

Kevin gave the prophet a look of confusion. "What do you mean? Are Adrian and Jake dead?"

The prophet smiled. "No, Kevin, they are not. In fact, I have a strong feeling that they are alive and well, performing a greater calling. You know it as well, Kevin, search your feelings and put away your logic and reasoning. Use your faith."

With these words, tears began to stream down Kevin's face. He had known all along that Adrian was alive. But without seeing him with his physical eyes, he couldn't believe it. He even knew that Jake was okay.

Kevin didn't know what to say.

President Scott recognized his loss for words and continued. "And, to answer your question about that strange ship and probes the news has been reporting on . . . who knows . . . only the Lord. But the scriptures have taught us only what the signs of the times are, not necessarily how they will come to be."

President Scott then placed his hand on Kevin's right shoulder. "Just remember, Kevin, rely on the Lord and he will show you the way. Have a good night, my brother."

And with that, Kevin watched the Lord's Prophet walk away surrounded by his security guards.

★ ★ ★ ★ ★

Skip, Jaskead, Ariauna, and Captain Morasea were all at the top of the stairs in front of the large wooden door.

"Are you sure this will work?" Ariauna asked.

Captain Morasea looked up at Ariauna from his kneeling position on the floor. "Don't worry. These charges will blow through a wall five meters thick."

"That's what I'm worried about. I don't want you to bring this entire temple down with your toys," Ariauna said.

Jaskead put his arm around his daughter. "Come, Ariauna. Let us leave the captain to do his work."

Ariauna didn't respond and began to follow her father down the stairs when Captain Morasea and Skip's communicators beeped. Skip grabbed his first and answered. "What is it?"

"Sir—"

"Lieutenant Ishae, is that you? There's too much static, and why can't I see you on the view screen?"

"Sir . . . c . . . Gn—"

"Lieutenant . . . I can't hear you. Repeat."

There was no response. Skip looked at Captain Morasea who looked back with the same bewildered look. "Captain, go and see what the problem is," Skip ordered.

Captain Morasea nodded, drew his gun, and made his way down the stairs.

"Jaskead, Ariauna, get back up here," said Skip.

Skip watched as Morasea turned and trotted down the stairs. Just as he turned the corner, Skip heard a gun blast. The plasma bolt nailed its target as the captain was thrown against the back wall. His lifeless and bleeding body slowly slid down the wall leaving a bright red streak of blood. Ariauna screamed. She and Jaskead jumped behind Skip for protection.

Skip quickly drew his gun and could feel Ariauna's trembling body on his while he waited patiently. Around the corner came two Gnol soldiers dressed in red battle fatigues and red battle helmets. They had their plasma assault rifles raised.

Skip raised his gun to get a shot off, but one of the Gnols threw an object up the stairs, and the two disappeared around the corner. Skip looked at the circular object and his eyes widened. "Grenade!" he yelled as he turned to cover Ariauna.

Jaskead lunged forward to kick the grenade back down the stairs, but it was too late. The deafening blast sent the three crashing through the door. Rock and wood splattered everywhere. Skip felt a sharp pain in his back and landed on the floor in the next room, his head hitting a piece of the wall.

When the smoke and dust settled, Skip slowly opened his eyes. Everything was blurry, and his body felt as if it had just been stabbed one hundred times. Finally after his vision cleared, he looked to his right. There, lying right next to him was Ariauna. Her forehead was bleeding, and she was unconscious. Skip prayed she was still alive. He then turned to find Jaskead.

There he was. About five feet to Skip's left. He lay there; eyes wide open, staring at Skip. Skip called out for him, but no answer. Skip tried to get up, but he couldn't. The only thing he could move was his head. He then looked straight ahead . . . and there it was; the answer to the prophecy.

He heard footsteps from behind and felt a fierce blow on the back of his head, causing his forehead to crash to the floor.

★ ★ ★ ★ ★

April 10, 2042 – Koroan's Palace

Celeste sat in one of the numerous luxurious leather chairs within her father's spacious office. She had never been in this office before. It was located on the thirty-fourth floor of the palace, just below the mysterious thirty-fifth floor and was immense. She estimated it to be nearly one thousand square feet of floor space.

She looked around the office. It was full of paintings and idols, all of which honored her father. Behind her father's gigantic wooden desk was a large window that encompassed the entire east wall. It was obvious why the window was so large. Celeste could just imagine her father peering out of the window daily, out upon the city he built to himself. She then looked to her left and saw what looked like an elevator entrance. She wondered if this was the elevator her father used to get to the mysterious thirty-fifth floor.

Celeste stood, and tried to loosen the ties that bound her hands behind her back for more comfort. It was useless. Whoever tied them did a good job. She closed her eyes and tried to loosen the cords with her new found telekinetic powers. It didn't work.

She was beginning to understand that in order for her to use her abilities she needed to use her hands. She figured there must be a connection between her mind and her hands. In fact, ever since her capture, she had her hands tied behind her back.

She sighed and sat back down. She was exhausted, hungry, and in need of a bath. The past two days had been miserable. She spent the last two days in the brig – in the basement of the palace – along with Bantyr, Kylee, and Sean. The other three didn't have their hands bound but were treated brutally by the guards.

Sean had been taken to her father. His inhibitors were taken out and tortured for information, and for no other reason other than her father enjoyed it. As a result, her father now knew where the second base was, and where Celeste's true loyalties rested.

Kylee and Bantyr, on the other hand, weren't tortured. Kylee was taken in for emergency surgery, and miraculously, her charred body was repaired; almost back to normal. If one looked hard enough, however, one would still be able to make out the areas where her skin grafts had been placed. It astonished Celeste as to why her father would permit Kylee's burned skin to be repaired. Bantyr, on the other hand, was left in the brig with Celeste, but he was beaten severely by the guards whenever they got the chance. Celeste knew, however, that her father wouldn't kill them. They were too important to him. He would use them to get to Adrian.

It was also obvious that Celeste's father was furious with her as well. She had demanded to see him several times throughout the two days. But the guards laughed and said that she was a disgrace to the Gnol race, and her father would just as soon let her die with the heathen humans. Until today; today, her father demanded to see her. As a result, the guards – without any regard for royal respect – dragged her to her father's office, with hands tied behind her back and blindfolded.

She was fearful. *What would her father do to her? Moreover, would he truly keep the other three alive?*

She heard yelling just outside of the door. She recognized the voices as her father's and Dorange's. The door slid open and in walked her father. He was no longer adorned in his usual white royal robe. Instead, he was dressed in similar black battle fatigues as Dorange. Only her father's contained more metals and patches demonstrating his power and might.

As her father entered the room, he turned his head and glared at Celeste. Never before had she seen such evil in her father's eyes. Koroan walked to the front of his desk and turned around. Dorange followed sheepishly. He looked like a dog that had just been beaten by its owner.

Koroan yelled with such volume it caused Celeste to tremble. "How dare you fail me!"

Celeste ducked her head in fear.

Koroan walked around his desk and slammed his fist down. The enormous desk split in two. "You had the heathen leader in your grasp, and you let him go!"

Dorange backed up as Koroan yelled so loudly that it caused the gigantic window to shake.

Dorange's voice trembled as he spoke. "Pl . . . Please your worship. I did not mean to fail. I—"

Celeste felt her draw drop. "What?" She questioned.

Koroan shot her a look. "You will not speak!" he barked as he approached Dorange. As a result, Dorange dropped to the floor.

Celeste had never before seen Dorange so afraid. He was now sitting on the floor with one arm raised, terrified Koroan would throw down a powerful blow. Koroan didn't deliver the blow Dorange expected, however. Instead, he began to pace back and forth with his hands behind his back. To Celeste, her father seemed to have switched his mood again from the monster he could become to the compassionate, caring father Celeste had once known.

Koroan slowly walked back to Dorange and gently lifted him with his telekinetic powers. "Yes, even though you have failed me in this mission, you have been more loyal to me than any other Gnol," he said as he turned and gave Celeste a look that caused her to tremble even more. He turned back to Dorange, letting him drop to the floor. "You can still prove your worth."

Dorange seemed to have stopped shaking. He then slid to the floor and knelt at Koroan's feet. "How, My Lord? Please . . . I beg of thee. What can I do to prove that I am loyal to my god?"

Koroan smiled at Dorange's reference to himself as a god. Celeste rolled her eyes. "If you want to prove your worth to me, Dorange, you will lead the attack against the new planet that has been discovered. . . . What is it called? Ah, yes . . . Earth."

Celeste was stunned. *How would her father know about Adrian's home world?*

Dorange quickly stood with a look of shock on his face. "But, My Lord, Earth . . ."

"You have an objection to that!" yelled Koroan, as he switched moods and lifted Dorange off the floor again. "You will do as I command . . . or . . . you will die!"

Dorange flailed his legs, and seemed almost to cry. "Yes," he whispered.

"What? I can't hear you!"

"Yes, My Lord," Dorange said with a quivering voice. "I will do as you command. For you are god!"

That seemed to please Koroan as he let Dorange drop to the floor. Koroan was about to say something else when his office door slid open. "I told you, I did not want to be disturbed!" he shrieked at the young Gnol guard who had just entered the room.

The young Gnol officer bowed and said, "Please . . . forgive me, your worship, but . . ." The guard stopped and looked at Celeste.

"You can tell me in front of her. She will soon no longer be a problem."

Celeste gave her father a puzzled and fearful look. *What did he mean by that?* She wondered.

The guard cleared his throat and continued, "Yes, My Lord. Captain Geraldus and his crew have just returned from the wormhole that they disappeared through four days ago."

"And?"

"And . . . he has found the location of this Earth."

A smile seemed to grow slowly along Koroan's face. "Good. Tell Captain Geraldus, he shall be promoted."

"Yes, My Lord. But . . . I also have some other good news."

"What is it?"

"Your lead scientists believe they have figured out a way to hold the wormhole open indefinitely. They wish to speak with you as soon as you are done here."

"Very well, Corporal, you can go now."

The corporal bowed and left the room.

Koroan seemed happy, at least for the moment. "Yes," he said and turned his attention back to Dorange. "Dorange, begin planning for an attack on Earth two months from today."

"Yes, My Lord."

"Good. You may go now, Dorange. I now wish to speak with Celeste alone."

"Yes, your worship," Dorange said as he began to leave the room.

Just before he got to the door, however, Koroan stopped him. "Dorange, wait."

Dorange turned around. He seemed frustrated that he was not yet allowed to leave. "What may I do for you, My Lord?"

Koroan walked closer to Dorange. "Remember, Dorange. Do not fail on this mission. If you do, you will not be able to imagine the consequences you will suffer."

Dorange swallowed. "Ye . . . Yes, My Lord," he said, and he whirled around and left the room.

After the door slid shut, Koroan stood in the middle of the room. He was silent and stared at Celeste for a long moment. Celeste could not look her father in the eye. She knew that she had disappointed him. Yet, she did not feel ashamed. She knew what she did was right.

Koroan took one step closer to Celeste and raised his right arm. Celeste felt her body become lighter as it levitated off of the chair she sat upon. Her father levitated her to him. She was now within inches of her father's face.

She looked into his eyes. They seemed to glow red from the blood within his capillaries.

"Tell me one good reason why I should not kill you now?"

Celeste felt her voice quiver. She had at times throughout her life been afraid of her father but never so much as now. "F . . . Fa . . . Father, I am your daughter."

Koroan's bloodshot eyes seemed to boil with anger. With a flick of his wrist, he threw Celeste toward the wall. With her hands tied behind her back, there was no way she could brace herself for the impact. She hit the wall and felt the air rush out of her lungs. She fell to the floor and rolled around trying to regain her breath. Koroan grabbed her and sat her in one of the chairs. "You are no longer my daughter!" he yelled.

Celeste didn't respond.

"How long did you think you could get away with this?"

Celeste looked at her father with the same anger in her eyes. "I was doing well for awhile."

Koroan backhanded her. Celeste felt her lip split and blood began to trickle down to her chin.

Her father then began to pace again. "Nevertheless, you are my daughter. I should kill you for your treachery, but . . . I won't. You will, instead be under house arrest. You will stay with your mother, your hands will always be tied behind your back, and you shall have two guards at your side at all times.

My high priest's daughter, Nichelle, will be brought in to assist you in your bathing and feeding needs."

Celeste stood and walked toward her father. She stopped and said, "I would rather die than be reduced to an animal!"

"I will not give you the satisfaction. I want you alive to see the sufferings and deaths of all those you truly serve." Koroan looked at his office door and opened it telekinetically. "Guards!"

The two guards, dressed in red battle fatigues, entered the room.

"Take my daughter to her mother's room. You are to never leave her side. Another shift of guards will replace you in twelve hours."

The guards nodded and grabbed Celeste by the arms. Celeste shook loose and turned back to her father. "Tell me something, Father. Why did you not read Dorange's mind?"

"I did not find it necessary."

Celeste shook her head. "Too bad . . . if you would have, you would have known who really killed Raqel."

Koroan walked closer to Celeste. "I already know who killed your sister who was loyal to me. It was that pitiful creature, Adrian Palmer."

Celeste's eyes narrowed as she spoke. "Are you sure? You never know who you can trust . . . right, Father."

Celeste's comments infuriated Koroan. He whirled around and raised both of his arms. The two halves of his giant desk, he had split in two previously, arose from the floor. With a deafening yell and wave of his arms, Koroan heaved the broken desk through the window. Glass shattered everywhere as the two guards holding Celeste's arms backed away. However, Celeste did not move a muscle. Strangely, she was gaining more courage the angrier her father got.

Koroan turned back to face his daughter. He was breathing heavily, his eyes wild with anger, and sweat dripping from his head. "How dare you question me that way? I am your father and more importantly your god!"

Celeste opened her mouth and was about to speak when her father stepped forward and grabbed her face just under her chin with his left hand. He lifted her off of the ground. "What do you know about loyalty?" he said. "Even though Dorange is not of my blood line, he has been more loyal to me than you have ever been."

Koroan dropped Celeste to the floor and looked at the guards. Take her to her mother's room. Her mother will soon be dead."

"What?" shrieked Celeste.

"Quiet!" yelled Koroan, as he hit Celeste again with the back of his left hand. She fell to the floor in pain. This time her father didn't hold back. She felt the blood rush to her right eye, it swelled up and burst as bright red blood splattered on the floor.

Koroan looked at the guards again. "As soon as her mother dies, inform me."

"Yes, My Lord," said one of the guards.

Koroan then turned and looked at his daughter with an evil smile spread across his face that sent chills down Celeste's spine. "Good," he said. "Because as soon as her mother dies, my daughter – the traitor – will suffer a public torture and execution."

CHAPTER 15

April 11, 2042 – Koroan's Palace

Tears rolled down Celeste's face as she sat on the edge of her mother's bed. She felt awful. Her right eye was swollen shut and her lip was swollen as well from her father's blows. Despite her injuries and how sad she felt for her mother – who was sleeping soundly just a few feet away – she felt a little better having just been fed and bathed by her dear friend Nichelle.

Celeste looked to her left. Nichelle sat in a chair, reading a book, her dark brown eyes opening and closing as she fought sleep. She brought her left hand up to her long brown hair and pushed it aside as she turned and smiled at Celeste.

Celeste was so grateful Nichelle was there. Nichelle was the only one she could trust now besides her mother. When Celeste decided to help the rebels, Nichelle was the only one she told. Nichelle promised Celeste that she would tell no one. She kept her promise because she had witnessed how her own father – Vlamer Kreuk, Koroan's High Priest and friend – had changed from a kind, gentle Gnol to a Gnol who now desired power and wealth above all else. Because of this, Nichelle vowed she would never tell, and that she would always help Celeste if she needed it.

A few hours earlier, Nichelle had been brought to the palace. She had a private meeting with Koroan and was ordered to stay with Celeste until

Celeste's mother died. Consequently, Nichelle also knew of Celeste's impending execution.

Even though Nichelle was there, Celeste still felt uncomfortable and embarrassed. Celeste had always been independent and didn't like being treated like a baby. It wasn't that Nichelle treated Celeste personally as if she was a baby. It was because her hands were still tied behind her back, which required Nichelle to feed and bathe her.

Celeste returned her dear friend's smile.

"Are you okay?" Nichelle asked.

Celeste nodded her head and took a deep breath. She then looked at the two guards dressed in their red battle fatigues at the doorway. These guards were different now from the guards who had taken her to her mother's room earlier.

The guard to her left was a big, muscular female with short red hair. Her fiery green eyes seemed to bore into Celeste as she stared, knowing full well the traitor Celeste had become. In fact, this new female guard was the one guard chosen to follow Celeste everywhere. She was in the bathing room when Nichelle bathed Celeste. Another female guard would replace her when her shift was over.

Celeste looked at the guard to her right. This guard was actually shorter than the female guard. He had short, blond hair and a patch of a goatee beginning to form around his upper lip and chin. It was obvious that this guard was barely in his twenties.

Celeste made eye contact with him. He quickly turned his gaze away, seeming shy if not embarrassed to look at the beautiful princess with her wet hair, and dressed only in her white robe.

Celeste forced a smile in his direction. He looked up and smiled back. Celeste knew that if she had any hope of an escape it would probably have to be through this young soldier.

Celeste heard her mother cough and turned back to her mother. Ciminae Chast looked old and frail despite only being fifty-six years of age. At that age, most Gnols were still young and energetic. Thanks to all of the new medical knowledge her father had revealed, the average life-span of a Gnol was roughly one hundred forty-three years of age.

"Cel . . . Celeste. Where are you?" Ciminae said as she tried to raise her head but couldn't.

"I am here, Mother," Celeste said, inching closer to her mother.

"Give me your hand."

"I wish I could, Mother. Father has ordered that my hands stay tied behind my back until . . ."

"What?" Ciminae said as she wheezed trying to breath. "Where are the guards?"

The two guards at the door made their way to Ciminae's bed. The male guard stood on the same side Celeste sat. Celeste made sure to smile at him. He smiled back shyly and then looked at the female guard on the opposite side of the bed. The female gave him an angry look, and he ducked his head.

Ciminae weakly turned her head to the left and looked up at the female guard. "I order you to unbind my daughter's bonds. I wish to hold her hand."

The female guard first looked at Celeste and then back at Ciminae. She opened her mouth, paused, and then spoke. "I am sorry . . . but I have been given a direct order from our lord himself. The princess is not to have her bonds untied, even if you order me to do so."

Ciminae gave the guard a stern look and then said, "Fine . . . if you will not let a dying mother hold her daughter's hand, then you will let her speak with her daughter alone."

The female guard looked uncomfortable. It was obvious that she wanted to obey the queen, but she couldn't. "I . . . I am sorry, Your Highness. That is also another order directly from our lord. He ordered us not to let the Princess out of our sight. Again, ev—"

"Yes, yes, I know. Even if I order it," said Ciminae, as she waved the guards away.

The guards returned to their posts, and Ciminae looked at her daughter. She coughed and spat out a small amount of blood.

Celeste was alarmed. Even though her mother had trouble breathing before, this was the first time she had ever seen her mother cough up blood throughout this strange illness. "Mother, are you okay?" she said. "Shall I call for the doctor?"

Her mother shook her head. "No . . ." She coughed again. "There's nothing the doctor can do. I will not live mu—" Blood spattered from Ciminae's mouth as she coughed.

Nichelle noticed and brought Ciminae a towel. Nichelle lifted Ciminae, so she wouldn't inhale the blood back into her lungs. Ciminae grabbed the towel and continued to cough into it. She coughed so much that Nichelle had to grab another towel because the first one had become soaked with blood.

Celeste felt helpless. She wanted so badly to help her mother. "Mo . . . Mother, are you okay?" she asked, beginning to cry.

Ciminae finally stopped coughing and nodded. "Ye . . . Yes. Sometimes I have these coughing fits, but . . . but this is the first time I have coughed up blood."

Ciminae tried to take a deep breath, but because of the blood and fluid within her lungs she wasn't able get the oxygen she needed. She tried again and gained some relief. She then looked at her daughter as Nichelle continued to hold her upright.

Ciminae wiped Celeste's tears away and smiled. Then she placed her own hands behind her ears and pulled out her inhibitors.

As she pulled, Celeste said in a whisper, "Mother, what are you doing? The guards will be able to read your thoughts." A flood of her mother's thoughts rushed into Celeste's mind.

Ciminae shook her head and pulled the inhibitors entirely out as she winced in pain. After the inhibitors were out, she leaned forward and embraced Celeste. Celeste began to sob as she felt her mother slide her hands behind her ears. Ciminae then pulled Celeste's inhibitors out. Celeste turned to look at the guards. They seemed not to have noticed what Ciminae did or had any indication that their inhibitors were out. She turned back to her mother and spoke to her telepathically. *Mother, what about the guards?*

Ciminae raised her hand to stop Celeste. She then looked at Nichelle and motioned for her to lean down. Nichelle leaned down; Ciminae hugged her, and commenced to take out her inhibitors as well. Once Nichelle's inhibitors were out, all three were able to communicate telepathically.

Ciminae was the first to send her thoughts. To Celeste, her mother's thoughts reminded her of when her mother was healthy. *Do not worry, Celeste. These Gnols are not experienced enough in their abilities to read our minds.*

Ciminae paused and looked at the guards. She continued. *We need to discuss how to get your cords untied, and how you are going to escape. I know that your father plans to have you executed as soon as I pass away.*

Celeste nodded. *How did you know?*

I know more than you know, my dear, Ciminae thought as she looked at Nichelle. *Nichelle?*

Nichelle moved to the other side of the bed and sat down, so she could better communicate with Ciminae and Celeste. *Yes, Your Highness*, Nichelle thought.

Ciminae raised her right arm and stroked the side of Nichelle's cheek with the back of her hand. *Nichelle, you have been such a loyal and trustworthy friend to Celeste.*

Nichelle smiled back as tears began to roll down her cheeks. Nichelle had grown to love Ciminae like a mother. When she was just a child, her own mother had died, and Ciminae had taken her in and practically raised her when her father was away. *Thank you, Your Highness,* she thought.

Ciminae continued. *Now, more than ever, Celeste needs you.*

Nichelle nodded.

Listen carefully, Nichelle. I do not believe I will last through the night.

Celeste cut in. *Do not think that way, Mother.*

Ciminae looked compassionately at her daughter. *It is inevitable, Celeste. Please do not be sad for me. Soon, I will not suffer anymore and will join our ancestors in the afterlife.*

She paused and wiped more tears away from Celeste's eyes. *Now, both of you listen carefully. When I pass on, Nichelle will accompany the female guard to notify your father of my death. It will be the female guard because she will want to be the one rewarded for notifying him.*

Yes, Your Highness, thought Nichelle. *What will you have me do when I meet your husband?*

You will not let the guard get to her destination.

What do you mean? Nichelle thought.

Ciminae pointed to the nightstand at the left of her bed. *There underneath the nightstand . . . feel.*

Nichelle glanced back at the guards. The guards were now sitting at the small table next to the door. The female guard was reading a small book, and the male guard was leaning back in his chair. He was dozing in and out of sleep.

Nichelle looked back at the nightstand, slowly slid off the bed onto her hands and knees, and felt the underside of the nightstand. There, in a small compartment on the underside of the nightstand, was a small plasma blaster. It was about the size of her palm. As a result, she was able to pull it out concealed. Then she slowly slid the gun into her right boot, just below her knee.

Once the gun was secure, she sat back upon the bed and looked at Ciminae.

Ciminae nodded. *Good, you will know what to do . . . and do not feel guilty, Nichelle; for we are at war, and, unfortunately, being a Gnol, we are on the wrong side of the battle.*

Ciminae then looked with intensity at Celeste. *Celeste, you will know what to do after Nichelle and the guard leave.*

Celeste turned and looked at the young male guard, then turned and forced a smile back toward her mother. *I do*, she thought.

Good, thought Ciminae. *Once you have taken care of the male guard. Dress into his uniform and put on his battle helmet that is underneath the table. Then meet Nichelle and get out of the palace using the secret passageway in your room.*

Yes, Mother.

Ciminae placed her left hand on Nichelle's hand and her right hand on Celeste's knee. *Now that we have your escape planned, I want both of you to listen very carefully. Your father, Celeste, has hidden so much from all of us. About a year ago when I had the strength, I demanded to see him in his private office. He refused to see me and his royal guards would not let me enter. But at that time, I was still able to use most of my telekinetic abilities. So, I easily moved the guards aside and barged into his office.*

Your father sat in the center of the room with his back to the door. He was meditating and in a trance. When I approached, I startled him out of his trance, and he stood. At the same time, his guards came rushing in. Your father stopped them and ordered them to return to their posts. He said that it was time I knew everything.

What did he tell you? Celeste thought.

Your father allowed me to read his mind, Ciminae thought as tears began to flow from her eyes. She tried to inhale another breath, but had another coughing fit instead. After she finished coughing and spewing blood into the towel Nichelle had provided for her, she lied back down and looked at Celeste with tear filled eyes. *It was at that time that I knew for a fact that your father was no longer the Gnol I grew to love and married. He was different. He desired power more than anything else.*

Ciminae reached up and wiped her tears away and continued. *I found out horrible things; things your father did, and the true source of his knowledge and power. I did not like what I learned. So, I threatened to tell his high ranking officers. He laughed and said that his officers would not believe me. I then threatened to tell you. That is when—* Ciminae stopped as she struggled to breathe.

Mother, you need to rest. We can continue later.

Ciminae shook her head. *No, I am afraid I will not last through the night, and you need to know the truth . . .* She stopped and coughed again, . . . *After I threatened to tell you, he became extremely serious and threatened me.*

Threatened you? Nichelle thought.

Yes, he said that I wouldn't dare, and if I did, Celeste would suffer.

Celeste inched closer to her mother. *How would I suffer?*

I asked the same question. That is when he went to his desk and pulled out a hypodermic needle. Using his telekinetic abilities, he held me in place and injected me with the solution that was in the syringe.

I asked what he had injected me with. He said that I would soon find out, and how you would suffer if I told anyone. Within hours, I had become seriously ill. That is when I found out that your father had injected me with an experimental, biological weapon that he and his scientists had tested on other Gnols. He planned to develop the weapon as an airborne agent and release it upon the humans. That is why I wasn't able to tell you. I knew that if you had found out who your father truly is, he would make you suffer the same as I.

Celeste was stunned. She knew her father had changed. But he had become worse than she thought he was. He was absolutely evil now. How could her father do this to the woman he loved? The only one he cared about was himself and what power he could gain.

Celeste gritted her teeth and thought: *What did you find out, Mother? What is his true source of power?*

Ciminae began to send her thoughts to Celeste but started coughing again. The cough was worse now, however. She struggled for oxygen and turned her head as more blood spurted from her mouth. Nichelle placed the towel underneath her chin and patted her back to help her.

After Ciminae was able to regain her breath, she continued. *I am sorry, Celeste. Using my telepathic abilities seems to have weakened me even more.*

Mother, what did you find out?

Do you remember when you were young, Celeste . . . back on Gnolom?

Yes.

Do you remember . . . it was about twenty-five years ago, Terrest time . . . when your father and Nichelle's father left on a hunting party, along with one hundred other Gnols from our tribe?

Celeste and Nichelle both nodded.

That was before we had any technology and our planet was dying. Do you remember?

Yes we do, Your Highness. Nichelle thought.

Remember, both of your fathers were gone for almost a year. We thought they had suffered some tragic end.

Celeste nodded and could see that her mother struggled more and more to breathe in the oxygen she so desperately needed. Her thoughts were also starting to become erratic. They were getting more difficult for Celeste and Nichelle to read.

Ciminae opened and closed her eyes several times as if she was fighting sleep. Celeste wanted to tell her to stop using her telepathic abilities, but she knew her mother wanted to tell her the truth about everything, and she wanted to hear it.

Ciminae continued. *Remember . . . remember . . . when . . . they . . . when they came back. . . . We were . . . were all so happy to see them alive, but . . . but your father, Nichelle, and your father, Celeste, were the only ones left from the hun . . . the hunting party. When . . . when they return . . . returned, they were different . . . remember?*

Celeste and Nichelle nodded again as they began to sob, seeing that Ciminae struggled to hold on.

Remember . . . remember . . . how both of your fathers were different. They had both gained so . . . Ciminae began to cough again. This time the coughing was more violent, and her body trembled with each one. After what seemed like several minutes, Ciminae continued. *Your fathers had brought back with them so much knowledge about new . . .* Again, she coughed and wheezed for air, . . . *about new and wonder . . . wonderful technology. They had even brought back these inhibitors that they had developed, and we gladly had them inserted . . . remember?*

Celeste nodded as the tears streamed out of her eyes, down her cheeks, and onto her mother's blanket. She was watching her mother – the woman she loved so dearly – die before her very eyes; the mother who sacrificed her own health and life to save hers.

Your father claimed he had been visited by a goddess. He . . . he cal . . . called this goddess the goddess of light. He claimed . . . he claimed that this goddess told him that he was the one who was the chosen . . . one. After that, your father and Nichelle's father changed our ancient scriptures, developed teams of people to create new technologies, and united every Gnol tribe. They made our ancient scriptures look like your father was the god of the Gnols! They took things out that . . . things that they claimed were not important.

What do you mean? Thought Celeste.

The most prominent scripture in our religion; the one that . . . the scripture . . . Ciminae wheezed as she tried to take another breath, . . . *the scripture that prophecies of the chosen one. The chos . . . the chosen one . . . he will be the one to unite two . . . two . . . peoples and two worlds. Your fa . . . . your father changed . . . he changed that scripture . . . he changed it to make it look like he . . . like he was the chosen one. . . . And most Gnols believed him because of his . . . because of his new found knowledge and power. For som . . . for some odd reason, he had more telekin . . . telekinetic and telepathic power than any other Gnol . . .* Ciminae was forced to stop again. She struggled for air, and blood began to seep out of her mouth. She fell back to her pillow; her body trembling as it struggled for oxygen.

Celeste could no longer read her mother's thoughts as her mother went in and out of consciousness. "Mother," she said. "Mother, are you okay?"

Nichelle grabbed the oxygen mask that was connected to the tank next to Ciminae's bed. She placed the mask over Ciminae's nose and mouth. It was no use. Ciminae's lungs were rapidly filling with fluid. She was drowning in her own blood.

The two guards noticed and walked to the bed. As the guards approached, Nichelle quickly placed Celeste's inhibitors back into her head behind her ears. Celeste winced in pain. Nichelle then backed away to the bathroom where she was out of sight of the guards and placed her own inhibitors in, then returned to assist Ciminae.

Celeste looked at the female guard. "Cut my cords! I need to help her!"

The guard glared at Celeste with her green eyes and said, "Sorry, Princess. Your father has made it abundantly clear that under no uncertain terms are your hands to be released."

Celeste opened her mouth and then shut it. She glared at the female guard with such intensity that the guard, for the first time, seemed intimidated. Thoughts rushed through Celeste's mind of what she would do to the guard if her hands weren't tied behind her back.

"Cel . . . Celeste," Ciminae mumbled, waving for Celeste to lean down.

Celeste looked back at her mother and leaned as close to her face as she could. Celeste could hear her mother desperately trying to breathe. "Mo . . . Mother," she said as she began to sob.

Ciminae looked into her daughter's eyes, grabbed her behind the neck, pulled her close, and said in a wheezing whisper, "The answers about your father . . . your father's mysteries lie on the top floor."

Because of Ciminae's wheezing and struggle for breath, Celeste had a hard time hearing her. "Mother . . . Mother . . . what . . . I do not understand?"

Ciminae looked so lovingly at her daughter, took one last struggling breath, and said, "The answers you seek are on the top fl—"

Celeste felt her mother's hand, that was on the back of her neck, go limp. Ciminae's arm fell to her side, and she layed motionless with her eyes wide open, staring at Celeste.

Celeste could no longer control her sobbing. She looked at Nichelle who was crying as well and approached Ciminae's lifeless body. Nichelle gently placed her hand over Ciminae's eyes and closed them.

As the guards moved away from the bed, Celeste heard the female guard. "I will go and inform Lord Chast of his wife's death."

★ ★ ★ ★ ★

As Nichelle left with the female guard, Celeste knew that was her cue to move. Even though her mother had just passed away, she knew she had to put the grief of her mother's loss deep down into the recesses of her emotions. She needed to look as happy as she could in order for her plan to work with the young male guard.

She stood and made her way to the restroom. The male guard began to follow, but Celeste stopped him with her look. She had made sure to not look angry. The look was more seductive than anything else. As a result, the young guard smiled shyly and ducked his head.

"If you don't mind, I need some time to myself," Celeste said.

The guard looked back at Celeste. It was obvious to her that the young Gnol was attracted to her. The thought almost made her sick, but she had to do what she had planned or she would soon be joining her mother in the afterlife as well.

The guard hesitated and stuttered a little as he spoke. "I . . . I am . . . I am sorry, Your Highness. I am not to let you out of my sight."

Celeste smiled compassionately at the young guard. "What's your name?" she asked.

The guard seemed taken back. "What? . . . Um . . . my name?"

"That is what I asked," said Celeste, as she slowly moved closer to the guard.

The guard backed up a little. "Uh . . . yes . . . my name . . . it's . . . uh . . . Gyrale."

Celeste walked to within inches of Gyrale's face. She leaned in and spoke softly into his ear. "Gyrale," she said. "That is a strong name." And then she eased off a little. She could tell that she was getting to the young guard. He was sweating and seemed very nervous. She continued. "Tell me, Gyrale. Do you find me attractive?"

Gyrale nodded his head but didn't say anything.

Celeste moved in closer and made sure he could smell her freshly bathed body. Gyrale gulped and tried to back away, but Celeste moved with him. "As you know, Gyrale, I am scheduled to be executed soon."

Again, the guard nodded.

"And . . . um, well, I was wondering, Gyrale. I haven't been with a man for such a long time." Celeste said, and then she giggled. "What am I saying? I haven't been with a man at all, and . . . Well, when I saw you, I knew you were the one I wanted to be with before my father had me killed."

"Y . . . you did?" said Gyrale, wiping his forehead.

Celeste nodded. She was disgusted and felt foolish. Never in her life had she acted like this, and she was ashamed even though she knew it was the only way to save her life. "You know, Gyrale," she said. "That other guard and Nichelle will not be back for awhile. If you could just untie my hands, I could show you things that . . . well, things that you could only imagine."

Gyrale continued to back up, and Celeste followed. The closer Celeste got, the more nervous Gyrale became. As he backed up, his left foot caught the rug that was next to Ciminae's bed. He flopped onto the bed, rolled over, and then back onto his feet on the other side. As he did so, Celeste saw the blanket that was being used to cover her mother's body, slide off.

Celeste turned her attention back to Gyrale who slowly made his way to the door. *This is not working*, she thought. "Gyrale, what are you afraid of?"

Gyrale continued to back to the door, and Celeste followed. "Uh . . . I . . . uh . . . I can't untie your cords."

Celeste forced a disappointed look upon her face. "Okay. If you will not untie my hands, there is something else we could do."

Just as he reached the door, Gyrale stopped. "Wha . . . what is that?"

Celeste moved closer hoping her gamble would payoff. "As you know, Gyrale, we Gnols can use our minds to simulate . . . uh . . . how shall I say . . . certain feelings? And because of our telepathic abilities our bodies can not tell the difference between what we are thinking and what is actually going on."

"Uh huh," Gyrale stammered.

Celeste walked right up to Gyrale and placed her right cheek on his left. It was easy for her to do so because Gyrale was about an inch shorter than she was. She then proceeded to – as she rolled her eyes – gently peck his cheek. She moved up his cheek to his ear where she whispered. "Take out your inhibitors so I can show you what I mean."

Gyrale backed away a little, but he didn't seem nervous now. Instead, he had a crooked grin on his face that gave Celeste an uneasy feeling, but she continued the act, nonetheless.

Suddenly, Gyrale grabbed Celeste by her arms and pulled her close. He then turned Celeste around and began to untie her cords. Celeste allowed a small smile to crease along her lips. She had finally gotten to him.

Once her bonds were free, Celeste felt her muscles in her shoulders relax. She then turned to face Gyrale and backed away. Gyrale tried to follow like a deprived animal, but she put up a finger to stop him. Then Celeste raised her hands.

Gyrale's eyes widened, and he reached for his weapon, realizing that Celeste had misled him.

Celeste also saw him reaching for his gun. As he did so, Celeste flicked her left wrist. Gyrale's weapon went flying across the room. And then, with her right hand, Celeste levitated Gyrale off the floor. Gyrale's eyes were wild with fear. He knew there was nothing he could do.

With a flick of her right hand, she sent Gyrale flying into the wall. Gyrale's body hit the brick wall with such force that pieces of brick fell to the floor.

Celeste let her arms fall to her side and dropped to the floor in near exhaustion as Gyrale's body dropped. She looked at Gyrale and crawled toward him. She placed two fingers on Gyrale's throat and felt a pulse. She was glad that she didn't kill him. After all, Gyrale was never actually a threat to her, but she knew he would suffer the wrath of her father.

Celeste wiped the sweat away from her forehead, moved to Gyrale's body, and proceeded to undress him.

★ ★ ★ ★ ★

"Tell me again, Madam, why did you need to come with me to inform Lord Chast of his wife's death."

Nichelle looked at the guard as they walked down the long, spacious corridor of the Chast's family's living quarters to the elevator. The guard was nearly a foot taller than Nichelle and obviously more muscular. *How am I going to do this?* She thought.

"Madam?"

"Huh . . . oh, I'm sorry. I am just upset about the queen's death and lost in my thoughts . . . sorry," said Nichelle. "What was your question?"

The female guard stopped and looked at Nichelle with suspicion. "I asked why was it you needed to come with me to inform Lord Chast of his wife's death?"

Nichelle thought for a moment. "Oh . . . well . . . um . . . Lord Chast also told me when I met with him that he wanted me to inform him as well. And . . . since I am the daughter of Vlamer Kreuk, his lordship's High Priest, it only makes sense that I am there as well."

The guard eyed Nichelle up and down. Nichelle worried for a moment that she did not believe her. Then she nodded and proceeded to the elevator again. Nichelle took a deep breath and tried to keep pace with the large guard.

Nichelle looked at the elevator as they neared it. *I'll have to do it in the elevator*, she thought. But when the elevator door opened, Nichelle's hopes of a successful mission began to fade quickly. There, along the back wall of the elevator, stood two palace guards. The male Gnols were dressed in the usual red battle fatigues that all palace guards wore. Rather than battle helmets, however, these two guards wore berets that indicated they were a higher rank than the guard Nichelle accompanied.

The female guard saluted the Gnol officers before she and Nichelle entered the elevator. The two officers saluted back, and the taller one on Nichelle's left – a large Gnol – spoke. "Private, what brings you and Madam Kreuk out this time of night?"

"Lord Chast wanted me to inform him of his wife's death, Sir. She died a few moments ago."

The Gnol nodded and said, "Very well. You may accompany us to the thirty-fourth floor. Lord Chast has called an emergency meeting with all of his officers. . . . Something about an attack on a planet called Earth."

"Thank you, Sir," said the female guard, as she stepped onto the elevator.

Nichelle followed and smiled at the two Gnol officers. They nodded back. There was no way Nichelle was going to try to kill the female guard now. She wasn't skilled with a weapon, and her telekinetic abilities were not even comparable to Celeste's. Even though she knew that she was probably more powerful than each individual in that elevator – combined they would tear her apart.

As the elevator ascended to the thirty-fourth floor, the smaller officer spoke. He was about the same size as Nichelle. "So, what kind of spectacle do you think Lord Chast will make of his daughter's execution?"

"I don't know," said the larger officer. "But, I will tell you this much. She deserves everything that is coming to her. She is an embarrassment to our way of life; the way she befriended those animals. I mean come on . . . those humans don't even possess the slightest power we do. I am glad that Lord Chast is setting an example by executing her. It will just prove even more how he is the chosen one."

Nichelle rolled her eyes.

Nichelle, personally, had never had contact with a human. But from what Celeste had told her, she knew that the majority of them were genuine and true. They may not have had the power, strength, or intelligence of Gnols, but Celeste seemed to trust them. And Nichelle trusted Celeste more than anyone.

"What do you think, Madam Kreuk?" the smaller guard asked.

Nichelle turned around and looked at him. "What do I think about what?"

The smaller guard laughed and looked at his friend. "Oh, c'mon. It's common knowledge that you and the Princess are best friends. You can't stand there and tell me that you agree with her execution."

Nichelle swallowed. The officer was right. She didn't agree with it. She would rather see Koroan, and her own father die for their sins than her dearest friend. "You are right in one aspect."

"In one aspect?" the guard questioned.

"Yes, in one aspect, I do agree with her execution because she has betrayed the Gnols. But on the other hand, I do not want to see my best friend die. After all she has done to dishonor us, she is still my friend."

The smaller officer nodded and said, "That's an interesting way of looking at it."

Nichelle turned back around and saw that the elevator was about to stop. When it stopped, and the doors opened, she was astonished to see that the entire floor that housed Koroan's secretarial staff was packed full of various Gnol military personnel. *This attack is certainly a big deal,* she thought as she stepped off of the elevator.

The two officers followed Nichelle and the female guard off of the elevator, and then made their way to another group of officers. Nichelle followed the female guard to the entrance to Koroan's office. The two guards standing at the door stopped them.

"Lord Chast says he is not to be disturbed," said the guard on the right. "What do you need, Private?"

"Sir, Lord Chast requested that I inform him personally when his wife had passed away."

"Well, that may be so . . . but Lord Chast gave us specific orders not to let anyone enter. He is in a private meeting with his generals and High Priest, Vlamer Kreuk," the guard said as he looked at Nichelle.

The private looked at Nichelle as well, and then turned back to the guard. "Very well, we will wait."

The guard nodded, and Nichelle and the private walked to the chairs that lined the outside wall of Koroan's office, and sat. Nichelle was sweating, and her stomach was in knots. Surely, Celeste had to be looking for her by now. She took a deep breath and tried to think of what to say when she encountered her father and Koroan. They obviously weren't expecting her, and what would she do if Koroan sent more guards back to the room with her and the private?

The door to Koroan's office slid open, and Dorange walked out first. He looked at the private and Nichelle and gave them a puzzled look. Koroan's two other generals, General Thourad and General Ochalt, came out of the office as well.

The private stood up quickly and saluted all three generals. They saluted back. "What do you need, Private?" Dorange asked as he continued to look at Nichelle with suspicion.

"Sir, I am here to notify Lord Chast of his wife's death."

Nichelle studied Dorange's face closely. She was curious to see his reaction to the queen's death. Rather than seem grief stricken over the death of a noble queen, Dorange's face seemed to glow with anticipation. Nichelle noticed and allowed a glaring stare to land upon his eyes. Dorange noticed and glared back. He then turned back to the private. "Very well, Private. You may enter."

The private walked toward the entrance, and Dorange began to follow. Nichelle, however, hesitated. She did not want to see her father, especially with what was going on. The private noticed Nichelle's hesitation, as well as Dorange. Nichelle met their gazes and grew extremely nervous. They both had a look of distrust. Nichelle stood quickly and followed.

All three entered the room as the door slid shut behind them. Koroan was sitting behind his new desk with his back to them. He faced his newly repaired window as he stared out amidst the lights of *Chast*. He looked as if he was deep in thought. Nichelle's father, dressed in his usual religious garb, sat in another chair beside Koroan. His back was also to them, and he seemed to be lost in his thoughts as well.

Dorange spoke first. "My Lord?"

Koroan and Vlamer both seemed to be startled out of their trances and quickly turned around. All three dropped to one knee and bowed in their lord's honor and then stood again. Nichelle looked up and made eye contact with her father. He gave her a questioning look.

"What is it, General?" Koroan questioned.

"The private has a message for you."

Koroan looked at the female guard. The private seemed extremely nervous in Koroan's presence. "Y . . . yes, My Lord . . . You wanted me to inform you of your wife's death."

"And?"

"She has passed on to meet the great goddess, My Lord."

Nichelle watched Koroan's reaction. She wasn't surprised. He showed no emotion whatsoever, no grief, sadness, or even happiness for that matter.

"Yes, thank you, Private," said Koroan. He then shot a look to Nichelle. "Nichelle, why have you come? I specifically told you to stay with Celeste at all times."

The private looked at Nichelle and stared. She opened her mouth as if she wanted to say something and then shut it again.

"Well?" demanded Koroan.

Nichelle looked at Koroan as she tried to hide her anxiety. "My apologies, My Lord. I must have misunderstood you. I th . . . I thought that you wanted me to inform you of your wife's death as well. Please forgive me."

Koroan's eyes seemed to glaze over and boil with anger. Nichelle noticed him take a deep breath. He was about to let out a bellowing yell when Vlamer cut him off. "Yes, My Dear. You must have heard our lord wrong. For you know, he does not make mistakes." Vlamer then turned to Koroan who was still seething with anger. "Please, My Lord, forgive her."

Vlamer's comments seemed to satisfy Koroan's ego. He changed moods again and walked to Nichelle. He gently placed his hands on Nichelle's upper arms. "Yes, you are forgiven. You must be distraught because of Celeste's pending execution?"

Nichelle nodded. "Yes, My Lord. I am. But I do agree with your execution order; for she has betrayed us and you most of all."

A smile grew along Koroan's face. He turned back to Vlamer. "Vlamer, my dear friend, you have raised a trustworthy and patriotic daughter."

Vlamer bowed his head and said, "Thank you, My Lord."

Koroan then turned his attention back to the female guard. "Private, inform the medical staff to take my wife's body to the morgue and prepare her for a proper burial. She shall have a funeral honorable of a queen the day after tomorrow."

The private bowed and said, "Yes, My Lord," and she left the office.

Koroan looked at Dorange. "General, escort Madam Kreuk back to my wife's room. Take Celeste and prepare her for execution at dawn."

A smile, as large as Nichelle had ever seen, graced across Dorange's face. "Yes, My Lord," he said as he bowed. He looked at Nichelle and turned to leave the room. Nichelle began to follow as the fear within her began to protrude throughout her body, causing her to tremble.

Just as they were about to exit Koroan's office, Nichelle heard her father. "Wait!" Dorange and Nichelle both turned around. Vlamer looked at Koroan. "My Lord, please may I go as well. I would like to pay my last respects to your wife."

Koroan smiled, walked toward Vlamer, and placed a hand on his shoulder. "Yes, my dear friend, you may go."

Vlamer bowed his head. "Thank you, My Lord." He then followed Dorange and Nichelle out of the office. As they approached the elevator, Nichelle began to panic again. There was no way now she was going escape. Her father and Dorange were probably the two most powerful Gnols behind Koroan.

Thoughts raced through Nichelle's mind. They were about to walk into Ciminae's room, with Celeste missing.

★ ★ ★ ★ ★

Celeste finished dressing, placed Gyrale's battle helmet on, and lowered the tinted visor. She punched the security code to unlock the door. The door slid open and there stood Nichelle with a panicked look on her face, as well as Dorange, and her father's high priest.

"Oh, Private . . . we were just about to enter," Dorange said.

Celeste didn't say a word. She stood motionless, trying to think of what to do.

Dorange gave her a strange look and stepped forward. "I know you do not want me to report you as insubordinate," he said.

Celeste's eyes darted back and forth between Dorange and Vlamer. She didn't know what to do. She knew that she could possibly take Dorange. However, Vlamer was a different matter. Even though she had grown extremely powerful in her abilities, she wasn't confident enough to challenge

Vlamer.

"Well . . . Private!" Dorange yelled. "When a superior officer and our lord's high priest are in your presence, what should you do?"

Celeste suddenly realized what Dorange was saying. She immediately stood at attention and saluted. Dorange saluted back as Vlamer stepped forward and moved Dorange out of the way. Vlamer stood within inches of Celeste's face as he eyed her up and down. "Take off your helmet, Private," he ordered.

Celeste thought about throwing Vlamer to the side, grabbing Nichelle, and escaping to her room across the hall, but she knew with Vlamer's strength and power that wasn't possible.

"Now, Private!" Vlamer demanded.

Celeste jumped back into her mother's room from the sheer volume of Vlamer's voice. As she did so, Vlamer followed. He noticed Gyrale's body on the floor and immediately raised his arms. Celeste tried to run around him, but couldn't. He had succeeded in holding her in place. Celeste felt paralyzed.

Vlamer continued to hold Celeste in place as he stepped forward. He grabbed Celeste with his right hand and with his left pulled off the battle helmet. "I have to say Celeste, I am impressed. It seems that you are gaining more strength in your abilities."

Celeste didn't say a word. She met Vlamer's gaze and just stared. Vlamer called out, "Dorange!"

"Yes, Your Eminence," Dorange said, stepping forward.

"Inform Lord Chast that his daughter has attempted an escape, but we now have her in custody."

"As you wish," said Dorange, backing away. Celeste watched Dorange back out of the open doorway. He stood next to Nichelle as he flipped open his communicator. As soon as he did, Nichelle frantically grabbed the gun hidden in her boot. She pulled the gun out and hit Dorange's hand that held his communicator. The communicator fell to the floor.

Vlamer turned around and saw what had happened. His daughter held the gun between Dorange's eyes. Dorange looked like a frightened animal. "Nichelle, what are you doing?"

"Let Celeste go, Father."

Vlamer looked shocked, which was just the distraction Celeste needed. Celeste grabbed Vlamer's arm and twisted. Because Vlamer was taken off guard by Nichelle, he wasn't prepared. He tried to resist.

Celeste twisted and jerked Vlamer's arm causing him to flip and land on his back. Celeste darted for Dorange and the door. Just as she was about to reach Dorange, she felt her legs give out. She fell, hitting her head on the hard marble floor. She looked up and saw Dorange snatch the gun from Nichelle. He then grabbed her and held the gun to her head. "Surrender, Celeste or Nichelle will die."

"No!" yelled Vlamer, as he grabbed Celeste by the left leg. Celeste turned her head and saw Vlamer raise his right arm. The gun flew from Dorange's grip to the back of the room. Vlamer looked at Celeste with fire in his eyes. He placed his other hand on the same leg and flung Celeste into the wall. Pictures fell, and pieces of the wall splintered all around Celeste.

As Celeste fell to the floor, she felt a painful gash open down her left arm. She resisted the temptation to grab it and focused her attention back to Vlamer. He approached her, seething in anger. "You will die now, Celeste," he said as he clenched his fist and threw a massive punch toward Celeste's face.

As Vlamer's fist approached, Celeste closed her eyes and focused. She quickly raised her right hand and pushed. She opened her eyes and saw Vlamer's body fly to the back of the room. His body smashed into the same brick wall she threw Gyrale into.

Out of the corner of her eye, Celeste saw Dorange grab his weapon from his belt. She raised her other hand. She mentally grabbed Dorange and flung him across the hall. He crashed through the door to Celeste's room.

Nichelle rushed for Celeste and tried to help her up.

"Look out!" Celeste shrieked.

Nichelle turned around. Her father grabbed her under the chin and lifted. "How dare you, Nichelle," he said. "You have brought shame to me. For that . . . you will die along with your friend."

Without hesitation or guilt, Vlamer hurled his daughter into the wall that separated Ciminae's room from the corridor. Nichelle hit the marble and wood wall head first. The force of Vlamer's throw caused her body to crash through the wall and hit the wall on the other side of the corridor. Celeste shuddered with dread as she watched in horror. She saw Nichelle's body go limp and knew there was no way she could have survived.

Before Celeste could focus her attention back to Vlamer, he clutched her by the throat and lifted. She tried to kick at him, but he was far enough away that her kicks were futile. She gasped for breath as Vlamer squeezed. He took her to Ciminae's bed and slammed her down beside her mother's body.

As Celeste struggled, Vlamer let a sinister smile spread across his face.

"Now, it is here, beside your mother, where you shall die."

Celeste saw the anger in Vlamer's eyes, and as he squeezed the life out of her, she wondered what had changed him and her father from loving, caring fathers to power-hungry, evil monsters. Vlamer squeezed tighter, and Celeste felt her strength begin to fail.

Celeste's vision went blurry, and her head began to feel light. She tried to struggle but couldn't. She closed her eyes and felt the tears stream out. This was it. In a matter of seconds, she would soon be with her mother in the afterlife. She opened her eyes again and looked at the ceiling. She could see her mother.

Ciminae was there, floating near the ceiling smiling at her daughter. She opened her mouth and said, "Remember . . . the source of your father's power." And then, she disappeared.

Celeste closed her eyes and let her body relax. She resigned to let herself be reunited with her mother. Just as she was about to pass into unconsciousness, she heard what sounded like a blast from a plasma gun. She quickly opened her eyes and saw Vlamer wide eyed. His grip relaxed, and he let go of her throat. Celeste felt the oxygen rush into her lungs as she coughed and took in deep breaths.

Vlamer stumbled away from Celeste, grabbing at his back. He fell back into a chair and looked toward his assassin. Celeste looked as well. There stood Nichelle with Dorange's weapon raised. Her head was split open, bleeding profusely. Her nose was smashed as well, and tears rolled from her eyes. She fell to the floor in a bloodied and sobbing heap.

Celeste rushed for her. She embraced Nichelle and gently lifted her from the floor. "Come. . . We do not have much time."

Nichelle glanced at her father as Celeste ran to the door. Celeste made it to the door and turned around. Nichelle slowly walked toward her father. Vlamer was still breathing and looked at his daughter. Nichelle stopped just out of his reach, stared at him for a few seconds, then quickly turned around and ran toward Celeste.

The two friends rushed across the corridor to Celeste's room where they could escape through a secret passageway Koroan had built within the palace that would take them outside of the city walls. As they approached Celeste's broken door, Dorange began to groggily move his head back and forth. Celeste knelt down on one knee and grabbed him by the throat. She reached behind each one of his ears and pulled out his inhibitors. His eyes widened as soon as he realized what she was doing.

He tried to struggle, but Celeste was too strong for him, as a result of his head injury. A flood of thoughts rushed into her head. Thoughts that she particularly didn't want to know, others that revealed his true identity, and others that suddenly were of vital importance to the rebel cause.

She broke her link with Dorange's mind and looked at Nichelle. "We have to get to the second rebel base now!"

★ ★ ★ ★ ★

The little boy looked up at his mother and father. They were both smiling at him. The boy looked to be almost eight years of age. Skip saw a very clear image of the boy, but not of his mother and father.

The boy had black hair and insightful, beaming blue eyes. His smile was nearly as bright as the sun, as his body seemed to glow from the light that was coming from the top of the temple pyramid.

The boy hugged his mother and father and waved good-bye as he entered the temple.

Suddenly, Skip flinched. His body had finally awakened from the deep sleep he had been in for days. He rubbed his head and realized that his head had been shaven, and he had stitches that extended from the top of his neck to the middle of his scalp.

He shook his head, trying to regain his blurred vision. He didn't know exactly how long he had been out of it, but he continued to have the same dream over and over again. The dream seemed almost real, and he actually thought he was living it. He had no idea what the dream meant, or why it seemed to replay in his mind. He wondered if it had something to do with what he saw at the temple after he had been blown through the door and lost consciousness.

Upon that thought, Skip suddenly realized he was fully awake and looked around. He had no idea where he was. He looked down and realized that he had been sleeping on a soft leather sofa.

As he scanned the rest of the strange room, he realized that he was in some sort of office. The office was big and spacious. Directly in front of him were two leather chairs with long backs. Behind the chairs was a large, shiny wooden desk, and directly behind the desk was another long backed black leather chair.

Skip blinked to better focus of his vision. The chair seemed to sway back and forth. He thought he saw an arm move out from behind the chair.

He continued to scan the room and saw that there was a large view-screen just above the person who sat in the chair. On the view-screen was what looked like a jungle background, machinery of all types, and thousands of slaves digging up the ground in the jungle, as well as Gnol guards dispersed among them.

He looked to his left and saw a gigantic painting of who he supposed was Koroan Chast. He looked back to the chair the person sat in and saw it slowly turn around.

In the chair sat a polished Gnol officer. He was dressed in official Gnol green fatigues – obviously to blend into the jungle background. Skip could tell from the stars on each of his shoulders that this officer was high up in the Gnol military. The officer had dark hair and a neatly trimmed beard.

He looked at Skip with intensity and seemed to study him. "Ah, Colonel Hendricks. It is nice to see that you have finally awakened. Allow me to introduce myself. I am Commander Polatis Schaal – Commander of the jungle slave camp of *Zikf.*"

Skip gave the officer a curious look. He had heard of the name of the slave camp before, but he couldn't recall where. "How did you know my name?" he asked as he felt behind his ears. His inhibitors were gone.

Commander Schaal moved to the front of his desk and leaned against it. "Do not worry, Colonel. Your inhibitors were taken out, but . . . for some odd reason, I was not able to read your mind. That is why you are here in my office and not in one of the slave quarters. I was able to gather the information I need about you from your female friend."

The mention of Ariauna caused Skip to suddenly stand. As he did so, his head began to spin, and he felt a sharp pain behind his knee in his cybernetic leg. Skip fell back into the comfort of the sofa and clutched his leg. He winced in pain and thought it odd that he was experiencing pain in it at all. Doc had told him that his leg would be able to sense touch, but not pain. However, this pain was almost unbearable. He wondered if it was malfunctioning.

The Gnol officer noticed Skip's pain. He gave Skip a congenial smile, grabbed a chair, placed it directly in front of Skip, and sat down. "Hmm," he said as she stroked his beard. "Our doctors scanned that cybernetic leg of yours. I have to admit, that is a pretty impressive piece of technology, especially coming from humans."

Skip glared at the officer. "What's that supposed to mean?"

Skip's question seemed to anger Schaal. He furrowed his eyebrows and glared at Skip for a moment. But just as quick, he changed his demeanor and smiled. He let out a small laugh and continued, "When we first took out your inhibitors, and I could not read your mind, we did a full-body scan to see if you had any implants hidden inside of your head. Needless to say, we did not find any, but we did discover that leg of yours. The only conclusion that I could come up with was either you have mastered the ability to block our mind probes or, and this is the most believable theory, whoever designed your cybernetic leg, placed inhibitors within it to prevent our mind probes.

"So, our computers searched your leg for inhibitors, but it seems that your leg is protected and encrypted with very complicated algorithms. As soon as our computers attempted a scan, your leg sent back an electronic pulse that downed our network for several hours."

Skip was stunned. He knew his cybernetic leg was impressive, but he had no clue that there could be inhibitors placed within it, or that it was encrypted. And if what this commander was saying was true, why didn't Doc and Sean tell him?

Commander Schaal continued to stare at Skip waiting for a response. Skip didn't say a word and looked at the view-screen. He looked back at the officer and said, "You said that you extracted all of the information about me from a girl. Where is she?"

The officer stood and turned back to the view-screen. "Computer . . ."

"Yes, Commander Schaal," the computer replied.

"Locate prisoner A-1209."

"Yes, Commander."

Skip watched as the view-screen focused in on a small group of slaves working on a hilltop. It continued to focus in until it located what it was looking for. There, in the center of the group and placing mounds of rocks into a hover truck, was Ariauna. Her head was bandaged, and she wore the same blue clothing as all of the other slaves. She looked as if she was in a trance.

Skip looked back at the officer. "What did you do to her?"

The officer returned to his seat and leaned forward. He was within a foot of Skip's face. "Nothing we do not do to all slaves," he said. "Ariauna is simply doing what we ask her to do. It is amazing, Skip . . . Can I call you Skip?"

Skip didn't answer. He felt his face flush red with anger and glared at the officer.

Schaal continued. "Okay, Skip. Anyway, as I was saying. The human mind is so frail and weak, and the Gnol's mind is so superior. It only makes sense that we control what you do. After all, we would not want you to hurt yourselves."

Skip wanted to take a swing at the officer, but he knew he would be ripped to pieces if he did. He took a deep breath. "So, you take it upon yourselves – the Gnols – to hurt us, so we won't hurt ourselves?"

Commander Schaal laughed as if Skip had just told him a particularly funny joke. "See, I knew you would understand."

Skip frowned at Schaal. "I meant it as a question."

"And the question was rhetorical, so you already know the answer," Schaal said, as he stood and walked to the painting Skip saw earlier. "Do you know who this is?" he asked, pointing at the painting.

Skip glanced at the picture and then back to Schaal. "I can only assume that he is your leader, Koroan Chast."

"Yes . . . but he is not just our leader, he is our god. And under the direction of the supreme goddess of light, he has saved the Gnol race and given us all this wonderful technology you see here today."

This time, Skip let out a small laugh. Schaal immediately turned his smile into a frown. He walked to Skip, clutched him by the collar of his rebel uniform, and lifted. "What is so funny? You must show more respect to your god."

Skip tried to knock Schaal's hand away, but it was useless. The Gnol was too strong. As Schaal held Skip in midair, Skip met his gaze and in a dead, serious tone said, "Chast is not my God. My God would never submit another person or animal – as you believe us to be – to tyranny or oppression."

Schaal looked as if he was ready to land a death blow to Skip's face. He lifted his fist, flung it forward, and stopped with his knuckle barely touching Skip's nose. He threw Skip back onto the sofa and resumed his seat. "Your God sounds weak."

Skip didn't respond.

"Well, your beliefs will soon change, especially after you have been here awhile."

"I thought you couldn't control my mind?"

Schaal seemed friendly once again and smiled. "That may be to my advantage."

Skip gave Schaal a puzzled look. "How so?"

Schaal stood and began to pace back and forth. He stopped and stared at Skip for a long moment. "It seems that I am in need of a new personal secretary. My last one . . . well, he could not think for himself. . . . I had to do all of it. As a result, I wasted a lot of time controlling his mind. Since I cannot control your mind, and since you seem somewhat intelligent – for a human – I have decided to make you my new personal secretary. This will allow me more time to run my camp."

"And how long will I be your secretary?"

Schaal seemed to look through Skip and said, "Until your death, of course."

"Well, I guess since I don't have any other option, I accept the position."

Schaal laughed at Skip's sarcasm. "You know, Skip. You are the first human I have ever held a conversation with. If you do what is asked of you and not cause any trouble, you will begin to see who your real god is, and you just may begin to see that we Gnols truly have your best interests at heart."

Again, Skip didn't respond. There was no way he would allow himself to be brainwashed by these monsters. He looked at the view-screen and saw Ariauna hard at work. He longed to rescue her from the hell she was in. She had told him once that being under the Gnol's mind control was like watching yourself from above. She wanted to resist every command that was given to her but couldn't. Her entire free will had been robbed.

Skip looked back at Schaal. "When Ariauna and I were brought here, was her father with her?"

"You mean the old man who was with you at those ruins?"

Skip nodded his head.

"He was killed. But do not worry; his body was cremated on sight."

Skip gave Schaal an intense look."

"What do you mean cremated on sight?"

"The old man's body was burned, and soon Lord Chast will have that heathen temple destroyed as well."

Skip tried to hide the panic in his voice. "When?"

Schaal smiled at Skip. "Oh, in due time."

Skip lowered his head. He didn't want to believe Schaal. The temple was too important. What he saw after he was blown through the door was too important to be destroyed. If his God was the true God, then he knew without a doubt that it wouldn't be destroyed. Somehow he had to get out of this slave camp and get back to the temple.

Another pain shot through Skip's cybernetic leg. Schaal saw Skip clutching behind his knee. "Problem with your cybernetic leg, Skip?"

Skip met Schaal's eyes. "No, I just had an itch, that's all."

Schaal looked at Skip with suspicion for several seconds, and then walked to the door. It slid open, and he called out, "Captain, you may come in now."

Skip watched as a gigantic Gnol walked in. Skip's eyes widened. He didn't know if he had ever seen anyone so big. The captain seemed to tower above the commander. Skip figured Commander Schaal to be about 6'3", which would have made this Gnol just about seven feet tall. Skip scanned the captain's body up and down. He wore a green T-shirt with green fatigue bottoms and black boots. The uniform reminded Skip of an army basic trainee uniform back on Earth.

The captain had large, rippling muscles that were accentuated by his shiny, ebony skin. One of his arms seemed as big as both of Skip's legs combined. The captain glared at Skip, and Skip quickly closed his mouth.

Commander Schaal seemed amused from the look on Skip's face. "Skip this is Captain Noran Belzar. He will be your shadow."

Skip gave Schaal a questioning look. "My shadow?"

"Yes, your shadow. Captain Belzar will never leave your side. He will stay in the room next to yours here at camp headquarters and stay with you every waking moment."

"May I ask why?"

"Well, Skip. Since I am not able to read your mind, I do not know what is going on in that head of yours. And because I do not know what you are thinking, I do not know if you can be trusted."

Commander Schaal turned to the captain. "Captain, introduce Skip to his new home and bring him back in precisely one hour. We have work to do."

The captain saluted and spoke with the deepest voice Skip had ever heard. "Yes, Commander." He motioned for Skip to follow.

Skip did as he was commanded and felt a sinking feeling deep within his gut. How was he going to plan an escape with this giant on him every waking moment of the day?

CHAPTER 16

May 31, 2042 – Conference Room of Base 2

Jake sat in the conference room of *Base 2*, listening to his father. Within the room were all of Adrian's senior officers: Jake, General Scott Hauler, Colonel Peter Sanchez, Colonel Aromos Jantear, the new doctor – Colonel Ithel Hopet – and of course, Celeste. Jake looked across the room at her. She sat next to Colonel Jantear. Jake looked at Colonel Jantear and felt a spark of jealously run through him. Jake had rarely talked to Celeste for almost the two months she had been at *Base 2*. She had attempted several times to talk to him, but Jake felt intimidated and almost afraid every time he was in her presence. As a result, he used every excuse he could think of not to talk to her. He used excuses like flight training exercises for the new pilots, briefings he had to go over with his father, etc.

Celeste, on the other hand, picked up on his signals and essentially stopped bothering him. And when Adrian assigned her and Colonel Jantear to work together on planning a rescue attempt for Bantyr, Kylee, and Sean, she began spending more time with Jantear. This made Jake even more uneasy because he could see that Jantear was not intimidated in her presence. In fact, the two almost seemed to have fun together. They were always laughing and smiling at one another, and this made Jake terribly nervous.

He knew he was falling for Celeste because he thought about her every moment of the day, but for some reason, he felt inferior and weak around her. A problem he had never had around women before. But Celeste was no ordinary woman.

Jake continued to stare at Celeste and imagined what it would be like if she had the same feelings for him as he had for her.

"Jake? . . . Jake?"

Jake saw Celeste turn to meet his gaze as well as everyone else in the room. Suddenly, his face flushed red from embarrassment, and he turned to his father. "Uh . . . sorry, General, I didn't here your question."

Everyone in the room giggled at Jake's reaction. It wasn't a secret that Jake had feelings for Celeste. Everyone knew it including Colonel Jantear who was the only one in the room not smiling.

Celeste smiled at him and turned back to face Adrian.

Adrian continued. "Jake, I asked, what are your numbers on battle ready pilots?"

Jake frantically searched his mind to recall the number he had figured just before the meeting. "Every *Wildcat 1* has a battle ready pilot. I have almost trained all of the pilots for the *Wildcate 2's* and their copilots."

"When do you expect to have them fully trained?" Adrian asked.

"By week's end."

Adrian lowered his head and shook it. Even though Jake had nearly enough pilots to fly the *Wildcats*, which consisted of nearly two hundred pilots and one hundred copilots, he knew as well as his father that there weren't enough men or firepower to combat the Gnol's battle plan.

When Celeste and Nichelle successfully escaped *Chast* and made it to *Base 2*, Celeste informed Adrian and Jake that she had seriously miscalculated the actual numbers in the Gnol military. She informed them that after she had read Dorange's mind, she learned that the Gnols had a military of about two million strong. That number was the same she had known to escape *Gnolom* when her father led the Gnols to *Terrest*. She had said, though, that number didn't surprise her because her father had so many secrets and had hidden so much from her.

Adrian also learned from Celeste that Dorange would be leading the attack on Earth. However, Jake sensed that Celeste was hiding something from Adrian; something about Dorange that she did not want to tell him. Besides Dorange leading the attack, they learned that the squadron going through the wormhole would consist of one command ship that Dorange would be on. The command ship would have a crew of approximately ten thousand Gnol military personal. There would also be three hundred eighty-four battle cruisers; two for each country on Earth. The battle cruisers would contain a crew of approximately five thousand personnel each. Also, each cruiser would contain approximately one thousand space fighters, one thousand hover tanks, five hundred assault vehicles, and five thousand *Chaties*. And, although the numbers would be miniscule compared to the military powers on Earth, Jake knew that the firepower the Gnols contained alone could take out the entire planet.

Adrian looked back at his senior officers. "This is your choice gentlemen, and lady," he said as he nodded at Celeste. "The Gnols have us severely outnumbered in manpower and firepower – especially considering we don't even have a thousand people in our military personnel. This is going to be a suicide mission. It's your choice. You can walk away now, and no one will question your bravery . . ." Adrian paused as he looked around the room.

Jake watched as one by one each person in the room stood – including himself – and offered his or her life to at least try and thwart the attack against Earth. As they did so, a smile grew along Adrian's face. He nodded and said, "Good. Then this is our strategy. We know the precise time the Gnols will try to go through the wormhole. It will occur at dusk two weeks from today.

"Jake and I will lead the *Wildcats* to the wormhole. We will be there waiting when Dorange attempts his entrance." Adrian then looked at Scott. "General Hauler, how many ground troops do you have prepared to defend the base."

"I have enough men to man every hover tank, ten assault vehicles, and every *Chati* in the fleet – approximately two hundred fifty soldiers," Scott said.

"Good. That just may be enough to defend the base. We know from Celeste that her father has planned a simultaneous attack of the base when Dorange launches his fleet," said Adrian.

Adrian then turned to Petey. "Colonel Sanchez, are the communication networks, computer network, and energy resources prepared."

Petey smiled at Adrian. "Yes, Sir. Everything is ready to go. Just let me know if you need any changes made."

Adrian returned Petey's smile. "Good," he said. He then looked at Colonel Hopet.

Colonel Ithel Hopet was the first Terrestrian to graduate from Doc's medical school he had established on *Terrest*. He was an intelligent man with a warm smile and inviting sense of humor. Hopet was in his early fifties with a full head of graying black hair and brown eyes. As Jake looked at the man who had replaced his father's best friend, he noticed for the first time how small the man actually was. Jake figured that the man barely stood over five feet tall and maybe weighed less than one hundred thirty-five pounds. Nonetheless, Jake knew that Colonel Hopet would make an excellent leader in his father's military because of his work ethic and genuine love for everyone involved in the rebel cause.

As Adrian spoke to Colonel Hopet, Jake sensed sadness in his father's voice. "Colonel Hopet, make sure your medical team is ready. You're going to have a lot of casualties."

"Yes, Sir," replied the colonel.

Adrian finally looked at Celeste. "Celeste, have you and Colonel Jantear finalized your preparations for the rescue attempt?"

"Yes, General," Celeste said. "Colonel Jantear and I along with fifty other troops will take an assault vehicle to *Chast* as soon as the attack on the base begins. My father will be so distracted with the attack, that he won't even suspect a rescue attempt."

Adrian nodded his head. He was about to speak again, when he remembered something he had forgotten to ask Celeste. "Oh, Celeste, any word from Nichelle and her people on the whereabouts of Skip and his crew?"

Sadness seemed to cover Celeste's face. "No, General. *Talead* has been crawling with Gnol soldiers for the past two months. There is no way Nichelle can get to the temple."

Adrian frowned at Celeste's response and sighed. "Very well, we can only assume that he has either been captured or . . ." Adrian paused and swallowed. Jake could tell that he was trying to stay strong. He then looked back up at Celeste. "Just inform her to keep trying to find a safe route to that temple."

Celeste nodded and said, "I will. She and her people have returned from *Talead* and are at the base now."

Adrian nodded, cleared his throat, and focused his attention back to everyone in the group. "Okay, if there are no further questions, everyone is dismissed."

As everyone in the room began to leave, Jake continued to sit in his chair. He leaned onto his thighs and cupped his head in his hands. The mention of Skip brought a lot of emotions to the surface that he didn't want anyone to see, especially Celeste. He missed his best friend and prayed every night that he was safe.

Jake began to feel the tears flow from his eyes. He rubbed his eyes and was about to stand up when he felt a gentle touch on his shoulder. He turned his teary eyes in the direction of the person who had touched him.

There stood Celeste with concern in her eyes. "Are you all right?" She asked.

Suddenly, Jake felt ashamed and embarrassed. He knew how powerful Celeste was and did not want to seem weak around her. He cleared his throat and said, "Uh, yeah, I'm just tired that's all . . . uh . . . I've got to go. I've got some pilots still to train."

Jake tried to walk away, but Celeste, with her strength, grabbed his arm and held him in place. He turned around and met her eyes. "You are not getting away from me that easy," she said. "We need to talk."

"About what?" asked Jake, as he glanced outside of the door. There, in the doorway, stood Jantear. He didn't look happy and seemed to wait impatiently for Celeste.

Celeste gently grabbed Jake's face and turned it to face hers. "Meet me in my quarters in two hours. I have to go now because I have some final plans I need to go over with Colonel Jantear." She smiled at Jake, leaned in, and gently kissed him on the cheek.

Jake watched as Celeste left the room. Now, he was confused more than ever. *What was that all about, and what did Celeste want to talk about?* Whatever the answers were, there was no way Jake was going to avoid Celeste this time.

★ ★ ★ ★ ★

As the scorching sun began to fade away beyond the horizon of the *Island of Vtasloget*, Skip began to feel some relief from the heat. He had been in the sun ever since he arrived at *Zikf*. So each day, when the day began to turn to night, he was grateful. Moreover, since his arrival, he had already learned many things about where he was and how that would help him with his escape plans. For instance, he learned that the mining camp of *Zikf* was located on the *Island of Vtasloget*, which was the *Tilicah* word for plentiful.

The Terrestrians called this the Island of Plentiful because it was loaded with precious ores, such as gold, silver, iron, and of course the priceless metal ore – *Omutx*; the metal that was nearly indestructible – except when barraged with plasma fire, bombs, or missiles of course, but still provided exceptionally strong armor, nonetheless – and used in the construction of buildings, vehicles, computers, etc. You name it; *Omutx* was more than likely in it. That is why the Gnols had the mining camp. It was their primary metal resource center for the Gnol's civilization upon *Terrest*.

Skip also learned that inhibitors were also made out of *Omutx*. And whenever he had a small amount of downtime, he would devise plans of how he could get enough *Omutx* to create enough inhibitors for his plan to work. But with Captain Belzar around twenty-four seven, there was no way he could collect any *Omutx* at all. In fact, the one time he tried to collect a small amount near a dig site and place it into his pocket, Tiny – as Skip affectionately called Captain Belzar – caught him. As a result, Skip suffered a severe beating at the hands of Commander Schaal.

He was still feeling the effects. His left eye was slightly swollen, and one of his ribs was still broken, which made it even more difficult for his task at hand.

"Next," he called out as the slave next in line stepped forward. The slave was shoved a little closer to Skip's desk by an armed Gnol. The slave hit the desk and nearly knocked Skip's computer into his lap. He caught the computer, looked up, and glared at the guard who had shoved the slave.

He then looked at the slave. "Ariaun—"

Captain Belzar slapped Skip in the back of the head.

"Uh . . .I mean . . . identification number, please."

He made eye contact with Ariauna. She seemed to plead to him with her eyes. For weeks, he had tried to keep an eye out for her but never caught a glimpse of her; not since he saw her on Commander Schaal's view-screen. He knew, however, that he would eventually see her with this new assignment Schaal had given him.

For the past two weeks, Skip had been sitting at the same desk in the middle of the mining camp, and entering data into a new slave database. Apparently, Lord Chast had issued a decree to all slave commanders on *Terrest* to catalog each slave by number, name, and date of birth. After each slave was catalogued, he or she would then be implanted with a computer chip into the back of his or her neck. This would enable the computer in each camp to keep track of each slave more efficiently, and most importantly, enable the Gnols to control their minds better. The slaves would also receive a bar code on the back of their hands to make it easier to identify them by a laser scan.

Skip had often wondered how it was the Gnols were able to control the minds of thousands of slaves at once, especially since most of the Gnols weren't that advanced in their telepathic abilities; only a select few were. He learned, before the new decree from Lord Chast, the Gnol military trained special agents called *Enforcers*. These *Enforcers* were superior in their telepathic and telekinetic abilities and sent out to all of the slave camps on *Terrest*.

Once an *Enforcer* arrived at a slave camp, he or she was given ten slaves for whom he or she would control, which was the maximum an *Enforcer* could control in a mind lock. Needless to say, with the number of slaves the Gnols had, and growing in number each day, they needed a new system.

So within the month, Lord Chast wanted every slave camp on *Terrest* to have installed a new computer system that controlled each slave in the camp with just four *Enforcers*. The *Enforcers* would work in shifts with only one *Enforcer* controlling the entire camp at one time. These *Enforcers* were to be connected to a new mainframe computer within the central administration building of each camp. From this central location, the *Enforcer* would send signals from his or her brain to the computer. The computer would then transmit the wireless signal to the chips each slave had implanted. Consequently, the *Enforcer* would be able to control and monitor each slave's movements and effort.

If a slave was lacking or the link to his or her chip was broken, the computer would then be able to identify the slave immediately based upon its new database. From that point, the guards would easily find the slave and repair the chip or worse, torture and kill the slave.

"A-1209."

Captain Belzar slapped Skip in the back of the head again. He snapped out of his trance and looked back up at Ariauna. "Um . . . number again, please?"

"A-1209."

Skip typed in the number and made eye contact with her again. He knew that, at the moment, the slaves were not under the mind control of their *Enforcers* because they needed their own minds to relay the information to the five hundred secretaries Schaal had lined up in the camp's courtyard. As Skip looked at Ariauna, he desperately wanted to reach out and rescue her. She looked horrible, and had lost the weight she had put back on since her last enslavement. She reminded Skip of a Jew in a World War II Nazi concentration camp.

"Name?" he asked.

"You know my name, Skip."

Her response caused Skip to stiffen. He knew that any kind of response out of the ordinary, especially a slave referring to a secretary by name, would bring dire consequences. The guard on Ariauna's right raised the butt of his rifle and landed it directly onto the back of her neck. She yelled out in pain and fell to the ground.

Skip launched himself from his seat. But before he shot himself over the desk and into the guard, he remembered Belzar was directly behind him. He sat back down as Ariauna groggily stood up.

Skip continued as he tried to hide his anger and emotion in his voice. "Name?"

Skip could not look at her while she glared at him. "Ariauna Tomwon."

"Date of birth?" Skip asked.

"*Fiseimb 16, 474*, or in English . . ." She sarcastically said, ". . . January 16, 474, *Terrest* time."

The guard, sensing her disrespect again, raised his rifle, but Belzar raised his hand. "That is enough, Private. Secretary Hendricks has all the information we need from her. Escort this slave to the implant station."

"Yes, Sir," replied the private. The guard grabbed Ariauna by the arm and dragged her to a chair about ten feet away from where Skip was sitting. As the guard dragged her, she never lost eye contact with Skip. Skip wanted to look away because her look wasn't a look of despair – as she had before – but now a look of anger. Skip knew that she probably thought Skip gave in as some of the other human secretaries had for better treatment from the Gnols if they worked personally for the officers. Skip desperately wanted to tell her that wasn't the case at all.

He watched as the guard strapped her into the chair. The Gnol medic approached her from behind and placed the implant gun directly under the base of her skull. Skip closed his eyes as he heard the swoosh of the implant gun. He opened his eyes and watched as the guard pushed her in the direction of another Gnol who stood nearby.

Skip shook his head. He knew, within a few weeks, Ariauna would never again have the free will to control her own mind. The combination of the computer and implant would keep her under the control of the Gnols twenty-four hours a day.

Skip felt the strong hand of Captain Belzar on his shoulder. Belzar squeezed, causing Skip to lower in his chair. "Hurry it up, Hendricks. We still have more slaves to process," Belzar said.

"Yes, Tiny," Skip said.

Belzar squeezed harder. Skip clenched his teeth in pain. "I told you . . . never call me that," said Belzar. "You will show more respect to your shadow."

"Sorry, Sir," replied Skip, as he gritted his teeth and looked up at the slave next in line. "Next," he said.

The slave next in line stepped forward. The slave looked to be in his fifties. Skip wondered if he had recently been enslaved because the man looked exceedingly well fit for his age. Rather than malnourished as most slaves were, this slave had his shirt off revealing his toned muscles and many scars, obviously from beatings, which was why Skip wondered how long he had been a slave.

"Identification number?"

The man looked at him with his crystal, blue eyes. He reached up and ran his hand over the white stubble of his shaven head. He smiled at Skip. Skip didn't return the smile. Instead, he gave him a curious look as to why the man didn't answer.

The same guard who hit Ariauna nudged the man with his rifle and said, "You better answer him now! And do not even think about shooting off that mouth of yours, or you will get another beating."

The man looked at the guard, gave him a smile, and in an accent that sounded remarkably familiar to Skip said, "Now, don't go gettin' your panties in a bunch, Creed. You know what happened the last time you tried to beat me. You don't want none of this again," the slave said as he hit his chest with his fist.

The guard seemed to back away at the man's response.

Skip was surprised. Never had he heard a slave refer to a Gnol by name before. And why did the guard seem intimidated by him?

Suddenly, Skip heard another slave about ten slaves back yell out, "You tell him, boss."

Skip looked at the slave who yelled out. Another guard stepped next to the slave and sideswiped him with his fist. The slave fell unconscious to the ground.

The slave with the familiar accent yelled out to the guard who had hit his admirer. "C'mon now, Tolpez. What'cha have to go n' do that fir. There was no harm done."

The guard, the slave called Tolpez, rapidly approached the mouthy slave. "Do not ever call me by my name." Tolpez shoved his rifle into the slave's chest. "You had better answer the secretary, now."

The slave held his hands up and backed away as he gave Tolpez a cocky smile. He looked at Skip. "My identification number is C-5698."

Skip typed the number into the computer and then asked, "Name?"

"Skyler Green."

Skip was about to type in the name when he realized what the slave had said. He paused and looked up. "What was that name again?"

Skyler smiled at Skip and confidently leaned forward on the table. "The name is Skyler Green, born on July or in *Tilicah – Feth* 10, 1986 or 454 if I was born on *Terrest*, which I wasn't. I was born and raised in Texas, U.S.A. on planet Earth," he said, giving Captain Belzar a cocky grin.

As Skip entered the data, he heard Captain Belzar laugh. "Well, Green. It looks like, in a few weeks, you will not have any free time to make your little potions you trade to our guards."

Skip looked back at Belzar and then back at the guards. Creed and Tolpez looked just as surprised.

"You fools," Belzar said. "You are dumber than I thought you were if you did not know that the commander and I did not know about guards trading drugs to Green and other slaves for special treatment. The commander is going to personally punish guards that have partaken in this heinous act of drug trading. But for now, take Green to the implant station."

The two guards grabbed Skyler and dragged him to the station. All the while Green kept his cocky smile on his face.

As Skip watched the medic implant the chip into Skyler's head, a spark of hope ignited within him. Adrian had previously told Jake and Skip that Skyler was cataloging plants and animals in the jungles of *Terrest* when the Gnols attacked. They never heard from him again, but now Skip knew. If Skip had any hope of escaping this hell, Skyler Green was the key.

★ ★ ★ ★ ★

As Jake walked down the corridor of the base, he reached up and wiped the sweat that began to drip from his forehead. That didn't help because his hands were clammy as well. He stopped at the door of Celeste's quarters. He took a deep breath and tried to calm his nerves. He didn't know why Celeste had this effect on him. He was extremely nervous to speak with her.

After waiting a few moments and trying to gain the courage to let her know he was there, he reached up and pushed the button to signal his arrival.

"Come in," Celeste said over the speaker.

Jake stepped forward into the door sensor. The door slid open, and there was Celeste sitting at her computer station. Jake looked around before he walked in. The room was the same as all the other quarters. In one corner was a bed. Next to the bed was a computer station, and in another corner, separated by walls, was the five foot by five foot bathroom. The rooms were modest, but they sufficed.

Celeste stopped working on her computer and turned around in her chair. Jake's mouth nearly dropped. She must have just finished showering because her hair was wet and she only had on a black robe. She smiled at Jake and crossed her left leg over her right, revealing a bare, left thigh. Jake tried not to look at her legs as she did so, but couldn't resist.

She was so beautiful. More beautiful than any other woman he had ever seen before.

"Well," she said. "You do not have to stand there in the open doorway. Come in."

Jake swallowed the lump that was beginning to form in his throat and stepped into the room. The door slid shut behind him. She motioned for him to have a seat on the bed directly across from her. Jake nodded, wiped his clammy hands on his pants, and walked to the bed. He sat down and forced a shy smile in Celeste's direction.

Celeste laughed.

"Wh . . . what's so funny?" Jake asked.

Celeste moved in a little closer toward Jake. Jake reacted by moving further back onto the bed. Celeste stood up and sat down extremely close to Jake on the bed. Jake didn't know what to make of it. He was excited that she was that close to him. Yet, he felt like a bumbling fool around her and thought for sure that she found that unattractive.

Celeste continued to smile at Jake and said, "Do you know why I wanted to talk to you tonight?"

Jake didn't respond. He just shook his head.

"I want to know why you keep avoiding me?"

Jake cleared his throat and moved a little further away from Celeste. She moved too. "I . . . I don't know what you're talking about. I haven't been avoiding you," he said.

Celeste rolled her eyes. "Come on, Jake. Every time I try to speak with you, you always have something to do. I want to know why?"

"Well, I'm busy. I need to get my pilots battle ready . . ." Jake paused and wanted to say what was truly on his mind but forced himself to stop.

Celeste, being as perceptive as she was, noticed. "What?"

Jake gave her the best puzzled look he could come up with. "What's . . . what?"

"Jake, I can read you like a book. You wanted to say something else but stopped. Please, tell me."

With Celeste's permission, Jake mustered up the courage to say what was truly on his mind. "Well . . . um . . . I was going to say that I was avoiding you because you seemed to be enjoying yourself with Colonel Jantear."

Celeste laughed again. As a result, Jake gave her an angered look. Celeste noticed and placed her hand on Jake's. Jake tried to pull away, but she held his hand in place. "Do I sense a bit of jealously?"

"No, I just . . . I could just see that you seemed to enjoy yourself around him, and I didn't want to get in the way, that's all."

"Aromos and I were assigned to work together to plan you brother's and sister's rescue from *Chast*. That is it."

Jake wasn't convinced and made eye contact with Celeste. She met his gaze. Jake wanted to turn away because he felt intimidated but continued to keep his eyes on her's. "That's not the impression I get from Aromos Jantear," he sarcastically said. "Aromos seems to think that you two are an item."

"And why would I be interested in Colonel Aromos Jantear?"

Jake shrugged his shoulders. "I don't know. Maybe because he's not intimidated around you or doesn't seem to be."

"Finally," Celeste said as she sighed.

Jake was even more confused. "Finally . . . what?"

Celeste met Jake's eyes again. "Finally, the truth comes out."

"Truth . . . what truth?"

"That is why you have been avoiding me. You are intimidated."

Jake tried to act surprised. "Wh . . . what are you talking about? I'm not intimidated."

Celeste didn't answer. She continued to keep eye contact with Jake and inched a little closer. As a result, Jake caved in and finally decided to be totally honest with her.

"Okay, okay, you're right," Jake said. "I am intimidated. I saw what you did at *Base 1* when the Gnols attacked. I've seen you use your abilities or superpowers—"

Celeste laughed and said, "Superpowers?"

"Yeah, that's not natural. Why wouldn't any human be intimidated by you? You're stronger than the average human, you can move objects just by thinking about it, and you can read minds. . . . Who wouldn't be intimidated?"

Celeste shook her head, and her smile disappeared. "You make me sound like some kind of monster."

For the first time, Jake noticed that he had said something that deeply impacted Celeste emotionally. He didn't know if he hurt her feelings or angered her. She moved away and Jake could see a small tear roll down her cheek.

You idiot, Jake thought to himself. He sighed and said, "Celeste, I'm sorry. I didn't mean to make it sound like you're a monster. It's just that I never would have imagined meeting someone like you, . . . and since I have . . ." Jake stopped what he was going to say.

Celeste wiped her eyes, sniffled, and looked back into Jake's eyes. "And since you what?"

"Um . . . since we first met, I haven't been able to get you out of my mind. I think about you night and day. I long to be with you, but I don't know if it's possible. That's why I avoid you."

Celeste let her smile come back. She gently placed both of her hands on Jake's face. "Why is it not possible?" she asked.

Jake shook his head. "I don't know. You're a Gnol, and I am a human."

Celeste continued to gaze into Jake's eyes. As she did so, Jake began to feel something he had never felt for another woman before; a deep respect and love.

"Jake," Celeste said. "Remember when we first met?"

Jake nodded.

"And did you ever wonder why I asked you out?"

Jake smiled shyly. "Yeah, I think about it a lot."

"When I first entered that room and saw you. I could read every emotion and thought in your mind. For some reason, I felt an instant connection."

"You did?"

"Yes, ever since that day, I have not been able to stop thinking about you either. I often wondered too . . . how can a Gnol and a human fall in love? But the more I thought about it, the more I realized it is possible."

"It is?"

"Yes, Gnols laugh and cry like humans. We eat and drink . . ." Celeste paused, moved closer to Jake, and looked deep into his eyes, ". . . We even fall in love."

Jake felt his face flush red and the lump that was in his throat came back. He let out a nervous laugh.

Celeste moved in closer and met her lips with his. A flood of emotions swept through Jake as he kissed her back. As they kissed, Jake realized that this kiss was different from any other kiss he had before. It wasn't a kiss of lust or desire. It was deeper than that. It was one of deep and abiding love.

Jake reached up and pulled Celeste in closer. The kiss seemed to last for hours, and Jake did not want to let her go. Finally, the two separated lips. Celeste looked passionately at him and said, "Now, if that does not convince you that it is possible for us to be together, then I do not know what will."

Jake chuckled. "I guess you're right, but . . ."

"But, what?"

"I still can't help but think—"

Celeste gently place two fingers on Jake's mouth to stop him. "Listen to me, Jake. You were there when Doc explained to you and Skip that the Gnols are human. His DNA tests upon me proved that our DNA is the same, with the exception of Doc's so-called *god-gene*. The only difference is our strength and how we use our minds. And if Gnols are human, then that means you have the potential to do what I can do."

Jake gave Celeste a questioning look. "What do you mean?"

Celeste slowly reached up behind her ears and pulled out her inhibitors. She then reached behind Jake's and was about to pull his out when he reached up and stopped her. "What are you doing?" he asked.

Celeste gave him that smile that made him melt and said, "Trust me."

Jake let go of her hands and allowed her to pull the inhibitors out of his head. Celeste then grabbed each side of Jake's face and looked into his eyes. All of a sudden, Jake's entire body felt relaxed.

"Close your eyes," Celeste said.

Jake closed his eyes and was astonished with what he saw. He could see Celeste through her mind's eye. He could read her thoughts and see her entire life in his mind. He now knew Celeste more intimately than any other person could know someone.

Then Jake heard Celeste in his mind. *Open your eyes.*

Jake opened his eyes and saw that Celeste still had her eyes closed. He heard her again. *You see the lamp on my night stand?*

Yes, Jake thought.

Get a clear visual picture of it in your mind and then close your eyes again.

Jake stared at the lamp for a few moments, memorizing every detail he could, and then closed his eyes. It was incredible. It was as if he never closed his eyes. In his mind's eye, he could see the lamp so clearly. Every detail was there: the crystal glass; the silk lamp shade; the light bulb. He could even feel the coolness of the glass, the softness of the silk, and the heat radiating from the bulb. He had imagined before, but never had he had an experience like this.

He heard Celeste again. *Now, raise your hand and imagine lifting that lamp and holding it.*

Jake did as he was instructed and saw himself in his mind grab the lamp with his hands and lift it about two feet off of the table. He heard Celeste again. *Now, open your eyes.*

Jake slowly opened his eyes and looked. To his astonishment, the lamp was there, hovering only about two inches above the nightstand. It was shaking violently and wasn't two feet in the air like he imagined it to be. But that didn't matter. It was still hovering.

Jake was so excited he lost focus. The lamp dropped back to the nightstand, tipped over, and fell, crashing to the floor.

"Oh, now you need to get me a new lamp," said Celeste.

Jake turned around with excitement all over his face. "Wh . . . how?"

"It was you, Jake. You did it. You see . . . it is possible for humans to do things you could only imagine. We are created in the image of God. Why wouldn't we have the potential to do what He and His Son can do?" Celeste then leaned in and kissed Jake again.

Jake kissed her back. And even though Jake barely lifted the lamp with his mind, he felt invincible. After their lips separated, he grabbed Celeste and hugged her tighter than he had ever hugged anyone before.

★ ★ ★ ★ ★

Bantyr was awakened by the wheezing and hacking cough of his older sister. He slowly opened his eyes and rolled off of the metal slab that was his bed. He rubbed his eyes and walked across the cell to the other metal slab his sister was lying on. Reaching down, he felt her face. She was burning up, and her blue prison overalls – the Gnols so generously gave them – were drenched. In a whisper, so the guards wouldn't hear, he called to her. "Kylee . . ."

She didn't respond.

"Kylee. You're burning up. What did they do to you?"

A day earlier the guards entered the cell by disabling the energy field that separated them from the prisoners and took Kylee and Sean while they were sleeping. Bantyr demanded to know why they took them, which was a mistake. Because of his insubordination and demands, he was severely beaten. He was still licking his wounds, as a result. He was grateful, however, that Koroan Chast ordered that all political prisoners in the brig of the palace keep their inhibitors in place. Only he and his high priest were allowed to take prisoners' inhibitors out and probe their minds for information.

Bantyr shuddered at the thought of what the less experienced Gnol guards would do to him if he did not have his inhibitors in. Strangely enough, however, neither Koroan nor his high priest had probed his mind yet. He figured they must have gotten all of the information they needed from Sean.

He called to his sister again. "Kylee . . ."

Kylee slowly opened her eyes and turned her face toward Bantyr. "B . . ." She stopped as she coughed, ". . . Bantyr is . . . is that you."

Bantyr looked down at his sister. He couldn't make out the details of her face because of the dim light in the cell, but he could tell from her fever and the shaking of her body that she was in pain. "I'm here," he whispered as he grabbed her hand.

"They . . . they did something to me."

Bantyr felt his eyes well up with tears. "I don't understand," he said. "You were fine before they took you?"

Kylee nodded her head and tried to swallow. Bantyr could tell that she experienced a tremendous amount of pain as she did so. "Whe . . . where's Sean?" she asked.

Bantyr looked in the direction of Sean's so called bed. He couldn't see because of the darkness, so he stepped over to it a few yards away and felt. Nothing. He made his way back to Kylee. "He's not here. They must still have him."

Suddenly the lights to the entire brig flickered on. Bantyr looked in the direction of the main entrance as he heard the doors slide open. Ten royal body guards, all dressed in red, walked in. The last guard carried Sean. Sean looked terrible. Both of his eyes were bloodied and purple, and blood trickled from his nose. He also looked to be going in and out of consciousness.

After the guard stepped in, Koroan and his high priest Vlamer Kreuk entered as well. Koroan was dressed in a white robe and looked extremely angry. Vlamer was dressed in his usual religious regalia and sat in his hover chair. It was rumored throughout the brig that the reason Vlamer now had to move around with a hover chair was because he was paralyzed from the waist down, as a result of a plasma blast to his spine – delivered by none other than his own daughter. Bantyr could only hope that was true because the rebels would then have another powerful Gnol on their side.

Bantyr heard the energy field, separating him and Kylee from the guards, disengage. The guard carrying Sean threw him into the prison cell and into the back wall. Bantyr cringed as he heard Sean's arm hit the wall and pop. He heard the energy field reengage, and the Gnols turn around to leave the brig. Before they did so, Bantyr summoned the courage he needed.

He stood up and approached the closest to the energy field he could get before it shocked him and threw him backwards. "Hey!" he yelled.

The guards, Koroan, and Vlamer all turned.

"What did you do to my sister?" he asked.

He heard the energy field disengage again. The same guard that threw Sean in rapidly approached and lifted him by the throat. "No prisoner speaks in the presence of the lord unless he is commanded to do so."

Bantyr kicked his feet and struggled for air. He then heard a bellowing command from Koroan himself. "That is enough, Captain! Let him go!"

Bantyr fell to the cold metal floor and clutched his throat. He saw the guard turn around and bow. "Sorry, My Lord," the captian said.

As the guard scurried away, Bantyr saw Koroan approach. Koroan lifted his right hand and gently levitated Bantyr about five feet off the floor. He gave Bantyr an evil smile that caused shivers to run down his spine. "Ask your question again?"

"What did you do to my sister?"

Koroan didn't respond right away. He looked Bantyr up and down with the same smile on his face. "Hmm," he said. "Very brave for such a young boy. You must have gotten that strength from your father."

"More than you know," Bantyr said with a glare.

Koroan's smile disappeared and his face flushed red with anger. With a twist of his hand, Bantyr flew through the air; his face stopping within inches of Koroan's. "Do not ever disrespect me again!"

Bantyr didn't respond. He knew that if he said anything else; Koroan would probably kill him right then and there. Koroan dropped him to the floor and walked over to Kylee. Bantyr wanted to get up and stop him, but he knew better. Koroan knelt down beside Kylee and rubbed the back of his right hand along her clammy face. All the while, Kylee watched him in horror.

"Such a pretty face," said Koroan, as he continued to stroke her cheek. "It is too bad she is nothing more than a despicable human. With her courage and stamina, she would make a valiant Gnol."

Bantyr felt the anger surge from within. He wanted so badly to pull Koroan away from his sister, and break his neck, but he knew that wasn't possible. He gritted his teeth and shook as he spoke. "What did you do to her?" he demanded.

Koroan slowly stood as he continued to look at Kylee. He turned around and met Bantyr's eyes. "She has been used for the cause."

Bantyr held Koroan's gaze. "Cause?"

Koroan smiled again and walked slowly toward Bantyr. Bantyr backed away, but Koroan clutched his left arm causing Bantyr to wince in pain. For a long moment, Koroan stared at him. Finally, he said, "Meaning, she was chosen as the test subject for new biological weapons that we plan to use to wipe out your father's renegade force."

Bantyr glared at Koroan. "You forget, Your Highness, my father has an advantage you don't."

Koroan furrowed his eyebrows and spit as he responded. "And what is that?"

"Your daughter."

With that comment, Koroan gritted his teeth and squeezed Bantyr's arm even harder. Bantyr screamed in pain as Koroan continued to squeeze until Bantyr felt his bone snap. Bantyr fell to the floor writhing in pain.

Koroan smiled again and turned to one of his guards. "Commander!"

The guard approached Koroan, knelt down, and bowed his head. "What would you have me do, My Lord?"

"These two male humans are of no further use to me. At dawn, have the two males in this cell sent to a slave camp. I do not care which one. Leave the female here. She is to continually be tested upon until she dies."

With Koroan's final orders, Bantyr forgot about his pain, jumped up, and lunged for Koroan. Koroan turned around, lifted his right palm and telekinetically sent Bantyr flying through the air to the back of the cell. Bantyr felt the bone crushing impact. He dropped to the floor and tried to look up. His vision went blurry and then darkness.

CHAPTER 17

June 8, 2042 – Rebel Base 2 on Terrest

Adrian stood upon the platform fifty-feet above the hangar floor and looked out amongst the rag-tag group of rebels he had led for fifteen years. Behind him and beyond a gigantic pain of glass were the large number of computer terminals, radar tracking systems, and rebel military personnel that would monitor the battle that was about to take place.

Adrian took a deep breath and wiped the tear away that rolled down his cheek. He looked over the men and women he would lead and felt sorrow. He knew that he was about to lead them into a suicide mission. He turned around and looked into the window. He met his wife's eyes. She gave him a warm, loving smile and nodded, giving him the encouragement he needed. Standing next to Anyta was Peter Sanchez. Together Petey and Anyta were going to coordinate and lead the attack.

Adrian glanced at Petey. Petey gave him that smile he always liked and gave him a thumbs-up. Adrian returned his smile and nodded. He slowly turned around and again looked out onto the fearful faces of his troops. He licked his lips and opened his mouth. "All of you are here today on your own free will and accord . . ." He paused as he scanned the hangar. Some of his troops were nodding, some looked eager to fight, but the majority looked like scared children, knowing full well they were about to walk to their deaths.

He took another breath and continued. "That is why we are all here. We are fighting for our free agency. Many of you know the horror of not being able to control your own mind. Many of you have told me your personal story of being enslaved in a Gnol slave camp. You have told me your stories of what it feels like when your mind is under the control of a Gnol. You have said that it is as if you are watching yourself from afar. Doing things you never would have imagined yourself doing . . ."

Adrian paused again. He saw many former slaves nodding their heads in agreement. Most of his troops had been former slaves and knew all too well the horrors of being under the mind-control of a Gnol.

Adrian made eye contact down below with his son. Jake smiled and nodded. Adrian continued. "For those reasons you are here to fight; to defend yourselves from the further enslavement and oppression of Koroan Chast. Koroan Chast believes that humans are here to serve him and his people. He believes that we are animals and cannot think for ourselves. That is one mistake he will regret . . ."

Adrian stopped as he heard clapping and small cheers break out amongst his troops. Feeling the confidence grow within him, he continued. "Yes, he has made a grave mistake; for he has underestimated us. He does not believe that humans are capable of fresh and new ideas, developing new inventions, and – most of all – making our own decisions. Well, this is the mistake he has made. For we can think for ourselves, we can create new and wonderful inventions, and we can develop new ideas!"

Applause and cheers arose from the mass of troops standing on the hangar floor. The cheers and applause grew louder as Adrian spoke. Each time, he spoke louder through his voice enhancer in order to be heard.

"Yes, Koroan has underestimated us. After fifteen years of war, he still has not succeeded in enslaving the entire human race upon *Terrest*. Each time he has nearly succeeded in crushing us; we have found strength from within and held on a little longer. And where do we get that strength you may ask?"

Adrian stopped and scanned the hangar. The countenances upon his troops' faces were beginning to change from a look of fear and dread to a look of sheer determination and confidence. He smiled and took another deep breath.

"That strength comes from our desire to be free. Five hundred years ago, your ancestors united *Terrest* into the most successful civilizations I have ever seen. Your leaders were good and righteous men who didn't care about wealth or power. They cared about you. They cared more that you were free to choose what you were going to do with your lives than they did about controlling you. Your ancestors and leaders truly understood what it meant to be free."

Again, applause and cheers exploded from Adrian's troops. Adrian felt a surge of electricity rise up his spine. His sorrow and dread was beginning to turn into faith and hope even though he knew the odds of a successful battle. He made eye contact with Jake and Celeste and continued.

"Almost two hundred sixty-six years ago on my home world, Earth. My forefathers did the same thing. They declared their independence and free agency from an enemy that oppressed them. No one at that time expected this rebellion force to win the war. They were severely outnumbered, and they were extremely inexperienced compared to their enemy. Despite those odds, they succeeded in winning the war, giving them their independence and free will to choose.

"Today, the Gnols have chosen a new world to enslave. A world populated by your brothers and sisters . . ." Adrian paused and felt his emotions rise to the surface as he thought about his brother back on Earth. "At this time, Earth has no idea that they are about to be attacked. We are the last line of defense.

"Each of you in this hangar today has been offered the choice of joining this small and overmatched military or living in the base with your families and working as civilians for the cause. Most of you have chosen to fight – to free your brothers and sisters that are still enslaved by the Gnols.

"Knowing this, each one of you has a choice to make today. We are about to go into a battle in which we are severely outnumbered. The odds of us winning this battle are astronomical. And even though we may not win the battle today, our fortitude and willingness to fight for the freedom of our brothers and sisters on Earth and for our brothers and sisters still enslaved here on *Terrest* will win us this war."

An eruption of cheers and applause resonated throughout the hangar. Adrian had a strange feeling of confidence overwhelm him. He knew the odds and yet, he truly believed that somehow by fighting today, they could win this war.

Adrian glanced to his left and saw Scott Hauler, his dear friend for all of these years and now one of his most trusted generals, thrust his fist into the air. "Now, I ask you my brothers and sisters, who will join me in this battle? Who will be willing to sacrifice their life for the lives of their brothers and sisters on Earth and *Terrest*? Who will be willing to sacrifice their life so that our brothers and sisters may be free?"

Adrian stopped and looked around the hangar. One by one, hands shot into the air. Adrian didn't notice one person within his range of vision that didn't have his or her hand raised. Even the young men and women barely over the age of sixteen had their hands raised.

After he scanned the entire hangar, he smiled and said, "May God be with us!"

★ ★ ★ ★ ★

Celeste squeezed Jake's hand. He turned to look at her with concern on his face. "Do not look at me like that," she said.

"Like what?"

"You look as if you do not have any faith that this mission will work."

Jake sighed and looked around the hangar that was busy with activity. Troops scattered to-and-fro as everyone prepared for a battle that they had no chance of winning.

"Jake," Celeste said as she grabbed his face and turned it so that she could meet his eyes. "Answer me. What is wrong?"

Jake shook his head. "I don't know. I just . . ."

"Just what?"

"I just don't want you in harm's way."

Celeste laughed, which caused Jake to frown even more. She stopped laughing and looked at him with compassion. "Jake, I do not understand. Just a few days ago you were afraid of me because of my abilities. And now . . ." She giggled again, ". . . you seem to want to protect the little lady."

Jake managed a shy smile and said, "Well you've grown on me, and I just worry about you that's all."

Celeste smiled at him and was about to respond when a short dark haired soldier approached Jake. "General Palmer," he said.

Jake turned and looked at the soldier. "Yes, Corporal?"

"Your *Wildcat* has had its preflight inspection and is ready."

Jake nodded and said, "Thanks, Corporal. Go and tell my father that my squadron will be ready to take off within ten minutes."

The corporal saluted and said, "Yes, Sir." And then he turned and made his way to Adrian.

Celeste grabbed Jake's hand and pulled him in close. She looked at the man she was growing to love more and more each day and hugged him. Their lips met for a few seconds and then they pulled away. "Be careful," she said.

"I will. And you take care of yourself as well."

"I will."

"Promise."

"Yes," Celeste said.

Jake gently placed both of his hands on Celeste's face and kissed her again. After the kiss, Jake whispered into her ear. "I love you, Celeste." He then turned and jogged to his fighter.

Celeste's spine tingled. Never before had a person that she was fond of told her that he loved her. She swallowed and managed to control the tears that were beginning to form in her eyes. At that same moment, she suddenly worried for Jake's safety as well. She wondered if she would ever see him again as they were about to walk into a no win situation that could cost them both of their lives.

★ ★ ★ ★ ★

Celeste walked up the ramp of the assault vehicle that would carry herself and her squadron to *Chast* where they would attempt to rescue Bantyr, Kylee, and Sean. She sighed as she stepped onto the ramp. She knew that this mission was extremely dangerous. *Chast* was heavily guarded and every Gnol within its borders knew who Celeste was, and of her loyalty to the rebels. That's why she would stay behind on the outskirts of *Chast*, and Colonel Jantear would guide the assault vehicle, that was disguised as a Gnol craft, into her father's great city.

Jantear and his men were already dressed in the standard issue black and red fatigues that the Gnols typically wore. The plan was simple. Jantear would lead his troops into the city, and from there they would enter the gates to the palace disguised as a squadron returning from the Gnol city of *Ciminae* to report to Lord Chast himself.

A few weeks earlier the rebels had stumbled upon an actual squadron of Gnol troops that were traveling from *Ciminae* to *Chast*. Colonel Jantear and his men ambushed the Gnol troops killing everyone, taking their uniforms, and stealing their identification codes. As a result, they now had the codes that would get them into the city and the palace gates.

The first part of the mission was straightforward. That not what worried Celeste. She was worried about the second half. Once Jantear and his men made their way into the palace courtyard, Celeste – from her position, outside of the city walls – would guide Jantear and his troops to the various secret passageways she knew of in the palace. She even knew of one that would lead them directly to the brig.

The difficulty in going through the secret passageways, however, was that her father never traveled within his palace via conventional means. He always traveled through the passageways. It scared her to death, the thought of Jantear and his troops encountering her father within one of the passageways. Sure they would have him outnumbered. But she knew what her father was capable of, and that is what scared her the most.

As Celeste stepped aboard the vehicle, all fifty troops stood and saluted. She saluted back and made her way to the front. She sat in the chair on Colonel Jantear's right and put on her head set. She heard Petey's voice. "All teams check in," said Petey.

Celeste heard Jake first. "Red team ready and awaiting orders to disembark."

"Roger that, Red Leader," replied Petey.

Then Celeste heard Adrian's voice. "Black team is ready and awaiting further orders."

"Roger that, Black Leader."

"Blue team is ready," said Scott.

"Roger that, Blue Leader."

Celeste paused before she spoke. She was lost in her thoughts about the mission and Jake. She wanted more than ever to stop this horrific war that her father had started and spend every waking moment with Jake. She didn't want to let him out of her sight.

She felt someone touch her left arm. She looked up and saw Colonel Jantear staring at her with concern on his face. "Are you all right?" he asked.

Celeste nodded and responded into her headset. "This is Yellow Leader. Yellow team is ready to go."

"Very well," Petey said. "Blue Leader your team will launch first and provide cover fire for the Red and Black teams, so they have a clear shot out of the atmosphere. We already know that the Gnols are already on the surface waiting for us to open the hangar doors. General Hauler, make sure you get those Gnol hover tanks first. From our surface readouts, they've got them lined up around our parameter with their cannons pointing into the sky. They anticipate we're going to launch space fighters."

"Roger that," replied Scott.

"Good. Red Leader, you will launch second. Go at full speed to get out of range of those tanks."

"You got it," Jake responded.

"Black Leader, your squadron is to launch immediately after Red team has left the hangar. Those *Wildcat 2's* carry more firepower to inflict enough damage upon those Gnol space cruisers near the wormhole, so don't waste any firepower on the surface."

"Roger that," Adrian said.

"Yellow Leader, your team is to wait approximately five minutes after Black team leaves before you launch. Hopefully, we will have created enough of a diversion that you can sneak past the battle. Ten *Chaties* will escort you far enough out of the battle area. After that, you're on your own."

"Roger that," Celeste replied.

"Very well, on my mark, Blue team launch," Petey said with a hint of anxiety in his voice.

Celeste looked up and saw the hangar doors slowly start to open. As the doors spread further and further apart, she could see the blue sky patched with white clouds. Out of the corner of her right eye, she saw the faint outlines of *Terrest's* two moons.

"Blue team, go!"

Celeste watched as Scott's squadron lifted off of the hangar floor. As the mass of hover tanks, *Chaties*, and assault vehicle ascended above the hangar doors, she could see flashes of plasma blasts and explosions.

"Red team go!"

Celeste saw Jake's *Wildcat* lift off of the floor first. She could make out the silhouette of the upper half of his body in his cockpit and longed to be with him. Once Jake's squadron reached the opening to the hangar, they shot off toward space like lightning bolts.

Celeste listened for Jake's voice in her headset. She could hear screams and orders being spattered all over the place as the battle began. She closed her eyes and said a silent prayer to the God Jake and Adrian had told her so much about for their safety.

"Black team, go!"

Adrian's squadron slowly approached the hangar doors and then shot off just as Jake's squadron had previously done. Again, she prayed for both Jake's and Adrian's safety.

"Okay, Yellow Leader, wait until I give you the order to launch," said Petey.

"Roger that," replied Celeste, as she looked to her left. Colonel Jantear sat in his chair with a mixed look of fear and determination on his face. His knuckles were beginning to turn white as he squeezed harder and harder upon the controls of the vehicle.

Celeste turned her head to look at the forty-three young men and seven young women that were willing to risk their lives for people they didn't even know personally. As she scanned their faces, some had looks of sheer dread. Others were wiping the tears from their eyes and trying to control their emotions as the fear of entering their first battle began to set in. There were other soldiers, however, that looked brave – at least on the outside – as their jaws were clinched taught and their eyes were full of rage.

Celeste looked above the soldiers and saw the man that would command the gun turret on the top of the vehicle. He clutched the cannon tight and Celeste hoped that he wouldn't prematurely fire. He looked down, made eye contact with her, and nodded.

Celeste returned the nod, turned back in her chair, and looked out of the hangar. There were explosions all over the place. She could also see red plasma blasts scattered throughout the sky. The sky was no longer blue. Instead, it had turned to a pale orange as the battle commenced.

"Yellow team, go!" Petey ordered.

Celeste saw Jantear clutch the controls tighter as he slowly ascended to the opening of the hangar. Celeste looked first to her right and then to her left. She could see the ten *Chaties* that would escort them out of the battle.

As the assault vehicle ascended out of the hangar, Celeste looked around. All over the battle field there were burning vehicles, and rebel and Gnol troops were scattered throughout, firing at will. Even though there was destruction all around, Celeste still felt good because she could still hear the voices in her headset of Jake, Adrian, and Scott giving orders.

Out of the corner of her eye, Celeste saw Jantear push the throttle of the vehicle to full speed. As he did, Celeste felt her body press against the back of her seat, and the assault vehicle darted off toward *Chast*.

As the vehicle sped through the mess of Gnol and rebel vehicles and troops, Celeste could feel the impact of plasma and missile fire upon their own vehicle. She was grateful, however, that the vehicle was heavily armed, and the fact that they could return their own fire with the soldier in the gun turret. In fact, she could hear the movement of the turret as the young soldier returned fire.

Suddenly, Celeste heard screams and two bright fireballs explode to her right. She looked and saw that two of the five *Chaties* on her right had been hit. "This is Yellow Leader! Two *Chaties* down! I repeat two *Chaties* down!"

"Roger that," Petey replied. "Maintain your course. You're almost out of the surface battle."

"Roger, th—"

Celeste turned around as she heard a loud explosion from the top of the vehicle. She looked up and saw the body of the brave young soldier go limp. She saw blood dripping down his arm and onto the turret's floor.

Celeste turned away. She returned to look as she saw two other troops open the hatchway to the gun turret and slowly remove the young soldier's body. One soldier gently laid his body on the floor of the vehicle as another young female soldier retrieved a blanket from the back and covered his body.

Celeste regained her composure and shot a look to one of the soldiers that removed the dead soldier's body. "Corporal, take over the gun turret."

The soldier climbed the ladder and secured himself into the turret.

As Celeste turned back to face the battle outside, she heard Petey in her headset. "Yellow Leader, report!"

"Our turret commander was killed. We have someone else manning the gun."

"Very well."

Celeste looked at Colonel Jantear. "How are you doing?"

Jantear's jaw was clenched tight, and he had a look of fierce determination on his face. Without looking at Celeste, he said, "She's keeping together, but I don't know how much longer she'll withstand this barrage of plasma fire."

Celeste looked out of the front windshield. She could see the gigantic grove of pine trees rapidly approaching. She knew that soon they would be out of the surface battle and onto *Chast*.

Celeste heard the static within her headset and the voice of one of the *Chati* pilots that was escorting them. "Yellow Leader, come in Yellow Leader."

"This is Yellow Leader."

"You're safe. For some reason, the Gnols decided not to follow you and stopped firing upon us. We're going back to help Blue Leader. You're on your own from here. Good luck!"

Celeste glanced at Jantear before she responded. For some odd reason, he didn't look surprised that they weren't being pursued. She turned back to look out of the windshield and said, "Thank you, Captain. And, good luck to you."

As the eight remaining *Chaties* turned around and returned to the battle, Celeste heard the voice of Jake within her headset. "Dad! Dad! No!"

★ ★ ★ ★ ★

Adrian pushed the button in his cockpit that would switch his *Wildcat* from atmosphere mode to space mode as his space fighter exited the atmosphere of *Terrest*. For a small moment before he joined the battle that raged ahead, he drifted back twenty-five years earlier the last time he was in space.

"What the—"

"What is it Captain," said Adrian to Captain Shultz, his copilot seated in his seat directly behind Adrian.

Captain Shultz, a young native Terrestrian barely out of his teens but an excellent navigator, pointed directly ahead and said, "Would you look at that?"

Adrian shot his head up and looked directly ahead. His draw dropped in awe of the sheer number of Gnol ships ahead of him. He knew that his men were severely outnumbered, but no one could have imagined what he saw before him.

Soon he would be flying into thousands and thousands of Gnol space fighters. Adrian could see Jake's squadron of bright red *Wildcats* scattered amidst the black Gnol fighters. There were plasma blasts and explosions everywhere. Adrian took a deep breath. "Red Leader, report!"

Adrian was relieved when he heard the static voice of his son within his flight helmet. "Twenty-six *Wildcat 1's* already down. There's too many of them. Black Leader, get in here now!"

Adrian squeezed his flight stick and said, "Black team engage!"

All one hundred *Wildcat 2's* darted off to join the battle. As Adrian entered the mass of space fighters, he maneuvered his fighter back and forth, dodging the plasma fire that was all around his ship. Within his helmet, Adrian could hear the screams of his brave pilots as they were obliterated.

"General, we got one on our tail!" Shultz yelled.

Adrian looked at his rear-view screen. Directly behind him and matching him move for move was a Gnol space fighter. "Captain, fire the gun turret."

Shultz pushed the button that activated the small gun turret that would fire a barrage of small plasma blasts at their pursuer. Adrian continued to watch the rear-view screen as the turret fired. He knew that the small blasts wouldn't do any significant damage to his enemy, but he hoped that it would distract him enough so Adrian could maneuver behind him.

As Adrian watched, he saw that the Gnol fighter was lining itself up for a shot.

"General, look out!"

Adrian looked up. He eyes widened as another Gnol fighter rapidly approached. He saw red plasma blasts exit the turrets in its wings. Without even a thought, Adrian yanked his flight stick to the left. His spacecraft banked left into a three hundred sixty degree roll.

Adrian looked out to his right and saw that he had barely avoided his and Shultz' deaths as the two Gnol fighters fired simultaneously. Both Gnol fighters landed direct hits on each other and exploded into two brilliant fireballs.

Adrian heard Captain Shultz let out a holler of total excitement. "Yes! Nice flying, General!"

Adrian allowed a small smile to crease along his face. It had been a long time since he had flown like that, and the adrenaline was simply astounding.

"Get him off of me!"

Adrian shot his head to his left and saw a red *Wildcat 1* speed past. Behind the *Wildcat*, was a Gnol fighter lining itself up for a shot. Adrian moved his flight stick back and forth as he flew his fighter into a direct line with the Gnol fighter. The Gnol zigzagged back and forth, trying to get Adrian off of his tail, and at the same time, line himself up for a shot on his prey. But Adrian matched every move the Gnol made. The second the Gnol appeared in Adrian's sights, he fired.

The blasts clipped the left wing of the Gnol fighter, causing it to spin out of control and into another Gnol fighter. They both exploded into bright red and orange fireballs. The blast was so bright that Adrian failed to recognize what was behind him before it was too late.

As he glanced at his rear-view screen, another Gnol had fired upon him. Adrian tried to dodge the blast, but it hit his right wing. He felt the shudder of his space fighter. He tried to regain control, but his right wing thrusters had been damaged. As a result, it was impossible for him to bank left. "Captain, can you get that fixed."

"Working on it now, General," Shultz said as he started typing into his computer.

Adrian looked again at his rear-view screen. The Gnol knew about Adrian's predicament and positioned itself for another shot. Adrian knew, by the way the Gnol fighter positioned his ship, that there was no way he could dodge the next plasma blast or missile fire. Then Adrian heard the tone he dreaded to hear.

The Gnol had locked itself onto Adrian's fighter and was about to fire a missile that would obliterate himself and Captain Shultz. Suddenly, Adrian saw the flash of a brilliant explosion. He looked and saw that the Gnol on his tail had exploded. He watched a red *Wildcat 1* fly though the fireball, and he heard his son within his helmet. "Dad! You okay?"

"Yeah, thanks."

"Dad, most of the Gnol fighters are retreating back to their battle cruisers. The wormhole must be opening soon. Take your squadron and afflict as much damage on those cruisers as you can. We'll hold off the rest of the Gnol fighters."

"Roger that," replied Adrian, as he thought about how grateful he was to have such a talented son. "Captain, how's that wing looking?"

Captain Shultz continued to type into his computer for a moment longer before answering.

"Captain . . ."

"Got it, General. She should be able to go now."

Adrian tested the fighter. He could now maneuver to his left just as if there had been no damage to his wing. He smiled and said, "Shultz, you're a genius."

"Thanks, General."

Adrian then turned his attention to the mass of Gnol battle cruisers that sat motionless just above *Terrest's* two moons. He hesitated for a moment as he thought about the odds he and his pilots were up against.

Ahead of him, he could see the three hundred eighty-four battle cruisers and the one command ship waiting for the wormhole to open. All of the Gnol ships reminded him of his *Mars I* space shuttle; the only difference being their colors, insignias, and, of course, their sizes. The Gnol Battle Cruisers were about five hundred times larger than the original *Mars I* shuttle, and the command ship about one thousand times larger.

Adrian swallowed and spoke into his comm. "Black Squadron, this is Black Leader. Engage the Gnol Battle Cruisers! I repeat, engage the Gnol Battle Cruisers!"

Adrian heard a series of *roger that's* as he sped off toward his targets. As his squadron approached, a barrage of plasma fire erupted from the cruisers.

"Evasive maneuvers!" screamed Adrian, as he dodged the plasma blasts as well.

As Adrian dodged the blasts, he tried to line himself up for a missile shot. It was useless. The firepower of the cruisers was too powerful. Adrian's pilots were getting picked off one by one.

"Dad, you have to retreat. You're not going to make it!" yelled Jake.

Adrian was about to respond when his fighter shuddered violently, and he saw a bright flash of light. He heard Jake yell something and felt his body spinning at a velocity he had never felt before. He opened his eyes and saw the surface of one of *Terrest's* moons rapidly approaching.

He gritted his teeth and used all of the strength he could muster to pull his fighter out of its spin. He knew that somehow he had to get his fighter upright so that it would land on its fuselage and hopefully skid to a stop on the surface. As the moon's surface quickly drew nearer, Adrian struggled with all of his might to control the fighter. He screamed, pulling on his flight stick.

Just before the nose of his fighter penetrated the surface of the moon, he was able to level the ship out and pull the nose slightly upward. The fuselage of the fighter hit the surface with such an impact that Adrian thought for sure he was going to be ripped to shreds. Gray dust and debris from the moon exploded out from underneath his *Wildcat*.

He opened his eyes again and saw that his plan, at least for the moment, had succeeded. But now, he had a new problem. His *Wildcat* now skidded along the surface with such velocity that Adrian was unable to reach his control panel and fire his reverse thrusters to stop. Just ahead, he saw a rock formation coming up fast.

Adrian's eyes widened with horror as he saw that his fighter was headed directly for a rock archway that was low enough to rip the top of his ship to pieces. "Duck!" he shrieked.

Adrian ducked his head as far as his seat's restraining belt would allow. Glass and metal splattered everywhere, and Adrian felt the back of his flight helmet scrape along the bottom of the arch.

After the fighter cleared the archway, Adrian sat up and looked directly ahead. Soon his body would be forever impaled upon the face of the cliff wall that his ship was about to meet. Adrian reached down to his right and pulled the ejection lever.

Adrian and Shultz were launched into the moon's thin atmosphere just as the fighter collided with the cliff's face. A brilliant fireball erupted, and Adrian felt the heat of the blast on his feet as he ascended toward space.

Adrian knew that the velocity of the ejection seat's ascent would send him and Shultz out of the moon's thin atmosphere and forever floating in space. He quickly pushed a button on the ejection lever, and reverse thrusters fired. The ejection seat slowly descended and landed softly onto the moon's surface.

Stunned, Adrian sat motionless in his seat for a few moments before he unbuckled himself. He called out for Captain Shultz. "Captain . . ."

There was no answer.

"Captain Shultz, are you all right?"

Again, no answer.

Adrian checked himself from head to toe. He wasn't injured anywhere; just sore from using muscles he hadn't used in a long time. He unbuckled himself and rolled onto the soft, dusty surface. He stood up and noticed that the gravity reminded him of his first trip to Earth's moon when he was training for the Mars' mission.

Adrian tried to call for Jake through his communicator, but there was no response. He then called out for Shultz again as he turned to the rear part of the ejection seat.

Adrian turned his head and almost vomited from the sight of Shultz's body. Shultz must not have seen the rock archway because not much was left of the captain. Adrian dropped to his knees in sorrow. As he mourned the loss of a promising young leader within the *Terrest* military, he noticed that the moon dust around him began to flurry.

He turned around and saw a Gnol transport shuttle landing about ten yards away from where he knelt. He quickly stood up and grabbed his sidearm attached to the left leg of his spacesuit. He raised his gun upwards just as the shuttle landed. He waited a few moments as the ladder lowered and the door to the shuttle slid open.

Adrian maintained his aim upon the open doorway and waited. A space helmet peeked out, and Adrian fired. Adrian missed, his shot hitting just above the doorway. He lined up for another shot when another Gnol stepped out and fired. The blast hit the bottom of Adrian's gun, causing it to fly from his hand. Adrian decided to surrender and raised his arms.

The two Gnols dressed in their red and black spacesuits approached Adrian with their weapons raised. One of them spoke to him. "Name and rank."

Adrian didn't respond.

"Name and rank now, or you're dead!"

Adrian waited a few seconds. The Gnol who spoke to him walked up to him and placed his weapon upon the shield of Adrian's helmet. He began to squeeze his trigger.

"Adrian Palmer . . . General Adrian Palmer."

The Gnol smiled and said, "Ah, General Dorange Gar would like you to join him on his trip to Earth."

★ ★ ★ ★ ★

"Dad! Dad! No!" Jake screamed as he watched his father's fighter spin out of control toward the surface of one of *Terrest's* moons.

For what seemed like hours, Jake just stared at the moon as his father's ship disappeared. Finally, he took a deep breath and said, "Red Leader to *Base 2* . . ."

He waited a few seconds for either Petey's or Anyta's voice. There was no response.

"I repeat . . . Red Leader to *Base 2*! Come in . . ."

Again, he waited. Finally after a couple of minutes, he heard Anyta's voice. Jake could tell from the sound of it that she was trying not to cry. "Thi . . . this is *Base 2*, Red Leader. Report."

"Black Leader is down. I repeat Black Leader is down. I'm going after him."

Jake could tell that Anyta hesitated before she spoke, but then she said something he didn't expect. "Negative, Red Leader. Your orders are to retreat back to base and provide air support for Blue Leader."

Jake was shocked. *What was she thinking*, he thought. "What? I don't understand. My dad needs help. I'm going down to that moon's surface."

Again, Anyta denied him. "Negative, Red Leader. Your squadron and the remaining Black Squadron are needed for air support."

Jake ignored Anyta's orders. He knew that his father had given Petey and Anyta full authority while they were in the battle, but he didn't care. He didn't want to admit to himself that his father might have been killed. He had to see for himself.

Jake pushed his *Wildcat* to full speed and sped off toward the moon's surface. Meanwhile, the rest of the remaining Red and Black squadrons retreated back to *Terrest* to aid in the ground battle.

As Jake drew nearer to the Gnol battle cruisers, they opened fire upon him. He dodged left and then right, avoiding the red hot flashes of energy. Just as he was about to enter the thin atmosphere of the moon, he heard Anyta again. "Jake, listen to me."

He didn't answer.

"Okay . . . if you're not going to respond, then just listen. I'm hurting just as much as you are. Every part of me wants you to go to that surface to see if the man I love is still alive . . . but . . . but you can't. We need you, Jake. The base is about to be penetrated, and the inexperienced pilots need your leadership. If you land on that moon, everything your father has fought for will be lost."

Jake felt the tears rush down his face. He didn't want to lose his father again. But Anyta was right. His pilots needed his leadership if they were going to prevent the Gnols from penetrating the base and destroy everything his father had worked so long to preserve – the free agency of his brothers and sisters.

Jake swallowed the lump that was in his throat and gritted his teeth. "Roger that," he said as he pulled on his flight stick and rolled out of the moon's atmosphere. As he neared *Terrest*, he looked at his rear-view screen.

He could see the wormhole open as the mass of warmongering Gnols entered it with the intent to destroy or enslave every human being upon Earth.

★ ★ ★ ★ ★

Celeste peered through her binoculars toward the entrance of her father's magnificent city. She was perched atop a small hill about three hundred yards away and well hidden from the cover of night and a small grove of pine trees that surrounded her. She was sure that the guards in their towers wouldn't be able to see her.

She continued to watch as Colonel Jantear guided the assault vehicle to the city gates. She looked around and counted approximately twenty-two guards within the vehicle's immediate vicinity. One of the guards held up his hand to stop the vehicle and waved for the driver to step out. Jantear stopped the hover craft just as the side entrance slid open.

Celeste adjusted the focus on her binoculars, so she could get a better visual of what was going on. As she did so, Jantear exited the vehicle from the side entrance and returned a salute the guard had given him. "So far so good," she said softly. She was relieved; at least for the moment that the Gnol's officer's uniform Jantear wore fooled the guard.

Her earpiece crackled, and she could hear the guard speak. "Uh . . . General . . . we were not expecting any troop movements today. What is your business?"

"We are returning from *Ciminae*," Jantear said. "We have standing orders to report directly to Lord Chast himself, and for you to not ask any questions. Understood."

"Uh . . . yes, Sir. Sorry, Sir. Do you have your identification codes?"

Celeste smiled and was impressed with Jantear's playacting. From his performance, Celeste knew that he came across as a legitimate and condescending Gnol officer. She watched as Jantear handed the guard the disk that contained the authentication codes. The guard inserted the disk into the small computer he was holding and examined the information.

After a few seconds, the guard looked up and then back to his screen. Again, he examined the information. He then looked back at Jantear and gave him a confused look. "Okay. It all checks out. You may enter."

Celeste watched Jantear return to the driver's seat. Once Celeste saw the vehicle enter the city and hover its way to the palace, she spoke to Jantear through the small communication devices they had on their collars and in their ears. "What was that all about?"

"What?" Jantear replied.

"That guard did not seem convinced about those codes."

"What are you talking about?"

Celeste was confused. She knew what she saw and could tell from the look on that guard's face that he was not sure about the information he was looking at. "Jantear, you saw that guard's face just as I did. And I could tell he was not convinced."

"You're being paranoid, Celeste. It worked, didn't it? We're in."

Celeste knew Jantear was right, but couldn't escape the feeling that something was amiss. She looked at her computer monitor that was next to her and could see that Jantear was nearing the palace gates. She continued to watch as Jantear went through the same actions he performed previously that got him into the city. The only difference this time, however, was that every one of his troops exited the assault vehicle and left it parked near the entrance of the palace walls.

She continued to watch through the small camera attached to Jantear's uniform as he and his troops neared the main entrance of the palace. "Okay, Celeste. We're at the main entrance," he said softly into his comm. "Where do we go from here?"

Celeste looked at her monitor and could see that Jantear and his troops were about to enter the entrance to the temple that honored her father and the goddess of light. She also thought that it was odd that there wasn't another Gnol in sight. In fact, the entire palace courtyard and temple floor of the palace, which was usually abuzz with activity, was strangely empty.

"Okay, Colonel. Enter the temple and scan the floor for any activity."

"You got it," Jantear replied.

Celeste heard Jantear issue the order and then saw him enter the temple from the camera on his uniform. She saw Jantear and his troops scattered about the floor with weapons raised, scanning for any Gnol activity. "It's clear," Jantear said.

"That is strange," said Celeste.

"What's strange? I'd say we're pretty lucky so far."

Celeste wasn't convinced that luck was on her side. She shook her head in doubt and responded. "That is strange because the temple floor is usually open to worshippers until midnight. It is only . . ." Celeste paused, as she looked at her timekeeper on her wrist, ". . .it is only nine thirty-two."

"Well maybe your father closed the temple because of the attacks on the base and the pending attack on Earth." Celeste thought for a moment. Jantear's reasoning made sense, but she still wasn't convinced. "Yes, maybe you are right, but I know my father. He always has a secret."

"Well, maybe," Jantear said. "But don't you think if he knew about this rescue mission, he would have stopped us by now."

"Perhaps."

"Okay then, Celeste, quit being paranoid and just tell me where to go from here."

Celeste looked at her monitor. "All right, you see those two huge statues to your right." Celeste saw that Jantear's body had turned, and she could see the statue of the goddess of light and her father. "Behind the statues is where you need to go."

Celeste watched as Jantear, and his troops walked to the statues. She could see the thirty-foot tall and twenty-foot wide *Omutx* walls that connected the heavy statues to the temple's wall.

Her earpiece crackled, and Jantear's voice came through. "There's nothing here, Celeste. It's just a wall."

"My father's statue . . ."

"What about it?" replied Jantear.

"Put your hand behind his left foot and feel."

Celeste saw Jantear place his left hand on the foot of her father's statue. He felt around the gold of the statue for a few seconds and responded. "What am I looking for Celeste?"

"Keep feeling."

Jantear continued to rub the gold on the foot of her father's statue. Suddenly, Jantear jerked his hand away, and the wall connecting the statues to the temple's wall dropped down into the floor. It always amazed Celeste how such a heavy, solid wall could drop down into the floor of the temple without so much as the sound of a pin drop .

"Impressive," Jantear said. "Now what?"

"You and your troops enter the compartment."

"Are you sure all of us will fit?"

"Trust me."

Jantear and his troops entered the secluded compartment behind the statues. Once everyone was in, the wall that had dropped to the floor for their entrance sprang back up, and the lights came on. Celeste saw Jantear's body turn as he looked around the compartment. "Now what, Celeste? There's nowhere to go."

"Look at the wall directly ahead of you."

"I'm looking. There's no door. No keypad. Nothing. It's just made of stones and cement. I hope you didn't get us trapped in here."

Celeste smiled. She enjoyed keeping Jantear on edge. "Just stand next to the wall and find the center stone."

After a few moments of looking the wall over, Jantear said, "Okay, I've found the center stone."

"All right. Get the hand that you took off of the general you killed from your ambush," Celeste said. She watched as Jantear motioned for one of his troops to give him a black leather bag he was carrying. The soldier tossed Jantear the bag. He caught it, placed it on the floor, and unzipped it. He reached in and pulled out a box. He opened the box and pulled out the hand.

"I was wondering why you had us cut that hand off of that dead general," Jantear said. "Let me guess, I place the palm of it onto the center stone."

"Yes," Celeste said. "Every general or above in my father's military has access to these secret passageways. The only way to get in and out is from a palm print."

"Celeste, if it was as simple as this, why didn't we just go over what I was supposed to and do it, instead of you guiding me?"

Celeste ignored Jantear's question. She knew the answer but didn't want to tell Jantear. When Celeste first planned the rescue attempt, she informed Adrian of the secret passageways of the palace and how to access them. Adrian told her that he didn't want anyone else to know about what she had told him because he was suspicious that her father had planted a spy amongst his ranks, but he couldn't figure out who it was. As a result, he didn't want her to tell Jantear about it, only to guide him. "Just put the hand on the stone," she insisted.

Celeste watched as Jantear placed the palm of the severed hand on the stone. She saw the familiar lights scan the palm and the voice of the computer she had heard so many times before. "You may enter, General Otholos."

Celeste noticed that Jantear backed up a bit as the stones folded up into the ceiling of the compartment. As soon as the wall disappeared into the ceiling, Celeste saw a bright flash of light and her monitor's screen went blank. "Jantear, what happened?"

Jantear didn't respond.

"I repeat. Colonel Jantear, come in . . ."

Again, there was no response.

Frustrated, Celeste grabbed the cloak she had brought with her just in case she had to infiltrate the palace on her own. She placed it on and put the hood of it over her head. She then looked into her binoculars to the entrance of the city. Instead of twenty-two guards as she previously counted, there were now only eight.

Before she left, she had decided to try Jantear one more time. "Jantear! I repeat, Colonel Jantear, come in!"

She waited a few moments for Jantear to answer. With no response, she sprinted toward the city gates.

★ ★ ★ ★ ★

Celeste entered the temple entrance and looked around. There was an eerie silence about the entire floor. Celeste was cautious. The only Gnols she encountered were the guards at the city and palace gates. She was able to handle the guards with ease, rendering each one unconscious.

She continued to look around as she walked in the direction of her father's statue. She felt the left foot of the statue and pressed the small indentation behind the heel of his gold boot. The wall separating her from the temple and the small compartment that led to the secret passageway silently dropped to the floor. As soon as she was inside, the wall shot upwards, and the lights flashed on.

Celeste threw off her cloak and examined the compartment. It was empty, and there wasn't a sign of Jantear or his troops anywhere. Celeste then took a deep breath and slowly approached the stone that was her key to the passageway. Her right hand was shaky as she gently placed it onto the cold surface of the stone. Her guard was up. She suspected that a trap lay behind the wall because this was the last place she had any contact with Jantear.

She kept her eyes glued ahead as the lights scanned her palm and the voice of the computer responded. "You may enter, Your Highness."

The wall folded up into the ceiling, and the lights within the passageway turned on. Celeste stepped slowly onto the damp, stone steps that led down to the palace prison. She walked down about thirty feet to where the steps ended and then she would have to take an immediate right down a long, narrow hallway. She slowed her pace as she approached the bottom of the steps.

At the bottom, she placed her back against the cold stone of the wall and peaked around the corner. Again, no one was in sight. She focused her sight toward the end of the hallway. She could see the door and the control panel that would give her access to the palace prison.

With no one in sight, she jogged to the door and pressed the only button on the control panel to the left of the door. The control panel ejected from the wall, and two small optical scanners rose from within the panel. She placed her eyes into the scanners and saw the lights scan her eyes. As soon as the scanners finished their job, the door slid open. With caution, Celeste walked into the darkness of the prison.

After she entered, the door slid shut behind her. She tried to look around, but the darkness utterly enveloped her. She couldn't even see her hand inches in front of her face. She now knew that something was wrong because there were always guards on duty.

She heard someone cough and groan in pain. The voice was familiar. She felt her way in the direction of the coughing and stopped just short as she heard the familiar buzz of the energy field of a prison cell. The prisoner within groaned again, and this time Celeste knew who it was.

"Kylee?" she whispered

Kylee coughed again, and Celeste could hear her move. "Cel . . . Celeste is that you?"

"Yes."

"Ge . . ." Kylee coughed and groaned in pain again before she could finish her sentence.

"Kylee, what's wrong? What did my father do to you?"

Celeste heard another cough, and could tell that Kylee struggled to speak. "Celeste you've got to . . . you've got to get out of here, now."

Celeste knew Kylee was right, but she wasn't going to leave without who she came for. "No, Kylee. I am not leaving; not without you, Bantyr, and Sean."

"Bantyr and Sean have been taken to a slave camp. I . . ."

Kylee began coughing and wheezing again. Celeste knew she was in trouble. She backed up to the back wall and felt her way to her right. She knew that somewhere on the wall were the controls that would open the energy field. She continued to feel and move. As she moved, she lifted her left knee. It collided with the guard's desk, and she almost fell in pain.

Ignoring the pain, she felt her way around the guard's desk and back to the wall. She reached her hands out and felt her way up the wall. Finally, she found what she was looking for – the control panel to the prison cell. She could feel the various buttons that controlled the lights and the cells. She wasn't sure which one opened Kylee's cell, so she decided to risk it and pressed all of the buttons.

She heard the snap and pop of the energy fields disabling among the numerous cells in the prison, and then the lights came on. Celeste turned around, and there stood her father. Startled, she flinched back into the wall and smacked her head. Her father, with a look on his face that terrorized her, reached out and grabbed her throat. He lifted her into the air and backed up.

As Celeste struggled for air and strength to escape her father's death grip, a guard approached Celeste from behind and bound her hands behind her back. Once her hands were bound, Koroan dropped her to the floor.

Celeste looked around the prison cell. All of the cells were empty except the one that contained Kylee. But Kylee wasn't alone in the cell. Jantear's troops were also with her and surrounded by several of her father's royal guards, with their weapons raised on them.

Celeste looked around and could not see Jantear anywhere. She looked at her father who still had the horrifying look on his face as his chest heaved up and down. "Where is Colonel Jantear," she demanded.

Koroan looked past Celeste and nodded. Celeste turned around and made eye contact with the guard that had bound her hands. "No . . . Jantear . . . why?

Jantear, with a smug smile on his face, walked around Celeste and joined Koroan, standing on his right. "Why do you think, Celeste?"

"I trusted you, and so did Adrian."

Jantear laughed. "Adrian Palmer is a fool and so are you."

"But . . . but you are a human. How could you betray your family?"

Jantear's eyes narrowed, and he gritted his teeth. Celeste could feel the anger seething from his presence. "My family . . . no, my family was killed in the attack on *Base 1*. My mother, father, and little sister were on that shuttle that was destroyed on its way to *Base 2*. So when you say family, Adrian Palmer killed my family. He is to blame."

Celeste shook her head and stood up. "No, Jantear. Adrian was only trying to protect your family. It was the Gnols that destroyed that ship."

With anger in his eyes, Jantear rushed to Celeste he raised his left hand, swung, and landed his fist on her right eye. Celeste fell to the ground and rolled in pain. She looked up at her father and saw a small smile grace along his face. He opened his mouth and spoke. "What do you know about family, Celeste? You betrayed your own father and everything you believe in."

Celeste struggled to her feet again and looked her father in the eye. "Believe in? I do not believe in terrorizing another person as you do. I do not believe that humans are inferior. I . . . I do—"

"Ah yes, Colonel Jantear here has told me everything about you and this human, Jake. From what I have been told, you have truly denied what it is to be a Gnol."

Celeste glared at Jantear. "How long?" she asked.

"Soon after we arrived at the second base. Needless to say, your father is very persuasive," Jantear said with a smile.

Celeste lowered her head and shook it.

Koroan walked to her, raised his hand, and wiped the blood away that trickled from her eye. "Now, My Dear, I offer you a choice."

Celeste looked at the man she used to admire and love, and held back the tears. "What choice?"

"You have a choice to stay here with me and become my daughter again, or witness the torture and death of first Kylee and then yourself."

Celeste narrowed her eyes. "Not much of a choice is it?"

Koroan just smiled at her.

Celeste looked at Kylee and saw the misery and pain she suffered. She looked back at her father and said, "If I promise to stay and never return to the humans, you have got to promise to stop doing whatever you are doing to Kylee, and let her stay with me."

Koroan smiled and nodded his head. "We have a deal."

A few minutes later as Celeste and Kylee were escorted to Celeste's old room, thoughts ran through her head. Thoughts mostly about Jake, and the terrifying thought that she would never see him again.

CHAPTER 18

June 10, 2042 – Slave Camp of Zikf on Terrest

Skip awakened in a cold sweat and was breathing rapidly. He quickly stood up and made his way across his small eight-foot by eight-foot room to the sink. He turned on the water and splashed the coolness of it onto his face. After he finished, he looked up and could barely make out his face in the darkness of the room.

The last three nights had been sleepless ones. He was no longer having the dream of the young boy and the bright temple. Now, he was having the same nightmare over and over again. The dream always began with Skip enjoying a summer barbecue with his family back in Springfield, Illinois. Just as his father finished saying grace, the blue sky above filled with red and orange, and chaos ensued. All around Skip, thousands upon thousands of Gnol soldiers surrounded his family, killing some and enslaving the rest.

In each dream, Skip always tried to rescue his mother, but just as he reached her, a Gnol would place his gun to Skip's head and pull the trigger. That was the moment Skip would always wake up in a cold sweat and out of breath.

Skip gritted his teeth and slammed his fists onto the sink, causing the mirror to shake. He was frustrated. For the last couple of months, he had the same peaceful dream over and over again. But now, he was having a continuing nightmare. What did it all mean? Was God trying to communicate with him, or were these dreams just a creation of his subconscious mind? Whatever the answers were, Skip couldn't sit around and wait in this slave camp anymore. He had to begin putting his plan into motion and somehow get into contact with Skyler Green.

Skip took a deep breath, turned around and began making his way back to his bed. On his second step with his cybernetic leg, he collapsed in pain. He let out a small scream and grabbed the back of his artificial limb behind the knee. The pain was almost unbearable, and he couldn't understand why.

Ever since he arrived at *Zikf,* he had been having trouble with his new leg. But now the pain was more intense. Skip sat up in his bed and pulled his pants off. He extended his artificial leg across the bed and examined it behind the knee. He looked closer and noticed an unusual dim red light blinking from underneath his artificial skin. With no sharp object in the room to cut away the skin, Skip pinched the area with his thumb and index finger and pulled.

He ripped the rubber skin away from behind the knee, exposing the metallic skeleton underneath. The red flash was undoubtedly brighter now without the artificial skin as a covering, and he now knew why he couldn't find anything wrong with his leg when he previously examined it because each time he did, it was in light.

Skip grimaced in pain again and touched the light with his finger. Just as soon as he did, the light switched off, and his pain immediately disappeared. Suddenly, three small objects protruded from his knee and emitted light. Skip's eyes followed the light and his jaw dropped with what he saw. Standing about two feet above him, was a small holographic image of Doc.

Skip sat up and whispered, "Doc?"

The hologram didn't respond, and Skip felt a little foolish for talking to what was obviously a computer program. After a few seconds, the holographic image of Doc spoke. "Skip, if you are viewing this message Sean and I programmed into your cybernetic leg, then you are in trouble."

Skip was stunned and wondered why would Doc and Sean pre-program a message into his cybernetic leg and not tell him?

"Perhaps you are wondering why we would pre-program a message into your cybernetic leg and not let you know?"

Skip smiled and said, "Yes."

"Well, the answer is simple," said the image. "Remember when you first learned about your new leg. You had the sensation of touch, but we programmed it so that you wouldn't feel any pain."

Skip nodded his head as Doc continued.

"Sean and I knew that the odds of you being captured by the Gnols were great. As a result, we hard-wired your leg to your nervous system. We programmed your leg, however, so that you only feel pain behind the knee when you are in trouble."

Skip was impressed with what Doc and Sean were able to do, but he was still confused.

"Perhaps, you are wondering why we didn't let you know about this fail safe in your leg," said the image of Doc.

Skip smiled at the coincidence that the holographic image of Doc seemed to know what he was thinking.

"We didn't tell you everything about your leg because the fail safe program installed in your leg is hard wired into your subconscious. In other words, if we would have told you, the program wouldn't have worked. We needed to keep you in the dark about the total potential of your leg. Also, if you would have known, any scans performed by the Gnols on your leg would have revealed everything about it, including the technology of the *Mind Inhibitors* used to block the Gnols' brain scans."

Skip was astonished. "Brilliant," he whispered. *No wonder the Gnols couldn't get any readings on my leg*, he thought.

The image of Doc continued, "Now that you know a little more about that computer you use as a leg, I want you to press the button that was emitting the red light earlier four times with exactly one second between each press."

Skip looked behind his leg and placed his finger on the button. He pressed it four times, timing each second between each press of the button. Just as soon as he pressed the button the fourth time, the artificial skin around his thigh enveloped and disappeared, leaving the metallic thigh exposed and revealing a numeric punch pad.

Skip slowly guided his finger to touch the pad.

"Don't touch the pad!" demanded Doc.

Skip looked up and pulled his hand away quickly.

"If you type in any numbers besides what I tell you to type, the code will never work, and your leg will self destruct."

A lump formed in Skip's throat, and he sat up a little straighter.

Doc cleared his throat and spoke, "Here's the code. One . . . seven . . . zero . . . five . . . one . . . zero . . . six . . . four . . . two."

As Doc rambled off the numbers, Skip memorized and committed each number to memory. He then looked at the numeric pad on the thigh of his cybernetic leg and carefully punched in the code, careful not to make a mistake so that the miracle of his new leg wouldn't self destruct. Just as he finished punching in the final number, the top portion of his artificial thigh containing the numeric pad, slid away. Skip's jaw dropped with what he saw.

Inside was a compartment, and inside the compartment were the tools he desperately needed to escape the slave camp of *Zikf*. Skip reached inside the hollow part of his thigh and pulled out a small gun. He examined it for a few minutes and then set it down next to him. He then pulled out a bag with what he estimated contained about one hundred *Mind Inhibitors*.

Skip slowly sat the bag of inhibitors next to the gun and was about to reach into his leg for the third and final key to freedom when the door to his quarters suddenly slid open. Startled, Skip jumped, and his hand hit the gun and the bag of inhibitors, causing them to fall between the bed and the wall.

He quickly turned around and met the angry, red-filled eyes of Captain Belzar.

★ ★ ★ ★ ★

Adrian's head ached horrendously, and the left side of his face throbbed in pain as he sat in the darkness of what he assumed was the brig of a Gnol spacecraft. He wasn't sure, however. After his capture, he was severely beaten to unconsciousness.

When he awoke, he was in the very place he sat now. The small cell was totally dark, and the only food that was provided to him in the two days since his capture had been the small slivers of bread already in his cell. The only water he was able to obtain was from the droplets of condensation that dripped from the pipes that crisscrossed along the ceiling of his cell. The pipes were the clues that led him to believe that he was aboard a ship because the pipes contained a cold liquid that he guessed cooled some sort of nuclear reactor powering the ship.

Adrian licked his dry lips and swallowed as he tried to ease the dryness in his throat. He slowly stood but nearly fell from the dizziness in his head. When he regained his balance, he stood on the only piece of furniture in his prison – a small wooden stool. He inched up on his tip toes and licked at the condensation on the cold pipes.

Adrian continued to lick as much moisture from the pipes as he could. When he couldn't scavenge for anymore water, he began to step down from the stool when the doors of his cell slid open. The brightness of the light outside of his cell pierced his eyes, causing him to wince in more pain. His heel caught the edge of the stool and he stumbled backwards cracking his head on the wall behind him.

Adrian shook his head trying to clear the cobwebs and opened his eyes. He saw two blurry images approach. He felt muscular arms grab him from under each armpit and lift him to his feet.

As the two Gnols pulled him from his cell, Adrian tried to keep their quick pace, but the weakness in his legs wouldn't allow him to keep up. He stumbled and decided to conserve his energy as he let the Gnols drag him through a long, sterile corridor.

Adrian's eyes began to improve as the Gnols continued to drag him. When they reached the end of the corridor, they turned right and made their way down another long corridor, and into what Adrian assumed was an elevator. When they entered the elevator, the door behind them slid shut.

"Bridge," one of the Gnols said.

Adrian felt the elevator lift upwards for about a minute. The elevator stopped, and the doors opened. Adrian's vision was back to normal, and now, he wished it wasn't for his worst fear was in full vision. Through the elevator doors and beyond the protective plasma shield of the bridge was the blue and green image of Earth. Adrian felt a lump form in his throat as he saw his home for the first time in twenty-five years.

He swallowed and felt a small surge of energy surge through his body. He shook loose. "Where's your commanding officer!" he said with anger.

The Gnol to his left looked angry and stepped forward to throw a punch into Adrian's face. But the Gnol on Adrian's right stepped around Adrian and stopped the Gnol before he delivered the blow. The Gnol glared at Adrian and gave him a knowing smile. The Gnol pointed to the left of the bridge and said, "He is through that door, and he is expecting you."

Adrian looked in the direction the Gnol pointed and made his way to the door. The thirty plus crew members working at various stations on the bridge immediately stopped working and stared at Adrian as he walked to the door. Adrian felt the anger surge through him, for he knew what they were planning to do. He looked at Earth through the bridge and stopped just in front of the door. The door slid open.

Adrian stepped into a spacious office about half the size of the bridge. The office was dimly lit, but Adrian could see a large crystal desk to his left. On the desk, were two computers and behind the desk was the long back of a leather office chair. The chair was swaying gently back and forth as its occupant stared at the planet outside of the giant plasma shield separating Adrian and his companion in the office from the vacuum of space.

"It's beautiful isn't it," said a familiar voice from behind the chair.

Adrian stepped closer to the desk and replied, "Yes, it is, but—"

Adrian was cut off by the familiar voice. "Twenty-five years. Has it really been that long?"

Adrian moved in closer. He recognized the voice as Dorange Gar's, Koroan Chast's right hand Gnol, but was confused and wondered what Dorange was talking about?

"Twenty-five years. Where has the time gone, Adrian? We were so young back then, and we had so many dreams of greatness."

Adrian's mind was reeling. The voice of Dorange Gar was so familiar and almost reminded him of an old enemy from his past, but how could that be? Adrian began to step around the desk when the chair slowly began to turn his way. Adrian stopped as the chair turned.

Adrian's jaw dropped after Dorange turned the chair around to face him. Adrian met the tear filled eyes of Dorange and spoke in almost a whisper of shock. "D . . . Don!"

★ ★ ★ ★ ★

"I can't believe you're playing that thing while we're here."

Adam stopped playing his holographic video game, looked up at his sister, and rolled his eyes. "What else is there to do? Dad has been in that meeting with the President for nearly three hours now."

Ashley sighed. Her brother had a point, but she also knew what an honor it was for the President of the United States to invite her father and his two children to spend a week in the White House while their father attended meetings in Washington D.C.

"Yeah, I guess you're right," said Ashley, as she rolled off of the bed and strolled across the Lincoln bedroom to the portrait of Abraham Lincoln. She stared at the portrait for a few minutes and then turned to the flat-screen television that hung on the wall. "Maybe there's a good movie on. Television . . . power on."

The television came alive, and a female reporter appeared on the screen. Ashley nearly fell from her feet with what she saw. "Adam!"

There was no response.

Ashley turned and looked at her brother who was fully engrossed in his video game. "Adam! Put that thing down and look at this."

Adam rolled his eyes, stopped playing the game, and looked up at the T.V. The video game fell from his hand as he stood up and moved closer to his sister. "What the . . . turn it up."

"Volume up," Ashley said.

The volume on the television went up, and both Ashley and Adam were able to hear the reporter's voice.

"It is still unknown as to who is behind this attack. There are rumors that a terrorist group is to blame, but that is not yet confirmed. . . . Again, for those of you just joining us, twenty minutes ago, just after midnight Paris time, Paris, France was viciously and heinously attacked by an unknown enemy. The attack has left nearly half of the city in ruins."

Ashley gasped as the next image on the television was of the famous Eifel Tower. The tower was in flames and was about to topple over. Again the reporter spoke.

"Wait . . . we're getting reports now of smaller aircraft coming in . . . wait . . . no . . . get a shot of that!"

Adam and Ashley watched as the camera man focused in on what seemed like thousands of aircraft swooping down from the air. The aircrafts were spewing what looked like red laser fire all over and laying destruction in their paths.

"Are those laser bolts?" Adam questioned.

Ashley was speechless. She continued to stare at the television with horror in her eyes. Suddenly, there was a deafening explosion just outside of the White House. The power inside of the Lincoln bedroom went out, and the room shook violently. Adam dove for his sister and tackled her to the floor just as hot, flaming fire burst through the windows.

The door to the bedroom flew open and two secret service agents bolted in. The agents grabbed Ashley and Adam and hurriedly escorted them down the hallway and down into the oval office where their father was located along with Michael Konrad, the President, and what seemed like hundreds of U.S. military personnel.

When they arrived in the Oval Office, Ashley broke free of the secret service agent's grip and rushed toward her father. She enjoyed the embrace of her father for a few seconds before she looked back up at him. "Dad . . . wh . . . what's going on?"

Kevin was about to speak, but was interrupted by a tall, lanky man with snow-white hair. The man stepped forward and looked directly at Kevin when he spoke. "That's just what we were discussing with your father before these attacks occurred."

Ashley looked at her father as he bowed his head in what seemed like defeat, and then back at the tall, lanky man. She glared at him and spoke. "With all due respect, Mr. President, why would my father have anything to do with this?"

President Clifford Galbraith first glared back at Ashley with his dull, gray eyes and then flashed his trademark smile, which always sent chills up her spine. "I am sorry," he said. "We're not blaming your father for this. It's just that there are no other explanations for what is happening here."

Ashley was confused and gave the President a look to show it. "It sounds like you're still blaming him."

President Galbraith stepped closer to Ashley while maintaining his same smug smile. "No . . . no . . . we are not blaming your father. It's just our satellite images have verified more than three hundred unidentified space crafts in orbit around Earth, all of which are similar to the space shuttles your father helped design and build."

Ashley looked back at her father just as a secret service agent whispered something into the President's ear. "Dad, is this true?"

Kevin looked at his daughter with a look of despair and a look that told her that he knew this would happen. "Yes, Ashley. The ships are similar to the design I helped NASA with, but—"

Suddenly, there was another loud explosion. But this time it wasn't outside. It was within the White House itself. Ashley heard gun fire as her brother pulled her by the arm and onto the floor. Ashley looked up and met the tear-filled eyes of her father who was lying on the floor in front of her. They ducked their heads again as the gun fire penetrated the Oval Office.

Just as Ashley turned her head to see where the gun fire was coming from, a secret service agent fell to the floor, clutching his head and screaming in pain. She jumped to her knees and turned around.

"Ashley! No!" Kevin shrieked as he grabbed her ankle.

Ashley's eyes met the black boots of the enemy that had penetrated one of the most secure rooms in America. Her eyes followed the body of the enemy up to its face. To her surprise she met the eyes of what looked like a human male, not a grotesque alien.

The man looked past Ashley. Ashley followed his eyes and noticed that he was looking directly at her father.

"Are you Kevin Palmer?" the man said.

Kevin staggered to his feet and replied, "Yes, I am."

The man gave Kevin an evil smile and began to raise his weapon.

"No!" screamed Ashley, as she jumped to her feet and instantly felt the fire, penetrating sensation of the weapon's blast penetrate her chest. Everything went silent as she stumbled back into her father's arms.

★ ★ ★ ★ ★

Dorange stood up from his chair and wiped the tears from his eyes. Adrian staggered backwards and fell back over another chair. He quickly regained his composure and stood up as Dorange stopped within inches of his face.

"That name no longer means anything to me," said Dorange with a quivering voice.

Adrian clenched his jaw and balled up his fists. "How could you . . . Don? How could you betray your own kind?"

Dorange narrowed his eyes and clutched Adrian by his flight suit. "I told you. That name no longer means anything to me." Dorange then lifted Adrian off of the floor and hurled him about twenty feet across the room.

Adrian screamed in pain as his back slammed against the cold, metal wall of Dorange's office. His body fell, crashing through a small wooden table and finally resting upon the floor.

Adrian closed his eyes, grimaced in pain, and wondered how Don managed to fling him across a large office.

Dorange laughed as he approached Adrian. "You know . . . it's funny, Adrian, how things can come full circle."

Adrian staggered to his feet in pain. "Wha . . . what do you mean?" he asked, meeting Dorange's anger-filled eyes.

"C'mon, Commander. You should know?"

"Know what?"

Dorange laughed, turned, and walked away. He walked to the large plasma shield with Earth in view. Adrian looked as well and could see small fireballs dotting the entire planet.

Dorange stared at Earth for a few moments and then turned to meet Adrian's gaze. "Revenge."

Adrian furrowed his eyebrows and cocked his head in confusion.

"Oh . . . I always knew you were as intellectually challenged as you were void in leadership abilities, Commander. Revenge. Revenge on you, Adrian. That's what I am talking about."

Adrian ignored Dorange's first comment and stepped forward. "Revenge? Revenge for what?"

"Hah, like you don't know," seethed Dorange, as he looked back at his former home, which anyone could tell was under full attack by now.

Adrian walked a little closer to Dorange. "Don . . ."

Dorange shot a look of pure hatred toward Adrian.

Adrian ignored it and continued. "Why would you want revenge on me?"

Dorange gave Adrian a wry smiled, placed his hands behind his back, and began pacing back and forth with the fiery image of Earth behind him. He ducked his head. "Revenge," he whispered. And then he looked at Adrian with intensity. "If it wasn't for you, Commander, I would have been a hero. I would have been the first human to set foot on Mars. I would have been looked to as a hero back home . . . but no . . . NASA had to pick you as Commander of the *Mars I* mission. As a result, you took my hopes and dreams away from me."

Adrian stepped closer and with frustration in his voice said, "How is that my fault. You know I had nothing to do with the selection process. When NASA chose me, I couldn't believe it. I thought for sure that they would choose you. That's why I made you my copilot on the mission."

"Copilot!" roared Dorange, as he turned and flung one of the computer monitors off of his desk.

Adrian ducked, turned, and looked as the computer monitor crashed into the wall behind him. He turned around and met the sweltering eyes of Dorange within an inch of his own. Dorange spit and gritted his teeth as he spoke.

"Copilot! You insulted me when you appointed me to that position. You knew who the better leader was, who would have led us safely to Mars and back home again. By making me copilot, you took everything away from me that I worked so hard for . . . everything!"

Dorange then grabbed Adrian by the collar with his left hand and set his left arm back into punching motion ready to strike. Adrian's eyes widened as Dorange's fist cut through the air to his face. He ducked and felt Dorange's fist skim the top of his head. Adrian dropped to his left knee and swung his right leg out, striking the back of Dorange's legs.

Dorange fell flat onto his back, and Adrian heard the air rush out of his lungs. Dorange rolled around for a few seconds, trying to regain his wind. Adrian stood up and looked over Dorange. For a brief moment, he almost lent Dorange a hand to help him up, but ignored the instinct, for he knew that Dorange would attack back. Instead, Adrian asked the question that had weighed heavily on his mind for nearly twenty-five years.

"Why did you abandon your crew when we crash landed on *Terrest*? All these years we thought you were dead. What happened?"

Dorange finally regained his wind and stood up. He glared at Adrian as he spoke. "I had to leave. I could not continue to stay with you and the crew. Especially . . . especially, considering how much more loyal they were to you, and how much they knew I despised you as our leader."

"But D . . . Dorange, we needed you. You needed us. There's no way we could have survived on a strange, new planet without each other."

"Hah," laughed Dorange. "As you can see, Commander, I survived just fine on my own. After I left you and the crew, I traveled for years on *Terrest*. I lived off of the land for almost fifteen years. The only thing that kept me alive was my motivation for revenge . . ." Dorange stopped and gave Adrian a look that sent chills down his spine. He then continued, "Revenge on you, Adrian, and your loyal crew."

"But I don't understand. How did you get involved with the Gnols? Not to mention, how were you able to fool Koroan into believing you were a Gnol yourself? You know how much he hates humans."

Dorange gave Adrian a cynical smile. "That was easy. His daughter—"

"Celeste?"

"No, you imbecile . . . his eldest daughter, Raqel. She found me and helped me to see what we humans can become."

Adrian gave Dorange a knowing look.

"Yes, Adrian, you know as well as I do that the Gnols are just more evolved species of human beings. She helped me to see that I could become so much more powerful than you, so much more intelligent, almost like God himself."

Adrian was stunned as he looked into Dorange's eyes. For the first time since he knew Donald Garrett his copilot, he was afraid of him. No longer was Don the egotistical, self-assured pilot he knew during his NASA training days. He was now truly someone else, Dorange Gar; a monster that craved power more than anything else.

Dorange walked strolled back to the plasma shield to look at Earth. Adrian could tell that Dorange's mind seemed to switch from one thought to another. After Dorange was lost in his thoughts for a few minutes, he turned, stared at Adrian, and continued.

"About six months after the Gnols attacked *Terrest*, I was camped near what is presently Koroan's glorious city of *Chast*. It was a tough winter. I was near death. My food supply had run out, and I had grown very sick. I almost conceited defeat by killing myself, but the thought of letting you win, Adrian . . . was unbearable. I—"

"Don, our lives aren't and weren't a competition."

Dorange spun on his heels. "I told you not to call me by that name!" he shrieked. He then shot both his arms out over his desk in Adrian's direction. Adrian felt a sudden, massive force of pressure on his chest, clutched it in pain, and dropped to his knees. It was as if someone was inside of him squeezing the life out of his heart.

After a few seconds, Dorange lowered his arms, and Adrian immediately felt the invisible pressure on his heart subside. Adrian slowly regained his composure and stood up. He knew full well the kind of potential power he and Dorange could yield because ever since Celeste had volunteered her services to the human cause on *Terrest*, she had been secretly training Adrian in the use of her Gnol abilities.

The only problem was that Adrian never truly believed that he could use his mind to move objects, let alone read another person's thoughts. Maybe that was why he could never move so much as a sheet of paper with his mind during his training sessions with Celeste. She had always told him that he needed to believe that it could happen. He never believed – until now. But there was another problem. Without gene therapy to mutate his DNA with the addition of the *god-gene*, there was no way Adrian could become as powerful as a Gnol.

"Yes," said Dorange, as he walked around the desk toward Adrian. "You can see now, Adrian, that I am no longer a mere human being . . ." Dorange stopped speaking for a few seconds and stepped closer to Adrian. Adrian stepped back until his back met the wall of Dorange's office. Dorange smiled, knowing he had the advantage and continued.

"While I was clinging to life, two Gnol soldiers – who were scouting *Terrest* for a place to build Koroan's glorious city – found me and took me to their leader." Dorange seemed to become emotional as he spoke. Adrian could tell that whatever happened to him was painful.

"Their leader was Koroan's eldest daughter. She was exquisite. The most beautiful woman I had ever seen and the most merciful. She was nothing like her father. She took pity upon me and instead of killing me or enslaving me in a slave camp, she made a deal with me."

"Wha . . . what kind of deal?"

Dorange let out a small laugh. "She told me that if I would join her royal guard as a body guard, she would teach me the ways of the Gnol, and she would never let her father know that I was actually a human."

"But what about the two Gnol soldiers that found you? Surely, they knew that you were human as well."

"Yes, but Raqel threatened that if they let anyone know about me, she would have them stripped of their military honors and shamed in front of their families, which is almost as bad as a dishonorable death in the Gnol culture. But . . . I always felt uneasy knowing that, besides Raqel, there were two others who knew about me. Ironically, however, you took care of that."

"What? How?"

"They were killed in battle, a battle that you led. I then decided to live up to my end of the deal, and Raqel lived up to hers. I never met Raqel's family while I was one of her royal body guards. Whenever she knew that she would be around her family, she would send me on training exercises with Gnol soldiers who were less experienced in their, shall we say skills. And when she found the time, she would train me personally. I also secretly received gene therapy.

"It was from those training sessions where we fell in love. But Raqel knew that her father would see right through me unless I could demonstrate the mental discipline he and his generals had. After about five years of training and therapy, she finally felt I was ready.

"After that time, Raqel had planted a new name and identity into the Gnol computer system, identifying me as Dorange Gar – the only son of a war chief and his wife back on *Gnolom* who sacrificed their own lives to save their only son's by giving up their spots on one of the transports off of the planet so that he may serve the powerful and great Koroan Chast."

Adrian looked at Dorange with apprehension.

Dorange noticed and stepped closer to him. "What? You find that hard to believe?"

At first Adrian did not want to answer, afraid of what the unpredictable Dorange might do, but he did nonetheless. "Yes, I do find that hard to believe. How was it that you and Raqel were able to fool Koroan, with his superior intellect and telepathic powers, into believing that you were a Gnol?"

Dorange's face seemed to change from one of beat, red anger to one of cynical happiness, as if he was glad Adrian had asked the question. He let out a small laugh. "Ah . . . you see, Koroan, probably the most ruthless leader I have ever known or heard of, has – at least until recently with Celeste's treachery – a soft spot for his beloved daughters. Of course, he had me checked out after I met him, and when some discrepancies appeared in my fabled Gnol military career, Raqel set those straight with her father. And you know what? He believed her. Can you believe it? He took her word over his most trusted advisors. Needless to say, I eventually fell into good graces with him, and upon learning about my ability to fly air and spacecraft, he made me general over his entire air and space force.

"But it got even better than that. I also learned that according to Gnol tradition. A tribal chief can only give the throne to a blood born son. However, since Koroan had only two daughters, his only choice was to give the throne to the Gnol husband of his eldest daughter. Little does he know that his own son-in-law is of the very race he so despises and longs to purge? Soon, however, he will see the error of his ways as he will be taken care of, and I – Dorange Gar – will ascend to the throne of a god!"

Dorange, with a look of such evil on his face that it sent spine-tingling chills down Adrian's back, hit his chest with his fist and looked up at the metallic ceiling in his office.

After what seemed like a few minutes of Dorange lost in his thoughts, Adrian shook his head and turned to look at his home world. It was horrifying. Even from this distance in space, he could see the destruction that the Gnols had inflicted. He continued to watch and could make out the small outlines of Gnol space fighters entering Earth's atmosphere. As he watched and Dorange lingered in his thoughts, a small seed of anger and frustration that had been bottled up for twenty-five years began to sprout.

Even when Don had acted totally irresponsible and unprofessional on their original mission, and abandoned his crew, Adrian had always tried to forgive him and see the good in him. However, with what he witnessed now and the memory of Dorange shooting Doc in the back, he now knew that all remnants of good left in Donald Garrett were gone.

Adrian turned his gaze to look at the gloating Dorange. He gritted his teeth and felt his heart rate rise. He then closed his eyes and tried to focus all of his frustration and anger into one singular thought.

There was a buzz on Dorange's communicator, located on the neck of his uniform. Dorange was startled out of his trance. "What is it?" he replied.

"General, this is Major Pontain on the surface. We have captured one of the targets, Kevin Palmer."

Adrian jerked his eyes open and stared in shock at Dorange. Dorange returned his stare with a look of victory and satisfaction. "Very well, Major. Hold the prisoner with the others and await further orders," Dorange said as he continued to give Adrian an evil smile.

"Yes, General," the major replied.

Adrian tried to speak, but couldn't get the words out of his mouth.

Dorange spoke for him. "Yes Adrian, one of the primary targets of this mission was not only to claim Earth as our own, but to capture your brother as well. He was going to be used as bait to bring the famous Adrian Palmer, the leader of the pitiful Terrestrian rebellion, out of hiding. But what luck. You just fell from the sky into my lap, and now we have you both. When Koroan visits his new conquered world, you and your brother will both be presented to him and eventually tortured and executed by Koroan himself. And I will reap the rewards."

Adrian wanted to lunge for Dorange, but he knew better. He knew that if he didn't focus his thoughts, Dorange would tear him apart with his abilities. Adrian closed his eyes again.

Within the depths of his soul, Adrian felt a powerful and strange emotion, yet it was oddly familiar. However, this feeling was also different in that it was more powerful. The feeling surged from his soul outward to his body. His muscles felt energized and potent. His mind was alert and more focused than he ever remembered it being.

Dorange's communicator buzzed again. Adrian slowly opened his eyes and noticed that his vision seemed sharper and clearer.

"What is it!" demanded Dorange.

"Sorry to bother you again, General. This is Major Pontain. I failed to mention on my previous communication that we also have the children of the target in custody."

Adrian took three steps closer to Dorange upon hearing the news that his brother's children were also captured.

Dorange smiled and looked at Adrian. "That is good news, Major. I am sure that his lordship would enjoy torturing and killing these children just before he does the same to Kevin and Adrian Palmer."

Adrian clenched his teeth and continued to focus all of his energy into one complete thought.

"Yes, General. Pontain out."

Dorange continued to stare at Adrian with the same smile on his face. "Ah, this is good news, Adrian. It looks as if the children of your brother will suffer the same fate as you and Kevin. It's too bad we don't have your children here as well. What satisfaction it would give me to see your entire family tortured and killed."

Adrian returned Dorange's glare while he continued to focus. The energy that he felt surging through his body was now at an all time high. He now felt ready. He slowly raised his left arm with his elbow bent and his palm facing Dorange. Dorange's expression changed from one of pure joy at his imminent victory to concern. He lunged for Adrian, but Adrian jolted his palm forward. Dorange's momentum stopped, and he flew backwards through the air. Dorange's body slammed into the plasma shield with Earth in full view.

Adrian watched in shock as Dorange let out a low grunt and fell to the floor. *It worked*, he thought. Just as he had visualized, he had used the telekinetic powers Celeste had taught him. The only difference this time, however, was – he believed.

Adrian saw Dorange lying on the floor struggle for breath behind the gigantic crystal desk. He slowly walked around the desk and stood above Dorange. "Call off the attack and release my brother and his children."

"Or . . . or what?" Dorange replied while he struggled to regain his wind.

"Or . . ." Adrian couldn't believe what he was about to say, ". . . or you won't live to see your victory."

Dorange laughed and raised his body to one knee. He looked up at Adrian with fire in his eyes and said, "Even if you kill me, which isn't likely, there is no way you will escape this ship, and my colonel will still make sure your executions are carried out."

Adrian knew Dorange was right. Nonetheless, if he was going to die soon, he was determined kill Dorange first. "Release them now!"

Dorange bowed his head as if he had succeeded to defeat, but Adrian knew better. Adrian reached down to grab Dorange by the hair and lift him up. Just as Adrian touched the back of Dorange's head, Dorange sprang to his feet and, at the same time, released a vicious backhand blow to Adrian's cheek. Adrian felt his jaw crack, and the momentum of the blow threw him back.

Adrian crashed through the giant crystal desk, and felt a sharp pain in his left leg as shattered crystal fell all around him. After he hit the floor, he tried to open his mouth but couldn't. His jaw was broken, and the pain swelled from his jaw to his head. He also looked down to where the pain was coming from in his leg and noticed a long shard of crystal stuck in the back of his thigh, extending all the way through to the front.

He immediately reached down to pull the shard of crystal out. But before he could grab the crystal, Dorange grabbed him by one leg and one arm and flung him across the room. Adrian immediately closed his eyes and concentrated. If he didn't focus all of his thoughts, the imminent collision with the wall of Dorange's office would certainly kill him.

Adrian extended his hand that was closest to the up coming wall and telekinetically stopped his momentum. He floated in midair for a few seconds and looked at Dorange. Dorange had a small smile out of the corner of his mouth as if he was impressed with Adrian's new found power.

Adrian dropped to the floor and groaned in pain as his leg with the shard of crystal impaled into it hit the floor first. He rolled over onto his back and looked at his leg. He noticed that he had already lost a lot of blood as there was a trail from where Dorange first picked him up to his present position.

"I have to say that I am impressed," said Dorange, walking toward Adrian. "But you are still not as powerful as me."

Adrian frantically tried to pull the crystal from his leg. But before he could pull it out, he began to float in midair. He looked at Dorange. Dorange had both of his arms extended and look of sheer hatred on his face. Adrian tried to move, but was frozen.

With a sudden upward motion of his arms, Dorange sent Adrian flailing to the ceiling of his office. Adrian's body slammed into the metallic ceiling, which caused it to dent. At the same time, Adrian felt the crack of his nose and several of his ribs. For a moment, Adrian thought he had passed out from the pain because he couldn't recall hitting the floor again. He opened his eyes and could vaguely see the blurry image of Dorange standing above him.

Adrian tried to move, but he couldn't. He was in a tremendous amount of pain and extremely weak from the loss of blood because of his leg wound. He heard Dorange speak. Adrian couldn't understand him because his hearing was like trying to listen to someone speak to him underwater. He closed his eyes again and screamed in pain as he felt another bone crushing blow to his chest. All of the air in his lungs exited his body. He opened his eyes and saw the blurry image of Dorange's fist preparing for another blow.

As Adrian struggled for air, his hearing came back. He heard Dorange.

"I have been dreaming for this moment as long as I can remember. Why give Koroan the honor of killing you, when it is all I think about day and night? We'll just say you died because of the injuries from your crash. Good bye Adrian Palmer."

Adrian continued to struggle for air and said a silent prayer. He knew this was it. Every moment of his life seemed to flash through his mind. He thought of his parents, then Melissa, then Gloria, and finally of Anyta. He then saw the images of his children – Kylee, Bantyr, Lexis, and Jake. Thoughts of Jake flashed through his mind. Images of Jake as a baby, a toddler, and little boy played like a lightning fast movie in his mind.

And then Adrian saw another image. Only this image was not familiar to him. He knew this memory was not his. Could he have died already? Was he witnessing something with his spirit while his body lay mangled in a pool of blood? He didn't know. He no longer felt the pain of his body. The image was so clear and so life like. It was as if his spirit was floating in midair witnessing something that brought joy to his heart.

Adrian saw himself sitting in a rocking chair in a dimly lit room. He was holding a baby boy. The baby was about 8-months old and turned his head to look at Adrian's spirit. The baby smiled, and instantly, Adrian's spirit heard the baby's mind.

Fight for your life, Grandfather. Fight!

In an instant, Adrian was back into his dying body on the floor of Dorange's office. He opened his eyes and saw Dorange as he began to deliver the blow that would certainly kill him. This time, however, Adrian's vision was clear and sharp, and Dorange seemed to move in slow motion. Adrian felt a flow of energy pulsate throughout his body. He telekinetically slid himself out from under Dorange's legs, jumped to one knee, and pulled the shard of crystal out of his leg just as Dorange turned around with a look of shock on his face.

Dorange bull-rushed toward Adrian, but just as fast, Adrian sent the long shard of crystal hurling through the air. Dorange noticed and tried to dodge, but the crystal was traveling at such a velocity that Dorange didn't have time to react. The crystal hit Dorange in the throat and sliced all the way through before it finally stopped, penetrating the metal office wall.

Dorange reached for his throat, pressed his communicator on his collar, and fell face down into his own pool of blood. His body jerked and squirmed as his life source drained out of him.

The door to Dorange's office immediately slid open, and several uniformed Gnol officers rushed in. Adrian felt weak again and barely felt a couple of the officers drag him off. Just before he lost consciousness, Adrian looked at Earth under full attack and knew that it wasn't time for him to die. Not until after his vision came to pass.

CHAPTER 19

June 15, 2042 – Koroan's Palace

Ciminae floated in the air, above Celeste's dying body. She was more beautiful than ever; more so than Celeste remembered her ever being. No longer was her spirit trapped inside its clay vessel, revealing her true beauty. Her ocean, blue eyes sparkled with pride as she stared lovingly at her daughter. Her long, flowing black hair seemed to wave in the wind along with her brighter than white robe, even though they were inside. And then her mother opened her mouth to speak. "Remember . . . the source of your father's power."

Celeste then grabbed her throat and tried to pull away the strong fingers that threatened to take away her life.

And then she was awake. Celeste coughed and inhaled the oxygen her body desperately needed. She sat up and wiped away the cold sweat that dripped from her hair. *How long was I not breathing this time?* She thought.

Celeste glanced over at the extra bed that was placed in her bedroom. Kylee was sleeping soundly; her body finally resting after Koroan ordered that all biological weapons testing done upon her cease. Celeste stared in admiration. She wished she could sleep just as soundly. Ever since her recapture, Celeste continued to relive her near-death experience the night her mother died and Vlamer Kreuk tried to kill her.

Thinking about the experience caused Celeste severe emotional pain. She placed her head into her hands and began to sob. She missed her mother desperately, especially now that she was in enemy territory. It seemed, now, that every Gnol on *Terrest* knew of Celeste's treachery. The only people she could trust were gone. Nichelle was with Jake and the rebels. And of course, the one who understood her most had passed on. She couldn't confide in Kylee because Kylee slept more than she was awake, trying to recover.

The thought of Jake caused Celeste to tremble as she cried. Oh, how she longed to be in his arms and feel the warmth of his body. At no other time in her life had she felt so low; so depressed. She was exhausted beyond comprehension and couldn't escape the pain by sleeping. Every time she fell asleep, she would relive the nightmare of her mother's death.

Frustrated now, Celeste gritted her teeth, looked up at the ceiling, and said out loud. "What am I supposed to do? Please, Mother. I don't know . . . help me."

"You know what you're supposed to do."

With the dim light of *Terrest's* full moons giving the room some illumination, Celeste spun on her heals and locked tired eyes with Kylee. Kylee was sitting up and had an expression of concern on her face. "Oh . . . Kylee, I . . . I didn't mean to wake you."

Kylee gave Celeste a warm smile and motioned for Celeste to sit beside her. Celeste rubbed the tears away from her eyes and made her way toward Kylee who seemed now more like a sister.

In fact, that was why Celeste didn't have her hands bound at the present time. She promised her father that if he wouldn't bind her hands behind her back, she wouldn't use her new found abilities. And her father, in turn, declared that if she even attempted in the slightest to harm the guards that guarded her room twenty-four hours a day, he would have Kylee brutally tortured and killed. Celeste agreed, and now here she was miserable and helpless.

She sat next to Kylee and looked into her warm, inviting eyes. Kylee smiled warmly and said, "You know what you have to do."

Celeste gave Kylee a look of confusion. "What do you mean?"

With a deep sigh, Kylee seemed to look through Celeste's eyes and into her soul. "Celeste, ever since I was brought to stay with you in your room, I have witnessed your dreams."

Celeste was shocked. "Wha . . . how?"

Kylee shook her head. "I . . . I don't know. It's weird. I don't know how else to explain it other than every time you have your dream, I actually witness the night your mother died. The only difference is that when your mother speaks in my dream she is speaking to me. She addresses me by name and tells me where to go to find the source of your father's power."

Celeste was speechless. How was this possible? Celeste and Kylee both had their *Mind Inhibitors* in. There was no possible way Celeste could have made a mind connection with Kylee. Unless . . .

"Maybe . . . I don't know. Maybe—"

Kylee cut Celeste off before she could finish. "Maybe, your mother is communicating with me as well."

Again, Celeste gave Kylee a look of puzzlement. "But . . . I don't understand. Why would she? What does she want me to do?"

Kylee shook her head. "Think about it, Celeste. What did your mother mean when she says remember the source of your father's power?"

Celeste looked down at the floor and thought for a few seconds. "I . . . I don't know. The night she died, she mentioned something about the source of my father's power. But so much went on that night. I can't. . . . Wait!" she said, jumping to her feet. She turned to face Kylee. "My mother did mention the thirty-fifth floor of this palace . . . that's . . . yes . . . that's where the source is."

Kylee smiled and nodded her head. "Well then, you know what you have to do."

Celeste shook her head as if in defeat. "But I can't. These ankle bracelets my father had placed upon us track our every movement. If I even take one step out of this room, my father will be alerted, and you will be killed. I won't let you die so I can fulfill my curiosities."

Kylee returned Celeste's look of frustration. "That doesn't matter now, Celeste. If your mother is communicating with me as well, then it is important; more important than me."

"Don't talk like that. I am not going to let you sacrifice your life."

Kylee motioned for Celeste to sit beside her again. After Celeste sat down, Kylee grabbed her hand and looked deep into her eyes. "Celeste, listen to me. You know as well as I do that I am as good as dead already."

Celeste shook her head and began to speak, but Kylee placed a finger to her lips. "Shh. No. Listen, Celeste. The poisons your father's scientists have placed into my body are slowly killing me. Your mother suffered the same fate. Perhaps, that's why she is communicating with me as well. You need to go. You never know. Maybe, whatever is on that top floor is the key to defeating your father and your freedom – the freedom to finally be with Jake."

As tears streamed down her face, Celeste shook her head. She looked at Kylee with compassion. She wasn't going risk Kylee's life for the sake of her own happiness, even if it meant being with Jake again. "No, I won't do it."

"Celeste, I'm dying anyway. You need—"

"There is an antidote you know."

Kylee's head snapped around to the entrance to Celeste's room, and Celeste jumped to her feet. "Commander Runa. Wha . . . how long have you been standing there?"

Commander Runa smiled warmly at Celeste. He was a young Gnol of small stature, probably around 5'8" in height, and in superb physical condition. Of all the guards that were assigned to guard Celeste's room, Commander Runa was the only one Celeste liked. He still treated Celeste like royalty, and whenever Kylee needed something, he took care of her with compassion.

As he walked in, the door slid shut behind him. "I'm sorry, Your Highness. I heard you two talking and entered to see if you were all right. You were so caught up in your conversation that you didn't even notice me enter."

Celeste returned Runa's smile. "You don't need to refer to me by that title anymore, Commander."

"What? Your Highness?

"Yes, you know my father outlawed my title as royalty. You know as well as I do that he has declared me on the same level as the human slaves."

"Perhaps . . . but to me, you are still the princess."

Celeste returned to her seat on the bed. "Thank you, Commander. But, please don't. For your sake."

Runa slowly made his way around Celeste's bed and sat directly across from Kylee and Celeste. "No, I need to, Your Highness."

Celeste gazed into Runa's bright, green eyes. She continued to stare and noticed compassion about him. Besides her mother and Nichelle, Celeste had never seen empathy in another Gnol. Most of the Gnols she knew were arrogant, greedy, and selfish, but Runa was different. "Why?" She asked.

Runa glanced at Kylee, smiled shyly, and then turned his attention back to Celeste. "Because . . . because I can see the goodness in you . . . in both of you."

Celeste gave Runa a look of apprehension. "You do know, Commander, that if my father finds you treating us like this, you will be relieved of your duties . . . or worse – killed?"

"Let me worry about your father," replied Runa. "And please, call me Nateal."

Celeste, still a little suspicious, looking first at Kylee and then back toward Runa. "Okay, Nateal. You said there was an antidote. And if there is, why didn't you let me know when my mother was suffering?"

Nateal Runa rested his elbows on his knees and looked intensely at Celeste. "Yes, there is an antidote, but I did not know about it until after your mother's death. I overheard your father mention it in a meeting."

Kylee sat up a little straighter and spoke. "What? Why didn't you let Celeste know when she was recaptured?"

Runa turned his attention to Kylee and smiled warmly. "Because I had to make sure it was true."

"And is it?" Celeste asked.

"Yes, I found out that your father's scientists conduct medical tests on human slaves at the medical facility a few miles from here. After I volunteered to lead the guard detail for you and Kylee, I—"

"Wait! You volunteered?" Celeste asked as she stood, glaring at Runa with mistrust.

"Yes, I volunteered because I knew that any other Gnol would have mistreated you and Kylee."

Kylee was now intrigued with this new Gnol she just met days ago. "Wait. So you're guarding us to protect us?"

"Yes. I will explain later, but first will you let me tell you about the antidote?"

Celeste sat back down and nodded along with Kylee.

Runa continued. "I was assigned to take a number of slaves to the medical facility. While I was there and waited for the scientists to finish their tests, I decided to do some looking around, and I found it. There is an antidote. It's in a vault within the heart of the facility and heavily guarded with military personal and security systems that I haven't figured out how to crack yet."

Kylee shook her head with doubt. "So if the antidote is as secure as you say it is, how were you able to find it by just snooping around?"

Runa gave Kylee a cocky smile. "Oh, I have my ways," he said as he stood up and made his way to the door.

"Wait!" said Celeste, jumping to her feet. "Where are you going?"

Runa held his hand up with his attention still toward the door. "I will be right back," he said as he left the room.

A few seconds later, Runa returned with his computer in hand. He sat back down on Celeste's bed, typed a few keystrokes onto the keyboard, and turned the screen to face Celeste.

Celeste's was shocked with what she saw. She was staring at the entire blueprint of her father's palace; every floor and most importantly every access code to secure locations. She looked back up at Runa. "Wha . . . How? Those codes are restricted. You don't have a high enough security clearance to have access to these codes."

Runa still had a confident smile on his face and said. "I do now. You see, Your Highness, while I was in the medical facility, I cracked into their computer system and found the antidote."

Celeste was about to speak, but Kylee spoke first. "I don't get it. Why would you want to help us, especially me?"

Runa placed his computer on Celeste's bed and looked compassionately at Kylee. He then looked at Celeste. "Do you want me to start from the beginning?"

Celeste gave Runa a small smile and looked at the clock on her nightstand. "I'm not going anywhere."

"Neither am I," said Kylee.

Runa nodded his head and let his expression transform into a serious look of determination. He then turned and stared with such intensity into Celeste's eyes that she wanted to turn away, but she couldn't. There was something familiar about Nateal Runa.

"Celeste, look at me. Do you remember who I am?"

Celeste continued to gaze into Runa's eyes, combing through her memory of who Nateal Runa was. Suddenly, her mind was back on *Gnolom*. She was ten-years-old again, preparing food with her mother and sister outside of their tent. She looked up and saw Nateal Runa waiving at her and her family. He looked to be about fifteen years of age.

Celeste snapped out of her trance and let a large smile grace along her face. "Nateal, you were part of my tribe on *Gnolom*."

Nateal smiled back. "Yes, we were childhood friends, and my name wasn't Nateal Runa. It was Tashak Arahad."

A flood of childhood memories engulfed Celeste's mind. She remembered playing childhood games with Tashak and her sister. She even remembered him being the first boy that she had ever thought she loved.

"You remember."

Celeste nodded in disbelief. "But . . . but I thought you were killed. My father said that your family suffered a tragic accident. He told my sister and me that you, your mother and father, and your sister were killed by a rival tribe that didn't believe my father to be the savior of the Gnols."

"Now, Celeste, do you believe everything your father says?"

Celeste shook her head. Nateal was right. Her father had lied to her most of her life. "But why didn't you let me know before?" she asked.

"I couldn't let you know. I had to keep my identity a secret."

"But why?"

Runa took a deep breath and let it out slowly. "Celeste, do you remember my father?"

"Yes, he was on my father's tribal council."

"Yes, and he was part of that last hunting party your father led before he and Vlamer Kreuk came back with new technology and abilities far superior to our own."

Celeste nodded her head. She remembered the night her mother died; her mother had told her that her father had led a hunting party of one hundred Gnols in search of food on their dying planet. Her father and Vlamer were the only two that returned. They had somehow learned of new and incredible technology that would take the Gnols from their dying world. In fact, it was from this trip that her father claimed he was visited by the goddess of light.

Runa continued. "My family was devastated when your father and Vlamer were the only two to return. I missed my father so much, but we did what your father asked of us. Things were changing so fast. Your father had factories built, computers assembled, space-craft constructed, and *Mind Inhibitors* produced by the millions. We even learned the new language of the goddess. My family and I truly believed that your father was the one prophesied in our ancient scriptures."

"But you don't anymore?" Kylee questioned?

"No. A few months after your father's return, we were asleep one night in our tent, dreaming of our exodus to our new world, when a man entered our tent. The man was terrifying. His body was scarred from severe burn wounds . . ."

Runa stopped and wiped the tears away that were beginning to trickle down his cheeks. Celeste placed her hand on his and spoke softly. "He was your father wasn't he?"

Runa looked back at Celeste with tear-filled eyes and nodded. "Yes, he told us not to follow Koroan; that he wasn't the one prophesied. He told us that Koroan wasn't visited by a goddess. It was actually . . ."

Kylee with anticipation in her voice responded. "What? It was actually what?"

Celeste could tell reliving the memories were painful for Runa. Tears now streamed down his face as he tried to force a smile at Kylee for her intrigue. "I . . . I don't know. He was just about to tell us when Koroan entered our tent. I have never seen such evil in anyone's eyes before. Koroan killed my father before he could finish telling us and then killed my mother and sister right in front of me. He thought that he had killed me, but he just rendered me unconscious. In fact, that's where I got this scar."

Celeste watched as Runa lifted his uniform shirt, revealing a three inch wide scar extending from the bottom of his neck to his navel.

"When I woke up, our tent was on fire."

"Yes," Celeste said. "I remember. That was the night my father told us that an enemy tribe had attacked."

Runa nodded and continued. "I was able to escape with the fire providing a cover. Another tribe, on their exodus to your father's new flying machines that would take them off *Gnolom*, found me. I was near death, but they took care of me and nursed me back to health. I was afraid that when it was time for the exodus, your father would recognize me and have me killed, but there were countless numbers of Gnols around, trying to get on the transports. I never saw your father, and he never saw me.

"When it came time to board the transport, the tribe that found me gave me another name, so my original name wouldn't come up in the computer registry. That's how I came to be so good at computers. I enrolled in the military computer training program your father started after his successful attack on *Terrest*. I learned how to crack security systems and invade other computer programs. That's all I focused on. I figured that's how I could reveal the truth that your father was a fraud. I thought I was alone, until I found out about you, Celeste."

Celeste was speechless and angry beyond comprehension. She wanted to sneak into her father's room down the hall and kill him. She never could have imagined the evil he had inflicted, on not only toward the humans but to her fellow Gnols as well.

Runa wiped the tears away and turned his attention back to his computer. He turned the screen to face Celeste. Celeste looked at the screen and noticed two blinking red lights in one of the rooms of the blueprint.

You see these two lights?" Runa asked.

Kylee and Celeste both nodded.

"These lights are signals from your ankle bracelets. If either of you exceed a distance of one hundred yards from this wrist band that is strapped to the guards in my detail, your bracelets will self-destruct."

Celeste and Kylee glanced at each other with defeat in their eyes. Celeste shook her head. How was she ever going to make it to the top floor to find out her father's secret, not to mention, obtain the antidote for Kylee and escape?

Runa seemed to know what Celeste was thinking. He looked at Kylee, again with compassion in his eyes. "Miss Palmer, can you walk."

"Please, call me Kylee. And yes, I can."

"Okay, Kylee, will you please leave the room and walk down the corridor to the elevator."

Kylee nodded, knowing what Runa had in mind. She got up, walked out of the room, and proceeded to walk down the corridor.

Celeste watched the computer screen as she did so. Her eyes widened, as the blinking light representing Kylee did not move. She looked back up at Runa as Kylee returned. Kylee made her way back to the bed and sat down. "Did it work?" She asked.

Runa smiled at Kylee. "Yes."

Celeste looked first at Kylee and then back to Runa. "Am I missing something here?"

Runa let out a small laugh. "No. The only ones that know the access codes to those bracelets are your father and his chief computer officer. But, unbeknownst to them, I was able to crack the codes and can now virtually place you anywhere in the palace."

Celeste jumped to her feet and hugged Runa. Runa nearly dropped his computer. After Celeste pulled away, Runa became extremely serious and said, "Now, Celeste, I suggest you go now; to discover your father's secret."

★ ★ ★ ★ ★

An hour later, Celeste managed to make her way to the elevator that led from her father's office to the mysterious top floor of her father's palace, using the access codes Runa had given her. When the elevator stopped, she felt her stomach turn over. A feeling of pure anxiety resonated throughout her entire body. *What secret lay beyond these doors?* She thought.

The elevator door slid open. Celeste stepped slowly, with nervous anticipation, into the pitch black room. Suddenly, light illuminated from a giant crystal chandelier, lighting the entire 5,000 square foot room. Celeste looked around. There were no windows. The walls were painted a bright white, brighter than any white Celeste had ever seen, which reflected the light and made the room even brighter. Celeste blinked to adjust her eyesight. Once her eyes were focused, she began to walk along the maroon carpet to the only items in the room.

In the center of the room was a black metal square pad that seemed to have a perimeter of about five feet by five feet. Celeste looked at it with curiosity and wondered what its purpose was. She then looked at the other item in the room.

About ten feet from of the metal pad was a ten foot gold statue of the goddess of light. She made her way to the statue and walked around it. She continued to scan the room for any more clues or items, but nothing.

She took a deep breath and in frustration began to walk toward the elevator. As she walked, she stepped onto the metal pad. The moment her foot touched the pad, the lights from the chandelier went out. She stopped and listened for anyone else in the darkness.

Unexpectedly, another light illuminated the room, but this light was different. This light seemed whiter than any light Celeste had ever seen. The light source emanated from behind her. With her guard up, Celeste slowly and cautiously turned around.

She nearly passed out from shock with what she saw. There floating about ten feet in midair, above the statue, were two bare feet. She slowly moved her eyes upward and saw a free flowing white robe, covering the body of the most beautiful woman Celeste had ever seen.

The woman was real. Only this woman seemed to be thirty feet tall. She had long flowing blond hair that emitted light of its own. Celeste locked eyes with the woman, and as she peered into the most beautiful blue eyes she ever looked upon, the woman spoke to her.

"Celeste, my child, it is so good to finally speak to you in person."

★ ★ ★ ★ ★

Celeste slowly walked down the hallway leading to her room. As she passed her father's room, she could hear his voice. It sounded like he was speaking with someone on his computer monitor. She knew that her father never slept, so it didn't surprise her that he was still hard at work. She also knew that her father was monitoring her current position, which told her that Runa must have successfully manipulated the computer system. If her father was to even suspect that she was a foot outside of her room, the entire palace would be on alert.

She tip toed quietly by her father's room, knowing her father's senses were acutely sensitive. As she walked toward her room, she saw Runa sitting at his desk outside of her room. Runa looked up from his computer with a look of anticipation. Celeste nodded and walked into her room with Runa following.

Kylee shot up from her lying position on the bed. Celeste noticed she didn't look well, but the eagerness Kylee had for what Celeste discovered superseded any physical discomfort Kylee may have felt. Celeste sat on the bed next to Kylee with Runa across on the other bed.

"Well?" Runa said with excitement in his voice. "What did you find?"

Celeste, with a look of confusion on her face, replied, "I don't know. I . . . I think I had a revelation from my father's goddess."

Kylee gasped, "That can't be."

"I know," Celeste said. "Everything your father and Jake have told me about Jesus Christ tells me that what I experienced couldn't be. She didn't have a physical body. It was like . . . like she was a spirit."

"Or a hologram," Runa interjected.

Celeste looked at Runa with bewilderment. "A hologram?"

Runa continued, "I've been monitoring the energy levels within the palace. I was curious to see what readings I would get when you entered the top floor. While you were there, the energy levels spiked. The readings matched the energy signature from hologram technology."

"But this wasn't a recording, Nateal," Celeste said. "I communicated and interacted with her."

"What did she tell you?" Kylee asked.

"Nothing that I didn't already know. She basically told me that she was the goddess sent to reveal new technology to the people of *Gnolom* and that my father was the chosen one. And that I needed to repent and follow him."

Celeste stopped and looked at Runa. "If it wasn't a recording, then I had to be interacting in person with her. She has to be somewhere in the palace or within *Chast*."

Runa looked down and thought for a moment. "*Gnolom*. . . . She has to be on *Gnolom*."

Celeste nodded. "That makes sense. Wherever my father went on *Gnolom* and learned about new technology, she has to be the source."

Kylee cut in. "But I thought *Gnolom* was a dead planet. How can someone survive on *Gnolom*?"

"Unless she is not alive," Runa stated.

It hit Celeste like a hammer. She remembered the story of how Adrian and his crew had to abandon *Mars I* in outer space. "A computer program!" Celeste looked at Kylee. "Kylee, you might remember more about your father's past. I know that *Mars I* had an artificially intelligent computer system. What was it they called her?"

Kylee thought for a moment and then looked up with a smile on her face. "*Maggie*. They called her *Maggie*. My dad's bother, Kevin, invented artificial intelligence." Kylee stopped, and emotions flooded to the surface. Tears began streaming down her face. "My dad always said that he somehow felt responsible for the Gnols coming to *Terrest*. . . . And he's right. It was *Maggie* and *Mars I* that gave Koroan the knowledge for new technology and a way to escape *Gnolom*."

Celeste put her hand on Kylee's. "There is no way Adrian could have known that abandoning *Mars I*, he would cause the enslavement of the Terrestrian people." Celeste then looked at Runa. "Nateal, we need to escape and get to *Gnolom*."

"I've already planned an escape. But we can't go for at least a week. Your father is scheduled to leave *Terrest* in a week to visit Earth. There is no way we can attempt an escape while your father is on the planet." Runa looked at Kylee, "Also, Kylee, you may not survive past a week. This will give me enough time to crack the security codes to the facility where they are keeping the antidote."

Celeste sighed. "Okay, we sit tight . . . but I have another concern. If my father communicates with the goddess of light or *Maggie*, he is going to know that I was out of my room and found the hologram."

Runa lowered his head and thought for a moment. "I might know a way around that. If it truly is a hologram, I can temporarily down the power to the top floor. I've already gained access to the power grid that powers the palace. I needed access to it to plan our escape."

Celeste smiled, amazed at Nateal Runa's ability to crack into the most secure computer system on the planet of *Terrest*. She had full confidence that they would be able to escape the palace, be reunited with Jake, and return to *Gnolom* to destroy the source of her father's power.

CHAPTER 20

One week later . . . June 22, 2042 – Slave Camp of Zikf

Skip stood next to Captain Belzar, waiting for the hover-truck of new prisoners to enter the front gate of the slave camp. The breeze blew through Skip's dark hair, which was now significantly longer touching the top of his shoulders. Skip scratched at the thick beard on his face and breathed in the air. The air was hot and thick with humidity; the smells of the jungle penetrating his senses.

Skip looked up at Captain Noran Belzar. Small beads of sweat dripped down over the brow of his ebony forehead. It had been over a week since Captain Belzar discovered Skip with his artificial leg open. Strangely, Belzar didn't say a word about it. Belzar only confiscated the items that Skip found in his artificial leg, including the key that would free all of the slaves from the Slave Camp of *Zikf*. Skip also wondered why Commander Schaal didn't torture or kill him for what he had discovered in his leg. Skip got the impression that Belzar didn't even report it.

Skip turned his attention back to the hover-truck as it stopped in front of them. The two Gnol guards escorting the prisoners exited the vehicle and opened the bay door at the rear of the craft. The prisoners, locked in shackles, filed out one by one. As the prisoners passed by Skip and Belzar, Skip scanned the tattooed bar codes on the top of the prisoner's right hands. Skip was shocked when he looked at the last two prisoners – directly in front of him stood Bantyr and Sean. Skip tried to make eye contact with them as he scanned their hands. But Bantyr and Sean kept their eyes down. Skip knew that they were already in the control of the Gnol *Enforcer*.

After scanning the prisoners, Skip turned around and began walking toward the camp's administration building with Captain Belzar at his side. Skip put his head down and let out a sigh. Feeling hopeless, he knew there was no way he could escape with Skyler, Sean, and Bantyr under the twenty-four hour control of Gnol *Enforcers*. In addition, without the item that Belzar took from him, there was no way he could wake his friends up from the mental prison they were in.

As Skip began to make his way back to the administration building of the camp, Belzar gently grabbed Skip's right shoulder to stop him. Skip stopped and looked up at Belzar. Belzar reached into the pockets of his fatigues and pulled out the item that Skip desperately needed. "Is this what you need to free your friends?"

Skip, astonished, reached out for the item. Belzar handed it to him, and Skip responded, "Wh . . . I don't understand, Captain? What are you doing?"

For the first time that Skip could recall, Captain Noran Belzar turned the corner of his lips into a small smile. "I had been up all night the night I found you with these items. I monitored everything the hologram said to you. When I entered your room, I wasn't angry. My eyes were red because I had been crying."

Skip looked at Belzar with confusion. "Crying?"

Belzar continued. "Earlier that day, a female prisoner gave birth to a baby girl. Commander Schaal ordered that the baby be killed immediately and that every male and female prisoner be sterilized."

Skipped nodded, knowing about the sterilization program, but he was unaware that a female prisoner had actually given birth. He continued to stare at Captain Belzar as tears began rolling down Belzar's face.

Belzar gritted his teeth. "What kind of person does that? This was an innocent new life. What kind of god enslaves and kills innocent people?"

Skip didn't know what to say.

Belzar continued. "The night that I confiscated those items from you, I was in turmoil about my own allegiances. I decided not to give the items to Commander Schaal. Instead, I had that last item analyzed. The disk is a computer virus. When inserted into the mainframe of our computer system it will kill all power to the camp, including the signal that the *Enforcers* use to keep the mind control of the prisoners. The virus is powerful enough to completely destroy the camp's computer and power systems. There will be no way for our experts here to recover."

Skip was speechless. All he could do was put his left hand on Belzar's shoulder.

Captain Noran Belzar managed another small smile and said. "Oh, and Skip . . . you can call me Tiny."

★ ★ ★ ★ ★

Adrian hadn't known how much time had passed. Ever since he was dragged out of Dorange's office after their battle, he had been locked up in solitary confinement in the same room on the Gnol ship that he had been in before. Kept in almost utter darkness and near death, he was given one cup of water a day and a small ration of food. For some reason, the Gnols were keeping him alive. They even repaired his leg.

He knew that the Gnol ship was on Earth now. He gathered that information from rumblings of the ship as it landed. Where it landed, he could only guess. Adrian felt in the darkness for the cup of water. He could tell that he only had about a sip left. Hoping that he had spread his water out throughout the day, he took the final sip. As he let the water wet the dryness of his throat, he wondered about his old copilot, Donald Garrett, or Dorange Gar as he was now known. Adrian wondered if Dorange was dead. There was no way anyone could have survived the wound that Adrian had inflicted upon Dorange.

Adrian also wondered how he had become so powerful in Dorange's office. He had tried to use his new found telekinetic powers when he was brought back to solitary confinement. However, they didn't work. He was surprised how he had so much power during the fight with Dorange, and yet before, he could barely use the techniques Celeste had taught him. And now here he sat again unable to access the powers.

Suddenly, the door to the room slid open. Again, the brightness of the hall lights caused temporary blindness. That was soon alleviated, however, as two Gnols blind folded and gagged him. They also tied his hands behind his back. The two Gnols grabbed him under his arms. They dragged him down the corridor of the ship to the hangar bay. The two Gnols then dragged him into a transport shuttle and buckled him into one of the passenger seats. Then the two Gnols exited the transport. As far as Adrian could tell, he was the only prisoner on the ship and the only one besides the pilot and copilot.

The shuttle took off. After a few minutes of flight, the shuttle landed. Adrian heard the shuttle doors open. He heard the voices of about four Gnols. "There he is. Take him to the holding cell."

Adrian again felt two Gnols grab him under his arms and drag him along the ground. Once outside the shuttle, Adrian could tell the day was hot. He also knew that he was being dragged along a lawn. Where he was, he had no idea.

The two Gnols dragged Adrian into a building. They then entered an elevator. Adrian felt the elevator move down to the basement of the building. After a few seconds, the elevator reached its destination. The doors opened, and the two Gnols dragged Adrian forward. After about fifty feet, they stopped. Adrian heard the buzz of the lock to a jail cell and heard the cell open. The two Gnols tossed Adrian into the cell.

With his eyes blindfolded and his hands tied behind his back, Adrian had no way to prevent his forehead from slamming into the concrete floor below. The blow nearly caused Adrian to blackout.

Adrian heard voices within the cell. He heard a young man's voice. "Who is it, Dad?"

There was a long pause as Adrian managed to make it to a sitting position with his back against the wall. He also felt blood drip from his forehead. Then, he heard a familiar voice.

"It can't be."

Adrian heard another voice of a young woman, "Dad, is that Uncle—"

Adrian felt someone kneel down beside him.

Again, he heard the familiar voice. "Yes, Ashley . . . he . . . he is your Uncle Adrian."

The man kneeling next to Adrian pulled the blindfold off of Adrian's eyes. After a few seconds, Adrian's eyes adjusted to the light. He looked at the man's face and then at the young woman and boy standing behind. He focused his attention back to the man kneeling in front of him. "Kev . . . Kevin . . . is that you?"

Kevin smiled and grabbed Adrian into a tight hug. "It's me Adrian. It's me, your big brother. Welcome home."

★ ★ ★ ★ ★

Jake peered through his binoculars. He and his team of twelve rebel soldiers were about one thousand yards away from the exit of the underground tunnel that led from Celeste's room within the palace to the outside of *Chast's* city walls. Jake and his team were hidden in a grove of pine trees on a small hill that overlooked the city. Jake put down his binoculars, pointed to the exit, and looked at Nichelle. "This is the exit?"

Nichelle nodded. "Yes. By the looks of it, Koroan isn't going to take any chances for Celeste to escape this time."

Jake looked back through his binoculars. There in front of the underground exit was a team of twenty-five Gnol soldiers. Jake recognized Colonel Aromos Jantear as the leader. Jake put down his binoculars again and squeezed the button that activated the communication's device on his neck. "General Hauler, do you read?"

Scott Hauler and his men of fifteen soldiers hid under the covering of the setting sun to the east about one hundred yards to the left flank of the Gnol troops. Jake heard the static voice of Scott Hauler on the other end. "Roger that, General."

"I've got twenty-five hostiles surrounding the exit. It looks like our source on the inside was right. Jantear betrayed Celeste."

Jake heard a grunt on the other end.

Scott replied, "When did Runa say the signal would begin?"

Jake looked at his watch. "At twenty-one hundred hours, Koroan's shuttle will leave the palace. We have to wait another twenty minutes after the sun sets. Runa will then cut the power and communications to the city. That's our signal to move. Make sure your men have their silencers attached to their rifles. Also, by using bullets, we won't alert the entire Gnol army that we're here."

"Roger that," replied Scott. "You do know that Runa has to come with us. We can no longer keep him in *Chast*. The Gnol computer experts are too good, and they'll trace the power and communication glitches back to him. That takes away the plans your dad had to invade *Chast*."

Jake sighed. "I know. But Celeste and Kylee are too important. We'll get another chance Scott."

There was a moment of silence on Scott's end, telling Jake that Scott didn't agree. "Roger that, General."

Jake looked at Nichelle, her hair now cut short covered by the camouflage battle helmet. Nichelle met his gaze and answered his question

344   Shaun F. Messick

before he even asked. "Don't worry, Jake. When Runa cuts the power, it will deactivate the motion sensors within the passageway, so they can make a clean escape. All we have to do is make sure Jantear and those Gnol troops are taken care of before they reach the exit."

Jake smiled and nodded. In the distance, he heard the rumbling engine of a Gnol transport shuttle. Jake peered back through his binoculars and watched as Koroan Chast left the planet.

Twenty minutes later, every light went off within the city of *Chast*. Jake immediately issued the order for Scott's team to move. Scott's team moved stealthily to within twenty-five yards of the Gnol troops.

Jake then raised his rifle and ordered his team of sharpshooters to open fire on the Gnols. The silencers on the rifles muffled the noise of bullets as they whizzed through the air, hitting their targets. Jake watched through his scope as one-by-one Gnol troops fell to their deaths. The remaining Gnols scattered.

"Go, Scott! Go!"

Jake watched as Scott and his team moved in silently eliminating the rest of the Gnol guards.

A few moments later, Jake and his team reached the exit. Jake looked at Scott. "Report."

"Twenty-four dead. Jantear is nowhere to be found."

Jake cursed under his breath. "He couldn't have gone far. Send a team out to search the perimeter."

Scott issued the order. Five rebel soldiers rushed to look for Jantear.

Jake and Scott looked at the exit. The exit was a set of double *Omutx* reinforced doors buried underneath a mound of earth and surrounded by pine trees. The doors had been welded shut. Jake gave the signal and two soldiers moved to the doors, placing charges.

After about ten minutes of nervous anticipation, Jake finally heard the sound he had been waiting for – three loud knocks on the other end of the doors. Jake waited a few second for the three, whom he hoped were behind the doors, to back away. Jake pressed the button that detonated the charge. There was loud hiss and then pop.

Two rebel soldiers moved to the doors and placed crow bars on each side. Both soldiers pulled the doors to the ground. As they did so, Jake and his men raised their rifles. Out of the smoke, Kylee exited the passageway. She looked considerably well, which told Jake that Runa must have successfully retrieved the antidote. Next, Runa walked out.

After hugging Kylee and shaking the hand of Runa, Jake walked to the edge of the passageway. Through the smoke, Celeste reached out and grabbed Jake's hand.

Jake was about to pull Celeste into him and embrace her when she was suddenly jerked away. Jake quickly pulled the plasma pistol at his side out and pointed directly between the eyes of Aromos Jantear. Jantear held one arm across Celeste's body, holding her arms. The other hand held a dagger at her carotid artery.

"Don't even think about it, Jake. She isn't even fast enough before I cut her throat."

Jake continued to hold his aim between Jantear's eyes. "Even if you do kill her, you won't get away."

Jantear gave Jake an eerie smile. "I don't plan on getting away."

Jantear quickly sliced Celeste's neck.

"No!" Jake yelled, firing two plasma blasts directly into Jantear's head. Both Jantear and Celeste fell to the ground.

Jake and Nichelle rushed to Celeste who was unconscious. Jake quickly placed his hand on her bleeding neck. "Medic!"

A medic rushed to Celeste with medical supplies in hand. He pushed Jake aside and examined the damage. "It isn't sliced all the way through. She'll live. I need stop the bleeding and suture her throat."

About an hour later, Jake walked to the back of the transport as it traveled back to the rebel base. As he walked to the back, he shook the hands of his men, offering them congratulations on a job well done. Nearing the back of the transport, Jake met the crystal blue eyes of Celeste, sitting up in the stretcher. Celeste with bandages around her neck and an I.V. in her right arm smiled at Jake and motioned for him to sit next to her.

Nichelle stood up from her spot next to Celeste, walked up to Jake and gently kissed him on the cheek. She whispered into his ear. "Job well done, General."

Jake smiled at her and watched her walk away. He turned his attention back to Celeste. He rushed forward, gently embracing her and kissing her ever so gently on the lips. Celeste kissed him back.

The two separated lips but kept their foreheads touching. Celeste spoke first. "I'm alright, Jake."

Jake smiled and with tears streaming down his cheek said, "I don't think I can live without you."

Celeste returned his smile and ran her free hand through his hair.

Jake then met her gaze. "Celeste . . . will you marry me?"

Celeste moved in, kissed Jake and then responded, "Yes, I want to be with you forever."

WORLDS WITHOUT END
AFTERMATH
BOOK 2

With the enslavement of the human race and all faith lost, the only hope humanity has is hidden in a prophecy given by Jesus Christ Himself on a planet 22-light-years from Earth!

The story continues with *Worlds Without End: Aftermath . . .*

After the initial attack by the Gnols, Earth lies in ruins with most of the cities destroyed and the majority of the population dead. Adrian Palmer remains in the custody of the Gnols who have established their capital in Washington D.C. as they await the arrival of their savior, Koroan Chast, to claim his new world.

Knowing full well of their execution, Adrian and Kevin find help from a group of rebels gathering in Jackson County, Missouri. Adrian knows that he needs to return to Terrest. But before he can escape, he and Kevin must face an old enemy, which may turn out to be futile.

Meanwhile, on Terrest, Jake and Scott are left to lead what's left of the Terrestrian Rebel military. Defeated and desperate, Jake and Celeste embark on an insurmountable journey to Gnolom and discover the true origins of Koroan Chast's power.

At the same time, Skip discovers new and old allies to help him in his escape from the slave camp of Zikf. Will he escape to continue his quest for the prophecy given by Jesus Christ? Or, is Koroan Chast the fulfillment of that prophecy?

The story continues as old and new enemies collide in a saga of faith, love, power, and war. A story that stretches across the galaxy in search of the key that will free humankind!

- For more information about *Worlds Without End: The Mission* and upcoming books visit www.EmpyreanPublications.com.

ABOUT THE AUTHOR

Shaun Messick currently lives in Shelley, Idaho with his beautiful wife and four wonderful children.

Mr. Messick earned his Bachelors of Science degree from Idaho State University in Secondary Education in 2001. In 2007, he went back to school and earned a Masters of Arts degree in Education Administration and Supervision from the University of Phoenix.

His passions include his family, writing and reading, and sports.

In 2011, he founded Empyrean Publications his own imprint to publish his books and future projects.

9892019R0023

Made in the USA
Charleston, SC
21 October 2011